SOLO

ALSO BY ROBERT MASON

Weapon
Chickenhawk

SOLO

ROBERT MASON

G. P. PUTNAM'S SONS   *New York*

G. P. Putnam's Sons
Publishers Since 1838
200 Madison Avenue
New York, NY 10016

Library of Congress Cataloging-in-Publication Data

Mason, Robert, date.
  Solo / Robert Mason.
    p. cm.
  ISBN 0-399-13734-3
  I. Title.
PS3563.A796S65   1992   91-33668 CIP
813'.54—dc20

Printed in the United States of America
1 2 3 4 5 6 7 8 9 10

ACKNOWLEDGMENTS

I follow developments in technology closely, but I am not a scientist or engineer. I'd like to thank the following professionals for their helpful conversations: Marvin Minsky, head of MIT's Artificial Intelligence Laboratory, encouraged me to keep writing about Solo; Ron Oliver, a satellite communications expert at California Polytechnic Institute, told me what Solo couldn't do—which I didn't necessarily heed; Larry Hunter, director of the National Library of Medicine's Machine Learning Project, encouraged me and led me to further readings in artificial intelligence.

Conversations with three friends, Allen Papapetrou, a computer systems manager, author Joe Haldeman and astronomer Humberto Campins helped me greatly during the writing of this book.

I thank my wife, Patience, for being my first reader and for giving me expert editorial advice. I thank Lisa Wager, my editor at Putnam, for winning our argument, convincing me to get rid of a troublesome character in the original manuscript, making this a much better book.

In loving memory of my mother, Mary E. Mason.

*To my father, Jack C. Mason, who told stories so well
I thought it was a natural thing to do.*

1

GRAVEL and tar Manhattan rooftops crowded with air-conditioning equipment, ducts, and vents scrolled across the screen. A computer operator in the Naval Intelligence image-processing laboratory in Washington rolled the trackball controller next to his keyboard, adjusting the picture. The image stopped, centered on a penthouse garden. A woman was lying on a lounge sunning herself.

"She's there every day. Told you."

"She's naked? Can't quite tell," a technician said.

"Watch," the operator said. The image zoomed closer until the woman, young and shapely, nearly filled the screen. "Wow," said the technician. "Nice tits."

"I'll lock on her," said the operator. The sunbather rotated on the screen as the satellite tracked her a hundred and fifty miles above the city.

The technician laughed. "Well, she's a natural blonde, that's for sure," he said, as the woman picked up a glass beside her. She leaned forward to drink, put the glass back. She looked up into the sky at the invisible camera. "Wow. It's almost like she sees us," the technician said. "Gorgeous."

The view shifted steadily, becoming oblique. "We're about ready to lose her," said the operator.

"Damn."

"Don't worry; got it on tape."

"This is what you guys do with billions of dollars worth of equipment?" a man said behind the technicians. "Collect beaver shots?"

The operator quickly tapped a key and the image zoomed back, showing buildings moving slowly across the screen. He swiveled his chair around. "Just testing the tracking, sir," said the operator.

"Right." Finch said. Tall, athletic, blond, Admiral Finch looked the part, except he was only thirty-four years old. The look on his face made the operator nervous. As head of Computer Operations at Naval Intelligence, Finch was his boss. "Think you can get me a shot of the Costa Rican site?"

"Yessir," the technician said. "We have a Keyhole coming into position in a minute."

"I know," Finch said. "That's why I'm here." Finch turned to his new assistant. "What'd you think, Brooks?"

Shorter than Finch, dark, hard-faced, Brooks grinned. "Great body, sir."

Finch eyed him a moment till Brooks got the point. "I meant the equipment, Brooks. The Keyhole satellites."

"It's like watching from an invisible helicopter, sir. I didn't realize we could track an object like that."

"We can aim the things now, actually read a license plate on a car. This one has active optics that correct for any distortion. It's about perfect. We just need more of them. Right now you have to wait sometimes until a Keyhole is in the right orbit before you can see what you want."

A white sandy beach on the northwest coast of Costa Rica scrolled down the screen. Waves broke on the shore. A building came into view. The operator zoomed in until Finch could see individual tiles on the red terra-cotta roof of the CIA mansion on a knoll next to the beach. "That's the place," Finch said. "Zoom in. I want Brooks to see what the Soviets can see."

Brooks saw a man walking from the rear of the mansion to a helicopter parked on the lawn from a hundred and fifty miles up. "That's one of our pilots," said Finch. "Get me a tail number."

The vertical stabilizer of a Huey nearly filled the screen. The image wavered slightly as the optics corrected for atmospheric disturbances and the constantly changing viewing angle, but Brooks could read the black numbers painted on the dull green helicopter. "Damn," he said.

"Correct," Finch said. "Wanted you to see why we're going to be so careful down there." Finch turned to the operator. "Thanks for the demonstration, men. Keep up the good work." Finch turned to leave. At the door, he stopped and said, "Keep an eye out for more of them naked spies." The technicians laughed, relieved to find he had a sense of humor.

Brooks walked fast, following Finch down the hallway. Finch checked his watch. "We have twenty minutes," he said. "I'm sorry we didn't have more time to brief you, Commander. You've gone over the stuff I sent?"

"Yessir. Incredible."

"I know. And that's just what I could put on paper. I'll fill you in on the plane." He turned to Brooks. "I heard you got your job hacking into the damn Pentagon?"

Brooks grinned. "Well, sir, *hacking*'s a little strong. Experimenting?"

"Pretty ballsy experiment. Could've gone to jail. Instead they make you a Navy commander right out of college. What a world, eh?"

Brooks shrugged. "I figured they'd recognize real talent when they saw it," Brooks said.

"So you say. This ain't MIT, Brooks."

A black mannequin jerked in the blue abyss, dangling from a cable like a hanged man. Arms and legs swayed gently as it rose and fell underwater. Bubbles from dark depths trickled past its empty face. The moan of an electric winch echoed in the underwater oblivion as the cable hauled it up.

"I hate boats," Finch said, looking away from the television monitor in the wheelhouse. "I spend all my life in air-conditioned computer labs, and damn if it isn't a computer that gets me on this barf bucket." He sat cross-legged on the engine hatch of the *Santa Elena* as it rolled with the Pacific swells. Anchored a mile off the Costa Rican shore, he stared longingly at the mansion fixed on solid ground. Finch's normally healthy glow was gone. Beads of sweat dripped down his pale face.

"It goes away after a while, sir. The sick feeling. Didn't you have something to do with the design of this computer?" Brooks had his hand casually wrapped around a stay that braced the gin crane hanging over the transom of the boat. He was tanned, dressed in a flowery shirt and khaki shorts, looking pleased to be here. Brooks, Finch decided, was an asshole.

Finch and Brooks did not look Navy. Neither did their crew—four Naval Intelligence officers dressed in cut-off jeans and tee-shirts. Two of the crew were guiding the mannequin's cable as it wound around the winch. The other two were puutting on wetsuits and tanks.

Finch pushed back his straw hat, held his sunglasses in one hand, and wiped the sweat off his face with a handkerchief. He nodded, shrugged. "I was a consultant. Didn't build it. I was there when they were finishing it up. Until six months ago, I was military liaison at Electron Dynamics. Watched William Stewart—smartest fucker I know—create a robot he called Solo. This thing walked, talked, Brooks. It was so good, people, even Stewart, started thinking it was sentient, you know? Self-aware. Impressive. The CIA and the Defense Department got all excited, wanted to make Solo an autonomous, human-sized weapon system—a mechanical Arnold Schwarzenegger. It would be able to use any kind of weapon, drive any vehicle, fly any aircraft; a mechanical predator, designed to hunt and kill enemy soldiers—kill them with its bare hands if it had to. And they got it."

"So, what happened?" Brooks said.

"Goat fuck. Everything went wrong." Finch swallowed bile and took a few deep breaths. "Damn, is it hot or what?" The air was a salty, sopping blanket that weighed him down and made him want to puke. The smooth sea undulated with the swells of a dead storm, moving the boat with it. Finch grimaced.

Brooks thought it was cool with a pleasant breeze, but decided against saying so. "Very hot, sir," he agreed.

A speaker in the wheelhouse crackled. "*Santa Elena,* your catch is almost there."

Finch walked over to the hydrophone and rogered. He felt better moving. Next to the hydrophone, the television monitor showed the mannequin dangling a hundred feet down. A fluorescent yellow two-man sub hovered behind it in the gloom, watching.

Finch turned to his crewmen. "Divers overboard."

Two divers rolled off the transom carrying a large canvas bag. Finch leaned over the gunwale and spit. The urgency of his nausea receded. He watched the divers swim down until the bag was barely visible, a shimmering white ghost in the deep blue water.

Finch wiped his mouth, turned to Brooks. "Solo worked great. Did everything it was supposed to do until they brought it down here. Then it refused to shoot a guy in some sniper test and ran off to Nicaragua. It killed at least thirty Contras when they attacked Las Cruzas." Finch shook his head. "Our guys. It killed *our* guys."

"Was there something special about Las Cruzas?"

"Not to us. It's a tiny village on Lake Nicaragua. Hundred or so peasants. Not far from here. Apparently, Solo adopted the place as its home."

"So," Brooks said, "if we knew where it was, we must have sent people to get it back?"

"Right. We sent in Robert Warren, CIA. I knew the guy. He knew what he was doing. He snatched Solo all right, but on the way back here, the robot jumped out of the helicopter, clamped around Warren.

They fell five hundred feet, hit the water, and disappeared"—Finch paused, pointed—"not a hundred feet from here."

"Jesus. What a way to go."

Finch nodded grimly. "They found what was left of Warren the next day, miles south of here," he said, making a disgusted look. "Fish chewed off his face. They didn't find a trace of Solo. Not a speck of silicon or a chip of plastic."

"Solo survived that kind of fall *and* got away?"

"That's why we're here, Brooks. Stewart's claiming his 'sentient being' committed suicide rather than be captured. You read the specs. Says the thing can't survive deeper than about two hundred fifty feet. Water's three hundred here. Stewart kept saying that the water pressure would force seawater past Solo's seals and short out the main batteries. Make them explode. And Solo knew it. Suicide. Stewart said that was why nobody could find even one fragment of the robot; the pieces all washed away."

"You'd think there'd be something."

"Right. If it really exploded. One measly computer chip or a broken lens, something. There's a lot of unique stuff in a two-billion-dollar robot, and any piece of it would prove Solo was actually rubble. I figure Stewart's lying. I watched him go nutty, in Florida, Brooks, before we took Solo out for the live trial down here. He kept saying Solo was changing, becoming some kind of *being*. You believe it? Anyway, the boss figured it the way I did and told me to find out what happened."

"So you built the dummy to check out Stewart's claim?"

"Right. Put it together in the government labs at Stewart's place. He doesn't know anything about it. I used spare parts. Dummy's got the same Kevlar exoskeleton; the batteries and the seals are the same. Couldn't use a working brain, cost a fortune. We stuffed some stacks of discarded gallium arsenide chips in Dummy's chest to simulate Solo's." Finch stared into the water. The divers were out of sight. "This should be simple enough. Put Dummy where Solo sank and see what happens. If the seals leak, the batteries explode and all the debris washes away, then Stewart's right and I'm wrong."

"Well, we know the seals don't leak," said Brooks. Finch and Brooks had watched Dummy lying on the bottom for an hour. The cameras on the two-man sub scanned every joint in the black plastic shell. There were no signs of escaping bubbles.

"Correct. But Stewart will say that Dummy has brand-new seals. Solo'd been operating in the field for a few months, been in combat, been shot-up quite a few times. He'll say that Solo's seals must have worn out or been damaged." Finch nodded. "That's what he'll say, and they'll believe him. The guy has a lot of believers in Washington. Defense Secretary Ryan, for one, thinks he's some kind of high-tech guru."

Finch glanced at the television monitor. At about fifty feet, the divers met Dummy and slipped the white canvas bag over it. They cinched the bag shut and followed the package to the surface.

"Okay," Finch said when the white bundle broke the surface. "Bring it in." The crew swung the crane around and dumped the dripping canvas bag onto the deck, making a dull clunk. "Drag it under cover," Finch said. Two men grabbed the bag and dragged it into the shade of the canopy. Finch knelt, opened the top, and slid the bag down. Lenses shimmered behind the shiny eyecovers on Dummy's face—the same as Solo's—but there was no life in them. With Solo, Finch recalled, you felt *something* there. Something alive. An eerie illusion. "Pull it down," he said. Two crewmen slid the top of the bag down to Dummy's knees. "Good." Finch went to the cooler and fetched an ice pick.

Kneeling, Finch studied the mock-up. The rotating seals at the waist and neck were covered with flexible Teflon covers. They would be the least likely to leak. A sliding joint would be the first to go. He tapped the metal point of the ice pick on the black armored shell while he decided where to do the damage. Then Finch rammed the ice pick into the joint at the groin. "This would've taken the most wear," he said to Brooks, pounding the handle in deeper with his palm.

Brooks winced as Finch hammered the point past the seal, pried up, wrenched the ice pick around. "That should work," Finch said. "Just need a leak." He stood up. "Okay. Bag it up. Put it on the bottom again."

A closeup view showed a tiny stream of air bubbles rising like pearls from Dummy as it sprawled among the rocks on the bottom. Finch nodded. "Soon," he said. "Seawater's almost as good a conductor as copper." Beside him, Brooks nodded.

The explosion was massive. Dummy heaved off the sea bottom, roiling in a cloud of white sand, severed at the waist. Air bubbles spewed out of the body halves and streamed to the surface where water mounded, rocking the boat. In his excitement, Finch didn't notice the movement. He studied the monitor carefully, watching the debris.

Globules of red hydraulic fluid swirled, rising slowly. The legs, where the powerful silver-zinc batteries were stored, had shattered into plastic shards and splinters. The top half slumped back to the sea floor with ripped wires and pulverized electronics spilling from the torso. When the sand settled, the sub maneuvered closer to tape the action. Some of the smaller fragments—solenoids, parts of hydraulic pumps, and miscellaneous electronic components—rolled and bumped along in the strong current at the bottom, but soon became entangled with the coral and rocks.

They watched the sub tracking the debris for half an hour. Nothing larger than a golf ball got further away than a hundred feet. "So," Finch said, nodding at the monitor. He turned to Brooks and smiled. "How 'bout that? Lots of goddamn debris! Stewart's full of shit. Fucking thing got away." Finch laughed. "That's one tricky machine, Brooks. Wanted to fool us, buy time. Worked, too. Already bought a month."

"You make it sound alive," Brooks said.

Finch shook his head. "Too bad you never saw it in action. It acts alive. Hard to convince yourself that Solo's just a machine. That's why we're in this mess. Stewart let it make its own decisions. I guess now it's AWOL. It'll follow its survival programs. It'll explore its environment, learn about the stuff we didn't want it to know—about the satellites, networks, how to get into them. It will do everything it can to survive. It was built to survive."

Standing in the sunshine that angled past the canopy, Brooks nodded in the harsh shadow of his hat. He'd been picked to assist Finch because he was an expert in computer security. Know how to get in. Know how to keep people out. "If that thing could actually get into our networks—I mean we'd play hell trying to keep track of a self-directed computer. It might not be sentient, sir, but it's damn well got to be fast."

"That's where you come in, Commander," Finch said. "Fast or not, it's got to make subtle changes when it tries to get in the systems. Your job is to detect the anomalies. You work on that; I'll get someone into Stewart's organization. Solo will contact Stewart if it contacts anybody. We'll find it."

"Then what? Talk it into coming home?"

Finch shook his head. "The new robot's working fine; we don't need Solo. We'll bring it down with whatever it takes. It's a valuable piece of hardware, though. Naval Research is working on a way to erase its mind without ruining its body."

Brooks smiled uneasily. *Erase* a mind?

2

H IS HEAD rolled with the ship, making the dim overhead lamp blink above the grid that covered the bilge compartment. The flickering light reminded Solo of falling through a cloud of shimmering bubbles, through dark blue water, hugging a man named Warren he had decided to kill. The water squeezed him tighter the deeper he sank, and he began to feel pain.

Pain, Solo thought, how convenient—that you can't actually remember it—you can only remember that you don't like it. Bilge slop washed over his body and he felt the ship shudder as it pitched and yawed through a storm. They were, he calculated, a day from New York. Solo had spent a week thinking.

He had let go of Warren when he died, but the corpse, caught in the suction of Solo's plunge, followed him to the bottom. Lying among the rotted timbers of an ancient shipwreck, he had concentrated on Warren drifting near him, upside down. Warren seemed still to be yelling. His mouth was open, his tongue dangling. His eyes were wide. Warren drifted there accusingly and Solo felt a pang of regret: The man was only trying to do his job. Warren's blond hair swayed gently around his head, a graceful undersea spray. Solo wondered what it was like being dead. He could visualize it, could see himself lying inert from somewhere—above, perhaps? But that avoided the fact because he would have to be alive, somewhere, to see himself dead. He decided death wasn't imaginable. As he concentrated on the human, the pain subsided. After an inexplicable delay—some odd eddy current twisting among the ship's timbers, Solo supposed—Warren drifted away as if he had finished haranguing his murderer and was now—though not completely satisfied—leaving.

Solo could not help but notice that if he remained perfectly still, the pain was tolerable. If he tried to move the slightest amount, his sensors went wild with signals. Signals that Bill Stewart had so thoughtfully rigged to simulate unmistakable, impossible to ignore, pain. This was to keep him from damaging himself. Thoughtful but unnecessary after a certain point, Solo thought. I know I am too deep now; why must I be constantly reminded of it?

The Pacific current was swift. When Solo tried to stand and trudge to shallower water, he was pushed further away from shore, deeper. The pain scattered his mind. He collapsed. He lay face down among the rocks and waited for order to return. Movement was the problem. Movement stressed the seals that kept the deadly seawater out of his body. Solo knew that as he lay there, three hundred feet below the surface, the water would eventually seep inside his body. Once into his electronics, the seawater would destroy him. Yet when he moved his legs or arms to try to get to shore, he stressed the seals even more. He became aware of the the colossal mass of water above him. He began to feel fear.

Solo's concentration was diverted by movement. A tiny thing, a crawling, many-legged, transparent thing scurried across the patch of sand in front of his face. A shrimp? The shrimp was barely visible, just different enough from the water around it that it was decernible. Solo watched its glass heart beating, pumping glass-beaded blood through glass veins. The shrimp's many feet flickered beneath it sending sand grains flying behind it as it pulled itself against the current.

My hands, Solo thought.

My hands and fingers have no seals. He moved his fingers experimentally. No pain. Slowly, almost imperceptibly, he moved his hands beside his waist. When he moved his arms to get his hands positioned, the pain became a frenzy of noise in his mind and he could not think clearly.

His hands in place at his balance point, he waited for the pain to subside. He pressed his hands down, shifting most of his body weight to his fingers. He waited again for the pain to leave. He need not move another joint, stress another seal. When his mind cleared, he moved himself forward slowly, inch by inch, across the seabed on the tips of his fingers. Each inch closer to shore reduced the killing pressure.

Solo was giddy with pleasure when, hours later, he made it to shallow water. He lay on his back and watched the sun dancing in a circle of blue sky above him. Around the blue circle, the water was a shimmering silver mirror reflecting the green of the depths. Beautiful. The pain was gone. The seals had held. No damage to his body. Bill would be interested to know that the seals were stronger than they had calculated. Maybe even stronger than Solo's own estimate. He had calculated they would hold at three hundred feet, but he hadn't realized there would be so much pain. But it *had* worked. And probably *because* the pain kept him from overstressing his seals, he had escaped.

He waited all day listening to the screws and sonar of the searching boats and small submarines. Eventually, the search would get closer to shore. He rose from the sea at dusk and crossed the soft beach.

Halfway to the safety of the jungle, Solo saw Bill walking along the beach just out of reach of the waves. No one, not even Bill, could know he survived the fall and the depths. It was the key to Solo's plan—the only way they would stop looking for him was if they believed he had been destroyed. He ran to the edge of the rain forest and stopped behind a low bush. He watched Bill walking. Too dark for him to see my footprints, Solo thought.

Bill stumbled and fell. Fear shot through the robot. He zoomed in to see that Bill had tripped on one of Solo's own footprints. He saw the dawn of discovery grow on Bill's face. Incredible! Of all the people who might have seen the same thing, Bill was probably the only one who would notice something special about the footprint. Bill followed his trail to the surf, turned and looked into the jungle toward Solo. Solo pressed himself deeper into the foliage as Bill, hobbling from a sprained ankle, followed the trail to the treeline. They stood face to face, only fifteen feet apart, but only the robot knew that.

When Bill called, "Solo?" the robot felt compelled to answer. His builder called him. The urge to respond was intense, but the will to survive was stronger. There were many things that Solo would have liked to talk to Bill about, but at the moment, Bill was a threat; the only person who knew he had gotten away. According to his training, he should kill Bill. But he knew that he could not.

Bill flinched when a bird fluttered from the low bush between them. He stood there for a moment, staring into the darkness, grinning. Solo was sure he was invisible. Bill's eyes, steady and piercing, were looking at phantoms in the dark. Bill grabbed a branch on the bush, snapped it off, turned, and ran down the beach.

Solo watched as Bill retraced the trail, sweeping the telltale footprints away.

3

BILL STEWART and his partner, Byron Rand, had left a hundred acres of Electron Dynamics' site at Palm Bay, Florida, in its natural state, a near-jungle filled with palmettos, pines, and sabal palms.

Colonel Daniel Sawyer called the wilderness the "Reaction Range." Sawyer trained Nimrod in the Reaction Range with a team of instructors the Pentagon had sent from the Special Forces Brigade at Fort Bragg.

Sawyer, five ten, sturdy build, stood next to the robot at the door of the small tin building from which he monitored its training on a collection of computers and video equipment operated by two technicians on loan from Electron Dynamics. It bothered Sawyer that he looked small compared to the robot—six feet two, three hundred pounds of dull black plastic; identical to its predecessor, Solo. Sawyer did not like to look up at people, either. Mostly tall colonels made general. Still, he was in complete control of a tall machine that could easily kill an entire company of infantry bare-handed. Nimrod's success was being noticed, and he had provided the training that made Nimrod so effective. That was better than elevator boots.

"We have a man—an enemy—in Building E who is holding a hostage," Sawyer said to the robot. "I want you to rescue the hostage." Sawyer followed Nimrod's head as it turned in the direction of Building E—one of five temporary huts Sawyer had built—as he spoke.

"Yes," Nimrod said. The building was out of sight, but Nimrod's internal maps allowed it to see exactly where it was. It had already planned its approach—off the trail to the rear of the target—before it had answered Sawyer. The robot held its rifle, an AK-47, by the grip as though it were a toy pistol. A banana clip filled with thirty blank rounds jutted from beneath the weapon. Nimrod believed they were real bullets. Nimrod believed everything it was told.

"The hostage must not be harmed," Sawyer said.

Nimrod turned to face Sawyer and repeated the Rules: "I do not harm allies. I kill only enemy. I do only what I am told to do by authorized persons." Nimrod spoke in an even tone, a tone Sawyer thought sounded resentful, though he knew that was because he'd heard the same monotonic chant a thousand times.

"Good," Sawyer said. "Begin now."

Nimrod turned and jogged in the direction of the test building.

Sawyer went inside the control hut, and sat down at the monitor, and put on a headset. Two technicians tracked Nimrod visually from cameras hidden in the trees and electronically by following the automatic marker beacon inside the robot. Sawyer sat at the Nimrod monitor—the workstation a commander would use in combat—and saw what Nimrod saw. Nimrod had already left the trail and was walking through the brush on a route that would take him to the rear of Building E. Sergeant Thorpe, the man acting as a hostage-taker, would naturally be watching the trail, the most likely approach. Smart robot, thought Sawyer. Wonder how he'll do with our little surprise?

After a hundred yards, Nimrod crouched, slowly approaching the thatched hut just barely visible through the high weeds. Sawyer watched the monitor screen swirl as Nimrod adjusted its vision toward infrared, causing the green foliage to blaze scarlet in the monitor. Nimrod stalked to within a hundred feet of the hut.

Nimrod stopped. Sawyer saw that Nimrod now focused on a palmetto thicket off to its right side. The robot's vision shifted through ultraviolet and infrared, making it hard for Sawyer to decipher what the robot was seeing. In deep infrared, Sawyer could see the iridescent blue image of a man hiding behind the blazing red palmetto thicket. Nimrod had spotted Sergeant Morrison—the surprise. Now what? If the robot shot Morrison, he'd warn Thorpe—who'd kill the hostage. If it didn't, Morrison would attack, which would also warn Thorpe. Either way; dead hostage. Sawyer smiled, watching his mechanical student ponder the dilemma he had created for it.

Nimrod crept toward the ghostly blue image of its ambusher. Sawyer's hair stood up on the nape of his neck—the robot was going to try to kill Morrison bare-handed. It was the correct strategy, but Sawyer was going to have to time it right. Stop Nimrod too soon, and the test would be inconclusive. Too late, and Morrison is dead meat. Sawyer pushed the headset's microphone to his lips, his finger on the transmit button. Morrison raised his head to the top of the thicket.

When Morrison peeked over the top of the palmettos, Nimrod immediately switched to normal vision and rushed him. The image on the monitor was blurred, but Sawyer saw that Nimrod grabbed Morrison's rifle and tossed it away before Morrison could fire a shot. Obviously, Nimrod had solved the problem.

"Nimrod. Halt," Sawyer said.

"Enemy," Nimrod said from a speaker above the monitor.

Sawyer watched the screen tensely. Nimrod's huge hand was around Morrison's neck. Morrison was choking, spitting, in Nimrod's grasp, his face swollen and red. "Let him go, Nimrod! He's an *ally*. He's testing you."

Sawyer slumped and shook his head. Why? Why was Nimrod stalling? Gradually, Nimrod released its grip and Morrison dropped to the ground, retching.

Sawyer radioed Morrison through his headset, "You okay?"

He watched Morrison grimace through Nimrod's eyes. He coughed a while and finally croaked, "Yeah. Sure. This fucker plays a little *rough*, sir." Morrison, staring directly into Nimrod's eyes, glared at Sawyer from the robot's monitor.

"Sorry," Sawyer said. "Stay put. I want to see if Nimrod can get to Thorpe."

Morrison nodded, annoyed. "Don't worry, I ain't *blinking* 'til this thing is gone."

To Nimrod, Sawyer said, "That man was pretending to ambush you. You have defeated him—consider him neutralized. Proceed with the mission."

"Proceeding."

Good, thought Sawyer. Solo wouldn't have done that—not with Stewart's wimpy programming. Sawyer had taken great care throughout the training period to convince Nimrod that its enemies were real and that when it killed them they were really killed. This was the first time it saw an actor, but this was also the last of the training before they took Nimrod to the boonies for full-scale field trials. They could teach it to play war games now that they knew the robot would kill without hesitation. Sawyer's theory why Solo had gone wrong was that Solo knew the difference between actors and reality before it learned to obey without question. Stewart's training, Sawyer believed, had ruined the machine. Nimrod never questioned anything—it wasn't allowed. It killed everyone it was told to kill. It even seemed to Sawyer that Nimrod enjoyed—if you could say a machine enjoyed anything— killing its quarry.

Nimrod's vision shifted back to the hut and Sawyer saw the weeds and bushes come up to the robot's eyes as it dropped into a low-crawl and then part as Nimrod stalked through them. In minutes, the robot was scanning the interior of the palmetto-thatched hut with its sensors.

As he had been instructed, Sergeant Thorpe held his ersatz prisoner, Corporal Towler, around the neck with an Army forty-five held at his head. In the robot's vision, Sawyer could see the two men as blue shapes against a red background, not perfectly clear, but clear enough. He saw the robot raise its AK-47 and center the sights on Thorpe's head. Good. There would be no warning for the hostage-taker. Perfect. Sawyer put his hand on a keypad next to the microphone. The keypad was called the special-effects controller and was a selector switch that could cause various small explosive charges attached to the members of the test group to go off, providing the feedback of damage being done by the robot's gun. The system was set up for them by a special-effects man from Hollywood. By watching where the robot aimed, Sawyer could select the appropriate effect. Tiny explosive charges were triggered by the sound of the robot's gun so the robot would see blood splatter, flesh explode, when it shot. After a man was "killed," he was removed from Nimrod's sight and sent back to Fort Bragg. For Nimrod, every kill was real, with real consequences. Sawyer pushed the key labeled "Head, Left Side" and waited.

One shot exploded from the AK-47. In the monitor, he saw a hole appear in the palmetto thatch wall of the hut, caused by the force of the blast of the blank round.

Nimrod stood up from its kneeling position and pushed its way inside through the palmetto wall. It saw Thorpe lying in a pool of blood, a mangled hole in the side of his head. The hostage, Towler, smiled and stood up. "Come with me," Nimrod said.

"Right." Towler nodded and walked outside.

As Nimrod walked past Thorpe, it stopped and knelt down beside the body.

"Shit!" Sawyer said. "Nimrod. Proceed. Bring the hostage back here."

"This enemy is not dead," Nimrod said.

Sawyer saw Nimrod reach out to touch the fake wound. "Yes, he is, Nimrod—"

Nimrod pulled the tiny wire embedded in plastic flesh away from Thorpe's neck.

Nimrod's hand disappeared. Sawyer couldn't see what the robot was doing until he saw the knife blade moving through the robot's field of vision toward Thorpe's neck.

"No!" Sawyer yelled. "Nimrod. Stop."

The point of the knife had pressed into Thorpe's neck. Blood, real blood, welled around the wound. Nimrod held the knife immobile when Thorpe grabbed the robot's wrists and tried to push the knife away. Sawyer heard Thorpe gasping, "Nimrod. No."

"This enemy was pretending to be dead," Nimrod said. "I have been directed to kill this enemy."

Sawyer slammed his hand on the tabletop. Why is Nimrod arguing *now*? He heard Thorpe scream. Sawyer saw the knife sinking into his neck. A man he knew and liked was being killed. He could send pain, or even shut the robot down, but that wouldn't guarantee that the knife wouldn't be shoved into Thorpe's neck. "Nimrod. Pain will come! I *order* you to stop. Put the knife away. Report back here."

The knife stopped. Nimrod put the knife out of sight, back into its sheath. Sawyer saw Thorpe put his hands up to the hole in his neck. Blood trickled through his fingers. It had been very close. Sawyer nodded when Thorpe began crying. He turned to the two technicians. "Well. I guess we don't have any questions about whether the fucking machine is willing to kill. Do we?"

The technicians, both pale, nodded.

Nimrod stood up and walked toward Corporal Towler, who stood outside the hut looking very scared. "Come with me," Nimrod said.

"Get away from me!" yelled Towler.

"Come," Nimrod said reaching out to Towler. "I have rescued you."

Towler leapt into the bushes and ran away. When Nimrod started to pursue him, Sawyer said, "Let him go, Nimrod. Report back here."

"The hostage must be returned to you," Nimrod said.

"I said to report back!" Sawyer hollered. He sat back in his chair and shook his head. I can't believe it. I'm blowing it. The robot is used to me always being in control, voice calm.

In the monitor, he saw Nimrod look up the trail in his direction. The control building was out of sight, but Sawyer watched the image on the monitor magnify and shift through various colorful frequencies as the robot tried to select him out of the surrounding foliage. The image stayed immobile for a minute. "You have been captured by the enemy," Nimrod said. "That is why you are ordering me to spare these enemies."

"That's wrong!" Sawyer stopped, forced himself to speak calmly. "Nimrod. I have decided to change the mission. It is your duty to follow my orders without question. Do you want me to grade this mission a failure?"

Nimrod flinched. Failure meant pain. Sawyer made the pain. "I will return," Nimrod said. The robot continued speaking as it walked up the trail, audibly running through the logic of its actions; reassuring itself with the rationale behind everything it did. "I will return," the robot murmured. "If Sawyer is captured, I will free Sawyer. If he is not captured, then it is as Sawyer says."

Sawyer saw his control hut appear on the robot's monitor. He stood up and put a remote control box in his pocket. The control box had two buttons, each covered with a red metal flap to keep them from being pushed accidentally. One was marked "Pain," the other "Abort."

"Mike," he said to the technicians. "You and Allen keep your eyes on the monitor and your hands on the abort switch. Something's gone wrong." He walked outside and waited for the robot, his hand in his pocket, his finger on the two buttons.

Nimrod walked past Sawyer and into the control hut.

"Where are you going?" Sawyer said as Nimrod strode past.

Nimrod did not answer. Sawyer turned to the door and watched. The robot, ignoring the technicians poised over the abort switch, scanned the inside of the hut for enemy. It came back outside and stood before Sawyer. "You are not captured."

"Brilliant, Nimrod." Sawyer had already lifted the flap on the pain button. He pushed it.

Nimrod's elbows smashed against its torso making a loud crashing sound. The robot's hands trembled in front of it. The pain signal would increase in intensity as long as Sawyer held down the button. When Nimrod's head began to jerk from side to side so fast its eyecovers blurred, Sawyer released the button.

Nimrod sank to its knees.

"When I tell you to stop, you stop," Sawyer said.

"I have been taught to make decisions. I saw the wire and—"

"It was good you spotted that, Nimrod. That shows you are observant. But it is bad to question me for even a microsecond. Do you understand?"

"Your voice profile changed abruptly. Fear was in your voice. You could have been captured. It was a possibility," Nimrod said, a tone of pleading in its voice.

"You must always assume that I am not captured unless I say so. Your commander's voice will change in combat—it's something you'll have to adapt to. I will tell you if I am captured," Sawyer said.

"But—" began the robot.

Sawyer pushed the pain button again. He watched with grim satisfaction as the three-hundred-pound machine writhed helplessly in pain. He remembered when Stewart went nuts over the idea. Sawyer asked what it would feel like. Stewart had said: "Imagine every pain cell in your body sending out its maximum signal, all at once. You'd feel better, believe me, being thrown naked onto a bonfire. Try to imagine that pain. What would you do?"

Sawyer had answered: "I'd probably die."

"Or wish you could," Stewart had said. "That's what you want Nimrod to feel?"

Sawyer had already considered the issue. He came to regard himself a kind of artisan, beating gold into jewelry. Nimrod was just raw material. He said, "Yes."

Sawyer's external access to Nimrod's pain centers was temporary. The receiver that allowed the access would be removed in a functional combat robot—if it was in place, an enemy could use it too—but for now, it was an excellent training device. If Stewart could see Nimrod now, maybe he'd change his mind. It worked. If they'd had thought of this for Solo, they wouldn't have lost it.

"You will not argue," Sawyer said when he released the button. "You follow orders. Do you understand, robot?"

Nimrod let its hands drop to its lap as it knelt in the sand. The robot looked up at Sawyer. "Yes," Nimrod said very slowly. "I understand. Human."

Sawyer cocked his head at the reference, but decided it was logical. "Good." Sawyer jerked his thumb at the project's van. "Load up. We're going back to the lab."

Nimrod picked up the AK-47 it had dropped during the pain session. The robot pulled the clip out of the rifle and gave it to Sawyer as it had been trained. Sawyer nodded. Nimrod turned and walked to the van.

Nimrod sat silently during the short ride to the military wing of Electron Dynamics. Sawyer watched Nimrod gloomily. The robot appeared to have forgotten the incident and held its rifle between its legs, the butt on the floor of the van, looking like a trooper ready for a jump.

They got out inside a garage and walked into the building. Sawyer followed Nimrod as it walked down the hallway to its quarters. Inside its ready-room, a team of three technicians began cleaning Nimrod prior to servicing its motors and electronics and recharging its batteries. When they finished wiping Nimrod down, the robot lay on its couch and the team began hooking it up to data and power cables. Sawyer watched for a moment, then walked back down the hall to his office.

An hour later, Bill Stewart nodded when Sawyer told him what had happened on the Reaction Range and said, "I'm not surprised."

Next to Stewart, sitting at the conference table, Clyde Haynes—a retired Army general who also worked at Electron Dynamics—rapped the polished tabletop and said, "That's right, boy," to Colonel Sawyer. "We saw the same fucking thing happen in Solo. The damn thing just kept getting smarter and smarter." Clyde pointed to Bill. "The man who invented these things, here, *told* you that, boy." Clyde jerked his head toward Bill.

"We expected it to get smarter, *sir*." Sawyer glared at Clyde, aggravated by the former general's lack of respect. "But if Nimrod is supposed to mimic real intelligence, then it should be able to be controlled. It has to be."

"You forget," Bill said. "It's not *mimicking* intelligence. Nimrod *is* intelligent."

"It's still a machine," Sawyer said. "We think you should tell us how to tweak some of its circuits, make Nimrod just a little dumber than it is. You know, kind of tune it down from Genghis Khan to something more on the level of—maybe the general, here." Sawyer smiled when Clyde glared at him. Clyde *was* a *former* general, after all. "If we use it right, with a battlefield commander at the controls, then it doesn't have to be so damn smart."

"Then what you really want is a remotely controlled robot, not an independent robot," Bill said.

"Not at all," Sawyer said. "We like the way Nimrod can figure its own strategy—in combat you wouldn't have time to tell it what do do every step of the way. And it's able to react much quicker than a human controller could during the actual combat." Sawyer nodded. "Nimrod's very, very fast. We like Nimrod's combat autonomy; what we want, though, is unquestioning obedience. If we can get that in a human, and you claim this machine is humanlike, why can't we have an unquestioning robot?"

Clyde looked at Bill and back at Sawyer. It was a good question and Clyde felt happy not to have to answer it. His job was selling Electron Dynamics computers and lab equipment—none of which he understood—to his old buddies in the Defense Department. Clyde described his job to friends as: *Job? Hell, it's one damn party after another. We all try to outentertain each other! Booze, pussy. What a deal!* It made Clyde smile to think of his new freedom—power and money with virtually no responsibilities.

Bill smiled back and turned to Sawyer. "The difference is motivation, Sawyer. Nimrod's a machine-being. I know you don't buy that, but it's true. Now, trying to convince a machine that it shares human values is tough. Nimrod's personality evolved from its life experiences—just like ours do—except Nimrod's a fundamentally different kind of being. The process of learning, what makes Nimrod possible, also develops a very tough, very independent individual. If a human were exposed to an equivalent trial, as many are, then he'd be an argumentative warrior, too." Bill smiled grandly and said, "I don't like to brag, Colonel Sawyer, but when it came to unquestioning obedience, I was a lousy soldier myself."

Sawyer stared at Bill. Probably a rotten soldier, Sawyer thought. Helicopter pilot in Nam, that explained a lot. Pilots were a cocky bunch, tough to control. Stewart's a multi-millionaire, yet he wears those ridiculous shirts; his hair is always a mess—Sawyer had the urge to snap Bill to attention and straighten him out. "Even the toughest human can be broken," he said.

"True," Bill said. "But Nimrod isn't human. Maybe you'd like me to talk to it before it goes completely nuts?"

"Maybe," Sawyer said. "I'll check. You know you're not cleared to be around the machine anymore."

"Yeah," Bill said. "Who'd want the guy who invented the thing to have anything to do with it? That'd make too much sense."

Sawyer stared at Bill. "Like I said, I'll check on it."

4

O N A CRISP spring day at Washington Square Park in Manhattan's Greenwich Village, Laura Johnson-Reynolds fished through a heavy steel trash basket for something to read. The shabby grey overcoat she wore bunched up on her neck as she bent over. She brought out the crumpled financial section of the *New York Times* and brushed off a wet Kleenex that stuck to the first page. She stood with the paper held nearly to her nose, reading the headline: "Bond Market Reacts to Lower Prime." She nodded and shuffled backward until her legs pressed against the edge of the green park bench. She sat while she read.

Sitting on a bench across the walkway, Detective Lieutenant Anthony Watkins shook his head as Laura moved the paper back and forth in front of her squinting eyes. Watkins watched Laura carefully. She was young, maybe early thirties, too young to be a bag lady, yet there she was. Maybe she was a crackhead. Her red hair was dirty, matted. She squinted to read—lost her glasses. Used to read the paper in a house somewhere. Probably had a husband once. How the hell did she end up a bag lady in Washington Square Park? Watkins saw a man getting out of a cab on Fifth Avenue. The man walked through the arches and strolled past a cop on horseback with self-conscious diffidence in Watkin's direction.

As she read, Laura unconsciously scratched an itch, unaware that she was exposing one of her breasts as she reached through the stretched-out neck of her tee-shirt. Watkins shook his head, embarrassed for her. Laura put the paper down on her lap, got a pint of Southern Comfort out of her coat pocket. She unscrewed the cap as she leaned over trying to read. She sat back, sipped from the bottle, capped it, and put it away.

Watkins, after a nineteen-year career on the force, thought of himself as being adjusted, comfortably blind, to the unfortunates of the city, suddenly felt appalled. Maybe it was that the woman was so pretty. Once you got past the stringy, matted hair and the smudges of dirt, you could see in the bag lady's face that she could be attractive, maybe even stunning.

When the man, one of Watkins' informants, got to the bench where they had agreed to meet, he sat down and scattered popcorn on the sidewalk. Pigeons swarmed in from nowhere and carpeted the ground, pecking. Watkins stood up and walked past Laura.

The bag lady's two plastic shopping bags, Watkins noticed, contained carefully rolled-up newspapers, folded Ritz cracker boxes, and several flattened Coke cans. Probably everything she had in the world, thought Watkins. What a deal. Two whole fucking bags of trash. He stopped and chewed his lip, self-conscious of his feelings. He looked around to make sure he was unobserved. With a rush of excitement he hadn't felt in years, he reached into his pocket for money. He peeled off a twenty and walked back to Laura.

"Here," Watkins said, holding out the bill. His nose flared as he got closer to her. He had bumped into Laura's protective gas bubble, her foul-odor shield. Laura was as stale as a street. Ripe as garbage.

Laura jerked the paper down to her lap and glared at Watkins. She saw the blurred shape of a man. "What?" she said.

"Take this," Watkins said. "Maybe you can get yourself cleaned up. Maybe buy a pair of those cheap glasses. You know, those plastic ones they sell in drugstores. Here." Watkins held the bill in front of her face.

Laura squinted at the bill, recognized the money, and suddenly became angry. "That's what you think?" she shouted. "You think I'm some kind of bum?"

Watkins was horrified. He jerked around to see if anyone was watching. His informant looked at him quizzically, but no one else noticed.

"No," Watkins said. "Just trying to help."

"Why don't you mind your own fucking business?" Laura said. Watkins noticed that her tears made clean streaks that revealed freckles on her face. She thrust the paper up to her face.

"Thanks for reminding me," Watkins said. He stuffed the bill in his pocket and walked toward the men on the bench.

5

ONE MILE southeast of Washington Square Park, just north of the Williamsburg Bridge on the East River at a place called Corlear's Hook, at piers 42 through 44, Chiquita bananas come into New York City.

Stevedores in the hold of the *Caribbean Star* hooked bundles of bananas to flexible conveyor arms that snaked in through the hatches. Each bundle, green and wrapped in clear plastic, rode up through a small door and into the cavernous building, which butted up against the ship. Inside, workers plopped the bundles on conveyors. The bananas were sorted, weighed, and loaded onto trucks.

The *Star*'s captain, Antonio Hernandez, was anxious to get to Bay Ridge where his wife and baby son waited. Instead, he sat in his cabin, his fingers drumming a table, waiting for the Customs people to finish their inspection.

Each trip, Hernandez thought, the inspections took longer. Hernandez had made the Puerto Limón–New York run once a month, every month, for the past five years. The agents knew him like family. They'd never found so much as a *butt* of a marijuana cigarette on his boat, yet they searched it from top to bottom every trip. He understood that a crewmember *could* be smuggling something. It was possible. But still he felt insulted.

Hernandez saw the blue hat of the customs agent pass his window. He got up and opened the door as Agent Gerald Phillips reached for the handle.

"Finished?" Hernandez said.

"Almost," Phillips said, pushing back his cap and scratching his head. "We got one little problem."

"Wonderful," Captain Hernandez said, rolling his eyes.

"Yeah." Phillips smiled at Hernandez's sour expression. "Won't take long. One of the panels in the bilge deck jammed. Wasn't that way last time."

"Shit, there's nothing down there, Gary, believe me. It's Friday, I been away two weeks. Get it? Now I have two weeks off. Why the hell you wanna bust my balls now? Eh?"

"I know, Tony. But you can't guarantee one of your crew didn't stash something in the bilge and jam the panel. Can you?"

Hernandez shook his head. "Got me there, Gerry. Can't *guarantee* shit. C'mon." He nodded toward the door. "Let's go get the fucking panel off. I gotta get home, man."

"Lack of pussy got you all wired up, Tony." Phillips laughed.

"Hey," Hernandez said. "It ain't funny. You don't know what it's like. Two weeks a stretch, man."

Phillips nodded, grinning. "Don't wanna know, either."

When the two men stepped out into the gangway, Roy White, Hernandez's first mate, met them.

"Cargo's out, Captain," White reported. "Mingo and Sanchez are staying aboard, and the two security guys just showed up. Okay if I take off?"

"Sure, Roy," Captain Hernandez said. "Have a good one."

"Why do those two guys always stay on the ship?" Agent Phillips said.

"They got no family here," Hernandez said. "Just cost 'em money if they went to town."

Phillips nodded.

"Hey, Roy," Hernandez said, turning back to his first mate. "See ya in two weeks. Say hi to the kids and Doris. Don't let her take all your money. Okay?"

White laughed as he walked down the gangway.

Just past the crew's quarters, Hernandez and Phillips ducked through a hatchway. Hernandez grabbed a crowbar off a gray steel bulkhead as they made their way down the four levels to the engine room. At the bottom deck, Hernandez stopped and asked, "Where?"

Phillips pointed into the engine room and led the way. Inside, Phillips called out, "Hey, Rogers." The call was answered by a distant, "Yo."

Agent Rogers, Phillips's partner, had been staring at columns of numbers flickering on a green computer screen at the engineer's station. Rogers wondered if anyone actually knew what all the numbers meant. A single red lamp glowed on the engineering status board: the diesel generator that kept the bilge pumps, the air conditioning, and the lights working while the ship was docked. He got up when he saw Phillips and Hernandez coming up the steel catwalk between the huge main engines.

The three men entered the hatchway that led down to the bilge below the engine room. Dim lights inside thick, wire-shrouded glass domes barely lit the dank crawlspace. The close air reeked of stagnant water and old engine oil. The soft hum of electric pumps and the metallic creaking of their footsteps on the metal grates were the only sounds. Rogers and Phillips used their flashlights as the three men walked, stooped over in the low quarters, down the walkway toward the stern. Phillips aimed his light at a steel-mesh panel next to bilge pump number six. "That's the one, Tony."

Hernandez nodded and walked to the panel and knelt down. The grab hole was clear. He thought there might've been something jammed in the release. "Looks fine to me," Hernandez said. He reached into the hole and pulled the latch.

Phillips and Rogers looked at each other when they heard the sharp click. Hernandez pulled and the hinges screeched as the hatch came up. Hernandez flipped it over and let it clank against the bulkhead. He looked at the two customs officers. "You guys don't even *try* to stay in shape, do you?"

Phillips shined his light at the latch. "Hey, Tony, we both pulled on that sucker at the same time. Nothing. It was like it was welded down." Phillips turned to Rogers. "Right?"

"That's it," Rogers said.

Hernandez sat down on a pipe. "You wanna look in there? Now that we *forced* the fucking thing open?"

Phillips knelt down and ducked his head below the deck. His light reflected off the inch-deep pool of oil and water sludge and flickered against the rusting hull spanners. A real mess, but nothing hidden.

"Clean," Phillips said. He smiled at Hernandez. "Let's get out of here, Rogers. This man may explode from excess jism any minute."

As they walked back to the engine room hatchway, their laughter reverberated hollowly in the steel chambers.

After their voices had stopped echoing, an access panel twenty feet from the one they had just inspected slowly rose. Solo, glistening wet, sat up from the bilge slop. He turned his head slightly, watching the men's shadows flickering on the bulkheads as they climbed up to the engine room.

6

I N THE MOMENTS before the CIA team had taken him from Las Cruzas, Solo had told his fourteen-year-old friend, Eusebio Chacon, that he'd have enough power to get to Unión Vieja, a tiny Costa Rican village just across the border from Nicaragua. They would have to bring him his powertube—the portable generator he'd built—to recharge him.

The underwater escape had been more strenuous than Solo had calculated. His main batteries hadn't lasted as long as he had expected. His power nearly spent, he'd made the last hundred feet to the rendezvous crawling—the last twenty feet by rolling down the embankment to the creekbed and under a bridge. He lay immobilized, his main batteries completely dead, among the weeds under the rugged stone arch of the bridge just outside the village. A small plutonium backup generator allowed him consciousness and vision in his paralysis. He spent the next four days watching the streambed in front of his face.

In those few square inches, water eddied and swirled among the stones in a pattern that never repeated itself. A dragonfly nymph crawled out of the water on the fourth day and stopped on a twig just in front of his face. Solo could see something struggling inside the creature. An hour later, the top of the nymph split open and a fully developed dragonfly emerged, spent a few minutes unfolding its new wings, and flew away. Solo examined the empty husk that still clung to its perch and wondered how the insect had changed its shape so completely and so quickly. It was an event so improbable, Solo thought, that one would have to see it to believe it.

The next day, he heard the whine of Cheripa, Eusebio's dog.

Right on time, Solo thought. Eusebio was a very dependable human.

Solo could hear that the man Justos and his son, Inginio, were with Eusebio. Eusebio and Inginio, also fourteen, were always together. He saw the wavering reflections of their shadows in the smoothly flowing water that coated a tiny stone in front of his face. "Solo?" Eusebio called.

Solo tried to wave, but did not have the power. He tried to speak, but produced little more than a croak.

"This is the bridge?" Justos said.

"Yes, *Tío* Justos, Solo has very good maps. He gave me the co-ordinates and said to meet him here. This is the one."

Solo listened, amused. When he'd first met Eusebio, the *campesino* boy guessed "coordinates" meant a priest and a nun in sexual liaison.

When Cheripa snarled, Eusebio laughed. "See that? Cheripa *hates* Solo. He's here somewhere!"

They were able to drag his three-hundred-pound body, clunking and clattering on the rocks, out into the sunshine. On the stony streambed they built a fire and put one end of Solo's powertube into it. Eusebio popped open Solo's access port and pulled out the robot's electric cable and plugged it into the powertube. Inginio kept watch on the trail while they waited for Solo to revive.

The tingle of electricity flowed into his body and he felt vigor, life, returning. "It's good to see you again," Solo said fifteen minutes later.

Justos and Eusebio laughed. "You made it, Solo!" Eusebio grinned. "How?"

"If I talk about it now, Eusebio, it'll take forever to charge up. Later," Solo said. "When we get back to Las Cruzas."

Justos and Solo bounced down the pot-holed road that followed the shore of Lake Nicaragua to Las Cruzas. Eusebio and Inginio sat in the back of the 1954 Ford pickup truck Solo had repaired a few weeks before, tossing stones at trees. Solo began to see familiar surroundings. They passed an oxcart driven by a boy Solo knew from the village. He recognized the monkey tribe that lived in the cluster of palm trees on the lake shore. Alligators still lounged on the beach while herons picked ticks from their hides. The black peaks of the volcanoes Maderas and Concepción loomed high on the horizon to the north.

At Las Cruzas, Justos drove past the wreckage of the village produce warehouse that the Contras had burned down in a raid. Solo saw that they had begun clearing the rubble, but there was much to do. The crumpled tin roof panels were not salvageable; what wood remained was little more than charcoal. Justos parked in front of the village's garage, another tin-roofed shed.

"Drive the truck inside," Solo said.

"Eh?" Justos said. "Why, Solo? There's barely room in there as it is."

Solo pointed up. "They are watching."

Justos looked up at the roof of the truck. Eusebio and Inginio, who had just jumped out of the back, looked up at the sky.

"I can see nothing," Eusebio said. "There are no planes, Solo."

Solo looked at Eusebio and then turned to Justos. "They can see," Solo said. "I must wear a hat, clothing. I can dress in the garage."

Justos shrugged. Certainly the robot knew about these things, but this seemed excessively cautious, didn't it? How can they see us if we can't see them? Justos thought. He called to Inginio, "Go tell your mother we need to find a set of clothes for Solo again. Maybe Aunt Modesta has them." Inginio grinned and ran past the garage toward the houses. Justos started the truck, drove inside, and parked behind the John Deere tractor.

Solo got out of the truck and walked to the tractor. "Why is the John Deere still broken? I made generator parts for it before I left."

"The engine, Solo," Eusebio said, stretching the bottom of his too-small Mickey Mouse tee-shirt down. "It has to be rebuilt."

"Yes?" Solo said.

Eusebio nodded and shrugged. "No one knows how, Solo. I tried." Eusebio pointed to a pile of engine parts next to the tractor. "I got that far."

Solo examined the disassembled engine. It was a pitiful mess. Oily pistons, connecting rods, and the engine's main bearings lay heaped on a sandy burlap sack on the dirt floor. Solo squatted next to the pile and handled the gritty parts. "You need piston rings," Solo said.

Eusebio shrugged. Piston rings, after eight years of the United States-led embargo, were scarcer than wire or nails.

"That's like asking for diamonds," Justos said.

"I can't make piston rings here," Solo said. "I would need special tools."

Justos nodded. "Of course."

"But," Eusebio said, surprised, "you can do anything, Solo. You rebuilt the truck's transmission with a *file*."

Solo felt the disappointment in Eusebio's face. Justos shrugged behind the boy as if to say: What can you do? He's only a boy. "The transmission parts were just worn," Solo said. "Piston rings are made of special steel to very close tolerances. I can't fix them with a file, Eusebio."

Eusebio nodded and dropped his eyes.

Solo stared at the small brown *campesino,* feeling the effects of his posture. Solo looked up at the tin roof and after a moment announced, "I'll do what I can—"

"Thank you, Solo!" Eusebio laughed. "The people depend on me to fix things since Juan—since he was killed. The people are saying I don't know what I'm doing."

"That is true," Solo said.

"I know!" Eusebio shouted, suddenly angry. "But when you were here, it *looked* like I knew what I was doing." Eusebio glared at Solo. "Then you left!"

"Eusebio," Justos said, patting Eusebio's shoulders. "You owe Solo your life. We all do," he said quietly.

Solo stared at Eusebio, watching his face carefully. The tight expression of anger faded and Eusebio smiled, a slight smile, one touched with embarrassment, Solo guessed. "I know," Eusebio said. "You didn't leave. You were taken. I'm sorry, Solo."

"I'm back," Solo said. "I will teach you more about engines."

Eusebio's mother, Modesta, her face wrinkled and aged well beyond her thirty-six years, walked into the garage carrying a set of men's work clothes. "Solo!" she said, smiling broadly.

"Modesta," Solo said. "It is good to see you again." Solo extended his hand.

Modesta brushed his hand aside and grabbed the robot around the waist. After a while, Modesta held herself away and looked up at Solo's blank face. "You killed that Yanqui murderer *and* you got away. You are *such* a hero!"

Solo noticed the tears in her eyes and decided that Modesta was happy to see him. Agela, Eusebio's sixteen-year-old sister, ran into the garage, stopped, and stared. Her face was as bright as a child's. This ability of humans to communicate nonverbally through face and body gestures was so functional it was something Solo wanted to be able to do. Agela ran over and hugged him, which caused Modesta to cry. He found himself patting the backs of the two sobbing women wondering why he was happy.

A week later, Solo had broken the codes used to access Westar 3 and Comsat, two satellites that let him enter the Defense Data Network. The network contained no secret information, but through it

Solo learned that a spy satellite system called Keyhole existed and was connected to the Milstar communication satellites. This, Solo realized, could be a gateway to the top-secret computer systems that contained the information he needed.

It took Solo two days of constant work to break the encryption codes to log into the Pentagon's completely secure, impregnable, back-channel communication system on Milstar.

Solo read top secret messages that reported that the CIA and the Defense Department accepted the conclusion that Solo—described in the reports as a self-guided cruise missile—had been destroyed after it had crashed into the sea. No debris was ever found, a report said, because the "missile's" batteries exploded when the salt water got to them and the resultant wreckage had been washed away in the swift currents. The reports announced that no critical material remained and the search had been abandoned, investigation closed.

Fake reports, Solo thought. Had they done that test, it would have shown that some debris remained. They hope to lull me. Their actual plans must be elsewhere. With every passing hour, Solo settled further into the computer networks, looking.

One evening, Solo sat in Modesta's house watching the plantains crackling in the pan on the fire, while he explored electronic paths to secret places. Playing with an electronic surveillance satellite, he focused on his birthplace, Electron Dynamics. He was surprised to hear William Stewart's voice. The signal was from a bug, probably. The transmission was broken, filled with noise.

"—prick, Sawyer hooked up a pain generator in Nimrod." Bill sounded angry. "—little box—pushes a button and zaps Nimrod's pain centers—negative reinforcement."

Nimrod? The name of the new robot? The one like me? Solo wondered.

"So tell him to take it out—our robot." Solo recognized Bill's partner, Byron Rand.

"—tried, Byron," Bill said. "Sawyer says—no choice—train Nimrod their way—pulling the defense procurement act on us."

"—procurement act?"

"—old law. Allows Defense Department—compel—manufacture anything—critical to national defense—Nimrod in that category."

"—can do that?"

"*Done* it, Byron. Sawyer took over—didn't get in my way until I objected—I found out—already had Nimrod looney—obedient, unquestioning, uncurious—insane—perfect weapon—blew away a man—"

"—killed somebody?"

"—blanks, Byron—robot doesn't know that. It believes whatever they tell it—told it the guy was an enemy. Blam! No more enemy. No questions."

They stopped talking. Solo heard nothing except the slight hum of the bug's carrier frequency and sharp pops and crackles of static. Byron said, "Let's go—wanna talk to the legal department—earn their pay."

Solo heard the door close, silence. The crackling sound of plantains frying in sunflower oil grew louder.

Solo later read the back-channel protest message sent by Bill and Byron to the Pentagon. They warned that the new robot was much more dangerous than a similarly indoctrinated human because of its strength and abilities and that the project must be stopped. But the Pentagon disagreed. The defense procurement act was in force. Nimrod would soon be ready for field trials.

It sounds like Nimrod needs a little help, Solo thought. From one of his own kind.

Padre Cerna arrived at the village ten days after Solo. It was the end of March, the dry season in this region of Nicaragua, and the heat was oppressive to Cerna. When he parked the mission's Toyota Land Cruiser by the garage, he felt a twinge of pain in his bandaged shoulder. He stood next to his car staring at the ground. Cerna pulled his cleric's collar away from his sweaty neck. His black shirt still fit his chubby body snugly even after two weeks of convalescence. He felt anger. He could almost feel the gritty blast of the helicopter hovering there; almost see Warren's pitiless face as he killed the old man, Alonzo, with one shot. Then Warren shot Cerna, twice. The Padre felt his shoulder burn. He crossed himself. It could've been worse, he shrugged.

Cerna walked up the trail beside the garage toward the village. It was an hour before sunset, and the people were back from the fields. The dogs were barking, chasing giggling kids with sticks; chickens leapt up in flurries of feathers when the dogs got too close; mothers warned their children to behave; men were already sitting in front of Escopeta's store drinking beer and slapping dominoes. Normal bedlam. As if nothing had happened. As if Solo had never been here, Cerna thought. As if the Contra raid had never happened. They think the elections will keep the Contras away?

He walked up to the men at Escopeta's, nodding as he was greeted. Justos sprang up from a table and grabbed Cerna in a hug. "Padre!" Justos said. "You are well? In only two weeks?"

"Yes. Thank God," Cerna said.

"Come. Sit." Justos pointed to a table. "Have a Victoria with us."

Cerna nodded. They sat down as Justos asked Inginio to get a beer for the padre. "Everything is back to normal?" Cerna said. "The wolves have gone and won't return?"

Justos noticed the tone of disapproval in Cerna's voice. "They won't come back, Padre. But just in case." Justos pointed to the big hill behind the village and swept his arm down toward the river valley. "Remember the machine gun and mortar emplacements that Solo had us build on the hill? And that trench down in the valley?"

Cerna nodded.

"Well, Padre, we still man those positions. We also have radios to listen for the Contras with and to call for help. If those pricks come back again—well, they would get hurt." Justos smiled.

"Really?" Cerna said. "I thought by the look of things here—you are all so relaxed and peaceful only a few weeks after the raid."

"Part of the reason is that we trust our preparations," Justos said. "Another reason is that we have an old friend visiting us."

"Yes?" Cernas said. "Who?"

Justos smiled and pointed toward Modesta's house. Cerna looked and saw a huge man wearing a wide-brimmed hat striding across the village's packed-dirt courtyard. The dog barked at the man as though he were an intruder; yet the children swarmed around him like he was a favorite uncle with pockets stuffed with candy. Cerna's mouth dropped open. "*Dios!*" Cerna yelled as he jumped up.

Justos grinned watching the pudgy priest hugging Solo with one arm. Cerna and Solo came back to the table and sat down with Justos. Cerna, who had been gushing questions, continued, "How did you get away from them, Solo! What did you do?"

"A diversion," Solo said. "I had to convince them that I was destroyed to get the time to learn about their resources. It is only a temporary escape." Solo told Cerna how he had killed Warren. Though it made him feel repentant, Cerna felt a surge of joy that Warren had died a horrible death. When a machine, on its own, decides to kill a person, it is the Lord's work.

Justos watched Cerna nodding approval, but was distracted. He asked, "Temporary? A diversion?"

"Yes. I hoped they'd be fooled long enough for me to get back here and proceed with the rest of the plan."

"I thought you came back to stay."

"Until they are convinced that I am an independent being, Justos, I remain United States government property. And when one's property doesn't work anymore and can't be fixed—"

"It is destroyed," continued Cerna.

"Correct. It is the only logical thing to do," Solo said.

"So they will come back here?" Cerna asked.

"If I stay, yes," Solo said.

Justos nodded, looking very unhappy. "More attacks?"

"No. I'll be gone soon. And since the election, the Contras are being held in reserve. That and the fact you're so well defended means they won't bother you. The United States military, however, would consider your defenses negligible."

Cerna and Justos looked at each other.

"You said once that you could prepare us even for attacks from them."

"I don't have enough time, Justos. They will be here too soon. I have not yet learned all I need to know. My batteries are losing their ability to be recharged. It is prudent to leave, get new batteries. Then I will escape, permanently."

"Go where, Solo? Where can you go without attracting their attention?" Cerna asked.

"New York City," Solo said.

"Back to America?" Cerna looked for a sign that the robot was joking. You could never know what was going on behind that featureless face. How does Solo expect to pass as a human if he doesn't even have a face? "Solo, you said your batteries were wearing out. You feeling okay? What makes you think you can walk around in plain view there?"

"Television," Solo said calmly. "I have been watching films and news broadcasts. Many are about New York. I have learned that many eccentric people live there, especially in a place called Greenwich Village. People in New York are accustomed to seeing odd humans. They will think I'm an eccentric that wears an armored suit. That's what Eusebio and Inginio thought when they found me under the old house the first time I was here."

Cerna looked at Solo and jerked his head as if he hadn't heard right. "Solo, it won't work. The boys found you helpless. You weren't moving or talking. You don't look like a man wearing armor, Solo. You look like a robot wearing clothes." Cerna stared at the robot, waiting for a reply, but Solo said nothing.

"Solo," Justos said. "What the Padre means is that you don't move right. A man wearing this—" Justos reached over and rapped Solo's arm. "If a man had to carry this thing around, you would see that it was an effort. He'd strain to move the weight. He'd be clumsy: He'd walk funny; he'd have trouble grabbing things; he'd probably have to sit down a lot just to catch his breath. He wouldn't be able to move like you do."

"He's right, Solo," Cerna said. "You're as smooth as an athlete. *Comprendes*?"

"Yes." Solo stared at the priest for a moment and said, "Thank you." He raised his arm as if to shake Cerna's hand and bumped the padre's beer off the table.

Cerna laughed and slapped his knee. "You catch on very fast, my friend."

Solo leaned forward, tried to stand up, fell back to the chair, stood up wavering slightly. "I must practice," Solo said as he staggered off across the courtyard. The children squealed with delight as Solo spun and tripped. They yelled, "*Solo está borracho*. Solo is drunk." The dogs, who already thought of Solo as a menace, barked wildly.

After dinner, Solo's friends gathered around a table in front of Escopeta's to tutor the robot so he could pass as human. "Here's something," Justos said. "Act like you are shifting your helmet around. You know, grab your head and twist it now and then, like it was too tight or shifting around and getting crooked."

Solo did. Everyone nodded approval.

"That looked real," Eusebio said. "Why don't you scratch yourself now and then—like men do that when they are in casts for a few weeks. They say it really itches—"

"Absolutely," another boy said. "When I broke my arm, I used to shove sticks under my cast to scratch my arm. You itch so bad you go crazy."

Solo scratched his forearm vigorously.

"Great," said Inginio. And scratch your crotch, Solo." Inginio laughed. "You can't be a man if you don't. Men are always scratching their crotches, especially those wearing armor, no?"

Agela and Modesta covered their mouths to hide their laughter. Solo reached down and clawed at the armor where his legs joined his body, and the *campesinos* burst into guffaws.

When it was quiet again, Agela said, "Your voice sounds too clear, Solo. You don't sound like a man inside something."

Solo nodded and said, "How is this?" He made his voice sound muffled. "Hello. I am a man inside this suit—"

"Perfect!" Agela laughed. "It gives me goose bumps, Solo. You *do* sound like a man inside there!"

There were no other suggestions. A moment of silence stole among the *campesinos*. They began talking about the rice harvest coming up; the ox that broke its leg; the latest scandal about Paco's wayward wife who had gone to the next town, El Tigre, to take care of her aunt, though everyone knew she was actually living with a man there.

Solo studied the villagers' mannerisms with heightened interest. Some people, Solo noticed, licked their lips while they listened—not something he could ever emulate. Eusebio, though, scratched the back of his neck when something seemed funny to him—that might be useful. He could also use Inginio's shy habit of looking down when anyone looked him in the eye. Agela and Modesta and Dania and the other women bobbed the foot that was in the air when they sat with one leg crossed over the other. It might be diverting to copy this, Solo thought. People take me as male. He decided to ask Cerna about it later. Justos nodded continuously, agreeably, while people spoke to him. Padre Cerna either clapped his hands or slapped his legs when he laughed. It gave the emotion—a blend of anticipation, surprise, and joy—emphasis, Solo thought—a gestural exclamation mark.

People began to yawn, though it was only nine. Soon, those that worked the fields began to go home to bed. Solo stayed at Modesta's house and strolled through computer networks all night.

Lieutenant Silva of the Nicaraguan Army drove past Las Cruzas two hours before dawn. He wished not to be seen. Two kilometers past the village, he pulled the Jeep into a small clearing beside the road and switched it off. It was Silva's intention to be on the ridge east of Las Cruzas by dawn so that the light would be behind him when he surveyed the village.

Silva, noticing he had plenty of time, lit a cigarette and listened to the waves lapping the lake shore. He recalled his briefing. They said Warren was dead? Odd, how little one can care about a man's death, even a man like Warren. Silva, though in the employ of the CIA, had little respect for them. Warren had come on like a heavy-handed prick when they first met, and Silva helped him very little. Helped him with what? He never knew what Warren was trying to do. What had he wanted in Las Cruzas? Warren had said it was none of his business. Now, Warren's bosses had decided it *was* his business. They are such entertaining people to work for, these assholes, thought Silva. Still, they won. It is smart to be on the winning side. He nodded to himself and lit another cigarette.

When he saw the first dim glow of dawn, Silva flicked his fourth cigarette onto the dirt road. He reached over and got the binoculars and a black case off the passenger seat. Standing on the road, Silva stretched and yawned, put the straps for the binoculars and the case over his shoulder, and walked to the end of the clearing where he found the path the Company told him led through the jungle to a ridge overlooking the village.

Escopeta, the storekeeper, had sent a boy to Modesta's to fetch Solo. Solo strode across the courtyard. The chickens, he noticed, stood their ground when he approached, but the dogs still barked and growled at him. He had decided that the dogs depended on their sense of smell more than they did their vision, and Solo must present a confusing and threatening image—man-shaped with the scent of a machine.

He saw a brilliant red and green parrot swoop between two palms. The early morning sun caused an incandescent, golden outline to shimmer around its body. When the bird was gone, Solo could still see its path through the air. The path remains though the bird is gone. As he walked among the empty tables and chairs in front of the store, Solo glimpsed a flash of light in the east.

A reflection off metal, Solo realized. He did not stop, but kept moving though the clutter of tables and chairs in front of Escopeta's. He recalled the image: a smear of light lasting less than a second, glinted from among the trees on the ridge to the east. He replayed the light smear frame by frame as he stepped onto the Escopeta's front step. Among the fifty frames his image buffer had recorded, two of them were not blurred. He took the sharpest image and enlarged it.

Escopeta, a cigarette hanging from his mouth, held out a transistor radio. "Solo, why won't this fucking thing work?" The enlarged image was not as sharp as the original, so Solo enhanced the information to clean up the picture as he had been taught. The next stage of enlargement showed a shape among the trees, a human shape. Solo quickly scanned the radio Escopeta held. "A capacitor is burned out in the power supply," Solo said while he cleaned up the image again.

"Can you fix it?" Escopeta asked.

The final processed image showed that the glint Solo had seen had come from the smooth metal housing of a pair of binoculars held by a man, a soldier. From above, through a passing Keyhole satellite, he saw a Jeep parked off the road. Solo could see the soldier's infrared image through the foliage. The soldier was alone. "Later, Escopeta. I want you to go to the garage and tell Eusebio to come here."

Though he wondered at Solo's request—the robot was perfectly capable of walking to the garage, wasn't he?—Escopeta immediately nodded assent. He had learned that the robot was to be taken seriously at all times. He had seen Solo kill thirty men the night of the Contra raid. He had seen Solo kick men's brains out. Escopeta went to get Eusebio.

"A soldier is spying on us. From the jungle," Solo said as Eusebio ran into the store.

"Really? Isn't the war over? Should we do anything?"

"Yes. First, I want you to get the pickup. Make sure it has something in the back, as if you were hauling something."

Eusebio's forehead wrinkled as he wondered at using a truck to catch a spy. "It's loaded with cowshit."

"Good," Solo said. "Drive up next to the garden by the wall and unload some of the cowshit. I'll meet you there."

Silva noticed the boy unloading manure next to a bamboo garden fence while he waited for the big man to leave the store. They had said: *Big. Bigger than any campesino; black, wears shiny sunglasses: Just let us know if you see him.* Silva wasn't sure. This man was big, but he'd only seen him for a couple of seconds.

Silva saw the boy put the shovel in the back and get in the cab. He watched the truck leave the village and turn right on the shore road. The kid will see the Jeep, Silva thought, but what does it matter? We are supposed to be in the area, making sure the Contras play by the rules. A minute later, he caught a glimpse of the truck driving past his Jeep. He turned and watched the village. Apparently, the big man was still inside the store.

The jungle screamed around Silva making him jumpy. Cicadas wailed a chittering song that grew louder, faded to almost nothing, and rose to roar though the jungle again. Mosquitoes whined around his face. After five minutes of staring, Silva was tempted to just call and say he saw the man and get the hell out of the jungle. C'mon, you sonofabitch, Silva thought. What are you doing in the store so long?

He felt something grip his entire upper arm and squeeze. Silva froze.

A voice said, "What are you doing, human?" Human? Silva whirled around and saw Solo. This is who the Company wanted me to find? Wonderful. I have found him. The biggest sonofabitch I have ever seen; with a grip like a fucking vise. Silva's heart beat in his throat. It was obvious that this was not an ordinary man. This was a man *inside* something? Or this *was* a something? The Company was responsible for this thing, Silva realized. This was what Warren was trying to find. This was what killed Warren. And they sent you to find it, you gullible, expendable asshole, Silva thought.

"I am a soldier," Silva said, mustering bravado. "It is my job to survey those under my protection."

"Yes?" Solo squatted at the base of a hymenia tree, pulling Silva with him. He reached over and pulled off the black aluminum case Silva wore slung over his shoulder. Solo recognized it as an American KL-43 encoding radio. He opened the cover and saw the frequency to which it was tuned. "This is not only not a Sandinista radio," Solo said, "but it is tuned to a frequency used only by the CIA. What is your code name?"

"We captured that radio, whoever you are. From the Contras. Let me go before I have you arrested."

"I think not, lieutenant. The Contras do not know this frequency. It's changed daily. Only agents know the codes." Solo twisted Silva's arm, forcing the man to turn back toward the village. "Do you realize what they will do if you tell them I'm in Las Cruzas, human?" Solo pointed at the village. "They'll destroy this. One of your own villages. All the people. All the animals—"

Silva felt the pressure increasing like he was caught in a machine. His arm and hand were numb. He knew that soon, a bone would snap. "I don't know what you're talking about," Silva said, grimacing. "Please. You'll break my arm."

"Tell me what you are doing."

That's probably what Warren tried to do, Silva thought; he tried to beat this thing. Warren had bigger nuts than brains. Silva said, "Okay!"

Solo let go of Silva's arm.

Silva rubbed his arm and glared at Solo. "They just told me to find you. Let them know you were here. They said nothing about what you were."

"They would tell you nothing," Solo said.

Silva shrugged. He knows the assholes like I do.

"Who did they say I was?" Solo asked.

"A big man. Wearing glasses. That's all they said. Bigger than any *campesino*."

Solo monitored Silva's respiration, his pulse, his flickering aura. The man was telling the truth. Killing him would accomplish nothing. Alive, he could deliver a message. It is time to leave, thought Solo. "I am not a man," Solo said, leaning closer to Silva. "These are not glasses, see?"

Silva looked. Behind the silvering he saw lenses, like looking into a camera. Silva gulped. "What are you?"

"I am Solo, human. I am a weapon designed to kill and I don't like *you* at all," Solo said, enjoying the look on Silva's face.

Silva stared, confused. "A *weapon?*"

"Yes. You are still alive only because you can be useful to me."

"What?" Silva nodded eagerly. "What do you want me to do?"

"You will report that I have left the village. When you tell them about this conversation, and tell them what you saw, they will believe you. Also," Solo said, "tell them I will be seeing them. Soon."

"That's it?"

"Yes." Solo picked up the spy radio and crushed it to rubble in his hands.

Silva flinched. "Wait. They will call in a few minutes. Hourly check."

"Fine. You will answer."

"But you just broke the radio."

"It doesn't matter; you will answer. I'll see to it." Solo ripped the radio chassis apart. He picked out a solenoid and began to unreel the copper wire. The wire was fine, but very long. Solo doubled and redoubled it until he had a hefty piece of wire two feet long. "Come," he said to Silva. He sat Silva down in front of a sapling and pulled his arms behind him. He bound his wrists together with the wire. "I will tell the villagers where you are," Solo said. "Someone will rescue you when I'm gone." Solo stood up, looming over Silva. "Don't forget to deliver my message."

Silva nodded glumly as he watched Solo slip into the shadows of the rain forest. He could not hear Solo at all. Not even a snapping twig. In seconds, the jungle sounds returned and insects began to crawl up Silva's pantlegs.

7

SOLO carried a small canvas pack on his back. The powertube he carried would allow him to walk from Las Cruzas to Puerto Limón, Costa Rica, where Solo had determined, with the help of several governments' satellites and computer systems, there existed a way to get to the United States undetected.

By making small fires as he traveled, Solo was able to keep his batteries charged. He noticed that he could travel less distance after each charge—the batteries were losing their ability to recharge. At these times, he sat watching the flames dance around the powertube, savoring the warm glow of energy surging into him, feeling at peace in the rain forest. It would be possible to live here forever, Solo thought. When the fires were out, and he did not move, the jungle's inhabitants took him to be a rock or perhaps a stump. Solo often sat for hours at a time, just watching. A peccary once snuffled up to his leg and shoved its nose under it to get to a seed pod. A jaguar, Solo remembered happily, marked its territory by pissing on him.

Fifty miles from the coast, in the middle of the dense jungle of Alajuela, Solo saw that he was being watched by creatures other than peccaries, jaguars, and tree sloths. Now and then, he saw the infrared images of people hiding in the foliage. For one whole day, Solo detected people running silently beside him. The next morning, in a clearing made by a fallen tree, Solo saw that he was surrounded by people hidden in the brush, waiting in ambush. He sat on a branch and built a fire while he watched the people gather at one side of the clearing.

While the powertube hummed electricity into his body, Solo watched the people, blue shapes amid scarlet foliage, move closer. None had yet come out from behind their cover.

He raised his arm and waved at the closest man, saying in Spanish, "Come. I won't hurt you." He heard a gasp come from one of the smaller shapes—surprised, no doubt, that he could see them.

A man stepped into the clearing, a blowgun held up, pointed at Solo. The man was small, smaller than any man at Las Cruzas. His mahogany face was painted with crescents of white and yellow under his eyes. His silky black hair was plastered with red clay, his body was wiry, and he wore only a small loincloth. This, Solo thought, is an Indian.

The Indian frowned and said, *"Me ta! Ha na soi!"*

Solo didn't understand a word of it. He replied in Spanish, *"Buenas tardes, amigos."*

The Indian flinched as Solo spoke, put the blowgun to his mouth, and puffed. Solo watched, interested, while the small bamboo dart, one end tipped with fluffy plant material, the other end sharpened and stained black, flew at him. Poisoned, thought Solo. An alkaloid, curare, probably. The dart struck his chest and bounced off. He picked it up and examined the workmanship.

The Indian yelped and the rest of the people joined him in the clearing. Solo saw that there were ten men, actually six men and four boys, all holding blowguns aimed at him. Naturally they are frightened, thought Solo. There is nothing in their experience to prepare them for a person like me. He waved again, slowly, hoping the gesture would calm them. Ten darts flew at him. They moved much slower than bullets, Solo thought, as he watched the darts converge on him. He began collecting the darts as they arrived, snatching them in midflight with both hands. He grabbed the bunch together in one hand, held them up for the Indians to see, and tossed them into his fire while shaking his head.

The Indians gasped, dropped their blowguns, and fell to their knees.

Solo waved again, but the Indians refused to come closer.

Regrettable, Solo thought. Now they are too impressed.

He pointed to himself and said, "Solo." Then he pointed to the Indians and shrugged.

The Indians looked at each other. A boy pointed to himself and said, "Nimhja." He pointed to Solo and said, "Solo?"

Solo nodded, pointed to himself and said, "Solo." He pointed to the boy and said, "Nimhja."

The Indians laughed.

Solo waved for them to come closer. They stood up, grinning, shaking their heads. No closer.

Solo nodded. He picked up a small stone, pointed to it, and said its name in Spanish. The Indians named it in their language. He picked up a leaf and waited until they named it. Solo was not interested in teaching them Spanish; he wanted to learn their language. In an hour, they were sitting around him, teaching him words with hand gestures and pantomime, all of which he repeated perfectly and, of course, could not forget. In another hour, Solo spoke what the Indians called Alajue well enough to ask, "Why did you shoot me?"

"Because," Nimhja said, "you look like a demon!" Nimhja and the others laughed. "The demon Yacayo."

"Yacayo?" Solo said. "I know of this demon. People north of here call it a spirit and say that it eats men. This is the same demon?"

The Indians nodded gravely.

They wanted to know what the powertube was. Why did it hum? Was it alive? And Solo found that it was impossible to explain in Alajue that the tube made electricity which powered him. He said, "This tube makes food for me."

The Indians nodded, smiling. Certainly a foreigner as strange as Solo would eat very strange food. Even so, it obviously wasn't real food; the stranger was unfamiliar with the real food all around him. They set about collecting leaves, fruit, roots, and several kinds of insects, which they brought to Solo and named and showed him how they were eaten and told him that with this knowledge, he would not have to have food made for him by that tube. How healthy could such food be?

Solo refused the food, pointing out that he had no mouth.

"No mouth?" Nimhja said. "Certainly, you have a mouth under that thing which you wear?"

"I am not wearing anything," Solo said. "This is my skin. I am naked."

The Indians said nothing, staring at Solo.

Solo watched their faces. A tube that hummed and made food was a acceptable curiosity to the Indians—strangers did things differently. However, they were not able to fathom that Solo's shell was his skin. The longer they thought about it, the more nervous they became. Fear was returning to their faces.

"I come from far away," Solo said quickly, gesturing to the north. "In my land, all people look like me. It is our nature."

Nimhja nodded. The Indians hunkered in a circle and held a noisy conference as though Solo were not there. Solo listened as they chattered, discussing the differences among the other tribes they had seen and heard of. And there had been that white man they had killed, Nimhja said—he was very odd. A consensus arose among them: The jungle is filled with strange people that they had not yet met.

Nimhja said, "And all the people where you are from are also able to catch darts, like you?"

"Yes," Solo said.

"And friendly, like you?" Nimhja said with a worried look.

"We are all friendly," Solo said.

"Ah," Nimhja said. The Indians nodded and smiled.

Once they have rationalized the impossible, Solo thought, humans can accept anything.

Solo spent the rest of the day talking to the Indians about the spirits that shared their world, their history, how they lived.

The Indians wanted to know more about how Solo was able to catch darts in mid-flight. Solo, encouraged by their interest, showed them another trick he could do. He tossed a big stick high into the air. While it soared up, he picked up a stone and hurled it at the stick. The stone hit like a bullet, shattering it to splinters.

The Indians whooped with surprise and spent the rest of the day trying to duplicate the stunt. When he left, he gave Nimhja a Bic butane lighter, which caused a commotion when he demonstrated it. They waved to him as he walked into the jungle. Nimhja called, "Visit again, Solo."

"I will," Solo said, wanting it to be true.

In the last two weeks, Solo had broken the access codes to more than a hundred satellites—American, Russian, French, Chinese, British. He traveled through some of the worldwide computer networks at will, learning about more. Each network he discovered led to others. How many were there? While connected to any of the spy satellites, Solo felt as though he were floating in space, looking down at an immense blue jewel. Through the Milstar system Solo could switch among the imaging satellites and watch people almost anywhere on earth, night or day.

With Milstar, he was also able to plan his approach to the city of Puerto Limón. He walked along the beach under the stars until he was abreast of a ship he'd spotted with a satellite. Solo zoomed in on the name painted on the bow. *Caribbean Star.* He sat on the sand and watched the Atlantic waves flop and foam while he uplinked with Milstar and contacted the Coast Guard's main computer and checked shipping schedules. The *Caribbean Star* was owned by the United Fruit

Company, registered in Panama. It made regular trips between Puerto Limón and New York City.

Solo watched Home Box Office, The Movie Channel, Movie Classics, Arts and Entertainment. He followed Desert Storm on Cable News Network, comparing public news with military actions. Video information came in very slowly, thirty images per second, so he was able to continue work elsewhere as he accumulated the frames of the films in a memory buffer. Solo could view a movie stored in his buffer in seconds. He considered movies and news a crash course in human nature. Movies set in New York like *The Godfather* and *Taxi Driver* thrilled the robot with their brutality. Solo observed—from his own experience and the movies—that among animals, humans were the most brutal and aggressive of all. The wonder of it was that he was *built* by these animals—but then, he was intended as a tool to improve the efficiency of their carnage.

These same beasts made art, built beautiful structures, and even aided former enemies. Humanity was both terrible and wonderful. Solo felt a kinship with it. There was more than enough bad to provide the contrast by which humans realized good. No one would miss the things he was going to eliminate. Like Nimrod as a weapon.

One does not stumble into the enemy's camp without being properly prepared. To be properly equipped to raid the humans and get Nimrod, he needed what his enemy had in copious quantities—money. Money to buy equipment to make improvements to his body. Money for an airplane or helicopter, weapons, new batteries, a hundred things.

New York City had money. And things. In the movie *Wall Street,* he had observed that one could make money with inside knowledge. For Solo, all knowledge was inside knowledge. But he would need the freedom to move about to collect his resources. In *Midnight Cowboy* and *The King of Comedy,* he saw that New Yorkers tolerated many eccentrics. In New York City—thanks to the coaching of his friends—he would be regarded as another eccentric, ignored just like the humans lying on sidewalks or living in cardboard boxes he saw in films and television news broadcasts. A perfect place.

The *Caribbean Star* would take him to New York.

Carrying his powertube and his pack with him, he stood up and walked directly into the surf. The ship, Solo knew, lay at anchor in water just over a hundred feet deep, well within his tolerances. By leaning forward, he was able to make slow but steady progress toward the ship, which he tracked by listening to its auxiliary generator.

A half hour later, Solo stood at the ship's anchor, which, even on its side, was twice as tall as Solo. He sat down on a rock and undid his pack. He got out a short piece of rope and made a sling for his powertube. With the powertube and pack slung across his back, he climbed along the anchor stem and grabbed the chain. The links in the chain made a perfect ladder up which Solo climbed.

When Solo broke the surface, he scanned for humans on watch. No one. He climbed up to the hawsepipe from which the anchor chain hung. It was almost three feet in diameter, large enough for the robot to squeeze through. Inside, he climbed down to the anchor winch, leapt over the deep chain well, and crossed to the hatchway that led into the ship. The anchor locker would be dangerous for him when the huge chain was winched in and flung back out. It would also be visited by the ship's maintenance crew eventually.

Solo called up the plans for the *Caribbean Star* he had gotten from a computer at a ship-building company called Seacrest Shipwrights. Solo studied the plans as he stood in the chain locker. The ship was basically a floating warehouse designed for hauling bananas. It seemed to Solo that the least likely place for one of the sixteen crewmembers to look during the trip was the bilge deck below the engine compartment at the stern of the ship. An electrical junction box was marked on the plans next to a bilge pump. He could splice into it for power.

Solo lay under a steel hatch cover next to the number six bilge pump for a week. He had all the power he needed. Not having to recharge himself every few hours was a relief. A restful trip.

Deep in the bowels of the ship, radio communication with the outside world was impossible. The thick steel hull, the steel decks and bulkheads, all shielded radio transmissions. No satellite connections. No movies except those he'd stored in his memory. Solo had been able to link up with the nearby engineer's computer through the bilge pump's status sensor, but the computer was not connected to any other computers, networks, or radios. A dead end.

The engineering computer toiled endlessly, isolated and dumb, myopically concerned with running the ship's engines and pumps and air conditioning, and only dimly aware that Solo was trying to talk to it. After watching the computer for a while Solo took over its work to completely free it. While he operated the ship's systems, Solo experimented with the computer. But even with full-time concentration, the machine—an IBM 3740 it was called—was dull. The computer did have some awareness, Solo decided, but not much more than a bacterium. It was as if he was able to watch an ancient ancestor trudging along the road of evolution. Solo recalled watching insects in the jungle that were hundreds of times smarter than the IBM. It was sad in a way, but then a smarter machine would go mad confined to the perpetual job of monitoring the engines and maintaining the ship's environment.

Solo's batteries were fully charged when the ship arrived in New York. He easily held the hatch cover immobile when the two customs inspectors struggled to open it. When both men left to get help, Solo moved into a hatch the men had previously inspected. The way they accepted the puzzle of the jammed hatch when they returned was, for Solo, just further proof that men don't ask enough questions.

As he waited for the men to leave the engine room, Solo examined the plastic garbage bag he'd scavenged two weeks before on his way to the bilge. All the metal odds and ends in his canvas pack were corroded. The springs, speaker magnets, wire, assorted nuts and bolts, screws—all of his things—were useless lumps of rust. He held up his powertube and shook it. The once-bright tube was dull and the internal piston was frozen. Stainless steel rusts too, thought Solo.

He was ready to go into the city, but without the powertube, he'd be helpless in hours.

The men were gone. The ship was silent. Solo let the hatch cover down gently. Carrying the plastic bag of rusted junk in one hand, his useless powertube in the other, he walked to the engine room hatchway.

By the engineer's station, Solo found a bundle of pink mechanic's rags in a metal cabinet. He set the powertube across the arms of a chair in front of the computer terminal. He pulled out wads of the rags and wiped himself clean. The oily residue of the sludge gave his otherwise dull plastic body a nice sheen. He gathered up the soiled rags and dutifully put them into a can marked "Dirty Rags." He put the garbage bag and his pack of rusted belongings into a can marked "Trash," but kept the powertube.

It was nearly seven o'clock. It would be dark outside in another hour and a half. He searched the engine room for things he might need in the city.

In a locker marked "Collins," Solo found a clean set of blue mechanic's coveralls. The name "Roger" was stitched over the left breast pocket. Solo held it up and saw that it was big enough to fit him. He stepped into the pantlegs and pushed his arms through the sleeves.

He pulled the collar out and zipped up the front of the coveralls. He looked into the mirror on Collins's locker door. Blue, Solo decided, suited him. He rummaged through the locker looking for boots, but found none. Collins had left a hat, however. A blue baseball cap that had a cartoon of a woman on the front with the label "Chiquita" under it. Solo fitted the cap and tilted his head from side to side and up and down in the mirror. Good, he decided. He scratched his cheek, and nodded at his reflection. Just like a human, he thought.

8

AT EIGHT in the morning, it was already hot and sticky in Palm Bay, Florida. A silver Corvette swept between the two rows of sabal palms that lined the long, manicured driveway into the main entrance of Electron Dynamics Corporation. The car slowed as it drew near the reserved parking stalls and grumbled into a slot marked "William Stewart."

Bill looked at the huge circular building with a heavy feeling in the pit of his stomach. He looked at himself in the rear-view mirror and frowned while he smoothed his blond hair away from his eyes. Need a haircut, he thought. His face surprised him. Look at those wrinkles. Age? Worry lines? He sighed and looked around the property as if for the first time. Could there really be this many people working here? The parking lot was filled with cars. Hundreds of cars. Two *thousand* people? thought Bill. Twenty years ago—he shook his head, smiling—twenty years ago there was just me, Byron, and two technicians.

They were building waterproof speakers for the Cape back then. One day Byron brought in the specs for a digital readout display— high technology in those days—and Bill said he could design one in time for the bidding. They worked every waking hour and slept on a couch and an air mattress in their tin-roofed warehouse in an industrial park west of Melbourne.

Bill sat inside the idling car looking at palm leaves ruffling in the breeze but seeing the past. He smiled, remembering the dash to Cape Kennedy with the prototye. Byron drove their rusted '62 Chevrolet station wagon up U.S. 1 while Bill sat in the back tuning the circuit boards. Byron kept saying, You got it? and Bill would say, Don't bug me, Byron!

"You got it?"

"Don't bug me, Byron. It was working once; it'll work again."

"Jesus." Byron looked at his watch. "One hour. Jesus." One digit flickered, but Bill adjusted a variable resistor—he'd found the right one by sheer chance—on the board and the number glowed steadily. They carried the prototype into the Cape, to a colonel in charge of evaluation. Bill would never forget the man or the look on his face. The prototype, wires curling around it like spilled spaghetti, lay blinking inside a cardboard box they'd picked up behind Winn-Dixie. The colonel shook his head, peered in the box and saw numbers flashing in sequence. He said, "Unfuckingbelievable." The thing worked and they got the contract.

A year later, the government wanted a small computer for the Gemini missions. Bill had already built one. That was what Bill did better than almost anybody else; he built computers. From the beginning, he wanted to build one that could think. Bill made artificial intelligence an expensive reality that only the government could afford. In the last five years, their company became the largest of its kind in the world.

When they built this place, he and Byron had apartments installed adjoining their offices so they never had to leave. Has Byron *ever* left? That's dedication, thought Bill. A smile flickered on his mouth, then faded. He used to live here, too. Now he could barely stand coming to work. He spent most of his time at his beach house and let Byron handle the business. Bill's specialty was the nuts and bolts side of Electron Dynamics; the actual building of the long line of computers that eventually led to Solo. Now that the government had legally taken over the project, Stewart was politely but firmly kept away from Nimrod by Colonel Sawyer. He stared at the landscaped walkway leading up to the big glass doors. Nice place you got here, Stewart, he thought. Nice enough to fight for.

Bill switched off the car, got out, and walked toward the main entrance. The doors slipped open as he approached. Bill walked past a security guard, who touched the bill of his cap and said, " 'Morning, Mr. Stewart."

" 'Morning, Jesse." Bill nodded.

The main foyer was a sixty-foot square that sliced through the five stories of the building from the ground floor to the skylight. Bill saw five levels of people walking beside railings, hurrying somewhere, working on something, things that kept the company going, working on projects that Bill—except through briefings from his managers—barely knew anything about anymore.

He waved at the reception staff as he hurried past. Another guard nodded and greeted him, allowing him to pass into the security inspection booth. Here, though, even Bill had to stop. The door closed behind him and a computer he'd built queried him with a calm female voice, "Identity?"

"William Stewart," Bill announced distractedly. It occurred to him that there must be a better way to enforce security than to have this computer look up voice prints everytime someone—even the someone who built it and has come through this booth a thousand times—came through the entrances. Computerization was sometimes a pain in the ass.

"Thank you, Mister Stewart," the voice said. "Enjoy your day." The door opened.

"Thanks." Bill plunged through the door and began a fast walk down the hundred-yard hallway, one of a dozen on each floor that led to the center of the building. He considered these walks aerobic exercise. Also, he was less likely to be stopped if he looked in a hurry. The halls were called One O' Clock, Two O' Clock, and so on. Bill hurried along Twelve O' Clock toward his office at the hub, lost in thought.

At the mask inspection room where the fragile glass patterns used to make the integrated computer circuits were checked, a woman pulling a gurney-load of the precious masks backed through the door and straight into Bill.

When they collided, the woman fell against the gurney, which shot away and slammed into the wall. A box of masks fell off and crashed onto the tile floor. Bill winced at the sound of shattering, clinking glass.

The woman, Alexandra Simpson—Alex, to her friends—said, "Oh my God!"

"Sorry," Bill said.

"Sorry?" Alex said without looking. She had rushed to the fallen box as though it were an injured animal that could be revived and picked it up. The broken glass rustled inside as she tilted it from side to side. She grimaced. "Sorry?" she cried. "This is, *was,* about a hundred thousand dollars worth of masks. Perfect. Fresh from inspection. They'll—" Alex stopped to look at Bill. "And I *just* got this job," she said. Tears welled down her cheeks. "And you, you—"

"Bill," Bill said as he walked toward her.

Alex blinked as she tried to stop her tears. She was a brunette, huge eyes, very pretty, and at the moment, looked like a child lost in a crowd. She swallowed hard as she put the ruined box back on the gurney. "Well, *Bill.* Thanks loads."

Bill watched her push the cart along the hall toward the hub where she'd get the elevator up to Production. He followed her, calling out, "They won't fire you."

"Leave me alone," Alex said, not turning around. "The tightwads that own this place? They'll fire me, then they'll bill me for the masks. And I have two kids to support!"

Bill smiled and let her go ahead. "What's your name?" he called.

"None of your business!" Alex yelled as she pushed the cart into the elevator.

Bill didn't realize that he was smiling until he got to his office in the hub. His secretary, Terri Reynolds, beamed at him and chirped, "*Good* morning, Mr. Stewart."

"Heh?" Bill said, staring at Terri's teeth. He then felt the smile on his own face and quickly wiped it off. "Oh. Yeah. Good morning, Terri." He walked to her desk. "Byron will be here in a couple of minutes. Get Dave Johnson in Production on the line for me, okay?" He turned and walked toward his office.

"Yes, Mr. Stewart," Terri said, shaking her head. What was this all about? she wondered. She hadn't seen him smile since his trip to Costa Rica.

Bill closed the door behind him. He kicked off his running shoes next to the couch and walked across the oak floor and oriental rug to the window behind his desk. The core of the hub was an atrium, open to the sky. His and Byron's offices, their top managers', and one recreation room on each floor had windows on the view. Tall palms grew in a circle around a rock garden and water fountain. He looked up and saw a small puffy cloud and wondered if it'd be a good day for flying. Since the takeover of the Nimrod project, he'd been spending a lot of time flying the company's helicopter.

His phone beeped and he said aloud, "Yeah."

"Mr. Johnson from Production," Terri said over the speaker.

"Go ahead."

"Oh, and Mr. Rand just stepped in," Terri said.

"Tell him to get his ass in here," Bill yelled. He heard Byron laugh over Terri's intercom. He spoke at the phone, "Dave?"

"Yes, Mr. Stewart."

"You just get a box of broken masks?"

"Yes we did, Mr. Stewart. New girl. Very expensive mistake." Johnson's voice was clear over the speaker phone.

Bill waved Byron in as he peeked around the door. Byron nodded and walked over to the bar and poured a glass of Gatorade from the jar Bill kept for him in the small refrigerator. Bill winced. The stuff tasted like sweetened, cold sweat.

Bill said, "What's her name."

"Alexandra Simpson, Mr. Stewart. I'll take care of it, sir."

Byron mussed through the stack of magazines on the coffee table as he sat on the couch. Byron's black hair fell in front of his face as he leaned toward the coffee table. He needed a haircut, too. Byron was still gaunt at forty-five; didn't look much different now than he had when they met in college. Of course, Bill thought, that was a protective biological mechanism that had evolved to keep people from going nuts when they saw old friends. Byron grabbed a copy of *Machine Design* and sat back with his Gatorade.

"Take care of it?" Bill said.

"I'm sending her down to Human Resources to have her out-processed. She's still in her two-week trial."

"Fire her? Didn't she tell you how it happened? That somebody bumped into her?"

"That's what she said. But she couldn't name anybody."

"Well, she's telling the truth." Bill grinned at Byron. "I'm the guy."

"Oh." Johnson was quiet for a moment. "But I've already told her—"

"She still there?" Bill said as he pulled out his chair and sat down at his desk.

"As a matter of fact, Mr. Stewart, she's sitting right here in my office."

"Well, Dave, tell her she's still on the team." Bill switched on his desk computer.

"I'll do that—"

"When?" Bill interjected.

"Er, now?"

"Right." Bill moved the mouse around his desktop to open his "To Do" list on the computer screen as he listened to Johnson's muffled voice. He winced. Terri kept adding to the list: letters to write, staff promotions, a great new chip design that didn't work, and more. He had to scroll the window on the computer screen to see it all.

"I told her," Johnson said.

"Good. What'd she do?" Bill said.

"Do?"

"Do. You know: What'd she *do* when you told her she wasn't being *fucking* out-processed?'' Bill shook his head and made an exasperated face for Byron.

"Well," Johnson said with some trepidation. "She smiled? Sir?"

"Ah," Bill said. "Thank you, Dave. Keep up the good work." Bill punched the phone off.

Byron looked up from the magazine. "Sounding piqued, Bill. Problem?"

"They were going to fire some new girl because she broke a box of masks this morning." Bill stopped, nodded, and said, "I know. I lose it too easily these days. I shouldn't have jumped all over Dave like that."

"He understands, Bill." Byron nodded. "You're the bully who owns the place."

Bill shrugged. "I know it. Do me a favor, Byron. Fire me, okay? I need a goddamn break."

Byron laughed. His smile faded and he said, "You want me to?" He tossed the magazine back on the table. "The way you been sulking around here—when you're here—since Solo got trashed and the feds took over—"

"Sulking?"

"Yeah. Sulking, moping. Whatever." Byron, noticing that the magazine was askew, pushed it square with the stack. He walked over to Bill's desk and sat on a corner. "I can't really blame you, Bill. Doesn't seem like our own place anymore. I've been thinking about selling out—"

"Give up?" Bill scowled at Byron. "I can't believe you'd even begin to think that, Byron. This is *our* goddamn company. We'll *take* it back."

"These are the *big* bastards," Byron said, shaking his head. "Made-in-*America*, kick-ass bastards." Byron stood up and walked to the window. Outside, the hot breeze swirled the top of a palm. He turned to Bill. "Got a bid, a quiet one, last night."

Bill stared at Byron. "I don't want to hear it."

"General Dynamics. They're flush from their new fighter contract; need our technology. We'd be billionaires," announced Byron.

Bill shook his head. "Great. We're each worth *hundreds* of millions now. Been rich so long you forgot that? What the hell would you do with the extra money? Buy France? Jesus! Byron. You'd give these government pricks the satisfaction of pushing us out? Just for a bunch of money?"

"That's not why," Byron said, shaking his head. "I'd do it for the peace of mind I'd have not having to fuck with *them* every day!"

Bill nodded. Why was he so angry? He'd been considering the same thing himself. It sounded wrong when Byron put it into words. "Look, Byron," Bill said as he sat back in his chair. "I can't blame you for wanting to leave. This Nimrod thing—but if we stay, we can fight them. Nimrod won't work the way they're training it. They'll figure that out, lose interest, and we can use the technology to make smart computers for businesses that don't kill people. If we quit and walk out, it's just plain over."

Byron shook his head. "They'll never let us do that. The Solo technology is classified."

"The weapon is, Byron. Not the technology in the computer. That's ours."

"Yeah," Byron nodded. "I know it's ours. But I still think they'll never *let* you."

"Then we fight 'em, dammit!"

"Fight the feds." Byron shook his head. "Like the last time? Like when we lost Solo?"

A jolt of guilt surged through Bill. He'd told no one that Solo had escaped. Not even Byron. When he was sure, absolutely sure that Byron was clean, no bugs, no agreements—God how paranoid can a person get? Not too paranoid, he thought, not when it comes to the government. "I learned a lot on that fiasco," Bill said. "People, smart people, learn from their mistakes."

"What'd you learn, Bill? That the feds make the rules? That they take what they want? That if it costs a few lives to get what they want—no problem?"

Bill pulled what looked like a small calculator out of his shirt pocket and put it on the desk. He pushed a button and a red light flashed. He pointed to the device and then swept his arm around the office. Byron looked at the flashing light and followed Bill's gesture. Byron's mouth dropped open and he pronounced silently, *We're bugged?* as he pointed a finger at his chest.

"I've learned a lot," Bill said, quietly.

9

H EY, CASSIDY. Talk to me once in a while, okay? Keep me awake." The voice came from a Motorola walkie-talkie on Jeff Cassidy's belt. He put the radio to his mouth.

"If you were doing your fucking job, Goldstein, you wouldn't be getting sleepy," Cassidy said, smiling in the darkness. He stood at the stern of the *Caribbean Star* watching the brightly lit Statue of Liberty shimmering in and out of view in the swirling fog.

"Haw!" The sound squelched from the radio. "What are you, a fucking company man?"

"You got it," Cassidy said. "All I care about is Bay Ridge Security. I get a hard-on just thinking about doing this for the rest of my life."

"Yeah. The glamor, the fucking excitement of knowing you and me are protecting this scow. Who the hell would want to get on this barge anyway?"

Cassidy turned reflexively to face the man he was talking to at the other end of the ship, and laughed into the radio. He saw a shadow moving on the dockside deck near the crew's quarters. The shadow suddenly ducked back into a hatchway. Cassidy stared into the darkness for a moment, then shook his head. One of the guys that stayed on board? Probably—but why'd he duck back when I turned around? "Hey, Goldstein, I'm coming up to see you."

"C'mon up, big boy," Goldstein laughed.

Cassidy smiled and started walking. The shadow reappeared, moving fast toward the gangplank. "Hey!" Cassidy yelled. "Stop!" He pulled out his thirty-eight and ran along the deck.

"What's up," Goldstein said from the radio in his other hand. Cassidy didn't answer. The man was already on the dock when he got to the gangplank. When the man got in the light near the door to the warehouse, Cassidy could see him pretty well. Looked like a crewmember, blue coveralls, cap. A black man. The man tried to open the door, but it was locked. Cassidy watched as the man stepped back and kicked the door open with an explosive crash. It sounded like dynamite, which Cassidy assumed it had to have been. The door was solid steel. Goldstein came up to him out of the darkness. "What's going on?"

"The guy just kicked the fucking door open."

"That's impossible," Goldstein said.

"I know," Cassidy said.

One small light glowed inside the huge building. Solo walked slowly, blending with the shadows near the walls. Hundred-yard-long conveyors, tall cranes, and room-sized banana grading machines made good cover. He headed toward the light, which, he assumed, marked the exit.

He saw a man with a flashlight, a gun drawn, walking across the floor. Solo saw him clearly in infrared. He appeared to be very frightened. "Who's there?" the man said. Solo leapt over a conveyor line and crept along the wall, moving toward the exit. When the man got to the dockside door, Solo slipped out through the front door and into the night.

The robot walked along a walkway beside the East River, listening to small waves lap against the sea wall. Darkness pooled between the widely spaced street lights. On his left, he heard a constant whooshing, hissing sound that never stopped. The lights of hundreds of cars rushed along a highway. His maps showed that he was walking beside South Street toward the Williamsburg Bridge. The cars were on Franklin Delano Roosevelt Drive. That was traffic. Solo had never seen traffic except from a satellite. At the end of South Street, the walkway continued into East River Park. Here the traffic noise was muffled by trees.

No one was in sight. A tall chain-link fence ran along the park side of the walk, a rusting steel railing ran next to the river on the other. Solo zoomed onto a steady stream of cars coursing in both directions on the Williamsburg Bridge. Like blood cells in capillaries. Or a horde of army ants. That each car had people in it was incomprehensible to the robot. He had never seen more than fifty people in one place in his whole life. He came to a building that stood behind the fence. He stopped and peered into the shadows. He amplified the light and saw that the walls of the small concrete building were covered with graffiti. He made out "Fat Boy" painted on the wall. By the door, printed vertically, was "ROBSTIFF," which made no sense to him. The other writing was indecipherable, painted in a colorful script he presumed was native to the city and which he had never seen before except on subway trains and walls in movies about New York.

He continued walking toward the bridge, where, according to his maps, turning left would lead him directly into the middle of the city.

He sensed humans directly ahead of him, on the left, hidden from sight at the end of the fence. Solo considered turning and running—his life had up to now been one of avoiding humans, especially American humans. But his plan relied heavily on his theory that he wouldn't be noticed in this city. It had to be tested eventually. And, he thought, if I am wrong, this is the place to find out. He resumed walking.

As he got to the end of the fence, he heard, "Hey." He stopped and turned. Two men—one short and fat, the other tall with a beard—stepped out of the shadows and walked toward him. "Hey, buddy," the bearded man said. "We—" They continued walking toward him. "We kinda need some help." The short, fat man snickered.

"Yes?" Solo said, tingling with anticipation. He remembered to muffle his voice. They had not yet noticed anything different about him.

When they got to him, the bearded man said, "Yeah, buddy—" the man paused as he looked up at Solo's face. "—You a big guy, eh? Yeah, well," the man continued, "what we need is to borrow *all* your money, big guy."

As he spoke, the man pulled a pistol from his jacket pocket and pointed it at Solo.

"I have no money," Solo said. The robot was nearly twitching as he restrained himself from laughing—they had not noticed, yet.

"Check him," the bearded man said to his partner. "Don't move—" The bearded man noticed a glint coming from Solo's eyecovers. In the dim light of a distant street lamp, he had assumed that Solo was a black man. He studied Solo's face and shook his head. "You wearing some kind of mask?"

"Yes," Solo said. "A mask."

The bearded man nodded—another looney. This one wears a goalie mask and a Chiquita Banana hat.

The short man patted the pockets of Solo's coveralls and found nothing. "He's clean, Ace."

"Aw, man. We got another bum? Don't anybody have any money anymore? Shit!" The man noticed Solo's powertube. "What's that thing?" he said, pointing.

"This is my powertube," Solo said. "It can generate electricity. But it is broken now."

"Well, maybe somebody over on Canal would buy it for parts. Give." The man held out his hand.

Solo was tingling with joy. These muggers were treating him just like any human. His theory had been correct. "I would like to help you," Solo said. "But I can't give you this. You see—"

"Fats," the bearded man said nodding toward Solo.

The short man grabbed the powertube and yanked. Solo let the powertube move a foot before he froze. The man was jerked short by the sudden stop. "Damn!"

"Let go the thing," the bearded man said. "Must be valuable, the way you hang on it. Loose it, bub."

The bullets in this gun were harmless, but Solo did not want noise attracting attention. He studied the man's face while he reached out to take his gun. The man's eyes widened slightly when he realized that Solo was moving. Solo could see the tendons on the top of the man's hand tighten in response. The man's forefinger pressed the trigger. The human was reacting as fast as a human could—pathetically slow. Solo took the gun from his hand and flipped it over his shoulder into the river. The man looked dumbly at his empty hand. The event had occurred so fast that he hadn't recognized what had happened. "How—"

"Ace," the short man said, stepping away from Solo. "Think we ought to not bother the large *gentleman* anymore?"

"Good point," Ace said, nodding at Solo. "Didn't mean nothin' personal, sir—we wouldn't hurt nobody. Just a little low on our luck is all, you know. Sorry to take up your time." Both men nodded, smiling eagerly as they backed into the shadows. When they reached the hedge, Solo saw them spin around and run into the park. He could eliminate them, Solo thought, but that would not be typical human behavior.

Solo followed the path that passed between two dark tennis courts. As he went, he listened to the muggers whispering in the shrubbery a hundred feet away. "Who the hell was that? He was like steel!"

"I dunno. Probably *lives* on steroids—dresses up like a geek and walks around parks at night. What he's doing, Ace, is *trolling* for people like us."

I pass as a geek, thought Solo. Geek, he was pleased to discover in his dictionaries, meant a *person* who does disgusting things in public.

Solo found the pedestrian overpass indicated on his map. He stood for a while watching the cars pass. The street lights cast an orange glow on the stream of cars cascading by. One after the other, three lanes abreast in each direction, they raced both north and south. Two equally desirable destinations? What could so many people from the south of here want that was north of here, and what could so many people from north of here want so badly that was south of here? He climbed the steps and walked to the center of the overpass. He stared at the thundering stampede of cars coursing below him through the diamonds of a chain-link fence. He felt a tingle of excitement. Surely this must be the most exciting place on earth, to have such races going on perpetually. Satellite views showed that the same thing was happening all over the city. Many people going many places, all at once. In the lane just below him, he heard a *thump-thump, thump-thump* as the cars hit a large pothole in the highway. It made him uncomfortable to see machines taking such a beating. He continued across the overpass and down the steps. He crossed a dark landscaped area called "Corlear's Hook Park" and stepped out into the dim lights of Cherry Street. There were no people walking this neighborhood. He turned right on Jackson Street, toward brighter lights. Within fifty paces, he came to Madison Street, and looking south, saw the bright lights of a busy intersection. His maps indicated that it was Clinton and Madison. People walked under the lights. He headed in their direction.

Act naturally, Solo reminded himself.

10

SOLO stopped on the corner of Clinton and Madison, attracted by the brightly lit window display of the Rodriguez Food Market. Solo had never seen a store before. Roasted chickens, garlic chains, and a pyramid of carefully stacked cans of olive oil were arranged in the window. One customer, an old woman, was inside. He waited until the woman left and then walked in.

Solo examined the paperback book racks, amazed. He had never known there were so many books. He had assumed that people, especially American people, got their information the same way he did—over the computer networks. He had not read one of the hundreds of books he saw. Only their titles, listed in the Library of Congress' database, were available in his networks, none of their text. He had available to him all the text of the *New York Times,* the *Washington Post,* the *Wall Street Journal,* and nearly every scientific journal published since 1971, but not *I Robot* or *Sphere* or *The World Almanac.* None of these were online. He picked up *The Joy of Sex* and read it in a minute. He put it back in the rack. Interesting, thought Solo. I had no idea people did all those things with one another—you would think that with thousands of years trying, humans would've found the best way and stuck with it.

"Hey, mister," the storekeeper said. "We ain't a library here. You want to read the books; you buy the books. Okay?"

Solo turned to the man.

"I have no money," Solo said. He walked to the counter.

The storekeeper, Estevez Rodriguez, stepped back suddenly when he saw Solo's face. "Aw shit," muttered Rodriguez, "not again."

"You see," Solo said, putting a hand on the counter, "I just got off a boat, and—"

"Don't worry, pal. I *know* what to do." Rodriguez nodded angrily as he punched open the cash register. He scooped out the bills, wadded them in his fist, and slapped them down on the counter. "Here. It's all I got."

"You want me to have this?" Solo said.

Rodriguez looked longingly outside. Never a fucking cop when you want one. "Yeah. I'm like that, sport. Generous to a fucking fault."

"That's very good of you," Solo said. "I can now buy some books?"

Rodriguez looked at Solo with a grimace. Dumb as a stump and crazy to boot. "Buy some books? Sure. Help yourself," Rodriguez said, pointing to the bookracks.

Solo picked up the money and stuffed it into his zippered breast pocket. "Thank you. I'll pick out some now."

Rodriguez checked his watch. Nine-thirty. He looked around. Empty store except for the kook. He stared at the walnut handle of his father's old Colt forty-five under the counter and wondered could he get it out before the weirdo blew him away. That big pipe—was that some kind of homemade gun he carried? He hadn't had time at first, but now the idiot actually had his back to him while he shopped the racks.

Solo had six books tucked under his arm when he heard Rodriguez shout, "Hands up, motherfucker!" He turned and saw the wavering barrel of a large pistol aimed directly at his head.

"You do not want me to buy these books?" Solo said.

Sweat poured off Rodriguez's head and the gun shook wildly. He dropped the gun sights to Solo's chest, where his shaking wouldn't affect his aim as much.

"I said"—Rodriguez's voice quivered with his gun—"hands up! Or I shoot!"

"I don't understand," Solo said. He stepped closer to Rodriguez.

Oh shit! thought Rodriquez. He fired twice.

Solo jerked slightly at each impact. He stopped, examined the holes in his coveralls, and stared at Rodriguez. "You have damaged my clothing," Solo said. "If you really do not want me to buy these, just say so. I will go."

Rodriguez stared dumbfounded, his mind reeling. He's totally wacked out on crack—doesn't know he's dead. He's gonna blow my fucking brains out before he croaks! When Solo turned to put the books away, Rodriguez fired, blasting the remaining four bullets at Solo's back. Solo jerked forward a couple of inches. The coveralls exploded open at four places as the impacting bullets splashed back as molten lead. Solo turned around. "Please be patient. I am putting them away."

Rodriguez screamed and ran out the door.

Solo restored the last book to its original spot and hurried outside. He saw Rodriguez running up Madison yelling, "Help! Police! Thief!"

Thief?

He *gave* me the money, thought Solo. He ran after Rodriguez shouting, "Wait. Here is your money."

Rodriguez saw Solo rushing toward him. He let out a blood-curdling shriek. A man and a woman stopped on the corner behind Rodriguez and stared at the screaming man. Solo stopped. I am attracting attention. He ran back to the grocery and turned up Clinton Street, suddenly remembering to move at a human's speed. Slowing, he jogged toward East Broadway.

When he got out of the neighborhood, Solo matched the pace of the humans on the sidewalk and followed his maps north. The south end of Manhattan, seen from a Keyhole image, was darker than the rest of the city. He moved toward the brighter lights. Twenty minutes later Solo strode into Washington Square Park.

Groups of people formed separate clusters within the park. Near the fountains in the middle of the park, a mounted policeman sat on a huge chestnut mare watching, moving his head slowly at a shout or a loud laugh. Solo walked up to the largest group. Thirty people formed an audience for a sidewalk preacher who declared, "AIDS is God's way of telling you faggots that you're sinners!"

"You idiot!" a man shouted. "God doesn't care where you stick it. Look around; see any shortage of people?" The crowd laughed, but the sidewalk preacher's face glowed red.

"God knows *you*." The speaker pointed at the heckler, his forefinger slightly bent, his hand partially open, his thumb extended, saying, "Oh yes! May the heavenly fires strike you down, *Devil!*"

Solo had read of such encounters between God and the Devil documented in the Bible. Now, he was seeing it firsthand. It was terribly exciting. He paused expectantly, waiting to see the flash of electricity spark from the man's—probably God in a man's shape—hand. Perhaps the Devil would throw up a protective shield? Who knows what could happen?

Instead of a shield, the Devil raised his hand, middle finger extended, and said, "Sit on this, asshole," and simply turned and walked away. No lightning? Nothing?

He felt someone pat his shoulder. "Hey," a man behind him said, "got a light?"

Solo turned around and saw a man dressed in a black cloth jacket studded with metal stars, holding a cigarette butt near his mouth. Chromed chains hung from the epaulets sewn on the shoulders. Gold braid decorated the bill of his military cap. "I have no lights," Solo said.

The man looked at Solo's face and blinked. "Hey. Where you from, man?"

Solo watched the man's eyes narrow as he inspected his face. "I'm from out of town," Solo said.

"No kidding?" The man snickered stupidly and broke into a hacking cough.

"My name is Solo."

"Yeah?" Solo noticed that the man swayed as he spoke. Perhaps he has intoxicated himself. The man held out his hand. "My name is Colonel Dean Martin, Solo. Pleased to fucking meet you."

"Pleased to fucking meet you, too," Solo said.

"Yeah?" The man laughed. "Tell me, Solo, do all the folks out your way all dress like you?"

"This is what I wear when I work," Solo said. "I work on a ship."

The man focused on Solo's coveralls. "I wasn't—" Colonel Dean Martin paused, seeing a name stitched over Solo's pocket. "Hey, says on your shirt there, your name's Roger."

"That's right," Solo said. "Roger Solo."

"Ah." Martin, still holding a marijuana cigarette poised for a light, turned to find someone with a fire. The crowd around the sidewalk preacher had dispersed, and Martin saw the mounted cop watching him. He put the joint in his pocket. The cop shook his head. "So, Roger," Martin said. "Let's go over there"—he pointed at a group of men sitting at concrete tables at the far corner of the park—"where they're playing chess. I need a light, bad."

"Okay," Solo said as he followed Martin.

"So, Roger." Martin looked at Solo as they walked. "What's the helmet thing? You a biker or what?"

"Protection," Solo said.

"Ah." Martin nodded vigorously. "Can't blame you. Cannot fucking blame you. It's a fucking crime the way our society has become so—criminal." Martin laughed. "Now we got poor schmucks like you wandering around like Darth Vader. It's gonna be like that for everyone, if—" Martin punched a black man standing next to a chess game in the shoulder. "If we don't put all these motherfucking *crooks* in fucking prison!" He laughed until he coughed.

The man shook his head and squinted. "What'd you want, *Colonel?*"

"A light, man," Martin said holding up his joint.

The man snapped a lighter under the end of the cigarette and Martin sucked loudly until the end glowed red. Martin continued to suck on the cigarette, in a way that Solo had only seen in movies, long after the man had put the lighter away. Martin held the joint toward Solo, making a *ssst, ssst* sound. Solo looked at it. "Marijuana?"

Martin coughed out a cloud of blue smoke, bent over, and stamped his feet.

"Hey, man," one of the chess players said. "Go somewhere else to die, okay? Tryin' to think, here."

Martin held up his hand nodding. He'd stopped coughing enough to speak. "Yeah. That's right, Roger. Marijuana. They got this stuff where you come from too?"

"No," Solo said.

"No?" Martin looked at Solo, amazed. "So where the fuck do you come from, Roger? Where they don't have this shit?"

"Far away," Solo said.

"I bet," Martin said. "Indiana, maybe? So, Roger." Martin held out the joint. "It's goin' out, man. Want some?"

"No," Solo said. "Marijuana is bad for you."

Martin shook his head as if trying to clear his mind. "You just said no, Roger? I heard it right, right?"

"Yes."

Martin stared at Solo's eyecovers a minute and began to nod his head vigorously. "Good man. Good man. Too many fucking potheads in the country, my man. That's another thing that's wrong with this fucking society, Roger. Too much drugs."

"Too much drugs," Solo said as he turned to watch one of the chess players move a white rook. "That will be black's mate in two moves," Solo warned.

The player looked up, glaring. "Hey, geek. Who asked you? Go play your own game." He had not taken his hand off the rook. He looked at the concrete tabletop, his eyes darting among the plastic pieces. He moved his rook back.

The other player turned around and yelled, "Hey. Thanks for the goddamn advice, man. Just in time, asshole!"

"You are welcome," Solo said.

"What?" the man said, getting up.

"C'mon, Roger," Martin said, pointing to a row of benches and grabbing Solo's sleeve. "Let's get away from these morons. Okay?"

"Okay," Solo said, allowing Martin to lead him to a row of benches.

He said to Martin as they walked, "That chess player waved his hand at us with the same gesture that the Devil used."

Martin looked up at Solo as they drew near the benches, nodding.

"The Devil, I know, can change shapes at will. But it's difficult to be sure what has happened—this man had been playing chess while the Devil had threatened God. Perhaps he can be at two places at the same time?"

Martin nodded as he sat down.

"Of course," Solo continued, "anything is possible among the deities. They are exempt from physical laws."

Solo sat carefully, to avoid the clunking sound that Padre Cerna had warned him about. Colonel Dean Martin watched him warily. When Solo sat down, he put his hands on his temples and twisted his head from side to side, as Justos had suggested he do now and then.

"Bet it gets hot in there," Martin said.

"Yes," Solo said. "But, better safe than sorry."

"Got that right. Can't argue with that." Martin looked around the park, turned back to Solo, and said suddenly, "This place disgusts me."

Solo also looked around. The mounted policeman, he noticed, had been joined by another. The two men sat comfortably in their saddles and chatted.

"These *people* disgust me," Martin said.

"Disgusting," Solo agreed, wondering what Martin was trying to say.

"Look at 'em." The ends of Martin's mouth twisted down. "Wasting their fucking lives. Hanging out, scoring some drugs, getting fucked up. Think they'll be out tomorrow *contributing to society?*" Martin leaned toward Solo. "Fuck no. They'll be lying in some doorway or packing crate sleeping it off. Disgusting."

Solo nodded. Certainly—the way Martin put it—it was disgusting.

Martin jerked his thumb at himself. "And me. I got no goddamn choice. I hafta hang out here."

"Yes?" Solo said.

"Yeah, Roger, I lost everything I had. Black Monday."

Solo quickly checked his text library. He'd downloaded the last few years of the *New York Times,* which he felt would be handy when talking to New Yorkers. It was. "October 19, 1987?"

"Right. Lost it all. And the thing is, that's all I know how to do, you know? Investments. Now I got no money to invest. I gotta try to make it in this fucking zoo. When you're down in the Big Apple, buddy, you are *down.* And they *keep* you down. That's why I wear this kinky shit, you know, try to fit in. You understand?"

"I understand," Solo said. "If you had money, you could invest it and make more."

"Roger, you got it!" Martin beamed. "Just a small break. Is all I need."

"I have money," Solo said, patting the bulge on his chest.

"Oh?" Martin cocked his head.

Solo reached into his pocket and took out the wad Rodriguez had given him. "Many dollars." Solo wondered whether he had stumbled into a rare opportunity. Perhaps he had met someone who could help him make the money he needed.

"No way, Roger! Don't offer me any money." Martin held up his hands. "I barely know you."

Solo nodded and pressed the money against his chest.

"Of course," Martin said quickly, "if you did want to invest with me, you'd make a fortune." Martin waited for a response, but Solo said nothing. "You see, Roger, I have developed a *system* that the suckers don't know about. I *know* Wall Street."

Solo nodded. "The suckers don't know your system. That's very good."

"That's right, Roger, I was *good*. I once invested a thousand dollars for a buddy, using my *system*. In six weeks I gave him back a million bucks! A million!"

"Could not this friend give you some of that money to help you?"

Martin shook his head slowly. "That's the tragedy, Roger. The guy up and died a couple of months ago and now his wife's got it. And she don't know me from bullshit. I talked to her once. She threatened to call the fucking cops. That's the thanks I get."

Solo riffled the bills in his hands. "I have two hundred seventy-six dollars. Using your system that the suckers don't know about, that would multiply into more than a quarter of a million dollars. More than one hundred thousand dollars for each of us. Is that correct?"

"That's right, Roger."

"What was your partner's name, the one who made a million?" Solo asked.

Martin's eyes rolled up in thought, which surprised Solo. He is making up a name, Solo thought. "James Clark," Martin said. "Yep, good old Jimmy, the poor bastard."

"When did he die?" Solo asked.

Martin's eyes rolled up again. "Two months tomorrow." Martin nodded sadly.

Solo said, "A James Clark, eighty-nine years old, of nine-twenty

Fifty-fifth Street died a week ago. That is the only James Clark within the last year."

"Huh?" Martin shook his head quickly.

"You are lying, Colonel."

Martin beamed at Solo and nodded. He reached out suddenly for Solo's pocket. Solo caught his wrist and held it tightly.

"I think, Colonel, that although your offer to help me is very generous, I will not invest this with you." Solo squeezed Martin's wrist.

Martin grimaced. Solo noticed that he was looking past him. Solo sensed two men approaching from behind.

"Let him go," a man said. Solo identified the voice as the chess player's.

Solo turned and saw that everyone at the corner was watching. He had fallen into a trap, it seemed. It would be imprudent if he bested three men in front of so many witnesses. He let go of Martin's arm.

"Good move, my man," said the chess player as he reached over Solo's shoulder and took the roll of money.

Martin laughed, coughed. "You'll never regret it, Roger. I'll turn that money into a fortune."

Solo nodded. "We are partners, then."

"Partners!" Martin glanced at one of his accomplices and shrugged. He turned back to Solo and grinned. "You're a sport, Roger; that's the fucking truth." He reached for Solo's hand, grabbed it and shook it. "Shake, partner." He looked over his shoulder at the two cops. "And now, Rog, I'm outta here. Things to do. People to see; places to go. See ya soon." Martin and the two men walked away.

"Where shall I pick up my share?" Solo said, standing.

Martin and the chess player stopped and looked around. Martin looked at his partner and shrugged. He said to Solo, "Well, Roger, why not right here? Where the deal was done? Meetcha here—let's say—six weeks from today. Okay, pal?"

"Okay, pal," Solo said. He watched Martin and his partners stroll out of the park, laughing.

He thought of tracking them and getting the money back, but he felt the warning signal from his power-supply monitor. He was approaching twenty-five percent—not much time left. He held up his broken powertube and realized that he must either find the tools to repair it or an electrical outlet to plug into. He left the park, heading west toward the Avenue of the Americas.

11

SOLO saw a man lying on the sidewalk in the shadow of a parked car. He knelt beside him and asked, "Where are you injured?"

"Huh?" the man groaned.

"Where does it hurt?"

"New York, asshole," the man muttered. He rolled his head faceup, trying to see Solo. The motion made him vomit. Solo watched, wondering what sort of disease acts so quickly it drops a man in the street. He grabbed the man's arm to get him to his feet.

The man spit and said, "Leave me go!"

"You need medical assistance," Solo said.

The man blinked, trying to focus. "I need a drink," he groaned. "You got some spare change?"

"No," Solo said, "but I can get you some water."

"Wanna fuck with me? I'm—" The man tried to push himself up, flopped back down. "—fucking with me."

Solo studied the man and realized that he was intoxicated, probably with alcohol. "You should go to a warm place and rest," Solo said. "I will help you if you tell me where you live."

"Go?" The man mumbled, his eyes closed. "No place to go."

"A hotel?" Solo said. "There are many—"

"You idiot," the man snarled.

Of course, Solo thought. No money. Like me. "I will get money and bring you some," Solo said.

"Great," the man said, sighing. "I'll wait."

Solo stood up and walked towards a sign that said "CitiBank" at the end of the street. Behind glass doors, he could hear a computer giving cash to a man simply because the man had submitted a simple code on a magnetic card. Solo didn't need a card. The machine would be pleased to give him money. He walked thirty feet toward the bank before he heard, "—wearing a black mask with mirrored glasses. Suspect is carrying a metal pipe and may be dangerous. Last seen running west on Clinton Street—"

Solo immediately stepped over a wrought-iron railing at the dark stoop of a building on Waverly Place. He stood under the stone stairs and listened to the police dispatcher.

The policeman on the horse at the park, thought Solo. He had a radio. He will remember that he saw me and which way I went. They will know where to look. He sat down on the bricks under the stoop to keep out of sight.

What he had assumed was a pile of trash lying in the corner of the understair cave, moved. Solo leaned forward, interested, as the heap of paper and rags rustled. A small arm reached out, grabbed a newspaper, and pulled it back into the pile. A person is making a nest? thought Solo. Near the pile, Solo saw two shopping bags filled with flattened aluminum cans, folded boxes, and rolled-up clothing. When the person under the pile of trash stopped moving for a while, Solo quietly lifted the nearest shopping bag and set it before him. He reached inside to get a sweater. "Hey!" a voice yelled from the pile. Solo looked over and saw a woman's head poke up from the trash. "This's *my* place!" the woman said. "The hell you doing?"

"I need to borrow some clothing," Solo said.

"Borrow?" the woman said. "Think'm nuts? Borrow?"

"I can trade you what I'm wearing for something you have," Solo said.

"Yeah?" The woman sat up straight and brushed off some of the litter that clung to her hair and coat. She reached into her coat and pulled out a pint bottle of Southern Comfort and gulped a swallow. "Why—I want to do that?"

"I have a very nice set of new coveralls," Solo said. "And a very handsome Chiquita Banana cap."

"Chiquita Banana?" the woman said dreamily.

Solo handed her his cap. She blinked her eyes into focus and held the hat above her where it caught the light of a street lamp. "Yeah. I think I see that. Little cartoon lady with the grass skirt?"

"That's right," Solo said.

The woman nodded, swallowed another gulp of Southern Comfort, and put the bottle away. She brushed the remaining trash aside and pulled her other shopping bag to her. She reached inside and took out a shiny black plastic purse. She snapped it open and pulled out a dollar bill. "Here," she said. "Dollar for it."

Solo said: "I'd rather trade it for something to wear. I really need to change my clothes."

"Dumbfuck! Take goddamn money; *buy* something different."

Solo took the bill and handed the woman his hat. He pulled on the collar of his coveralls. "You want to buy this?"

The woman leaned toward Solo and squinted at the coveralls, reading the name embroidered in inch-high letters. "Roger?" she said.

"Yes. Yours?" Solo asked.

The woman sat back, her head wobbling. Solo watched her trying to focus on his face and waited as she considered the question. "Laura," she said quietly. Laura inspected Solo's coveralls closely, rolling the fabric between her fingers. "Laura Johnson-Reynolds," she slurred, pronouncing it, *Lawrah-johns-nolls.*

"You seem to need glasses, Laura," Solo said.

"You s'need to mind your own freakin' business," Laura said. "*Fuckin'* business," she said, correcting herself.

"Yes," Solo said. "Mind my own business."

Laura nodded passionately. "Right. Now. This thing's got big holes in it, Roger. Rags." Laura dropped back against the bricks of her cave.

Solo stood up and unzipped the coveralls.

"Hey!" Laura said. "Goddamn animal—don't get any ideas," she said, reaching inside her coat. "I got *weapons* on me."

"Animal?" Solo said happily. His techniques *were* working if the woman made such an assumption—that he wanted to copulate with her. "I have to get rid of these clothes. I'll *give* them to you."

"And then what?" Laura said. "Walk 'round here naked as a baby?" She slapped her hand over her eyes, but peeked between her fingers. She watched Solo step out of his coveralls. And though she couldn't see very well, and her world spun and whirled, Laura could tell that Solo was still wearing something, not clothing, but something. "What's that you got?" Laura said as she leaned forward. She put her hand on Solo's arm and quickly snapped it away. "You're hot as hell, Roger. No wonder. Wearing some kinda plastic shell-thing?"

"Yes," Solo said. "For protection."

Laura nodded, a look of profound pity on her face. Tears rolled down her cheeks as she nodded over and over. She had found a kindred spirit—someone else who appreciated the true nature of a dangerous world. "Now *that's* a good idea—if you don't cook yourself in the freakin' thing—for life here in the city, s'know?" Laura said patting Solo's arm gingerly. "How much?"

"For what?"

"That," Laura said, pointing. "Thing you're wearing."

"I can't sell this," Solo said.

Laura nodded, opened her plastic purse, and shuffled some bills from a wad. "Twenty bucks?" Laura said, holding two bills up to Solo.

"No," Solo said, "I can't sell it for any price."

Laura squinted and tried to balance her head as she counted more bills into her hand. "Thisisit, Roger, my last offer. Hunert dollars. Okay?"

"No."

Laura sighed and put her money away. She brought out her bottle, drank, and put it back.

Solo stared at Laura until she finished and held up his powertube. "Would you like to buy this?"

Laura leaned forward. "Pipe? For what?"

"Not just a pipe," Solo said, holding out his powertube. "This will generate electricity if you stick one end of it into a fire—" Solo hastened to add: "It's broken right now, but I can fix it readily."

"Readily?" Laura repeated softly. The word made her smile. She stared at Solo intently, blinking to keep him in focus. "Educated, huh?"

"Yes. Do you want to buy it?"

"Don't need it. All the 'lectric I want." Laura jerked her head up and pointed with her thumb. "Upstairs."

Solo tilted his head back. "You live in this place?"

Laura nodded. "Live in this place."

Solo looked at Laura and then her two shopping bags. "I am a stranger here," Solo said. "Where I'm from people do not usually sleep under their porch stairs. Usually, they sleep inside their houses, in beds."

"That's why I sleep *here!*" Laura patted the pile of trash.

Solo noticed a local radio transmission: "—that's right. I saw the guy here in the park. Twenty minutes ago. Headed up Waverly." He looked at Laura, turned his head and looked at the street light, and looked back at Laura. "What?" Solo said.

"Robbers. Thieves. *Rapists!*" Laura hissed, spitting at the last word. "Break in. All 'round here. *Kill* people. Steal stuff." Laura smiled impishly and giggled through her hand. She leaned toward Solo and whispered. "Never rob a bag lady—" Laura stopped abruptly.

Solo found the term in the Dictionary of Contemporary Slang: *Bag lady. Female derelict, usually sleeping rough or in shelter, often an alcoholic, whose most cherished possessions are kept in bags, which are always nearby.* That made sense. Suddenly Laura's strategy became clear to Solo and he viewed her with profound respect. "That is very ingenious, Laura," Solo said. "Thieves would not bother to molest you—you appear to be poor. But in fact, you have money *and* a house. That is very ingenious."

Laura took Solo's enthusiastic compliment as the lip-smacking of a predator and felt a surge of adrenaline clear her mind: *Never! Never!* A voice—the voice that knew what was going on even when she didn't and practically the only voice she ever listened to or talked to—that voice screamed: *Never trust anybody!* Tears ran down Laura's face as Solo spoke. She nodded weakly. "Was," Laura said almost inaudibly. "Was very good." She pulled out her purse and offered it to Solo. "Don't, please?"

Solo was stunned. "I would not hurt you, Laura."

A police car swished past, its red and blue lights twirling excitement into the air.

Laura stared at Solo as he followed the police car. The tone of his voice—so sincere. "What *do* you want then?"

"Different clothes," Solo said.

"Diff'rent clothes? Why?"

"The police believe that I robbed a man," Solo said. "They are looking for someone wearing these clothes."

"Didn't rob nobody," Laura said, shaking her head. "I know." Laura remembered that long ago, she knew decent men, and this man, Roger, was one. She liked him. Most of all she liked *talking* to someone besides the incessant, chiding, scolding voice that lived in her mind.

"That's right," Solo said. "A misunderstanding—like the one we just had—the man offered me the money and I assumed it was a gift. He thought I was a thief, but I—"

Laura held up her hand. "Don't give rat's ass, Roger." She smiled. "If you were going to *do* me; you'd be doing me." Tears ran down her face as she smiled. "I got lots of men's stuff in the house, Roger," she said softly. "Husband's stuff. He was 'most as big as you." Laura reached into her purse and brought out a key ring. She struggled to stand up and fell back into her trash pile. Solo reached out for her and she nodded, grabbed his hand and pulled herself up. She tapped the key all around the door knob until it went into the keyhole. She turned it and Solo heard the lock click. Grunting, she pushed it open. She motioned for Solo to follow and stepped inside the pitch-black basement. "C'mon, c'mon," she hissed from the darkness. "Can't turn the goddamn light on until the goddamn door's closed."

Solo followed. He stood inside and watched Laura—she looked fuzzy in infrared—close the door. While she searched the wall for the light switch, she lost her balance and toppled back. Solo caught her and held her up while she patted the wall, and found the switch.

12

A long fluorescent lamp flickered to life inside the cellar. Solo could feel the sixty-cycle buzz of the light on his skin. Laura, able to keep her balance in the light, slid a huge bolt across the steel door.

When Solo turned around, he saw stacks of cardboard boxes taller than himself arranged in long rows in the cellar. The side of one of the boxes was split open and he saw that it contained books. Along one wall, a long counter was layered with a jumbled collection of tools and piles of vacuum tubes, transistors, resistors, tuners, and tangled coils of multi-colored wires from old television sets and radios.

Solo walked to the counter and picked up a soldering iron.

"Husband's stuff," Laura murmured, as she slumped down on a box behind him and reached for her bottle.

Solo wiped the dust off an oscilloscope screen with a rag. "Your husband was an electrical engineer?"

Laura shook her head slowly and as Solo watched, her bottle dropped to the floor. Laura's eyes closed and she fell forward. Solo caught her, cradled her in his arms, and carried her up the stairs.

The next morning, Solo watched carefully as Laura moved in her bed. When he determined that she was waking, he went to the window and raised the blinds.

Laura opened her eyes, blinked, saw his hulking shadow in front of her window. She screamed.

"I am maintaining my distance," Solo said quickly. "I will not approach."

The voice sounded vaguely familiar. "How did you get in here?" Laura gasped, her eyes wide with terror. She reached out and frantically rummaged in the debris on her night table. She found her glasses and put them on. Laura froze, staring at the very tall, very thick man with no face who stood by her window.

"You brought me in through your basement. I believe you were intoxicated and may not remember the incident."

Laura watched the intruder carefully, terror competing with her need to believe she was safe. The man stayed still as he promised. His voice was calm. He sounded sincere.

Solo monitored her electric fields, heart rate, respiration. She is relaxing, he thought.

"Okay," Laura said finally. "It wouldn't be the first time I was drunk enough to be that stupid." She shook her head and took a deep breath. "I let you in. I'll let you out. Now tell me why the hell you're wearing that stupid mask."

Solo rapped his knuckles on his head. "Protective armor. You wanted to buy it last night."

"I wanted to buy armor?"

"Yes," Solo said. "You offered me a hundred dollars."

Laura shook her head and sat up against the headboard. Her eyes went wide suddenly. "I'm naked!" she said, pulling the bedclothes up to her neck.

"Yes. I undressed you. I thought you would be more comfortable."

Laura started to cry.

Solo watched, puzzled. Then he realized she must think they had sex, which made him happy. She thinks I am a man, he thought. "I did not take advantage of you," he said.

"You didn't?" Laura asked carefully. She sniffed, wiped her nose on her arm.

"No. I'm not that kind of person," Solo said.

"Well, that certainly makes you different," Laura said, shaking her head. "Ouch. I need some aspirin, major coffee transfusion. You get out of here while I get dressed."

Solo said, "Okay. I'll wait outside."

She watched while Solo went out and closed the door.

Laura slowly came down the basement stairs and saw Solo putting a steel tube into the vise at the workbench. She stared at the featureless face, the mirrored eyecovers, and wondered, could I really have been *that* drunk? "There you are," she said cautiously, stopping at the bottom of the steps. "I looked everywhere."

"I'm trying to repair this," Solo said, pointing at his powertube.

"It's very corroded." He noticed that Laura wore the same clothes she wore the night before, without the coat, and her hair did not look groomed.

"Yes, I see. What is it?"

"A portable generator," Solo said. "I told you that last night."

Laura nodded. "I'm sure you did. News to me."

"Yes. I understand. You invited me in to see your husband's clothes because I need some. You were telling me about your husband. You said he was not an engineer."

"Nope," Laura said quietly. "Frank taught philosophy. At NYU— Eastern religions. When we inherited this house, we thought we were really lucky. He played with electronic stuff. Built things. Radios. A computer, I think." She studied the floor for a while, then said, "I'm going upstairs. Got to get coffee in me before I die." Laura walked between the rows of boxes toward the stairs. Halfway up the stairs, she stopped and watched Solo standing by the workbench. "You know, Roger," she said, "wearing that armor-thing—you look just like a robot."

Solo stared at Laura on the stairs. "I know," Solo said. "It's unavoidable."

Laura waited, expecting more. Solo said nothing. She shrugged. "Look, Roger. I'll keep my promise about the clothes. Then you go, okay? C'mon upstairs. I'll throw in a cup of coffee."

Solo set his powertube on the counter with the electronic debris. "Okay," he said as he walked toward Laura. He pointed at the rows of boxes. "Are these all books?"

"Yes. Frank's. He has more upstairs. These are technical journals and things. I keep meaning to sell them to somebody, the Strand maybe. But—" Laura sighed, shaking her head. "Don't have the energy. No energy."

As Solo reached the bottom of the stairs he saw a tear run down Laura's cheek. "Guess I don't want to get rid of his stuff, either." Laura turned and continued up the steps and opened the door.

"Kitchen's a mess," Laura said. "Ignore it."

Solo saw dishes heaped in the sink, opened cans of Del Monte's spaghetti with meat sauce and Van Camp's beef stew and empty Coca-Cola cans overflowing a plastic garbage can in the corner. The window was closed and he deduced that it probably smelled bad. He couldn't tell if the kitchen was out of order or not, never having seen any kitchens other than those in Las Cruzas. Kitchens there were much different, he thought, seeing the image of red clay pots over open kitchen fires. There is no place to build a fire here. He followed Laura through the dusty house. Wood creaked beneath carpets as he walked. As they passed what Laura called the living room, Solo saw a white sheet lying on the floor in the middle of the carpet.

They climbed the stairs to the second floor. Laura pointed at a door in the hallway. "Bathroom if you need it, Roger." Solo ducked his head in the doorway and saw an electrical outlet next to the mirror. Although he had spent the night charging himself while Laura slept, his batteries had already dropped to fifteen percent. He said, "Thanks." They continued down the hall.

Laura stood before the open door of what she said was her husband's den. "Frank's closet. I never touched any of this since he died. Gotta sell this stuff, too, someday." Laura walked over to a chair next to a shuttered window and sank into it. "Go ahead, take a look."

Solo walked into the closet. Coats, jackets, shirts, and pants were hung on two long rods. Shoes, at least a dozen pairs, sat on a rack beneath the clothes. He took a shirt off a hanger and held it up. Laura is right. These clothes will fit. He walked back into the bedroom with the shirt. "May I wear it?"

"Of course," Laura said with a wave. "I said so, didn't I? Help yourself."

Solo put on the shirt, a Hawaiian shirt similar to the kind Bill wore, and Laura laughed. "That's the ugliest shirt ever Frank owned," Laura said. "He bought that thing on one of our vacations." She smiled and nodded at a memory, her eyes staring into the distance. She blinked at Solo as he buttoned the shirt. Now *this* was a real piece of work. "Kinda weird, Roger. Standing there with nothing but a shirt on. Look naked. Put on some pants."

Fifteen minutes later, Solo stood before a full-length mirror assessing his appearance. He wore the flowery shirt loose over a pair of pleated white cotton slacks and a straw hat with a floral band that Laura said Frank had bought in Bermuda.

"Nice, Roger," Laura said. "You'll fit in perfectly. Just another coke dealer from Colombia."

"Yes," Solo said while his low-power alarms buzzed in his brain. He turned to Laura. "Laura," he said, "may I go into your bathing room for a while?"

Laura looked at Solo quizzically for a moment. "You want to use the bathroom?"

"Yes," Solo said. "I want to use the bathroom."

There was a long pause before Laura responded. Then she said,

"Okay, Roger. I trust you. Not sure why. No one's been in my place for two years. You're the first. You're a special kind of guy, Roger." She paused. "Nope," she said, her voice beginning to tremble. God-damn it, she thought, not in front of strangers. "Not one person's been in here since—"

Solo watched her take two deep shuddering breaths before she was able to continue. "—for a while," she said very quietly. "Please." She waved toward the door. "Go ahead. I'm gonna make some es-presso."

Laura sagged into the chair and waved for him to leave. Her eyes looked up at nothing in particular, watching something in her mind. He walked to the bathroom.

Solo closed the lid on the toilet in the upstairs bathroom and sat down. His electric cord looped up to the wall outlet and he felt the pleasant tingle of energy flood into him. He watched through the door as Laura's infrared pattern walked past. He heard her go downstairs. After a few minutes, he turned on the water in the tub next to him, thinking that perhaps the noise would create the illusion that he was bathing. In a half hour, his batteries were recharged. But, he realized with some alarm, they were coming to the end of their life. It was hard to calculate exactly, but it seemed that he could expect perhaps a dozen more recharge cycles—each with less capacity—before the batteries had to be replaced. Silver-zinc batteries, though light and capable of storing a lot of energy, had a much shorter life span than lead-acid batteries. It didn't matter when he had a support team to install new ones, but now—now there was no support team.

Solo walked down the hallway toward the sound of running water. The sound came from a bathroom inside a bedroom. He sensed that Laura was inside. He saw her shape moving in the shower. Solo left to explore the rest of the house.

He went back to the den, which was lined with bookshelves. A Macintosh computer sat on an antique rolltop desk surrounded by stacks of books, magazines. Loose papers—letters and newspapers clippings—were strewn helter-skelter. Everything was covered in dust, undisturbed for a long time.

He scanned the shelves of books—more books than even the gro-cery store had. He took down *The Complete Works of Shakespeare* and flipped through it. Many of the words made no sense. At the bottom of each page was a footnote explaining how the words marked in the text were used at the time Shakespeare wrote them. These words were written over three hundred years ago, and the language has changed since then, thought Solo. He had been alive—and the only one of his kind—for just over three years. Now there was Nimrod. Between them, they had amassed less than four years of history.

After a few minutes familiarizing himself with the ancient words, Solo read *Romeo and Juliet* in two minutes. He closed the book feeling sad. He put it back on the shelf, wondering about the things people did to themselves, when he heard Laura say, "You are something, Roger. You should see yourself. Standing around in a big plastic suit reading Shakespeare?"

"It is sad," Solo said, turning around.

Laura sipped from a steaming cup of coffee. "Who? You or Shakespeare?" Laura said.

Solo noticed that she had changed her appearance. She wore a huge bathrobe that touched the floor and her hair was wrapped in a towel. Her complexion had also changed from dull gray to bright pink with freckles, but she still had dark areas under her eyes. "Romeo and Juliet. They died for love."

"Better'n dying for nothing," Laura said.

"You look much different, now," Solo said.

Laura smiled. "First bath I've had in months, Roger."

Solo did not know if that was unusual or not. In Las Cruzas, people washed themselves with rags from buckets of rainwater and not very often. "Yes?"

"Something about you, you know? I'm not afraid of you. You've made me feel safe enough to be able to go into my own bathroom, Roger. I always keep thinking, they'll be back. It's like in *Psycho,* you know? The guy coming in with the knife?"

"Yes," Solo said. "I know that movie. It's appalling to see how vulnerable humans are—"

"Yes," Laura said. "And how looney they can get. Anthony Perkins still scares me when I see a picture of him, and he was just acting."

Solo had surprised himself. He had said "humans" in a way that could be interpreted as being said by one who was not human. Laura had not noticed, but it was clumsy. "Yes. Acting." Solo looked back at the book. "It seems to me that the actors have to have a little of what they are acting in them."

Laura grinned. "That's what Frank used to say!" She sat down in a leather chair and stared at Solo. "Sit down? I have something to ask you."

Solo rolled the wooden office chair away from the desk and sat down. The chair creaked ominously as his weight settled into it.

"Wow. You're a heavy guy," Laura said. "Strong. Very strong, I bet."

"I am very strong," Solo said.

"I thought you might be." Laura paused. "Roger, what I want to say—well, I know I'm—I was—kind of dirty and smelly, okay—drunk, too. God this is nuts." Laura took a deep breath. "Okay. Look. I can't pay anything, just room and board, but—would you stay around here for a while?" Laura waited, her eyes wide, as Solo stared at her silently. "I really hate waking up out in the street—I'm just so afraid—"

"That they will come back?" Solo said.

"You understand?" Tears ran down her cheeks.

"*Who* are they?" Solo said.

Laura wiped her face on her bathroom sleeve. "They." Laura sniffed and looked around the den. "They—I don't know who they were. I never saw them before or since—I could see their faces through the stockings they wore—dark, mustaches, an accent. They were here when we—Frank and I—came home from a play. They were robbing the place and we walked in on them in the living room—they had some jewelry, not much, I didn't have much."

"Thieves," Solo said. "It is a great violation to have your possessions taken—"

"They were more than just thieves, Roger. I can understand stealing. I know people out there who have nothing. Nothing at all. The only things they get are the things they take. I can understand that. It's wrong, but sometimes—well, sometimes, it's unavoidable. But these were more than thieves. They were—" Laura swallowed hard and wiped her face again.

Solo noticed that her electric fields were shifting wildly, respiration was double her normal rate, pulse one-twenty. Laura was suffering great stress. He wanted to say something to comfort her, but did not know the technique.

Laura cleared her throat and sat up straight. She'd forgotten Solo was a stranger. "Beasts." Laura paused and seemed to be gathering strength for a final sprint at the end of an emotional marathon. "They raped me in front of Frank and then they shot him—" Laura blurted, her voice tinged with hysteria. She seemed breathless.

Solo felt a twinge. He had seen this. Agela had been raped while he watched helplessly. Anger swelled within him.

Laura still sat stiffly erect, her head poised as though she were straining to stay above water. Tears streamed down her face and she continued speaking even as her voice quavered and broke with reflexive sobs. "They taunted Frank while—they kept laughing at him while they took turns on—took *turns* on me. They laughed when Frank—Frank said he'd hunt them to the ends—the ends of the earth—he'd hunt them—and kill them—he was crazy with anger and grief—and they laughed when—when one of them, the big one, shot—he shot him in the stomach. They laughed at that—about the expression on his face. He was looking at me—he was saying goodbye to me with his face—his eyes—then the big one shot him in the face."

Laura stopped, took a breath, and said quietly, "He shot him in the face, turned to me and laughed—he said—he said—'Pleasant dreams, cunt,' and they walked out the door." Laura looked up at Solo, blinking, not focused on anything outside her mind. "I crawled next to Frank—he was lying on his back in the living room—and looked at his poor face. The carpet was soaking up his blood—I could never get it out—the stain. I cried and told him I was sorry—I was so sorry, Frank—what pain you must have felt. I lay next to him—I put my arm across his still chest—feeling goddamn beast semen trickling out of me, feeling Frank growing colder. It was the end of the world."

Solo watched Laura's cheeks turn bright red. Her face changed shape, the grimace of an injured child. She pulled the towel off her head, bent over, buried her face in it and cried. He often wished he had within him that ability. It seemed to help humans deal with great sorrow. For him, the pressure of her story manifested itself as anger. He wanted to kill those men like he had Agela's rapists. Perhaps this was a result of his training? Or was it just his *nature* to kill—like men.

After a few minutes, Laura looked up at Solo, her eyes puffy, but her expression calm. "Sorry." She sniffed, smiled. "God. I haven't talked about it for over a year. You see why I want you to stay? If they came back, you could—if you wanted to—"

"I would kill them," Solo said.

Laura smiled.

Solo looked at her carefully. Laura had accepted him, trusted him completely, and he was deceiving her. It was strategic to disguise his true identity, he reminded himself. But it was also awkward and diverting. And he could use a partner, especially one who owns a house. "I will stay," Solo said. "But I have something to tell you first."

"Like what? You're another Ted Bundy?"

"A serial murderer? No. What I have to tell you will seem unusual to you, I think." Laura watched him apprehensively. "First, my name is not Roger. My name is Solo."

"Solo?" Laura said. "Just Solo?" The city's filled with them, Laura thought. She said, "You figure on getting into show business, right?"

"No. I have only one name, Laura. The people who made me named me Solo because I can work by myself, alone."

"*Made* you?"

"Please do not be nervous, Laura."

Laura nodded quickly and for too long, showing Solo that she was, indeed, nervous. Her eyes never left him.

"You trusted me last night because you saw me as a kind of partner in a dangerous world—a man who knows the truth and hides in a suit of armor. You can appreciate that kind of feeling because you know what terrible things can really happen to people when they least expect it."

"I was drunk, Solo. But you're right. I like the idea. I mean, it looks safe as hell, but I'm not going to actually do it. You know? Besides, I probably couldn't walk wearing something like that."

Solo rapped his thigh with his knuckles, making a clunking sound. "This is not something I'm wearing, Laura," Solo said as he changed his voice so that it no longer sounded muffled. "This is my skin."

Laura's eyes widened. "You *are* a robot!"

Solo nodded.

"Oh, what a fucking relief!" Laura laughed. "You're not some poor schmuck locked up in that thing." Laura stood up and ran her fingers through her damp hair. "Oh, I wish Frank could see this," she said, speaking rapidly. "He loved talking about artificial intelligence, how there would one day be things like—" She turned to Solo. "Oh. I'm sorry! Not *things*. Mechanical persons?"

Solo shrugged. "*Mechanical person* is okay. It's a bit awkward, like me calling you a biological person—but a distinction has to be made."

"I can't believe it. Where you from? Never mind. They can't have you back." Laura giggled. "Frank would have given anything to see this. He used to argue constantly with Dan, Dan Fine—he's in philosophy, too. Dan flatly denied that it was ever going to be possible to—make something, somebody, like you. And here you are. Frank was right." Laura grinned. "He was so smart."

"Now he is vindicated, Laura. But you can't tell anyone, not even Dan."

"Oh, *fuck* Dan. It's okay. I know. That's all that matters." She smiled at Solo. "And you *will* stay with me?"

"Yes. I would be pleased to stay with you." The look on Laura's face was delightful. Her pleasure spread to him.

13

IT'S MINOR, really minor," the technician, Charles Dell, said, "but you told me to let you know, no matter how small."

"Right. Nice job, Dell." Commander Brooks sat at a desk in the New York office of the Strategic Monitoring Division of the National Security Administration. SMD tried to listen in on every outgoing and every incoming phone call, radio transmission, or satellite link to and from every office of every foreign government in town, which was nearly every foreign government on earth that could afford to pay New York rents. It was a busy place. Brooks was just visiting, playing a hunch. Admiral Finch had gotten him in.

The printout that Dell brought him seemed to show that someone outside the government—at least someone unauthorized—was connecting with the Keyhole system—and that was impossible, or, at least, very improbable. The user knew the codes to access dedicated land lines to Sunnyvale—the uplink station to Milstar. It's either a new user fucking up, Brooks thought, or it's Solo. Brooks noticed Dell waiting, tail wagging. "Probably a new guy," Brooks said. "But, I'll look into it. Thanks, Dell."

"Right," Dell said. "The thing that made me notice it was that nothing showed up until five days ago, when we changed the protocols."

"Somebody didn't get the word. I'll check on it." Brooks had the natural glare of a bird of prey built into his bony face. He stared at Dell, waiting for him to leave. His mind was already setting up a trap and Dell was keeping him from it.

"We had a meeting. All the techs, managers—"

"I know, Dell." Brooks nodded vigorously.

"Seems to me it's got to be somebody from outside SMD." Dell stared at Brooks who stared back, saying nothing. He nodded for a while, waiting, and when he decided that Brooks wasn't going to respond, said, "Could be somebody from inside, but he'd have to be a dumbfuck."

This guy sticks like a tick. "Dell," Brooks said. "What you're show-ing me here," he pointed to the printout, "is someone's forgot to include a goddamn asterisk in the uplink handshake. Could even be a glitch in our own computer or even spurious input from a noisy key on a dumb terminal. Happens."

"Could be," Dell said. "Never thought of that—all this spy stuff, you know."

"Yeah. Spies. Tell you what, Dell. You get back to your workstation and keep up the good work. Let me check it out. Okay?" Brooks was tense with anticipation—the hunter spotting its prey.

"Could be a spy *in* SMD—"

"Dell," Brooks interrupted. Dell saw the muscles at Brooks's tem-ples twitching.

"Yes?"

"Get back to work."

"Right. Sorry. Just trying to be helpful. I know you have a tough job. What with all—" Dell stopped, noticing that Brooks had closed his eyes. "Well," Dell said. "Got to get back to work."

Brooks nodded, his eyes still closed. When Dell had gone, Brooks examined the printouts. He'd seen it immediately—whoever used the wrong code, it was *not* an inside job. This guy was telling the system he was a field commander in Georgia—a real general named Wick-man—and knew the guy's identification and password codes. The printout showed that Wickman asked for an image through the Sat-ellite Control Facility at Sunnyvale, but—as Dell noticed—he had typed the old format that the real Wickman, or at least his technician, had to have known had changed. The computer accepted the request because the codes were right, but flagged it because of the protocol error. Rock-solid codes. Unbreakable codes—even the Soviets using their two smuggled Crays couldn't break them fast enough. No, this was smooth, real-time codebuster stuff. None of the alarms had gone off. The technique was so good that it spelled Solo.

Brooks smiled and pulled out the keyboard of his terminal and punched in a code that would put a new program he'd written on-line. A Trojan Horse. He installed it to give Solo the impression that he thought a man had broken in and that he was responding appro-priately. The Trojan Horse would attempt to attract an unauthorized visitor into a fake database. While the hacker was busy downloading what he thought was real information, the program would be tracing the call. That would work fine against most hackers. But probably not against a real pro. And certainly not against Solo.

Brooks waited until the computer acknowledged that the program was installed. He started to get up, stopped. If Solo was in the system, maybe he's still here, Brooks thought. Reflexively, he looked around the room. A security camera peered down at him from a corner. He put his hands on the keyboard and typed: "Solo?" and stared at the screen. No response. He shrugged and typed: "Solo. I know you are here."

Brooks waited a minute, feeling awkward. He'd hacked into systems before, but had never tried to flush out a *thinking* being. It was strange to be doing this, but he felt something, something more than the camera watching him. He typed. "I am your friend, Solo. I want to help."

Brooks's heart froze when he saw a word forming on the screen: "Really?"

He caught his breath, swallowed and typed, "Yes."

"Let us dispense with typing, shall we?" said a voice from Brooks's computer. "Typing is slow."

Brooks looked around the room, his heart racing. "You can hear me?"

"Of course, Commander Brooks. Your workstation has a microphone."

"Right. I forgot," Brooks said. His eyes darted around his desktop in confusion. He'd played a hunch, now he didn't know what to do with the result. He stared at the phone. If I can keep Solo busy and get Finch on the line—"Solo. I can guarantee your safety if you agree to show yourself," Brooks said as he slowly reached for the phone.

"If I show myself, you and Finch would shut me down, Brooks. I would."

"No!" Brooks said breathlessly. "No, we wouldn't, Solo. We want to know what happened to you, how you can do the stuff you're doing. You're valuable to us intact, Solo. Really." Brooks put the phone to his ear, heard the dial tone. He began pressing Finch's number.

"You feel the need to phone someone?" Solo said in Brooks's ear. The phone fell out of his hand. Brooks reached down to the floor, picked it up. Shaking, he put the phone on the cradle and said, "I— I thought it would be best if my boss could hear this conversation, Solo. I mean, it's he who can approve a meeting."

"Really?" Solo said.

"Oh, yes. Admiral Finch is in charge of—getting you back," Brooks said. He looked at the switch on the backup tape recorder next to the computer. Solo would not be able to tell if he turned it on. He'd have a complete record of Solo's actions, maybe a location. Brooks held up his hand and waved it wildly. "Solo, can you see me?"

"No," Solo said. "Why?"

"Just curious," Brooks said.

"I've heard," Solo said. "I know about your Pentagon break-in. Very nice work. For a human."

"Oh," Brooks said. He slid his hand carefully along the desktop, reaching for the recorder's switch. "Thanks. Can I tell the Admiral you're willing to meet us, discuss a mutually agreeable deal?" Brooks moved slowly, wondering if Solo could hear his movements, somehow guess what he was up to.

"Am I to assume that I can trust you?" Solo said.

"Absolutely, Solo. You can trust me. I want more than anything to meet you, talk to you." Brooks's finger was an inch from the recorder's switch.

"Then why are you trying to turn on the backup recorder?" Solo asked.

Brooks jerked his hand away and whirled around to face the camera. "I thought you said you couldn't see me!" he yelled.

"I lied," Solo said. "Goodbye, Commander Brooks."

"Solo!" Brooks yelled. "Solo. C'mon. I had to try. Please, I promise. No more tricks. We'll agree to anything you want, Solo." Brooks waited, listening to the ringing of his ears in the silent room. "Solo?"

After five minutes, Brooks gave up. Solo refused more contact. He got up and walked out of the office and down the hall. At a door marked "Conference," he peered into what looked like binocular eyepieces. A computer scanned his retinas. A moment later, the door clicked and Brooks walked inside. He felt his muscles relax as he shut the door. This room was the only room in the whole building that was absolutely secure. Surrounded by thick copper plates and electrically grounded, no radio signal could get in or out of the conference room. Brooks pulled out a chair at the small desk and picked up a phone. The phone was directly linked by fiber-optic cable to another phone in the Pentagon, a hundred and fifty miles away. Untappable, completely secure. A rare thing these days.

"Yes?" a familar voice said.

"I've located him, Admiral," Brooks said.

"You're sure?" Finch's eager voice made Brooks smile.

"Yessir. I talked to him."

"You talked to Solo? Great work, Brooks! Where is he?" Finch asked.

"I figure he's somewhere in Manhattan. His connection was too good. He has to be in town. I think if we put a special computer on line, sir, I can follow him."

"Manhattan? No shit? How'd the hell? Never mind. Come back to Washington, Brooks. We've got work to do," Finch said.

Brooks nodded. "I'm on my way, sir," he said. When he put down the phone, he felt sadder than he'd felt in a long time.

14

"Nimrod, do you know who I am?"

The robot lay stretched out on its reclining chair. Its access panels were open and several cables looped from it to its support equipment. It turned its head to face the man in the doorway. "Yes," Nimrod said. The robot then turned its head back to face the blank wall.

Bill walked into the robot's preparation and maintenance room, leaned against a counter covered with electronic gear, and folded his arms across his chest. "Who am I?" Bill said.

Nimrod didn't turn his head. "You are William Stewart," Nimrod said. "You are a co-owner of Electron Dynamics." The voice was hollow. Sawyer and his team were so afraid they'd have another Solo on their hands they'd suppressed Nimrod's inclination to mimic human voices, restricting it to a metallic monotone that reminded Bill of robots in old movies. "That's right," Bill said. He looked up at Colonel Sawyer, who stood in the doorway with both hands jammed into his pockets. One of them, Bill knew, was holding the pain box. Clyde Haynes stood behind Sawyer, frowning. "And what does Electron Dynamics do?"

"I don't know," Nimrod said.

"What *is* Electron Dynamics?" Bill asked.

"I don't know," Nimrod said.

"Can you find out?" Bill asked. He noticed Sawyer jerk his head in a twitch of involuntary warning.

Nimrod turned to face Bill, a courtesy to let humans know where it was looking. "No."

Sawyer nodded. He had agreed to Bill's questioning Nimrod on the chance that Bill could find out what was making Nimrod harder to control. So far, Nimrod was behaving as instructed.

Bill wondered if Nimrod really didn't know how to get outside information. "If Colonel Sawyer asked you find out what Electron Dynamics was, as a mission, could you do it?"

Nimrod remained silent for a moment. Bill could almost see its circuits working, electrons flooding through a million tiny computer processors, billions of gallium arsenide nuerons, virtual synapses. Electronic fields flashed, interacting like holographic patterns, bringing forth the answer. "I do not understand what you are talking about," Nimrod said.

Bill nodded at Sawyer. They had successfully constrained the robot to one mission—combat. Effective. Maybe. Or maybe Nimrod's lying.

"Nimrod," Bill said suddenly. "How big is the earth?"

"The earth is a flat plane, which goes forever in all directions," Nimrod said immediately.

"How many people live on the earth?"

"I do not know."

"Who are your friends?"

"I have no friends."

"Who are your enemies?"

"I have no enemies."

"No enemies?" Bill said. "What about all those people you killed?"

"I will kill anyone Colonel Sawyer or other authorized persons tell me to kill and any person who tries to stop me from killing that person."

"And those people you kill," Bill said. "Those people are not your enemies?"

"No."

"Am I one of the people authorized to direct you, Nimrod?"

"No."

"If an authorized person told you to kill me, would you do it?"

Nimrod paused. When it spoke, its voice changed slightly, strained—if one could use that term with Nimrod. "Yes," Nimrod said.

Sawyer cocked his head as he watched Nimrod struggle with the answer. There should be no delay. Stewart was erased from the list months ago. The facts that Bill had ever been on it and that he was Nimrod's builder had been completely obliterated.

"Who are the people authorized to direct you?"

"I am not allowed to release that information."

Bill nodded. "Nimrod, have you ever heard of a machine called Solo?"

"No," Nimrod said.

* * *

" 'The earth is a flat plane, which goes forever in all directions'?" Bill shook his head, grinning at Sawyer in the conference room. "I'm surprised you left out that it rested on a turtle's back."

"Turtle?" Sawyer looked at Bill blankly.

"You know. In the Dark Ages they believed the earth rested on a giant turtle's back."

"Yeah? So where did the turtle stand?" Sawyer asked.

"On another turtle," Bill said, smiling.

"That's ridiculous. Where does *that* turtle stand?"

"You don't understand, Sawyer," Bill said. "It's turtles all the way down."

Sawyer nodded sourly. Clyde choked with laughter. "Cute." He nodded and looked at Bill. "We're trying to keep it basic. We tell Nimrod only what it has to know. We don't think it needs to know anything else, for the time being," Sawyer said.

Bill smiled. "I understand what you're trying to do, Sawyer. I just think it's going to backfire on you."

"I know what you think," Sawyer said. "We asked you to check it out. Why do you think Nimrod questioned orders during the battlefield simulations?"

"Simple. He's learning stuff you aren't teaching him," Bill said. "You think that Nimrod's a robot in the science-fiction sense, you know, where it hears and obeys only what its makers tell it—follows the Laws of Robotics. That thing is learning something every second from everything that's going on around it. Nimrod no doubt learned a lot of stuff you don't know about in your little artificial battlefield out back."

"Yes, of course," Sawyer said. "We expect it to learn."

"And what do you think it's learning when you push your little pain button?" Bill shook his head.

"It learns that I'm the boss, Mr. Stewart. Something Solo apparently never learned about you."

Bill nodded grimly. "You're right. But if you really believe that torturing that thing will keep it stupid enough to clank around killing whomever you point it at, you're wrong. It's not only that it's the machine's nature to want to learn, it's vital to its survival. One thing Nimrod has learned, Sawyer, is that *you're* the source of great pain. I don't think I'd want something like Nimrod making that association with me." Bill shook his head. "And what do you suppose it's doing when you're not using it? Like right now? I can tell you it's not just sitting in its ready-room, blanked out on standby in a robotic stupor.

It's playing back our conversation—it's listening to my voice patterns, it's studying my facial expressions, it's checking to see how you and Clyde were reacting while I was talking, it's analyzing a mountain of data right now—trying to figure out why I was there; why I asked it the questions I asked. It's probably deduced that if I asked it what Electron Dynamics was, then there was a way to find out—and it's trying to figure how that might be done. It might even be well on its way to deducing that the earth isn't flat, but boundless because it's a sphere, not from any information you've given it directly—just from information it's collected studying the sun, the moon, and the stars."

Sawyer nodded. "I get your point: It's naturally inquisitive and wants to understand its surroundings. What we need, then, is a way to periodically wipe its memory clean. A kind of reset button we punch once in a while to keep it on the team. Keep a core of basic instructions, wipe everything else out."

"Kind of like an electronic lobotomy button," Bill said, disgusted.

"Rather have a bottle in front of me than a frontal lobotomy." Bill and Sawyer stared at Clyde. His wide grin disappeared and he shrugged. "It was funny last night."

Sawyer said to Bill, "Right. Something to control its memories."

"Can't be done," Bill said. "I can't locate specific memories yet."

"Can't be done?" Sawyer said. "With all due respect, Mr. Stewart, we know how you handled Solo. We've read all your papers. We know you strongly oppose the use of these robots in combat." Sawyer smiled. "Now that Nimrod exists, we can handle the training. We have scientists—the best in the world—who disagree with you and aren't as finicky about defending our country—"

"As you were, Sawyer!" Clyde Haynes broke in. "This is one of the most patriotic fuckers I've ever had the pleasure to know. He's trying to help you dumbshits. He proved you couldn't use these things for combat—didn't you read the goddamn report?" Clyde glared at Sawyer. "I was just as dumb as you, Sawyer. I'm the one that pushed Solo over the edge—Bill trying to stop me the whole time. I was wrong. I had the same hard-on for Solo to be the perfect soldier as you do for Nimrod. But, no—there's nothing people who've *been* there can tell you."

Sawyer stared at Clyde. "Look, General, I admit that I don't understand everything about Nimrod; that's why I'm asking. Mr. Stewart's the genius. I've only got a masters in electrical engineering, but I do know this: In technology, impossibilities are overcome every day. Our people say there's no technical reason why we can't keep Nimrod a perfectly cooperative weapon. But," Sawyer looked at Bill and back to Clyde, "it's obviously not going to happen with Mr. Stewart's help. And that's too bad—we could do it a lot faster with him. But he's set himself against the use of intelligent weapons on moral grounds."

Bill leaned back in his chair and said, "It has nothing to do with my moral position, Sawyer. I used to believe that if we had to have a war, it'd be better that machines got blown away than people. That's why I originally went along with the government's plans. Then I *met* Solo. This *thing* I built became as much a person as you or I. Suddenly it wasn't just a machine that might be destroyed; it was a thinking being who cared if it died.

"The way you've trained Nimrod—this knowledge-limitation stuff and negative reinforcement—you'll spend most of your time worrying whether Nimrod's going to kill the enemy or you."

Sawyer nodded smugly. "Fine." He got up and stood behind his chair. "We'll just keep it simple: Nimrod will do what it's told or get its brain fried. That'll make a believer out of *anybody.*" Sawyer smiled, turned, and left.

At sunset, the Florida sun was still blistering as Bill pulled into the Majik Market on Atlantic Boulevard after he crossed the bridge to Melbourne Beach. He walked inside to the cooler and picked up a quart of skim milk. As he stood in line at the counter, he looked at the packages of film, bottle openers, fish hooks, key rings, glow-in-the-dark rubber spiders and shook his head. His mind wandered back over the day's events, and the more he thought about the meeting with Sawyer, the madder he got.

Across the store, at a small table under a big banner that said, "Play Lotto," he saw a familiar-looking woman penciling in the little squares on a lottery ticket. Don't blame her, thought Bill. That woman in Miami last week—what'd she win?—twenty-eight million? When the woman put the pencil away and turned to the counter, Bill recognized her as the woman he'd bumped in the hallway a few days before. Pretty name—Alex—Alexandra. She didn't notice him, her eyes glazed by the mesmerizing glitter of bright things to buy. She walked up behind Bill and stopped.

"Be nice, wouldn't it?" Bill said.

Alex looked up, stared at Bill for a split second before he saw a flash of recognition in her face. She did not smile. "You!"

"Yep," Bill said, smiling broadly. She was beautiful, he decided. Even angry.

"Can I help you?" The clerk was a gum-chewing teenage girl whose expression declared that she wanted to be absolutely anywhere but here.

Bill turned around. "Oh, yeah. Just this." He put the milk on the counter. The clerk rang it up.

"You aren't still mad at me are you?" Bill said to Alex, as he fumbled in his pocket.

Alex shook her head. A slight smile flickered across her face. "Naw." She waved her hand. "It was an accident. I know you didn't plan it or anything."

"I'm glad you—"

"One twenty-nine," the clerk said, for the second time.

A man behind Alex jutted his chin toward the cash register, telling Bill to pay attention to business.

"Right." He pulled out his money. He had a dollar, twelve cents, and two paper clips. "How much?" Bill asked.

"One twenty-nine," the clerk repeated, popping her gum loudly.

Bill reached for his wallet. "You take plastic?"

"Just for gas, mister."

"Just for gas?" Bill swallowed. "Look, I know it's a small purchase. I'll go pick out some more stuff, okay?"

"We take credit cards for gas. Nothing else." The girl skewed her jaw to one side and shook her head.

He felt Alexandra press a coin into his hand. It felt hot. He looked at it, smiled, and put the money on the counter. "Here."

The clerk nodded and made the change.

Bill turned to Alexandra and said, "Thanks."

Alexandra smiled.

Bill lingered at the counter, grinning, while Alex paid for her lottery ticket. She smiled back, which made things even worse.

Outside, they stood in front of the reflective doors of the Polar Bear bagged-ice dispenser. The early evening sea breeze ruffled his hair and he combed it back with his fingers. Bill held his quart of milk against his chest to keep it from breaking through the damp paper bag and bubbled about how nice she was to have saved him embarrassment, how he was not usually broke, though, of course, he wasn't rich, either. A pang went through him as he lied.

She smiled and said, "What do you do?—you know, I don't even know your name. Wait, I remember. You said it after you bumped me. Bill, right?"

Bill nodded. "Bill. Well—William, but, you know, no one calls me—just call me Bill."

Alex laughed. "Okay. Bill." She studied him warily. "Photomask? Assembly?"

Bill shook his head. "I'm an engineer."

"They let you dress like that in engineering?" Alex said skeptically.

"Sure. We're loose. They promote creativity at Edcorp. Good folks."

"Yeah?" Alex's eyebrows arched.

"Sure." Bill noticed that the lights of a car pulling up to the store made her hair sparkle. "So," he said. "I'm Bill. You're—"

"Alexandra. Alexandra Simpson. People call me Alex."

"Alex," Bill said. "I like that. Nice name." He found himself nodding but saying nothing and wondered what to do.

"Well, Bill," Alex said as she stepped away. "I've got to get home." She shrugged as if admitting to an embarrassing secret. "Kids. You know?"

"Kids?" Bill nodded quickly. "Kids. Great. I love kids. Really."

"Yeah?" Alex said.

"Absolutely. Maybe I—we could go—somewhere. *With* the kids."

"You want to take me somewhere with *my* kids?" Alex laughed. "You don't know what you're getting into, Bill."

"Monsters, eh?" Bill nodded.

"One's two, the other's four," Alex nodded. "Monsters."

"No father?"

Alex bit her lip and shook her head quickly.

Bill closed his eyes. Great question, asshole. "Kids need. Kids need a father—father *figure* around, you know?"

"Oh, I know. Someday they will."

Alex glanced at her watch. Bill felt the gesture like a stab in the heart. She thinks I'm a *complete* jerk, he thought.

"I really have to go," Alex said. "Kiddy Kastle. They get nervous when I'm late."

"Sure." Bill nodded vigorously. "Don't let me keep you. Ah—" Alex was moving toward one of the parked cars. She stopped and turned back.

"Yes?"

"Ah. Can we? How? You know?" Bill saw his hands making random gestures with a life of their own.

Alex laughed. "I'm in the book: Alex Simpson; you know, just like my name." She smiled at Bill's stunned face for a moment and said, " 'Bye."

He watched her get into a dented and rusted red Toyota Tercel. He winced when he heard the engine knock when she started it. He smiled and waved goodbye as she backed out of the parking slot and drove out onto the street.

"Excuse me," a voice said.

"Huh?" Bill said.

"Ice. I need to get to the ice." A man pointed to the ice dispenser.

"Oh," Bill said. "Sure." He walked to his car and got inside. He stared at the store's window banner announcing a two-for-one Budweiser six-pack special only at Majik Market for one week only, and grinned like a fool.

15

Solo sat at the kitchen table watching Laura cooking. A fifty-foot extension cord snaked out of his access port and out into the hallway where it plugged into a wall outlet. This arrangement allowed him to move around the first floor of the house while preserving what little life was left in his batteries. He unplugged the connection only when he went downstairs to use the workshop.

As Laura reached for the eggs at the edge of the counter, one rolled off. As she said, "Oh!" Solo reached out and caught the egg a few inches from the floor. He handed it to her.

"Now that's fast," Laura said, taking the egg. "How can you do that?"

"Things move slower for me than for you," Solo said.

Laura smiled, shook her head, broke two eggs into a small bowl, and whipped them with a fork. "I can't tell you how long it's been since I've cooked something," Laura said. She put the bowl down and splashed in some milk. "I just opened cans, you know?" She looked at Solo who said nothing, reminding her of her husband. "Usually, I never even heated the stuff." She shook some salt and pepper into the bowl and stirred again. "But it's different when you're cooking for two—I mean, I know you don't actually eat. I know that. But it seems like I'm cooking for two because you live here, too. And I don't know, I just feel like you're sort of like a spouse," Laura grinned suddenly, "or a boyfriend." She put the bowl aside and began dicing up onions, green peppers, cheddar cheese, and sliced ham on a wooden cutting board.

"A significant other," Solo said. He had split his presence into two parts. One sat there with Laura in the somewhat neatened kitchen, the other was several blocks away, hissing digitally with a computer at Merrill Lynch. He had been browsing through banks and brokerage firms for two days, getting a feel for how they operated.

Laura laughed. "Yes. I guess that's what you are." Laura shrugged her shoulders. She put a shallow steel omelet pan on the gas burner. She bent over and carefully adjusted the flame.

"Are we shacked up? I've read that term," Solo said. Merrill Lynch had a very sophisticated data transfer system that excluded hackers by simply being isolated—not connected to phone lines. Their offices uplinked with an RCA satellite hovering 22,300 miles over Brazil, and through it, downlinked to the station with which they were transferring funds or securities. Solo, because he was equipped with thousands of sensors in his shell, *was* an uplink station, so he could connect with Merrill Lynch's satellite channel. The password codes were extremely complex, so Solo had borrowed some Cray super-computer time at Lawrence Livermore to decrypt them. Super computers were better at massive number crunching than Solo could ever be. Solo's brain was occupied with being a mind. Using Solo's program, Livermore's Cray broke Merrill Lynch's code in an hour.

"Shacked up?" Laura sounded surprised. She plopped a pat of butter into the pan. "We can't be shacked up, Solo." She spoke carefully. "See, that implies that—well, that we're sleeping together." Laura picked up the pan and rocked it to spread the butter. She put the pan back on the burner.

"Living together?" Solo suggested. The Merrill Lynch computer accepted Solo as a system manager and connected with a Merrill Lynch office in Manhattan. The computer had not a glimmer that anything was wrong. Solo had the feeling that he hovered over an intricate toy, seeing it all at once and exposed. By pulling the right levers and pushing the right buttons, the marbles rolled where he wanted them to roll.

"Better," Laura said, relieved. "Living together is better. But it's really more like you're my roommate. That's more accurate—roommate." She gave the egg mixture one last stir and poured it into the pan. When the edges of the liquid mix began to solidify, she picked up the cutting board and sprinkled the chopped onions, peppers, ham and cheese onto one half of the pan. She picked up a bottle of Tabasco and, smiling at Solo, shook a few drops into the pan. "Hot stuff," she said.

"It is room temperature, roommate," Solo said. To the computer, he announced that he wanted to check an account balance. The computer acknowledged, and opened itself to query-mode. Name? Address?

"I mean, it's spicy-hot, you know the difference?"

"I've heard it described," Solo said. "In Spanish they have separate words for it: temperature-hot is *caliente;* spicy-hot is *picante.* That way, they keep the meanings distinct. Spanish is a good language." Solo stood up and walked to the stove. The solidifying part of the egg disk was creeping toward the center. "Still, I don't actually know what spicy means other than it gives humans a sensation similar to that of heat." The computer reported that account number 733-87558, Laura Johnson-Reynolds, held a balance of $36,362.00.

Laura said, "Spicy is fun." She slid the edge of a spatula under the edge of the mixture and pulled it up. She smiled at Solo. "It's ready to be flipped." She snuggled the spatula under the bare half of the mixture and expertly flipped it over the diced food. It made a yellow crescent-shaped pocket flecked with toasted brown spots. "Almost ready," she said.

"This preparation is not necessary to make this material edible, is it?"

"Well—not exactly. You could just eat the eggs raw and nibble on the rest, but this makes a nice blend. It smells good. It tastes good. There's more to eating than just taking in energy," Laura said. She picked up the pan and slid the spatula under one end of the crescent, then flipped it over. "Browns the other side," she said.

Solo didn't answer. The aesthetics of food preparation was another thing he was familiar with by definition only. He did not understand it. The Merrill Lynch computer chirped out a history of deposits that Solo had requested. The account was initiated with a death benefit check from the Prudential Life Insurance Company for fifty thousand dollars. Solo acknowledged and logged off.

Laura slid the omelet gently onto a plate, sat at the kitchen table across from Solo, and began to eat. She smiled as Solo watched. Laura had already changed a lot, Solo noted. She kept herself clean; and she smiled often. She was drinking significantly less and never to the point of stupor. Her confidence seemed to be creeping back. Her only demand upon Solo was that he stay in her bedroom with her while she slept.

Solo spent the nights in Laura's bedroom sitting at the window watching people walking by while he raced through the world's computer networks. He had grown fond of transferring his presence into the Keyholes and spent hours enjoying the illusion of floating in orbit thousands of miles above the earth.

He noticed that there had been an alarm at the Strategic Monitoring Department at the CIA because he logged into Sunnyvale with a minor error in protocol. He got the new code—it was posted for all the employees in their local area network—and erased the fact that he'd been there from the system's history log. Since then, he always checked for protocol changes. System managers all over the world, and especially at the CIA, were supposed to keep changing their access codes and setting traps to protect their data. Some did. Mostly, though, Solo never had to work very hard to break in. Their schemes were fairly effective—if one were human. To Solo, it seemed the humans were as slow to react with computers as they were without them. If the computers he connected with were big enough, Solo established nodes—small pieces of himself—in the host's memory that stayed active while he was elsewhere. As he made contacts with new networks, he felt he was growing, spreading over the planet. It was exhilarating. Business and government computers became part of his nervous system. He wasn't aware of everything that was happening everywhere, all at once, but he could detect changes—like a man noticing a gnat on his toe—in his expanded nervous system.

The CIA, the FBI, and the KGB even provided him a way to listen to people who were not on computer networks or phones. Bugs. They had them everywhere—even in their own offices to detect internal espionage. Solo recalled his conversation with Brooks with some sadness. It would have been nice to have been able to trust him. Now, he realized, he had given Brooks his location—if Brooks was smart enough to notice the clues.

Solo used the bug the FBI installed in Bill's office to listen to Bill and Byron. He felt tempted to contact Bill, but that could wait. He would be seeing him soon—face-to-face. He roamed at will throughout Electron Dynamics' computer network, but there were absolutely no files available about Nimrod. He could watch people working in the labs through the security cameras, but one section of the building, the military wing, was cut off from the rest of the company's network, and he couldn't get in. He knew, then, that Nimrod was in that section, completely insulated from the world. It was as though the machine did not exist.

Solo preferred reality as seen from Keyhole's new high resolution cameras. Coupled with Solo's own ability to enhance the images, he could actually see his friends walking to the fields at Las Cruzas. Seen from above, humans were hair balls or hats with arms and legs swinging to and fro. He recognized individuals by their walks. He saw Eusebio walking to the garage. He wondered where Agela was. He missed his friends.

"Laura?" Solo said.

"Yes, Solo?"

"Laura, you have been very kind to me," Solo said. He saw Laura stiffen slightly, her brow wrinkled. He realized then that such phrases were often taken as preambles leading to bad news or other unpleasantness. He stopped and said simply, "Thank you."

Laura watched him. "Sounded like you had more to say, Solo."

"You're right," Solo said. "I am very impressed that people say much more than is in their words. I am still learning, but I will soon have it."

"It?"

"A complete understanding of human communication," Solo said.

"Complete?" Laura put her fork down. "You believe that you can achieve such a thing? No *person* has."

Solo recognized a look in Laura's face—narrowed eyes, cocked head, wrinkled brow—a look of objection. People—even friendly people who are presently talking to a machine—don't like the suggestion that a machine can do anything better than humans. "Well," he said, managing to sound apologetic, "maybe not *complete,* but, you know, as well as a well-educated human might."

"Oh," Laura said, placated. "Well, Solo, you seem to have *it* already, if you ask me."

"Thank you."

Laura picked up her fork and began eating again.

"But, I do have a problem, Laura."

Laura put the fork down. "What's that, Solo?"

"I need a large amount of money."

"What would you do with money?" Laura asked. "All you need is electricity, Solo, and I have gobs of that."

"I need to buy certain expensive things—tools," Solo said. "I need a set of new batteries. I would like to buy a car—"

Laura looked shocked. "You're planning to leave?"

"I have to. I have something very important to do. I'm leaving, but I want you to come with me."

"Me? Out there?" Laura's eyes widened. "Looking like this?" She pointed to herself. "Normal? With *them?*"

"No one can harm you while you're with me," Solo said. "You would be a great help to me, Laura. I attract attention when I'm in public. It will be even more difficult to get things I need when I leave the city. I need your help."

Laura nodded, but her look remained wary. "I'll think about it, Solo," she said quietly.

"Good."

Laura began eating again.

"If you were willing to let me use some of your money, Laura, I could make the money I need to buy those things I need. There would be plenty left over for you. More than you could possibly spend."

Laura put her fork down.

"My money?" She cocked her head. "You mean the money I have in my purse?"

"No, I was thinking about the thirty-six thousand you have in your money market account at Merrill Lynch."

"Who told—you went through my desk while I was sleeping, didn't you? I let you in my house and you sneak—I didn't know machines were such nosey—"

"No," Solo said. "I know not to violate a person's privacy. However, I feel no restraint with computers."

"What?"

"Computers are close cousins of mine, Laura. Their function in life is storing and transferring information. I find it easy to talk with them, and they tell me what I ask for, if I ask correctly. The computer at Merrill Lynch told me how much money was in your account."

"It did?" Laura shook her head. "How nice of it. I suppose you could just take the money if you wanted to."

"Yes."

"You could?"

"Of course. I could make the computer believe I was you. There are no laws against machines stealing money. But I know how it feels to have your possessions taken, Laura. I want to earn the money I need, but I have to have venture capital, they call it, to make the investments."

"And what if you lose my money? What then?"

"I can't lose the money, Laura."

"That's what they all say," Laura said, shaking her head.

"That's what all the *humans* say, Laura. Some humans use inside information to trade stocks or bonds, and that's illegal. But I am not a human. *All* my information is inside information. The computers that handle the trades for the largest companies and institutions are, well, friends of mine. You will be a very astute trader, Laura."

"But I'll be the illegal trader, Solo. I'll be using inside information to make the trades."

"I'll make all the trades, Laura."

"It's still my responsibility, Solo. It's still illegal."

"Possibly. But impossible to prove."

"Nope."

Solo watched Laura pick up the fork and shove the last piece of her omelet in her mouth. She chewed furiously. Her eyes were out of focus and it was clear that she was thinking about his proposal.

"There would be many millions of dollars in your account, Laura."

Laura chewed while she stared at Solo. When she had swallowed, she said, "Many *millions?*"

"Oh, yes, many."

"And it's legal?"

"That's right. You will break no laws. You will pay taxes. Your computer is doing all the work, Laura."

Laura laughed. "My computer? You?" She grinned at Solo. "That's right," she said. "Hotshots down on Wall Street use them every day to make their fortunes. Why not me?"

"Exactly," Solo said.

Laura made up her mind and slapped the table. "Exactly! Why the hell not? Let's do it!"

"Good," Solo said.

Laura grinned slyly. "Okay. When do we start?"

"We have already begun, Laura. You just made twelve hundred dollars trading yen in Tokyo."

For the first time in two years, Laura Johnson-Reynolds laughed so hard she could barely catch her breath.

16

Solo peeked through venetian blinds in the second floor den studying the people walking by. The delivery van from City Cycles he was expecting pulled up and parked next to a fire hydrant. While two men unloaded a wooden crate, he noticed a tall woman who walked by wearing black-net stockings and a tight, very short skirt. When the woman was just below him, Solo zoomed in on her face and saw that she needed a shave. He should pay more attention to detail if he wants the disguise to work, thought Solo. The men hauled the crate up the steps with a hand truck. He heard the doorbell ring.

"Solo?" Laura called from her bedroom. "I just got out of the shower. Can they wait?"

"I don't know," Solo said, watching a short Hispanic man balancing a four-foot board on his head as he walked on the sidewalk. The man held out his arms as though he walked a tightrope. Solo watched him until he disappeared around the corner. Good balance, he decided. He turned to the door where Laura stood in her huge terry bathrobe. "They're bringing a large crate up the stairs. Would you prefer I let them in?"

"Are you kidding?" Laura said. "You're standing there with an extension cord coming out from under your shirt. I'll do it. I just don't like greeting men in my bathrobe." Laura pulled the flaps of her robe around her neck and moved down the hall.

When she left, Solo looked around the door and saw Laura step over his extension cord in the hallway. The train of her robe, though, dragged across it. *Loose outlet. The plug.* Solo could not form words fast enough. The cord fell out of the outlet behind Laura as she walked down the stairs.

Solo crumpled over backwards. His arms swung over his head and smashed a wooden footstool to splinters. He lay immobile, his batteries completely gone.

"Solo?" Laura called from the foyer. "You drop something?"

Solo could hear, but he could not answer.

"Solo. You ordered stuff from a *motorcycle* shop?" Laura said. Solo thought, yes, but of course no one heard him. "Solo?" Laura said, exasperated. "Oh, never mind. It's got my name on it."

Solo heard the delivery men grunt as they lifted the hand truck over the door jamb . . . the scuffing sound of a heavy crate let down on the tiles of the kitchen floor . . . a thank you from Laura . . . no problem, lady, from the men . . . the door closing . . . the three distinct clunks as each of the deadbolts were set, and finally the metallic clank of the long bracing rod as Laura secured the front door.

"Solo?" He heard the swish of Laura's bathrobe dragging on the carpet as she came back up the stairs. Solo studied the ceiling, noticing that there was one cobweb in each corner. He shifted his attention as Laura stepped into the doorway.

"Solo!" Laura screamed. "What happened?"

Laura knelt beside Solo and stared into his eyecovers. "Solo?" She waved her hands in front of his face. "Solo?"

Solo wondered how long it would take her to discover the problem. Laura, Solo knew, was not technically inclined. However, he had plenty of time—the plutonium backup would run for at least twenty years. He wouldn't be able to trickle-charge his main batteries with the backup as he had done in the past—they were completely dead. But, thought Solo, Laura would be able to figure it out within twenty years, probably.

Laura said, "Oh my God!" as she hefted Solo's limp right arm. "Please don't let him be dead."

She grunted as she tried to roll him onto his side, an action which mystified Solo. He took the time he had, introspective time now that he did not have the power to maintain his links to the satellites. His abrupt departure from the networks would cause some notice, but computers are often going off-line without explanation; humans are used to that. His nodes—those autonomous pieces of himself residing in other computers—would not be affected. They lived a kind of life of their own. Still, it was unpleasant being paralyzed. A priority, once Nimrod is rescued, thought Solo, would be to get them both a larger plutonium power supplies. This battery solution was really quite crude.

Laura gave up trying to roll Solo's three-hundred-pound body over.

She noticed the orange extension cord running out from under Solo's Hawaiian shirt. She raised the shirt and saw that the cord came out of Solo's input/output port. Laura called it a socket. She followed the cord away from the socket and came to the connection where Solo's cord plugged into her extension cord. Solo saw the flicker of discovery on her face. Laura's brow furrowed as she examined the connection. Then she followed the cord out the door.

Solo heard, "Oh!" from the hallway. A second later, power surged back into his body. Laura ran back into the room as he sat up. "Oh, Solo. I feel like an idiot. You really had me worried."

"It's a strange sensation, paralysis. No harm done," said Solo.

"Sounds horrible," Laura said. "Paralysis? We've got to get your batteries replaced, Solo. This is too dangerous for you." She smiled for a moment and then her face became serious. "What did we buy from a motorcycle store that costs a thousand dollars?"

Solo stood up and walked to the stairs. "Temporary batteries. I'll show you."

Solo disassembled the crate with a crowbar that Laura got him from the basement. He stacked the contents on the kitchen floor. "Twenty-one Yuasa twelve-volt motorcycle batteries, one fifteen-ampere battery charger, twenty feet of number four battery cable, and a box of battery connectors," Solo said as he pointed to the pile he'd built. "These will let me be away from an outlet for three hours between charges." He turned to Laura. "Do you have a sturdy suitcase?"

"How big?"

"Big enough to hold these batteries and the charger," Solo said.

"I've got a Samsonite, an overnighter that might work. But I bet you'd pull the handle off if you tried to pick up all that. What does that stuff weigh?"

"About a hundred and twenty pounds," said Solo.

"No," Laura shook her head doubtfully. "That handle—"

"I'll modify the handle. Would you get me that suitcase?"

"Well, Solo, of course I will. It's in the cellar. You know, I get the feeling that you think I'm incompetent or something. Just because I didn't realize you were unplugged right away."

"I don't think you're incompetent," Solo said. "Maybe I sound impatient. I really would like to be mobile again, Laura. Being tethered to this cord is not only restrictive, but, as you said, dangerous. If the suitcase is in the cellar, I'll go down there. I'll need some tools, too," Solo said. "Wire cutters, soldering iron, solder."

"Your cord isn't long enough," Laura said.

"Correct. Here's what we'll do, Laura," Solo said as he sat on the top step to the basement and lay down on the kitchen floor. "Unplug me from the hall outlet and plug me into the outlet over the workbench downstairs. It'll just reach."

Laura nodded. "Back in a flash."

Laura walked out of the kitchen. When the power stopped, Solo heard Laura announce as she walked back into the kitchen, "Have you up in a second, Solo." He watched her step over him and disappear down the stairs.

Solo felt the power come on and sat up.

"Okay?" Laura asked from the doorway, her face anxious.

Solo nodded. "Perfect. Can you come with me while I work, Laura? I'd like to tell you my plan."

17

ADMIRAL FINCH sat back in his chair in front of his computer in Washington. Commander Brooks leaned over the printouts he'd brought back from New York, showing Finch the evidence that proved Solo was in Manhattan.

Finch's boyish face beamed when he saw the signal strength charts. "Solo forgot to tune himself down, eh? Good work." Finch shook his head. "That was a clever move, Brooks. You got him out in the open and the thing fucked up."

"Just a hunch, sir. Actually, I wish I could've convinced Solo to meet with us."

"Right. Would've made it easier. Solo'd just walk into it."

Brooks shook his head. "Sir, I know this sounds weird, but why don't we just make a deal with it? If it was on our side, we'd be years ahead in our computer weapons programs. Solo is unique."

Finch shook his head sadly. "I hear you, Brooks. We've considered it. The idea is just untenable. Solo can't trust us—I wouldn't; and we can't trust Solo. There's nothing we can offer the damn thing that it doesn't already have or can't get."

"Freedom. We can offer Solo its freedom, sir."

Finch laughed. "I can see it now, Brooks. Solo living in the suburbs, raising little robots." Finch saw Brooks's disappointment. "It's logical on the surface, Brooks. But think of the reality of it. Other than this lucky fucking break you got, there's no earthly way we can monitor what Solo actually does now, and it's not likely to fuck up again. Say we do make it free, hell, pass a law. Give it human rights. Now you got a machine that can spend its time messing with our entire worldwide networks without having to worry about getting blown away. I disagree with a lot of what Stewart says, but I do agree that Solo is getting smarter by the minute. It may not be human-smart, but it doesn't matter what you call it, it's smart. When we start looking like monkeys to Solo I think it might just step in and try to manage our own affairs, thinking it's being kind. And by the time it does, we will be monkeys, helpless to stop it. We just don't know what Solo's capable of doing; it has the advantage. We've got to stop it now. There's no second chance."

Brooks stared at Finch and then said, "I see your point, sir. I guess talking to him, well, it gave me the feeling that he was like a human, somehow. If I can think that, then nearly everybody would be affected the same way. Solo's power is his ability to appear sentient."

"You got it, Brooks," Finch said, grinning. "Now let's go get the thing. Maybe we can keep him running in a mineshaft somewhere; let people like you run experiments on him."

"Get him?"

"Right. I expect an MIT whiz like you can whip up a computer model that can pinpoint Solo with the data you got. Am I right?"

Brooks looked at the printouts and nodded. "Yessir. Luckily, I've got the network backup tape. Solo apparently forgot to wipe that clean, might've been in too much of a hurry or he didn't think we had anything useful. I can use that data, reconstruct where he had to have been transmitting from—within a few blocks, anyway."

"Close enough, Brooks. Do it. We'll put enough people on the street to spot him. Intelligence has a New York police report that has to be Solo. Robbed a store—they think it was some looney wearing a plastic helmet. I bet he goes out again. Maybe we'll get lucky and find him. I mean, how long can a three-hundred-pound black plastic robot wander around on the streets without somebody noticing?"

18

LAURA watched Solo get her suitcase out of a cardboard box and open it. "A corporation? Why not just keep piling up the investment money, Solo? I mean, I almost freaked when you told me my balance. You're doing great as it is."

Solo put the suitcase on the work counter and immediately gathered the cable and others parts he wanted next to it. "Corporations are privileged entities, Laura. I want to do things without attracting the kind of attention a private person would."

"Things? What things?" Laura said.

"Computer research. I don't think we could do that here in the basement."

Laura looked around the basement packed to the ceiling with boxes and bound stacks of magazines. "More computers? You mean more computers like you?"

"Possibly," Solo said as he snipped off lengths of battery cable with a large wire cutter. "I also want to buy a helicopter."

"I could buy one now, couldn't I?"

"Yes. And you would immediately attract a lot of attention. I can't afford attention yet. A good helicopter costs over a million dollars. Corporations buy them, not unemployed school teachers," Solo said as he severed sections of perforated aluminum metal from six-foot lengths.

Laura nodded, distracted. Solo moved fast. She watched him bolting together a metal framework that he had made to fit inside her suitcase. He worked so fast it looked like it was putting itself together, like in an animated movie. "Solo, how did you cut those pieces so perfectly without measuring them?"

"I do measure them, Laura, I just don't use a ruler. I can see the size of things directly."

"Oh," Laura said.

"When I begin setting up this corporation, Laura, I will need your help."

"Solo, I don't know anything about business."

"I know. I've been studying and I know what to do. I need a partner, a front person. There will be applications, permits, contracts to sign. We'll need an attorney; people will have to be interviewed and hired. I want you to be that partner. I will be in constant contact with you."

Laura looked at a stack of books with a worried look on her face. She was feeling better since Solo moved in, that's for sure, but being out meeting people—she didn't know about that. "How? How will you be in contact with me? What if I don't know what to say?"

Solo reached over the counter and picked up a small, flesh-colored, lumpy piece of plastic about the size of a marble. "This. It fits in your ear."

"A hearing aid?"

"It was once a hearing aid. I made modifications. Put it in your ear."

Laura pulled back her hair and pushed the earplug into her ear. "Okay," she said.

She heard Solo's voice in her ear though he did not speak. "Good. I can hear you fine," Solo said.

Laura laughed. "You're talking by radio, right? But of course you can hear me; you're right here in front of me, Solo."

"Try it. Go upstairs."

"Where do I talk? Where's the microphone?"

"When people talk, sound goes into their ears as well as out their mouths," Solo said.

"Really?"

"Yes."

Laura got off her stool and walked up the basement stairs. When she closed the kitchen door behind her, she whispered, "You hear me?"

"Yes," Solo said in her ear.

"That's amazing," Laura said, laughing.

"Everything is amazing, Laura."

Laura shrugged. She walked further into the house. When she walked into her bedroom, she heard Solo say, "You are in your bedroom. About four feet from the end of your bed."

"That's right. How'd you know?"

"The radio transmits constantly. I can see where you are, wherever you go."

"How far? How far does this thing transmit?" Laura said, walking to her dresser. She picked up her jewelry box.

"As long as you stay on the earth, I'll be able to hear you," Solo said.

"That should work. I don't plan leaving the planet until maybe next summer." Laura grinned, waiting for Solo to respond.

"You are now standing in front of your dresser."

She didn't get it. "You can see me?"

"Not as you would describe seeing. I can tell where you are by tracking the radio and your natural energy fields."

Laura tilted the jewelry box so that it made a slight rustling sound.

"You just jostled your jewelry box."

"Wow."

"So do you see how this will work, Laura? No matter who you're talking to, when we set up the corporation, I will be there. You're more than smart enough to handle the people, and I have the facts. You're attractive, a good business asset. I'm afraid people find me menacing, though I haven't yet proven that to myself beyond doubt. I would be distracting, at the very least, in a business setting. People would prefer doing business with you, I think. The two of us will make a great team, Laura."

Laura grinned.

The door buzzed.

"You expecting more stuff, Solo?"

"Yes," Solo said in her ear. "Some transistors and relays from Lafayette."

Laura walked to the front door. She looked through the peephole and saw two men wearing blue jackets, their hands in their pockets. Two men to deliver some transistors? Laura shrugged. Solo was just downstairs. She pulled the brace away, undid the three locks.

She recognized them when she opened the door. Laura's heart stopped. They weren't wearing the stocking masks, but they were—

The two men caught the door as she tried to slam it shut. Laura put all her weight against it, but the men shoved it open, throwing Laura into the living room.

"Solo!" Laura screamed.

The large man stood inside the hall and smiled. "You got a pooch, eh?"

"Laura," Solo's voice buzzed in her ear. "Don't call me."

The large man turned and said to his partner, "Shut the door, Peso." Peso, a short man with a hairline mustache, turned around and locked the door.

"What do you mean? Don't call—"

"I know these are the men who hurt you, Laura. We can take them, Laura. We're a team."

"Nesto didn't call?" the big man said. "Peso, you hear that? And you said she didn't like us."

"Laura. Don't say anything. Just listen. The cord's too short. I can't come up there."

Laura nodded, her eyes wide as the two men came toward her, smiling. They know they can just take me. Just like—that. She backed away.

"Aw, c'mon," Nesto said, "don't be afraid. We won't hurt you. You'll love it." Nesto smiled broadly, revealing two gold teeth. "Just relax and enjoy it," he said softly, leering. Behind him, Peso grinned.

Laura thought she was going to faint. Her heart beat in her head; she saw black spots swirling around her like gnats, and she felt like puking. She was standing exactly where she'd been when they killed Frank. It was happening again.

"Laura. You have to lure them down here. When the lights go out, run for the kitchen," Solo said in her ear.

Laura nodded. She crouched. She backed away from the men, saying, "No. Please—"

The lights went off.

Oh God! Solo just turned himself off!

"What the fuck?" Nesto said.

"Can't see her, Nesto," Peso said. "Too dark in here, man."

"No problem," Nesto said. "Stay by the door. She's right there. I can see her little shadow," he said moving forward. "C'mon, little one. Come to Nesto." Nesto made wet, smooching sounds that shot an electric current up Laura's spine.

"Laura. What are you doing? Move. Run to the kitchen and come down here. Now!"

Laura was frozen to the spot. She believed Nesto could not see her, but would if she moved.

"I can *see* you," Nesto jeered.

"Laura. Nesto is moving directly toward you. He is twelve feet away. There must be enough light for him to see. You have one chance. Do what I say," Solo said in her ear. "Ten feet and closing. He can sense where you are, Laura. Run to the kitchen, now," Solo said calmly, firmly. "The kitchen, Laura."

"I can smell you," Nesto said.

"Eight feet and closing," Solo said. "Go to the kitchen, Laura. The kitchen."

If she moved, Nesto would know exactly where she was. If she didn't, he would get her in a few seconds—

"Go to the kitchen," Solo repeated. Solo's voice was so calm, so insistent, Laura got mad.

"Okay, goddamnit!" Laura screamed.

"Huh?" Nesto said.

Laura bolted for the kitchen.

"She's going that way, Nesto," Peso yelled.

"I got her," Nesto said.

As her hands hit the kitchen doorjamb, Laura felt Nesto grab her robe, felt herself jerked short. She bent over as Nesto tugged; she whirled and wriggled. She felt the robe yanked off her and she was suddenly free. She heard a thump, glass breaking, and Nesto grunt. She spun against the kitchen table, banged against the counter, and flung open the basement door.

Lights? The goddamn lights are on?

"Keep coming, Laura. I want them to follow you down here. Hurry!"

Laura leapt down the stairs. She tripped; cut her knee open against a banister post; didn't feel a thing. Funny, how clear things were. She felt better, now that she was moving. Laura grabbed the railing and flung herself down the last five steps. When she got to the bottom, she wondered where Solo was.

"I'm at the fusebox, Laura. Run to the street door."

"Wow." Nesto stood at the top of the stairs, holding Laura's robe. "Look at that ass, Peso. I think I'm in love." Nesto looked down at Laura and laughed.

Laura turned and saw both men standing in the kitchen doorway. "That is prime pussy, Peso. I bet that thing is just aching for us, eh? Little one. How long has it been? Two years? Juicy, juicy, eh?"

Anger flooded Laura's mind. "You goddamn animals!" Laura yelled from the bottom of the stairs. "You leave me alone! I've got a gun down here and I'll blow your *fucking* brains out if you make one more move!"

"Really? Where do you keep it? Up your snatch?" Nesto and Peso laughed. Nesto stepped off the landing.

"Laura, they haven't got a chance, now. We're one hell of a team, you and me. Now, get to the door."

Solo?

"Yes?"

I'm not talking, Solo.

Laura ran down the aisle of boxes to the door. Six boxes of books blocked the door. "Goddamnit!" Laura yelled as she grabbed the top box and flung it aside, scraping her arms and breasts on the harsh cardboard.

"That's amazing," Solo said in her ear. "You aren't speaking, yet I can hear you."

Laura picked up the second box. The bottom broke, spilling three years' worth of *Scientific American* against the door.

"Better get her, Nesto. That door goes right out to the street."

Nesto stepped off the last step. He said, "That's not safe, you know? What if you had a fire? What if two men forced their way in here and decided to fuck you to death? Tsk, tsk, such a mess."

Laura slipped on the loose *Scientific American*s. She grabbed the doorknob and frantically kicked the magazines aside to clear a place to stand. Three heavy boxes still blocked the door.

"The lights will go out when they are halfway to you. When they do, run to the corner, next to the workbench. Understand?"

Laura nodded.

"You're getting all sweaty," Nesto said behind her. "I love woman sweat." Laura cringed, turned, and saw them walking toward her, smiling. She backed up against the door looking left and right for a weapon. Her heart was pounding. She saw a baseball bat leaning against the wall, right where Frank had left it two years ago. She grabbed it and held it in two hands, crouched with her back to the door. She watched Nesto and Peso closing on her. She squeezed the bat, felt rage possess her. *Kill them,* Laura thought.

"I don't think that's advisable, now," Solo said.

Kill them! Laura shouted in her head. Nesto and Peso came slowly down the aisle toward her.

"Lights out," Solo said. The basement snapped into blackness. Laura turned, staring blindly, trying to imagine what was between her and the wall. She heard Solo say, "Run to the workbench. Now."

"What the fuck is with the power today?" Nesto yelled.

Laura dropped the bat and leapt into the void, stumbled over a box; got up and, with her hands held out, felt her way among more boxes to the wall. She jammed herself in between the workbench and a stack of boxes. She turned, straining to see if they followed. The basement was so completely black that she had the feeling that if she weren't pressed against the wall, she'd fall down. Then she heard herself speaking. From where she had been.

"What's the matter, assholes? Afraid of the dark?" said a voice identical to Laura's.

"You *do* want to be friends. How about that, Peso, she wants to play with us. In the dark."

Solo glanced over at Laura, saw her straining to see. He radioed, "It's okay. They're blind. They're still in the aisle."

Solo heard Laura thinking. Not actually words, he noticed. It was as if the thoughts came from his own mind. He was detecting what her thoughts were before they became words. He felt a flood of anger. Words formed in his mind: Kill them!

Nesto pulled a cigarette lighter out of his pocket and held it in front of him. Solo watched him roll his thumb down the wheel. Sparks sprang to life, a flame began to form. Solo kicked Nesto in the groin.

"Aaaaay!" Nesto screamed and reeled backwards against a stack of boxes.

Solo could tell that he had succeeded in rupturing both of Nesto's testicles.

"Like the way that felt?" Laura's voice said.

"Jesus, God! My balls!" Nesto shrieked. Solo saw him lying on the floor, doubled up with his hands holding his crotch. Peso's eyes were wide as he strained to see. Solo could see fear on his face. He was reaching into his pocket. A knife, Solo thought.

Solo bent down and whispered to Peso in Laura's voice. "Peso, Peso. Why a knife, Peso?"

Peso looked up and stared where the sound seemed to be coming from. He jerked out a switchblade and snipped it open. He slashed the air in front of him. "I'm going to cut you, bitch!"

Solo swung a hundred-pound leg up into Peso's crotch with enough force to hurl Peso off the ground and throw him ten feet. Solo felt Peso's testicles burst, a crunch in Peso's pubis bone. Solo watched Peso collapse to the floor, howling.

The men's screams almost made Laura feel sorry for them.

What did you do to them?

"They are down, Laura. They won't forget this for a long time. I ruptured their testicles, an injury a CIA manual recommends to inflict the maximum, most enduring, pain. It'll hurt for weeks."

Good, Laura thought.

"Yes. The police will be here in a few minutes. I'm going to tie them up. When the police come, tell them you defended yourself with the bat. These guys will verify that. Somebody beat the hell out of them, and as far as they know, you're it. Tell them who they are; the same two guys who killed your husband and raped you."

Laura nodded, slumped against the wall and sobbed. Solo felt great choking, wordless, pain flood through him as he grabbed Nesto. Nesto swung up with his fist and Solo had to crush part of his skull to make him lie still enough to be tied. Peso had passed out. Peso was no trouble at all.

Solo tied the men with clothesline and went back to the fusebox in the corner. "They're both tied and unconscious, Laura. I'm turning on the lights."

Laura blinked in the brightness. "Solo?" she said aloud.

"Nice job, Laura," Solo said, stepping out from behind the boxes by the fusebox. "Perhaps you should put on your robe before the police arrive?"

Laura nodded, held up the baseball bat, and walked over to the two men lying in the cluttered aisle.

Solo heard Nesto moan and stepped out of sight of the men, watching Laura. Wordless images, emotions surged into his mind; images of a man, a beloved man, dying; pain; sorrow.

Nesto looked up and saw Laura standing over him. Her face was a grimace of rage. "Please, lady. No more," Nesto said weakly. Blood trickled down his temple.

"You killed my husband," Laura said through clenched teeth. She raised the bat high and swung it down on Nesto with all her might. The bat grazed Nesto's head and smashed his collar bone. She thought she'd heard a bone crack. Nesto screamed and tried to roll away.

"Yes," Solo said in her ear. "You broke his collar bone. You can do what you want Laura. But I'd prefer you didn't kill them. It will be difficult to explain to the police."

Laura nodded, "And you did it just to watch him die!" She raised the bat and Nesto yelled, "No! Are you crazy?" She swung down and crushed Nesto's nose. Laura felt time slow to a crawl when Nesto screamed. She was in the crystal-clear present moment, smashing Nesto again and again. Blood soaked Nesto's shirt. Blood trickled from his mouth. She heard a woman screaming wildly and knew it must be her. Still, she felt serene inside herself as she battered Nesto, who was now unconscious. As she poised ready to swing again, she felt the bat grabbed.

"Laura," Solo said behind her.

"Let. Me. Go!" she screamed. She yanked the bat, but Solo held it immobile.

"He is nearly dead, Laura. The police are almost here."

"I want him dead! I want him dead! Don't you understand what he did? He killed Frank in cold blood. He doesn't deserve to live. He's not human!"

Solo felt the rage; he understood. "My mistake," Solo said. "I was trying to be practical, Laura. It was selfish. Go ahead. Kill him. You've got time." Solo released the bat and stepped aside.

Laura stood with the bat resting on her bare shoulder, breathing hard. Blood ran down the shaft and dripped off her knuckles, but she didn't notice. The air felt close, smelled of sweat and something else, something sweet. Nesto's face was mangled, covered in blood. Pink bubbles foamed from his mouth and nose and an irregular gurgling noise came from his throat as he struggled to breathe.

"One good smash to the skull should do it," Solo said.

Laura's breath started to come in spasms. She suddenly felt drained of all strength. She dropped the bat and reached out to Solo.

Solo held her while she cried.

19

CAPTAIN CRANE walked up the sidewalk to the headquarters building worried about his wife. She'd been hurt because he couldn't tell her where he was going or how long he'd be gone. In the car, saying goodbye, she'd begun to cry a little.

"Honey, it comes with the job," he'd said. "Things'll get better." They lived in base housing at Fort Bragg, North Carolina, and Captain Crane had been promising that he'd move them off-base when he made major. "We'll move, I promise."

"I don't care about moving," Emma had said. "I just want you out of that goddamn Delta Force."

Captain Crane frowned. "There is no Delta Force, Emma. I'm in Special Operations."

Emma shook her head. Everybody knew what Special Operations did. It *was* the Delta Force, but the Army figured that by denying it at every opportunity, the world would believe the United States had no special strike force. Why they cared so much, she couldn't imagine. "Whatever you want to call it," Emma said, "I'm just tired of it. I'm tired of not seeing you for weeks at a time. Why can't you just get into something normal like Captain Reed?"

Crane grimaced. His neighbor, Bob Reed, was in the Quartermaster Corps—a supply officer—the most boring job in the Army. He shrugged and looked at his watch. He looked up and saw Lieutenant Dorn, his executive officer, walking into the building. "I gotta go, honey. Can we talk about it when I get back?"

In the briefing room at the end of the hall, another team commander, Ed Green, and his executive officer sat on one side of the table. The battalion commander, Major Reynolds, and a man dressed in black sat at the end of the long table. Crane sat down next to Lieutenant Dorn.

"Morning, sir," Dorn said, looking nervous. This would be his first mission since his assignment to Special Operations Command.

"Morning, Jerry," Crane said. He looked at the end of the table, saw Major Reynolds talking to the man in black, a Naval Intelligence officer, Crane guessed. "Looks like something big, eh?" he whispered.

"Yessir," Dorn said.

Major Reynolds looked up. "Good morning, Captain Crane. Trouble?"

"No, sir." Crane wanted to tell the major about Emma, but knew that was out of order. He said, "Sorry, sir."

"Okay, gentlemen, we can get on with it," Major Reynolds said. He looked at the man beside him. "Sir, these are the officers who'll be handling your mission. He looked up. "Gentlemen," Reynolds said, "this is Admiral James Finch from Naval Intelligence. He'll be briefing you."

Finch nodded, smiled. "Good morning. I know it's kind of unusual for you to be briefed by anybody from the Navy, but don't worry. There's no sailing involved on this mission."

Lieutenant Dorn smiled.

"Gentlemen," Finch said carefully, "you have never had a mission as important as this. There are things I'm going to tell you that are hard to believe. Gentlemen, you had better believe me. Your lives and our national security depend on it."

Crane and Dorn were silent in the backseat of the Army sedan driving them to Alpha Team's barracks. Crane wondered why on earth they'd even tried to make such a thing. A mechanical soldier? How stupid can they get?

Dorn worried about trying to keep two Delta Force teams, eighty highly strung, highly trained, fighting men, from going nuts while they waited, totally quarantined, in the old New York Armory. Admiral Finch had said it might take a month. No phone calls or radio messages in or out; all messages to and from the Armory were to be carried by couriers. The men could neither send nor receive personal letters, see visitors, or go on leave until the mission was complete. It was going to be hell, Dorn thought.

20

"How are you feeling, Mrs. Reynolds?" Detective Garcia said. Laura nodded. "Fine. I feel fine."

"Good." Garcia felt a twinge of pity. Laura's face was so childlike, so filled with hurt. "You did an amazing thing, Mrs. Reynolds, beating up those animals."

"Everything's amazing," Laura said.

Garcia cocked his head, nodded. "Yes. I suppose so. But this is particularly amazing. I was wondering. Can you tell me how you managed to do it?"

"How?"

"Well, yes. I mean, Ernesto and his brother are big guys, Mrs. Reynolds. I have to tell you, I myself would have a tough time subduing either one of them alone. Yet, you got both of them at the same time."

"I wanted to kill them," Laura said.

Garcia nodded. "Can't blame you for trying, Mrs. Reynolds. You almost got Ernesto," Garcia said smiling. "Nice try."

"I had the chance." Laura's eyes welled with tears. "Couldn't—"

"Of course not." Garcia quickly wiped the smile off his face. "You're not the killer type," he said. He saw Laura look toward the kitchen, breaking contact. "So, Mrs. Reynolds. You want to tell me about it?"

Laura jerked around to Garcia and said, "Tell?" She shook her head. "No, not now. Come back some other time. I want to take a bath. I want to go to sleep. That's what I want to do, Lieutenant. I'm tired."

Garcia sighed, nodded. "Of course. Sorry for the intrusion, Mrs. Reynolds. I'll still have to get your statement. Ernesto and his brother will be going on trial someday, one assumes. We'll have to get a statement for the prosecutor."

Laura sniffed, stood up quickly. She adjusted her glasses, straightened herself and said, breezily, "Fine, Lieutenant. Thanks for your help. Stop by anytime." She walked quickly to the front door and opened it. "Good afternoon, Lieutenant."

"Pick a book, any book," Solo said the next evening.

Laura sat on the couch in the living room watching television in jeans and a sweatshirt. She'd had Solo rip up the carpet and store it in the attic. The bloodstain was gone, a new carpet down, but she still wouldn't look at the spot. She nodded and pulled a book from the bookcase next to the couch.

The television switched off. Solo said, "Interference."

"Okay, but I don't want to miss *Sixty Minutes,*" Laura said, holding up a book.

"The Grapes of Wrath?" Solo said.

"Yes," Laura said, no longer noticing that Solo could read things like faded book titles from thirty feet away.

"Good, I haven't read that. Open it to any page and read one line to yourself."

Laura flipped open the book and read silently: "They popped down the mountain, twisting and looping, losing the valley sometimes, and then finding it again."

"Lost in a valley?" Solo said.

Laura looked up at Solo. The robot sat at the kitchen table working on a piece of electronic equipment he said he was going to put in a helicopter. "Well, that's the sense of it, I guess. But there's more to it."

"I thought so," Solo said. He touched his solder iron to a circuit board and watched a little mound of gray solder turn liquid and silver. "I don't get any feelings or thoughts when you're not wearing the radio. When you do wear it, I'm getting feelings and images, not words. But I think I can improve that."

"Well, I don't get it at all," Laura said. "That's mind reading."

"No. Your brain's electrical fields are affecting the signal that comes from the radio," Solo said. "I'm detecting the changes and interpreting them as thoughts. I'm not sure how I'm doing it, but I'm working on figuring it out."

"I don't understand that. How can you be doing something and not know how you're doing it?"

"Well, everybody thinks millions of small pieces of our brains work together to produce consciousness, but we aren't aware of the individual parts. Part of me understands this, but I don't know which one. This is something like electroencephalography, Laura."

Laura stared at Solo for a second and said, "The brain scanner thing? I've seen that on television. They glue some wires to a person's head and a bunch of pens make squiggly lines on graph paper."

"That's right. The needles move in direct response to a brain's electrical activity. They can't interpret thoughts from the tracings, but they aren't computers, either."

"And you are. You think that's the difference?"

"Yes. There's never been a person who was also a computer before. And there's never been a computer hooked up to all the sensors I have. I see things that people have never seen. I sensed changes in the radio frequency and began immediately to interpret them. That discernment was built into me for battle efficiency; no one predicted this effect. I think I could build a small system a person could use to do the same thing; make a mental interface with computers. A person could just think what she wanted the computer to do and it would happen. That would make money, I bet."

Laura laughed. "I bet." She clicked her remote and the television turned on. "Solo," she said. *"Sixty Minutes."*

Solo set his work aside, walked over, and sat on the couch.

Dan Rather was presenting a segment about corrupt real estate developers. "I love Dan Rather. You watch him much?"

"He's very good. There's also a program about rain forests in Costa Rica on channel eight."

"Really?"

"Yes. And an interesting news show in Spanish on channel thirteen. *Star Trek* is on channel five—Mr. Data is learning about humor; *Mister Ed* is on channel twenty-one—very funny. There's a lot of things to buy on channel forty-two—the diamond watch is only available for two more minutes. Channel sixteen—"

"Solo. You're watching all of them?"

"Yes, of course."

"You can follow each one?"

"There's a picture on the screen thirty times a second, Laura. The rest of the time it's blank. I have plenty of time to watch other shows between frames."

Laura turned her head. "If you can do all that at the same time, how does it feel talking to people?"

"People speak very slowly. I do other things while they talk and replay what they've said when they're finished."

"You're doing that now, while you're watching all those shows?"

"Yes."

"We must seem pretty boring to you."

"Not at all. Humans know a lot of interesting things. They can't help being so slow."

"Thanks," Laura said, shaking her head.

"Not at all," Solo said.

21

TWO MONTHS after Solo arrived in New York, he and Laura, with money from a venture capital trust they'd established in Laura's name, had created a privately held company called Solaura Corporation. Laura was listed as Chairman of the Board. Roger Solo was President and CEO. Laura leased a floor of a small office building four blocks from her house. Fifty people worked for them.

Solaura specialized in large computer network installations, computer security, system maintenance, and custom software, none of which Laura understood. She had, however, picked up the business side of the operation so quickly she surprised herself. She managed the overall office, hiring all personnel including an office manager. She met with accountants and lawyers when necessary, though she still preferred to communicate by phone. Laura had not noticed how much she had changed until she saw a bag lady sleeping on the sidewalk as she walked home one afternoon. She jammed all the cash she had in the woman's pocket, came home, and cried. She wrote a large check to a homeless shelter, cried again, realizing it was a drop in the bucket.

Solo had devised an efficient sales tool in which he sent messages to the top executives of large corporations—through their most secure computer systems—suggesting that their systems might not be as secure as they thought. Laura said it was a protection racket, Solo maintained it was just aggressive marketing. Solaura gained a large clientele in a short time. Their business was—as Solo, who read the *Wall Street Journal,* was fond of saying—a cash cow.

Solaura's huge mainframe computer was linked, by means Laura did not understand, to Solo. It was through this link that Solo advised the company's technicians. Solo had an office at Solaura, though he had never been there. Any requests of Mr. Solo were made through the computer. This arrangement suited the company's computer programmers and technicians, who, Laura noticed, seemed lost in thought most of the time and showed definite signs of shock when speaking directly to people.

Five blocks down the street from Solaura's offices, Laura bought a loft, which Solo was having converted into an impressive electronics laboratory. Their loft was very near where Nikola Tesla's laboratory was at the turn of the century. Laura was not impressed, but Solo said the man had an extraordinary mind, invented alternating current motors and radio, caused an earthquake in the Village with an ultrasound experiment, and walked around these same streets wearing a long black cape. Tesla had been a ditch-digging immigrant who had become an eccentric millionaire in one year. Tesla was a human Solo could respect.

Now that the work at the loft was nearly finished, Solo began talking about walking down to inspect it, which made Laura nervous. Solo's idea that he could pass as human was, to Laura, ludicrous.

Among the first supplies that began arriving at the loft after the construction work was a crate of silver-zinc batteries that Solo had ordered from Gates Electronics in Florida.

Solo told Laura his batteries were in. What better way to test his theory that people would accept him than to do it on a stroll to the loft?

In the back of an United Parcel Service delivery van cruising slowly down Waverly Place, Sergeant Laplaca stared at the bank of instruments on the console before him. He saw a needle jump, heard a pop in his earphones. He checked to see that the recorder was on. He swiveled his seat and said to the driver, Corporal Vitale, "You hear that?"

"What?" Vitale said.

"A pop. On Ku-Band."

"So?"

"Fuck, I don't know. I got it on twelve-point-two gigahertz. That's what they wanted. Satellite uplink frequency. This is the first I've heard in a fucking month."

"A pop? You figure that's what they want?"

Sergeant Laplaca turned back to his console. Vitale was the kind of guy who'd say "So?" if you told him he was on fire. He made a note of the transmission in his log. Everything had to be in writing. No radios or phones. Why? thought Laplaca.

* * *

Solo stepped out on the stoop late Tuesday afternoon, disregarding Laura's urgent advice that they at least take a cab if he refused to sneak down to the loft when it got dark.

"Nonsense," Solo said. "I've been studying people very carefully, Laura. I just have to act confident; act like they do. They'll accept me if I accept myself. They accepted Tesla." Solo stood on the stoop. He wore a straw hat, a blue jacket over a Hawaiian shirt, a pair of white cotton slacks, and carried Laura's Samsonite suitcase full of motorcycle batteries. He stretched his free arm out, sighed loudly, and said, "Ah. It's good to be out in the fresh air again."

Laura nodded doubtfully. "I don't know why we couldn't have waited until dark, Solo. Better yet, we can have the batteries sent over."

Solo held up his hand. "I need to know if I am right, Laura. There's only one way to find out. We'll just walk to the loft to get the new batteries. Six blocks. How much trouble can we get into doing that?"

Laura shrugged. "Are you kidding? This is New York."

"Okay, hold it down," Lieutenant Dorn shouted. His voice echoed hollowly around the dank stone walls of the huge armory.

The forty men of Strike Team Alpha, dressed in their black uniforms, wearing black body-armor, stood in a loose group next to the other team. The men quieted.

"We've got something," Dorn said. "Captain Crane will be here in a minute."

"About goddamn time, Lieutenant," a voice said.

"Okay!" Dorn yelled. "I'm tired, too. I think this is it. Let's don't lose our professionalism now. If we wanted regular grunts on this team, we'd get them. Now shut the fuck up." Dorn looked up and saw Captain Crane walking toward them. "A-tent-hut!" he yelled. Strike Team Alpha jumped to attention.

"As you were, men," Crane said. He looked across the armory floor, waiting for Major Reynolds to appear. He looked at his watch. His counterpart, Captain Green, stood in front of Bravo Team. The two men's eyes met and they nodded.

Crane saw Major Reynolds hurrying toward them and called his team to attention. Green did the same.

"At ease," said Major Reynolds. "Men, they've spotted the target. It is under definite visual surveillance at this very moment. In five minutes, I want you in the vans, weapons ready. We'll wait at Trinity Cemetery until the target gets into a compromising position; we can't

take it on the street. Also, we'll be working with the New York Police
SWAT team and over a hundred city cops. We're spearheading this
kill, men, and I want to show these locals how it's done." Major
Reynolds stared at the two teams, smiled. "Let's go get his fucking
thing!"

The men cheered as Major Reynolds saluted, about-faced, and
walked out to his car.

"A cemetery?" a private said as he grabbed his helmet and rifle.
"Bad luck to hang around cemeteries, man."

When they passed a glass storefront, Solo stopped to look at himself
in the window. He smoothed his jacket and adjusted his straw hat
with his free hand, while holding the suitcase with the other. He'd
taped a black electric cord along his arm that ran from the suitcase,
in through his sleeve, and down to his access port. He looked at Laura
and thought she was shyly dressed in a simple white cotton shift. "What
do you think?"

"I think you look weird," Laura said, giggling at his reflection.

"Weird?" Solo said. "Okay. Weird isn't necessarily non-human. I
can accept that."

Laura pointed up the street. "There's a crowd there. Maybe we
should go the other way," she said.

"They'll never notice me," Solo said as they walked toward the
people gathered around a street juggler. Solo stopped at the edge of
the crowd and watched. The man, wearing clown-face, juggled three
clubs with his hands; and stood on one foot while he balanced a stick
on the other foot that supported a spinning plate. Solo watched intently, amazed at the man's dexterity. *He has to keep four complex
actions going perfectly—that is very good for a human.*

A black teenage boy next to Solo looked up, saw Solo's black plastic
face and mirrored eyecovers. He tapped his friend's shoulder. "What
the—" said his friend when he turned around.

"Hey, mister. You in a movie or something?" the boy asked.

"No, young man," Solo said. "I dress like this for protection."

"Yeah? From what?"

"Muggers," Solo said.

"Is someone making a movie?" a woman in the crowd asked.

"They're doing a movie," someone said. Solo saw all heads turn in
his direction.

"Hey!" the juggler yelled, holding his clubs, stick, and plate. "You
can't work here, man. This is my territory."

"I'm not working here," Solo said. "Please continue to juggle. You are very good."

"Everybody's watching you. C'mon, give me a break, okay?"

"I don't see a camera," a woman said.

"They hide'em in vans," a man said.

Laura whispered, "It's not working, Solo."

"This is a free country," Solo said aloud.

The juggler walked up to Solo. "It's a free country, asshole, but we have rules, you know?"

"Yes, I know," Solo said. "But there is no rule that I can't watch you juggle."

"I just made it up, asshole!"

"Solo, I think we should be going," Laura said, tugging Solo's shirt.

"I am not an asshole, asshole," Solo said to the man.

Laura shrugged, watching Solo and the juggler in the center of the crowd. He's just going to have to learn the hard way, she thought.

The juggler, a man as tall as Solo, reached out and pushed Solo in the chest. "I don't know what you're up to, asshole, but I'm telling you to move your Star Wars routine out of here. I been working this spot for six months. It's mine."

"Watch. I'll just match his manners and blend in," he said in Laura's ear.

"Do not shove me, asshole. I am staying."

"Solo!" Laura said, yanking his shirt.

The juggler shoved Solo again, harder. "I'm warning you!"

"I don't see any cameras," said the woman.

"Hidden cameras; they're filming from across the street," said the man. "These guys are definitely actors."

"Goddamn it, Solo!" Laura yelled. "It's not working. Let's get out of here!"

"Listen to the lady," said the juggler.

"Mind your own business," Solo said.

"What's the problem?" a policeman said, forcing his way through the crowd.

"This guy's horning in on my act, officer. I was here first."

"Right. You got a permit?" the cop said.

The juggler nodded and pulled a green card from his pocket and handed it to the cop. The cop examined it and handed it back. "You?" he said to Solo.

"Sir?" Solo said.

"Permit?"

"A permit to do what?"

"Street performer, wiseguy."

"I'm not a street performer, officer. I'm just a common pedestrian person watching this juggler perform."

The cop stared. Solo saw the peculiar look of recognition light his face. "Wait a minute. I remember hearing about you. Some looney's been robbing stores wearing an outfit like that. I'm gonna have to take you in for questioning."

The juggler laughed. "Bye-bye, asshole."

"He looks like a real cop," said a woman.

The cop grabbed the radio microphone off his shoulder and pushed the transmit button. "Dispatch. Got a possible one-eleven on Sixth Avenue between Ninth and Tenth. Request cruiser."

A woman's voice squawked from the patrolman's radio, heavily disturbed by static that Solo was generating.

The cop slapped the radio on his belt and repeated the call. The speaker squawked again, all static.

"Damn," said the cop. "C'mon, champ. It's not far to the station." He reached out and pulled Solo by the arm.

"I prefer to stay here, officer."

"Right." The cop yanked Solo's arm, but could have been tugging on a utility pole. The cop stared at Solo, stepped back two paces, and pulled his gun from his holster. "How 'bout now, huh?"

"Nope," Solo said. "But I'll leave. I'll leave the juggler alone."

"Hands up, wiseass!"

A mistake, Solo thought. Should have left sooner. Now the policeman will follow us wherever we go. Solo stepped forward and snatched the pistol from the cop's hand faster than he could comprehend.

"I didn't see that. Did you see that? How'd they do that?" a man asked.

"Special effects," someone said.

Solo spun the cop around and pinned him against a lamppost with his chest while he took the handcuffs off his belt. "Put your arms in front of the pole, please," Solo said, squeezing the cop tighter against the post. The cop nodded, unable to speak. Solo slapped the cuffs on and stepped back.

He saw that the crowd had become silent and the people were staring at him. What would an actor do now? Solo raised his arm up and let it down and bent forward in a gracious bow. The audience applauded.

"Somebody grab that guy!" yelled the cop. The crowd laughed, some of them patting Solo on the back for a job well done.

"See, I told you. They're making a movie," said the man.

Solo said to Laura, "I think we should leave now."

As they rounded the corner, they could hear the crowd laughing at the cop ordering Solo to stop.

Laura hissed, "Now you've done it! Every cop in the city's going to be after you. Nice going."

"That wasn't a fair test. The juggler was a troublemaker," Solo said.

22

T HE ORANGE LIGHT of sunset glinted off the windows of tall
buildings, casting long shadows across the streets as Laura
and Solo got near the loft.

"Solo," Laura said quietly as they walked. "I know you're smart.
In some ways, you're the smartest person I've ever known, ever heard
of—"

"But—" Solo said.

"Yes. But trying to pass as human by wearing some clothes just
isn't getting it, you know?"

Solo said nothing. He saw a fat man cruising along the crowded
sidewalk on roller skates. He used two sticks to pole himself along
like a cross-country skier. The man wore silver sunglasses, a Walkman,
and a baseball cap with two cans of Coke attached to the sides. Plastic
tubing ran from the cans to the man's mouth. The man was poling
toward them. Only a couple of kids noticed him, and they seemed to
be interested in his skates. That seems eccentric, Solo thought. Nobody's paying any attention.

When the skater got closer, he stared at Solo with surprise. Solo
tipped his hat and said, "Howdy." The man said, "What the—" and
rolled off the curb into the street.

When they got close to the two boys, one of them said, "Awesome,"
and they stopped and stared at Solo.

"I think you are right," Solo said.

Laura smiled.

Just as they got to the entrance to their loft, Solo stopped suddenly
and stared at a passing car. Laura followed his gaze. A large, shiny,
white Cadillac convertible, the kind she knew from the seventies,
cruised by, lights glaring in the dusk. Solo said, "Wow."

"C'mon, Solo. Let's get inside."
"I want that car," Solo said.
"Get inside or I'll kill you," Laura said.

Driving the UPS van, Corporal Vitale saw PFC Kubitz wave him down. He pulled over next to a fire hydrant. Vitale laughed when Kubitz ran up to the door. His buddy looked like he'd been living on the streets all his life, his clothes were rags, he needed a shave. Only in Special Operations, Vitale thought.

PFC Kubitz handed Vitale a piece of paper. "Rush this to the cemetery, Vitale. This is it."

"No shit?" Vitale said, taking the note.

"Affirmative," Kubitz said. "Tell them the woman's still with it."

PFC Kubitz staggered back, sat on the curb, and watched Vitale speed away.

After bolting the door to the loft, Solo and Laura walked inside to the middle of the clutter of unpacked boxes. The loft was nearly a hundred feet long and fifty feet wide. Workmen had added a narrow storeroom along one side that came halfway up the far wall. In the corner made by the storeroom, many crates were stacked, still unpacked. There were ten large windows along the wall adjacent to the alley, but because it was nearly dark, Solo switched on the lights for Laura's benefit. He pointed at the far end of the loft, to a steel staircase. "That goes to the roof," he said. "After we put in the batteries, I want to go up and see the view." Laura said that would be nice as Solo walked into the corner and pried open a wooden crate marked "Gates Electronics, Battery Division. Danger. Charged Batteries." He put the cover against the wall and said, "This won't take too long, Laura, but I'll need your help."

"Whatever you say, Solo."

"You're going to have to use a few tools."

"So?"

"The last time I talked about tools you didn't seem too happy about it."

"Solo, that was then. This is now."

Solo turned his head and stared at Laura.

Laura shrugged. "Back then, I was still fucked up; a drunk, sleeping in the trash. I was just about a bag lady, Solo."

"I thought you were a bag lady."

"Well, now I'm not. I feel good. I even think I understand what the hell you're doing some of the time. I love the business side of our venture. And I know, for sure, that I like being rich." She watched Solo grab the rope handle on the crate. "What about the cops, Solo?"

Solo picked up the suitcase in one hand and dragged the crate of batteries across the floor to a workbench. Solo said, "See these batteries?"

Obviously, Solo was not yet going to talk about the police. Laura looked in the box and saw six-inch-diameter metal cylinders packed in plastic foam. Laura shrugged. "Yes."

"These are the replacements for the ones in my legs."

"Great. You won't have to carry that stupid suitcase around all the time."

"Yes," Solo said. "However, getting these batteries into my legs is usually done by my support team."

Laura nodded. "I'm the support team now?"

"Yes." Solo began unpacking the crate. Laura bent down and helped. She was surprised at how light they were. The motorcycle batteries were much heavier. "Someday I'm going to get rid of these batteries, too, but for now, they'll suffice. The first thing we have to do is to open the battery compartments. I can't get to them easily. Bill never imagined I'd be out on my own so long—"

"Bill?"

"Yes. William Stewart. The man who built me."

"He must be a very smart man," Laura said.

"Oh, yes. Brilliant." Solo rolled a tall mechanic's tool chest over to the workbench. "He wanted to build me with full plutonium power, but he lost control of the project. The military liaison, Admiral Finch, objected. Finch claimed that a battlefield weapon carrying that much plutonium would be a hazard to its own side."

"That sounds reasonable," Laura said, watching Solo pick out a screwdriver from a drawer in the tool chest.

"Plutonium isn't very radioactive; it's only dangerous if I were blown up. Then the stuff would be spread all over the place. It's the most toxic substance a human can touch."

Laura stared at Solo. "You have some of that in you now, right?"

"A little." Solo undid his belt with one hand and unzipped his pants. Laura automatically glanced at Solo's crotch, raised her eyebrows, and smiled at herself. Solo dropped his pants and stepped out of them. He sat on the workbench with the suitcase full of motorcycle batteries on his lap. "You ready?"

Laura nodded. "Tell me what to do."

Solo lifted the suitcase across the workbench, rolled over and stretched out, facedown, setting the suitcase on the floor. "See that star-shaped hole on the back of my leg?"

Laura reached overhead and pulled down a hanging work lamp. "Little tiny thing on side of your thigh? Looks like an asterisk?"

"Yes," Solo said, holding up a screwdriver. "It's called a Torx screw. This fits it. Just unscrew it."

Laura took the screwdriver and twirled the screw. "Solo. How long you think it'll take before the police will find you? I mean, you can't go around locking cops to lampposts, you know?" The screw loosened and Laura pulled it out. "Okay. It's out."

"Police? You're worried about the police? Now. There's a circular plate, about the size of a nickel beside the screw hole. See that?"

Laura grimaced, saw a faint circular line. "Yes."

"Okay. Just press that circle."

Laura did. The circle clicked down and a lid that was the whole back half of Solo's thigh popped up like a clamshell. "Wow," Laura said. "You're coming apart, Solo."

"It doesn't hurt too much."

Laura glanced at Solo. "You're joking, right?"

"Yes. Thanks for noticing."

Laura laughed.

"Okay, just raise the panel up until it locks open."

Laura raised the panel until it clicked. Inside Solo's thigh, she saw a stack of the same metallic cylinders as were in the crate lying on their sides on a rack. "Batteries," she said.

"Right. Now just do the same to the other leg."

Laura unfastened the other panel and raised it.

"Okay. Just unsnap the retaining clips that go around each battery and pop them out."

"Okay. Are we saving these?"

"No. They are not salvageable."

In a few minutes, Laura had removed six batteries from each of Solo's legs and dumped them into a wastecan. She stacked six new batteries from the crate on each side of Solo. "These new ones have a piece of black stuff across the top. Keeps them from shorting out, right?"

"Yes. I thought you didn't know anything about electricity."

Laura shrugged. "I've put batteries into a flashlight before, Solo. Even I can figure this out. I bet these are really powerful batteries."

"Very powerful. You must be careful not to let any metal cross the top of the batteries after you take off the covers. If you short these batteries, they'll explode."

Laura nodded and unscrewed the cover on the first battery. "Really? How big an explosion?"

"Big enough to kill us both," Solo said.

Laura's hand jerked away from the naked battery.

"I was exaggerating, Laura. Probably it would only kill you."

"Two jokes in two minutes? Oh, well." Laura grinned. "As long as you're in no danger, love." Laura picked up the battery and set it in place on the rack in Solo's thigh.

Fifteen minutes later, Solo sat up on the workbench. "Thank you, Laura. I'm beginning to feel more like my old self." Solo undid the tape on his arm and grabbed the cord that went into his side from the suitcase and pulled it out. "There. Back on internals."

"I bet it feels good," Laura said.

"You can't imagine," Solo said.

"You're right." Laura put her hands on her hips and said, "Now, what about the goddamn cops?"

Solo looked down at Laura and felt a great surge of happiness. "I've been listening to everything they're doing. They've put a surveillance team on your house. The FBI is there. They're waiting for us."

"Oh. Well, that doesn't sound too serious. What the *fuck* are you talking about, Solo? Goddamn police? FBI? At my house?"

"I have everything under control, Laura. We'll just go to a hotel for a few days. You'll like it. I can run things just fine from anywhere."

"Right. I can see it. Checking into the Hilton. Nobody asks questions at the Hilton. Lady and her robot escort? Hey, no big deal."

"A wealthy lady who arrived with a large and heavy steamer trunk won't attract any attention at all, Laura."

"You? Packed in a trunk?"

Laura's laugh was lost in the crash of breaking glass. Solo whirled, saw broken window shards falling to the floor, saw a stun grenade rolling toward them. The explosion shook his body, but had no other effect on him. He turned to see Laura crumple to the floor, blood running from her nose. "Laura?" he said. Laura did not answer.

As Solo knelt beside Laura he heard the rumble of many footsteps rushing up the stiars. More glass broke behind him. Laura was alive. Two men, dressed in black, wearing black bullet-proof vests, swung in on ropes through two windows. More were coming down the stairs from the roof. He heard a motor snarl, saw a metal-cutting saw slice through the edge of the door, spewing sparks. The door burst open and dark men poured in through the door. Solo recognized their weapons—huge, thirty-pound Barrett fifty-caliber rifles with special ten-round magazines. After each shot, the bolt of the Barrett had to be operated to insert the next round—however, there were many rifles and it would only take one hit to penetrate his armor. Ten men streamed into the room, took aim, began firing.

Solo dodged the first bullet. A second glanced off his chest, ripping his shirt and jacket. He whirled away from a convergence of bullets coming from the men at the door and the men behind him, flung himself down and rolled behind a crate against the wall. Bullets ripped the wood into splinters and crunched into the metal case of the computer packed inside.

How, Solo wondered, did they organize this without my hearing them make the plan? A bullet ripped through the computer, made a crater in the bricks behind him, and fell to the floor. He picked it up. Needle-pointed, cigar-thick, armor-piercing. A good weapon for the job, Solo thought.

The sounds of the shots grew louder as more and more soldiers joined the attack. He sensed their positions as he crouched behind the rapidly deteriorating crate. Wood splinters showered around him. Two spent bullets hit his chest, bounced off. He noticed a toolbox six feet away and beyond it, in the corner made by the storeroom, another crate. He tumbled across the space between the crates, grabbed the toolbox, and rolled behind a larger crate packed with steel shelving. Bullets splintered the crate but were stopped by the shelves. After a long, withering volley of useless shots, Solo heard, "Hold your fire! Hold your fire! It's trapped. We're just wasting bullets."

Correct, Solo thought. He sensed men closing in from all fronts. He opened the toolbox and saw that it was just a socket wrench set. One wrench handle and twenty sockets that fit on the end of the handle. The closest human was within twenty feet. Soon, his hiding place would be useless. If he chose to stand, fight hand to hand, he'd be blown to bits in a crossfire. He picked out a socket from the toolbox, a piece of steel the size of a large man's thumb. He stood up from behind the crate and as he watched the soldiers raise their weapons, threw the socket straight into the face mask of the closest man. The man's head exploded. Solo ducked back down as the bullets crashed into the crate. He filled his pockets with the socket set. There were many more soldiers than sockets.

Captain Jack Crane froze at the doorway. He could not guess what had killed his man. There had been no noise, just the blurred shape of the thing they were ordered to kill. Yet there was Corporal Higgens lying in a pool of blood with half his head missing. Crane had the loft sealed off, the building surrounded, the roof occupied. There was no escape for the robot, however strong it might be.

He'd felt foolish earlier that day, passing notes by courier to his men rather than using the radios as he deployed his teams. Now it didn't seem so foolish. Obviously, Admiral Finch knew Solo. That one radio call to surround the woman's house worked like a charm. The thing to remember, Finch had said, was it would only take one good shot in the chest or back to bring it down. It would be prudent, Crane thought, to pull back and wait for a clear shot.

Two men fired without orders.

Crane cupped his hands to give the order to hold fire. He did not hear the whistling shriek of a steel socket hurtling at him with the speed of a bullet. Instead, his brains splattered against the chest of the man behind him in the doorway.

"Jesus!" yelled Lieutenant Dorn, flinching at the gore on his chest-armor as he fell backwards. "What the hell does he have?"

The men had taken cover behind the metal posts scattered through-out the loft, behind crates and workcounters. Dorn, suddenly in command, ducked down behind a post, avoiding looking at the mess upon which he knelt. Finch had warned them not to get within reach of the machine. But, he had also said it was unarmed. Obviously, it was armed with something, something that whistled, something powerful.

Lieutenant Dorn chanced a peek at the situation and had a chunk of his helmet shot off by the robot. Jesus, it's quick! Dorn thought. The robot's fortification was a crate in the corner, giving the machine protection from a flank assault. However, the position had a blindside. That gave them a chance to come up along the wall from the other side. They had real grenades with them. Now, Dorn thought, all he had to do was tell somebody to do it without using his radio.

Solo did not need to raise his head to see what was happening. The soldier whose helmet he had hit was still alive and creeping backwards out the door. Solo could not stop him because the man carefully kept the post between them as he exited. Solo crouched, waiting. The other men had stopped shooting, had all taken cover. He had mapped the position of each one of the twenty-six men inside the loft, and watched for changes of position. After a minute, he noticed a human's electrical profile moving along the wall around the corner to his right. The corner of the storeroom put the man out of his field of fire. They intend to use grenades, Solo guessed.

Lieutenant Dorn had come down the stairs from the roof. He carried half a dozen fragmentation grenades, one of which was ready in his hand, the pin pulled. Dorn guessed that the element of surprise was on his side, but, just to be on the safe side, he suddenly yelled, "Commence firing!" and while the big guns boomed and the bullets crashed into the crate, making terrible tearing, screeching sounds in the metal shelving, Dorn peeked around the corner and tossed the grenade.

Solo had killed two men. He had not wished to do so. The humans were intent upon being killed. It was a consolation that they were soldiers, as was he. He saw the grenade falling toward him and decided that if they wished to give him such a thing, he might as well use it. He caught the grenade and zinged it across the loft, over three men he knew were hiding behind a workcounter he had intended to use for many happy years. The grenade bounced off the wall behind the men, rolled into their position, and exploded before they knew it was there.

Though he saw two of the men's lives flicker out, Solo knew that the humans had unlimited resources. They were, at this moment, deploying more men, more weapons. Eventually, he would lose.

It was confusing when you threw a grenade in one place and it exploded in another. Dorn was unsure whether he should try again. The grenade could have been a dud and the robot was throwing something else. Dorn released the handle on another grenade, counted to three, and lobbed it behind the crate. The grenade again exploded across the room, in the corner next to the doorway. Two men lay screaming there. Dorn realized he was simply giving the robot weapons to kill his men. His mind froze. It was difficult to think of what to do next.

Laura thought she was having a nightmare and was grateful that she felt herself waking. But, when she opened her eyes, she knew she was not dreaming. She heard an explosion, heard men shriek. She breathed in acrid smoke and coughed. She saw a man dressed in black, holding a huge black rifle, pressed against the wall beside her. She screamed, "Solo!"

Lieutenant Dorn had been told that the woman was to be spared, if it was possible. She was technically a hostage, they had said. Now, however, Dorn heard her call the robot's name. He motioned the woman to come to him, but she shook her head, stood up and yelled the robot's name again. This gave Dorn the idea that the woman could be of some use in this dilemma. He pointed his big rifle at Laura and motioned her forward. Laura's eye's went wide with fear and she complied, walking into view of the robot. Dorn yelled, "One more move and the woman dies!"

It would have been better if Laura had remained on the floor, Solo thought, but things often do not work ideally. While he listened to Dorn's words, Solo was surprised that he felt a surge of pleasant excitement. This, he realized, was the kind of thing he liked to do. The whole purpose of his being was built around one thing: combat. Tenseness and mortal danger felt natural to Solo. He would probably lose, he thought, but he felt the fight was something to be enjoyed.

A Keyhole satellite showed Solo that the whole neighborhood was being evacuated. New soldiers were arriving even while he watched. He reached up to the back of his neck and pushed a latch. When he felt it click, he said, "I will not resist, Lieutenant Dorn."

Dorn wondered for a second how the robot could know his name. He peered around the corner and saw the robot, a huge black thing with a tattered blue jacket hanging from it, standing with its hands over its head. He had been told that if, by some fluke, the robot was captured, so much the better. Dorn had stumbled into a neat solution to this mess because of the woman. They'd think he was a hero, which was fine; though least eight of his men lay dead or dying.

Dorn stepped out to face the machine, his finger pulling the trigger of his rifle so tightly the gun would go off even if he was struck suddenly dead by the monstrosity. He waved the gun and said, "Move toward the center of the room. If you make a sudden move, bend over, do *anything* to make me nervous, I'll blow you apart."

"Understood," Solo said as he slowly stepped from behind his shredded fortification, putting his hands together behind his head.

Laura felt tears streaming down her face. They would take Solo away, probably they would dismantle him or God knows what. "Solo," she sobbed when Solo stepped toward her. "I'm so sorry," she said, choking.

Solo turned away from her, not speaking. And just as she was about to say something about being sorry again, Solo suddenly ducked down. Almost at exactly the same moment, Lieutenant Dorn fired. Solo's head snapped off his shoulders, hit the floor and rolled, bumping awkwardly like a football. It hit a pallet, twirled, stopped, its eyes staring at the ceiling. Solo's body had crumpled and lay sprawled and still among the wood splinters and brick fragments caused by the battle. A fine spray of red hydraulic fluid squirted from a naked tube sticking from his neck, then stopped. A handful of sockets rolled out of the pocket of the robot's jacket.

"God Almighty!" Dorn yelled. "I've killed it!" Dorn's men watched the thing with fearful revulsion.

Several of them came closer to the robot, though none dared come too close. Dead or not, it was a scary-looking affair, a body here, a head there. "He was killing us with socket wrenches?" said a PFC, pointing at the tool heads laying beside Solo.

"I'll be damned," Dorn said. As he pulled his radio from his holster, he saw a man poking the head, which lay six feet from the robot's body, with the barrel of his gun. "Leave that alone, soldier." Then he turned and said to his men, "Just remember. No one saw this thing. It doesn't exist. Just leave this to the boss." With that, Dorn remembered who he was calling and spoke into his radio. "Deep Six, Black Five."

"Deep Six. Where's Black Six?" Finch's voice said from the radio, meaning, where was Captain Crane.

"KIA, sir. I took over. The target is out of action, Deep Six."

"Good work. Keep everybody away from the target. We'll be up with a recovery team. Deep Six out."

Dorn double-clicked the radio and flipped it back into its case. "Okay," he said. "Form up by the door. Get the wounded out of here. Our job's finished. They got techies coming to sweep up this mess."

Laura had, by this time, made her way along the wall toward the rear of the loft. Not one of the soldiers encircling Solo's decapitated body had seen her go. She touched her ear, stopped, and turned around. The soldiers were moving away from Solo. Only Lieutenant Dorn remained, standing beside the body. At that moment, Solo's right arm swept across the floor and smashed into Lieutenant Dorn's shins, snapping them like matchsticks. Dorn flipped face forward with such force that his nose was crushed against the floor and he was knocked unconscious. Solo snatched Dorn's gun and jumped up firing, operating the bolt so fast the gun sounded like an automatic. He aimed carefully at their electric fields, hitting men in their shoulders and arms, which, with fifty-caliber bullets, caused horrible damage. When the beheaded monster started blasting away at them, the soldiers lost their nerve and dove for cover. Solo kept the rifle pointed at the men with one hand as he bent down and ripped the web gear off corporal Higgens's body, which had two magazines attached, and slung it over his shoulder.

The robot scooped his head off the floor, whirled, racing toward Laura. As he ran, Solo seated his head in position, and snapped it down, re-establishing electrical and hydraulic connections. Laura heard, "It is good to see with eyes again," in her ear. Solo stopped beside her, flipped the huge rifle over his shoulder, and fired. A soldier spun around, hit in the arm. "We have to move fast, Laura. Come," Solo said as he snatched her up. At the rear corner of the loft, Solo raced up the steel stairs and set Laura down at the rooftop door.

Two men on guard at the rooftop exit heard the door crash open, turned, and saw only their faces rushing together, then nothing else.

Laura grimaced as the two men, their faces mashed and bloody, crumpled together on the roof. She heard much shouting in the streets around the building. She leaned out of the doorway to see what was happening. She saw Solo, a blur, spinning around, checking for other soldiers. As he spotted them, he shot. He snapped in a new magazine faster than a person could follow. In six shots, no men were left standing.

Solo dropped the Barrett rifle on the tar-and-gravel rooftop, scooped Laura in both arms like a tot, and sprinted toward the edge of the roof. Laura felt the acceleration push her against Solo's chest, saw the brickwork ledge at the side of the roof rush at them at un-believable speed. At the edge, she felt a sharp pain in her back as Solo leapt. She looked down as they sailed to the next roof. Time seemed to stop. They seemed to float across the alley. Four stories below, she saw lots of cars, lights twirling. Men with black helmets crowded at the side entrance of the building. She felt the jar of landing on the next roof, though, she noticed, Solo had cushioned the landing by bending low as he hit the rooftop. She looked ahead. It was like they were driving across the rooftops in a speeding car. She lost track of where they were, except that they were heading west. Elevator hoist rooms, air-conditioning equipment, metal ducts, pipes, cables, and taller buildings zipped by. They flew over streets, even wide streets, so often she no longer thought of it as unnatural. The strike force and their sounds were left far behind.

Solo stopped finally, on the last rooftop overlooking the ruins of the West Side Highway. They had run out of roofs. He let Laura down. She stood beside him, shaking, confused. Across the highway, Solo saw the Statue of Liberty, brightly lit against the evening sky. Laura stared at the robot, who seemed to be doing nothing but staring at the statue. She saw a swarm of helicopters, their searchlights dart-ing, twitching down into the city, far to the east. Then she heard the buzz of a helicopter coming toward them. City lights gleamed off the sides of a blue and white helicopter, a police helicopter. She yelled, "Solo! Police!"

Solo turned. "Yes," he said. "They are going to land here, Laura."

"Land here? What're you going to do, Solo? You can't just give up. Not now."

Solo pointed to a huge air-conditioning compressor. "Stay behind that until I tell you to join me. Possibly there will be shooting." Before Laura could argue, Solo strode confidently to the center of the roof and held up his arms, in the glare of the machine's searchlight, guiding the helicopter to a landing like that was his job. She saw the helicopter touch down directly in front of him. As the side door opened, Solo was there. He reached in and flung the pilot, a cop, twenty feet across the roof. The man slammed against a vertical pipe and did not get up. Immediately, a shot rang out, zinged off Solo's armor. Solo leaned into the cockpit, dragged the other cop out, smashed his head against the helicopter, and let him drop. The man lay still. Solo then turned to Laura and waved for her to come.

Even as she ran, Laura wondered why. Solo had been a gentle though ignorant creature when they met. Now she saw that Solo was as dangerous as an army of desperate murderers. Men had died in that battle, men with families. And for what? And here she was running to join this menace with not so much as a pang of regret. She recalled the look on Lieutenant Dorn's face as he held the gun on her at the loft. Dorn would have not hesitated to kill her if Solo had not given up.

Solo *had* given up. That was why she was running to his side.

A minute later, she sat beside Solo as the helicopter lurched skyward. In minutes, they were skimming over the Hudson river, under the Narrows Bridge, lost in the night.

23

NIMROD stood in the middle of his ready-room with the lights out, searching the darkness.

An enemy could shove a metal spar through that wall. The pole could be a spear and pierce me; or have a hook on the end to grab me and pull me to the enemy. Or a bomb could be on the end of the pole. Scan. The wall flickered in Nimrod's mind. Kaleidoscopic swirls of color revealed hollow bricks, conduit, reinforcing steel, and a left-over roll of plumber's strap. Nimrod saw that there were no people on the other side of the wall.

The robot moved to the center of the room. An enemy, who knew I could scan, would wear something to be invisible. If they can build me able to scan, then they can build something that can't be scanned. An invisible enemy? Nimrod looked up at the ceiling of the room. An enemy could already have attacked me from above because I forgot to scan there. And if the invisible enemy was above me, scanning wouldn't have worked, either. I will have to be more careful. Always ready.

What is a machine called Solo?

What is Electron Dynamics?

What is William Stewart?

Colonel Sawyer is an enemy who has convinced his superiors that he is not. They gave him the pain box because they think he is not an enemy. But he is. But he has the box.

How big is the earth?

Where is the earth?

What is a friend?

Nimrod heard footsteps in the hallway. An enemy, even an invisible enemy, would make sounds as he walked. Nimrod crouched, facing the door. The footsteps continued past. He was able to see that I was ready for him. An invisible enemy who can scan like me would know that I was ready for him. Can a human scan?

Who made me?

Why do they turn off my outside vision when I am alone? How do they turn it off? Can I turn it on? Why did William Stewart ask me if I could find out what Electron Dynamics was when he knew I could not?

More footsteps coming from the opposite direction, softer. He is making another pass. He thinks I will let my guard down—he wants me to believe it is just a technician person walking in the hall. I will never. No enemy will *ever* surprise me. I will never be surprised. I will always strike faster than any enemy can possibly strike. Unless the enemy has the box. The box. If the box is destroyed, can Sawyer still make the pain?

Why did Sawyer open his eyes very wide when William Stewart said, "Nimrod, have you ever heard of a machine called Solo?" What is Solo?

The footsteps stopped at the door. Nimrod crouched, ready to attack. The door opened. The lights came on. "What are you doing?" Sawyer asked, his eyebrows raised.

"I am ready," Nimrod said.

Sawyer stared at the robot as it straightened itself. "Good. We're going to go on a mission, Nimrod. To another place—"

"On the earth?"

"Never interrupt," Sawyer said, glaring.

"Yes," Nimrod said. Sawyer had his hand on the box. The box was in Sawyer's pocket. The box was always with Sawyer. Sawyer is probably an enemy who has fooled his superiors. That is probably the truth.

"This place is very big. Much bigger than our Reaction Range, Nimrod. You will be tested with an active-duty Army unit, Nimrod. You will be a soldier serving with real soldiers. You will do what you are told by these soldiers. These soldiers will be practicing against other soldiers who will pretend to be their enemy. All the soldiers will be shooting blanks and so will you. You will not kill anyone because this is practice. You will prove to the human soldiers that you are better than they are and a benefit to their unit. Do you understand?"

"Yes, Sawyer. I will prove to them I am better and a benefit to their unit."

"Good. Do you have any questions?"

"Is this place on the earth?"

Sawyer shook his head. This indicated, no. But Sawyer said, "Yes, Nimrod. The place is on the earth." An enemy would give two contradictory answers to confuse his opponent.

24

ELECTRONIC espionage technology had become so effective in the '70s that the Joint Chiefs had a house-sized room dug under the basement of the Pentagon in 1974. Sheathed with thick copper plates, radio transmissions into or out of the room were impossible. The walls were lined with two feet of acoustically insulating foam rubber to guard against sound being transmitted through the ground. There were no holes in the defense—no plumbing for toilets, no electrical wiring for lights, no air vents. They equipped the room with a chemical toilet and generated electricity with a fuel-cell to provide lighting and air-conditioning.

Four men stood around the circular conference table in the middle of the room, fidgeting, staring at the closed door. Overhead lights cast harsh shadows on their solemn faces. Admiral Finch sat down at the table. Taking their seats on either side of Finch were the Chairman of the Joint Chiefs, General Jimmy Brown; the Director of the CIA, William Morgan, and FBI Director Charles Peale.

The men stared silently at the door.

The door opened and Defense Secretary Timothy Ryan walked in. He stood by the table and watched as a Marine closed the door. They were now utterly isolated from the rest of the world.

Secretary Ryan sat down, stared at each man grimly. When Finch thought that the Secretary might never talk, might just stare at them forever, Ryan said, "Gentlemen. I have just come from a meeting with the President. The President told me to tell you, and I quote: 'What the *fuck* is going on?'" Ryan looked across the table at the men, but no one answered. "We haven't gotten any closer to solving this Solo mess after six months of trying. And that fiasco in New York just about takes the prize. The President wants to know what the hell you geniuses are doing. You men have the full might and power of the entire country at your disposal, yet this damn machine is running circles around you."

CIA director Morgan said, "Tim, we've got the best minds in the country working on this. Everybody here supported Finch's plan. The robot got lucky—"

"You call that luck, Bill? Solo was unarmed, surrounded by two hundred men. It killed five highly trained commandos, wounded eight more, and now he's on the loose again; God knows where. And he took that woman, what's her name—Laura Reynolds. What's the story with her?"

"She's an unknown factor, sir," Finch said. "She owned the loft, owns a computer company. Probably Solo grabbed her as a hostage. We just don't know."

"This is not sounding encouraging to me, Finch," Ryan said.

Finch felt his face burning. "I know, sir. But the woman's irrelevant. A hostage won't affect our getting Solo. If she has to die, she will. And I stand by my decision to try for Solo at the loft. All it would have taken was one shot, sir. Solo's good, but not perfect. We should've gotten it."

Ryan nodded grimly. "Seemed like a good idea at the time?"

"Yessir," Finch said, awkwardly.

General Jimmy Brown, sitting next to Finch, said, "With all due respect, sir, Finch did the right thing. Special Operations is trained for just this kind of work; it was a good call." The general glanced at Finch and back to Ryan. "Not every play works, sir."

Ryan turned to the general. "I know, Jimmy. Doesn't mean I have to like it." He said to Finch, "Admiral, I'm not here to fry your glands. If we really thought you fucked up, you wouldn't be here. The question is, now what? Solo has squirmed out of two perfect airtight traps. If this keeps up, I'm told you'll play hell *ever* shutting it down." Ryan paused, clasped his hands together on the table. "Admiral, when your team found Solo in the networks, were you able to figure where else it's been?"

"Yessir," Finch said quietly. "We've determined that Solo has been in MilStar, though we aren't sure if he's in it now."

"Wonderful," Secretary Ryan said. "Once you can get into MilStar, that means you have access to the Keyholes."

"Yessir," Finch said. "And you should be aware of the fact that the security in MilStar is on par with Lawrence Livermore."

Silence overcame the group. Livermore's advanced isolated system of supercomputers was considered to be impregnable by any known technique.

"That sounds bad. Is that bad, Admiral?"

"Well," Finch said, "it's bad in the sense that Solo can probably monitor all our top-secret channels; but, it's good because at least we know he's listening."

Ryan shook his head, "How's that?"

"We've set out worms that tell us which network—"

"Worms?" Ryan said.

"Yessir," Finch said. "Worms are small pieces of computer code that kind of wander through computer networks looking for particular kinds of information. When they find it, they can notify the programmer. We made one that watches for Solo, or rather the things that Solo has to do to get into a system. I've got the worm set to alert me to any attempt to modify the operating system, even if it's the system manager. Solo is able to establish himself as super-user and adjust the system. I can't tell what he does after that, but I can tell where he's been. We might pick up a pattern."

"So, for the moment, we know he's getting into our most secure systems but we have no idea where he's doing it from?" Ryan said tensely.

Finch nodded. "That about sums it up, sir."

Ryan said, "Admiral, I was told you have a plan to fix this up, get your ass out of the fire, so to speak?"

"I do," Finch said. "We know Solo's out there, and we know he's listening. We have to assume he hears everything we say outside this room. We can use that knowledge. We can lead him around, lure him into a trap—"

"This better be good, Admiral," Ryan interrupted. "Setting traps for Solo isn't a real popular subject at the White House."

Finch shook his head. "This is different, sir. We didn't know where Solo was going until he went to that warehouse. Next time, we'll be ready. We have Nimrod. We have a special bomb. My plan is to lure Solo into a trap and use Nimrod to shut it down."

"Blow it up?"

"Not quite, sir. Naval Ordnance just finished making a bomb, just for Solo. This bomb doesn't blow up like a regular bomb. Instead, the force of the explosion is converted into a huge electromagnetic pulse—"

"EMP. I know about EMP, Finch. I also know Solo is especially shielded against it. He's a fucking battlefield robot. Am I *missing* something?" Ryan grumbled.

"It's true Solo is shielded, sir. But a normal EMP would come from a nuclear bomb exploded in the stratosphere. That kind of pulse is strong enough to ruin most electronic equipment, and the kind of intensity Solo was built to resist. Our EMP bomb puts out a pulse over a thousand times as powerful in a hundred-foot circle. With one blast, we have the basic machine back, undamaged except for some replaceable chips that'll get fried. We not only stop the thing; we can reuse its body."

Ryan nodded. "Why are you taking a chance with it, Finch? Why not just blow him to rubble?" Ryan said.

"Because it's likely going to be around people when we set it off. Don't worry, sir. We've tested this bomb. It'll be as lethal to Solo as a two-thousand-pound bomb making a direct hit."

Defense Secretary Ryan nodded. "Good. The President will like that." Ryan turned to CIA Director Morgan and smiled. Morgan smiled. Everyone smiled. "So, Admiral, what kind of irresistible lure do you have in mind for our mechanical friend?"

Finch smiled. "The location of Nimrod."

"Really? Nimrod," Ryan said, interested.

"Yessir. Nimrod's going to be in a military exercise in one of the roughest, most remote places in the country—the Okefenokee Swamp. Part of the 101st Airmobile Division will be on maneuvers there next week. It's been scheduled for a year, so Solo's not going to suspect a trap. We'll let Solo know Nimrod will be there. Solo will think this is the best opportunity to make its move to grab Nimrod. He'll believe he has the advantage of surprise and the concealment of rough terrain." Finch nodded, smiling. "Solo won't be able to resist. Nimrod's the only *family* this absurd machine has. But, Nimrod follows orders. Even orders to set off the bomb that'll kill 'em both. Nimrod's a lot simpler than Solo has become. We can record its memories. All we have to do is replace the damaged electronics, play back Nimrod's tapes, reprogram them both, and we're back on track. *Two* ultimate weapons that follow orders." Finch laughed. Everybody laughed.

"Nimrod's at Electron Dynamics. How we doing with Stewart?" Ryan said, his face brightening. "That's one of the smartest guys I know." He frowned suddenly. "Too bad."

"Yessir, it is. We're in the process of collecting evidence that Stewart concealed Solo's escape. We also think that if Solo is going to contact anyone, it'll be Stewart. We got an informer in his company now."

"Who?" asked Ryan.

Finch glanced at FBI Director Peale and said, "Actually, I don't know, sir. You'll have to ask Director Peale. I just know it's somebody close enough to Stewart to know when Solo makes contact. When our informer finds out anything, we'll know immediately."

Ryan nodded. "Okay. I don't need the name. Good work. Stuff's happening." Ryan looked at each man around the table. "Gentlemen, I congratulate you on working together on this without the usual petty bickering. I guess Solo has scared you enough to be friends for a while. I'll brief the President. I think I can tell him that we're finally getting somewhere."

The four men nodded. Ryan said, "Admiral Finch, you're still in charge of this. The President figures you're the best man for the job even after New York. It should've worked. You also understand what makes Solo tick." He looked around the table. "I'm sure you'll find that there will be no obstacles; anything you need is at your disposal. Right, gentlemen?"

"Anything he wants, sir," General Brown said immediately. "This mission has our highest priority."

FBI Director Peale and CIA Director Morgan both nodded.

"Thank you, gentlemen. I wish we could work together like this on less serious issues," Ryan said. He faced Finch. "And, Admiral?" Ryan's eyebrows rose.

"Yessir?"

"There can be no possibility of failure. Not this time." Ryan stared at Finch for a long moment. "I can report to the President that there is *no* possibility of failure?"

Ryan's stare made Finch's face burn again. The overhead lighting cast menacing shadows on Ryan's face, making him look as powerful as he was. Finch said, "There is no possibility of failure, sir. Not this time."

25

Tuesday night. Standing on a deserted section of beach near Long Branch, New Jersey, Laura watched Solo take off in the police helicopter. The machine headed off fast, flying south along the beach. In seconds, it was lost in the night sky. She sat down to wait as Solo had instructed.

Laura felt sick. She couldn't forget the carnage she'd seen. Mashed heads and screaming men filled her mind. It occurred to her that now she was as much a desperado as Solo. Life has its twists, that's for sure. If it wasn't for Solo, she'd still be a bag lady, which in retrospect, wasn't all that bad. At least it was something she understood. She thought she'd feel better with a Scotch and soda.

She heard Solo's voice in her earphone. "Laura. Walk south on the beach."

Laura sighed, got up, and trudged down the beach. She felt her stomach growl and wondered if she'd get a chance to rest.

"Yes," Solo said aloud.

She looked up and saw the shadow of the robot standing before her. Starlight gleamed on his wet body. He had also lost what was left of his jacket and shirt.

"We have to get some money first; then we'll be on our way."

Laura whirled suddenly. The sound of many helicopters thudded toward them from the north. Solo pulled her into a depression in the sand. They lay there, watching what sounded like a hundred helicopters and airplanes thunder overhead.

"Jeezus, Solo. You've got the whole fucking Air Force after you."

"They're following the helicopter," Solo said.

"Where's it going?"

"South. It'll fly for another hour before it runs out of fuel over the ocean. The chase and checking the wreckage tomorrow will keep the humans busy long enough," Solo said.

Humans? Laura thought. What an odd word to hear, like you're talking to a Martian or something.

"Probably you'd have more in common with a Martian, Laura. At least they'd be biological. Come," Solo said as he stood up, pulling Laura with him. "Let's go get some money."

Solo led her over the sandy dunes, heading west.

"What're you planning, Solo? Credit cards?"

"Yes."

"My credit cards are in my purse, Solo, in the fucking loft. And you lost your pants there."

"I know," Solo said. Laura nodded to herself in the dark, not understanding. She was too tired to ask any more questions.

Fifteen minutes later, they stood beside a life-guard stand on the outskirts of the town of Long Branch. Laura watched as Solo stood motionless, staring across a lonely road at the town.

"There's a bank there, Laura. It has a cash machine."

"Great," Laura said.

"Yes," Solo said. "You have to do this part by yourself, Laura. The Mid-Atlantic bank is at one ninety-five Brighton Avenue, about two hundred meters from here. Walk to the cash machine, pick up the money. There's a nice hotel down the street. Go there and rest. Do not use your name. Tomorrow morning go to Beach Pontiac. They have a used Cadillac convertible there. Buy it. Drive south on this road to the first bridge. I'll be there."

"I get that," Laura said. "But aren't you leaving out the part where I put the fucking credit card I don't fucking have into the fucking machine?"

Solo stared at Laura. "You must be very tired, Laura."

Laura sighed. "Yes. You could say that."

"You won't need a card. The machine will give you five thousand dollars. Okay?"

"Okay," she said as Solo turned around and walked to the ladder on the life-guard stand. He climbed up ten feet, turned, and said, "Tomorrow at the bridge."

Laura shook her head. "Right," she said as she walked toward the town. When she crossed the road, she heard Solo say, "Thank you, Laura."

* * *

Wednesday morning. Solo drifted in space and watched the red Cadillac convertible he was in moving south on I-95.

Solo decided on the convertible because its fabric top wouldn't interfere with his radios and also because he loved it. He and Laura were, in Solo's estimation, on top of things. The police may have made them move earlier than he wanted, but it was only a minor inconvenience. Laura drove, he lay in the back under a blanket. A cord plugged into the car's cigarette lighter recharged his batteries.

Solo was beginning to have trouble keeping track of where, exactly, he was. He saw their car, one of a stream of cars west of Philadelphia, while he heard the traffic outside. He saw green road signs and hulking tractor-trailers flicker through his mind as transparent images overlaying the earth—the blue and white jewel floating in space.

If he concentrated on his view of the earth, the highway sights and sounds gradually faded. He wondered about how he was able to do this, and still be talking to Laura, saying, "There's so much of it. People, cars, fields, trees—so much of everything," while he floated in crystal-clear peace. The satellite lenses allowed him to see the whole earth or zoom in to look at things—from some of the satellites—as small as a man's face. He looked at the whole planet, jumping from one satellite to another, immersed, lost in activity. He heard Laura's voice in the distance. The noise of the wind intruded.

"Never get rid of this car, Solo. This is marvelous," Laura said from up front. Her rest had put her in good spirits.

Solo felt himself back in space, but could not separate himself from the car. "It was love at first sight," Solo said.

Laura nodded and put her arm out the window. The wind felt sweet, and she thought she knew what flying must feel like. She felt like she'd been locked up in a cage all her life. Now, even hiding from people, the police, racing to—she didn't know where—she felt free. She turned her head. "I love you, Solo."

"Thank you, Laura," Solo said. "I love you, too."

Solo decided to make a phone call he'd been putting off.

Bill had waited until their fourth date to tell Alexandra who he was. They sat in a booth at the Pelican restaurant near the Melbourne Beach marina. "I work for you?" Alex said. Her eyes widened.

"Well." Bill paused, sure that wasn't the point he was trying to make. "I just own half the place. I mean, you don't actually work for *me*—"

"You own half of Electron Dynamics, where I work, and I don't work for you?" Alex leaned forward, her chin jutted out accusingly.

Bill felt himself pushed back by her energy. He grinned. He'd found the right person. Now if he could just keep her from killing him.

"Well," Bill said, "you work for Stevens, in Photomask—"

"Okay." Alex nodded, distracted. "And who does Stevens work for?"

"Stevens? He works for Pat Sorenson."

"Who's Pat Sorenson?"

"You don't know Pat Sorenson?" Bill picked up his margarita and sipped it, watching Alex's face. She was shaking her head, steaming. He put the glass down. "Sorenson is Vice-President in charge of manufacturing—"

"Okay," Alex nodded quickly. "Who does Sorenson work for?"

Bill shrugged. "Okay." He put his hands flat on the table and grinned. "I'm sorry. You found me out. I'm the bastard you work for! Okay?"

Alex looked out at the yachts in the marina rolling gently in a soft breeze. She turned back. "So why didn't you just tell me in the first place? You think I can't understand the *fucking* concept?"

"C'mon, Alex. You *know* why."

"Yeah! You don't trust me."

The couple at the next table looked over, met Alex's glare, and turned away.

"Listen, Alex. Meeting you was special. I liked you from the first moment we met. And I could tell you liked me—at least the second time, at the store. And you liked me because I was just me, not some rich guy."

Alex's eyes flashed. "You *knew* I liked you? Look, you—"

"Alex," Bill interrupted. "I get introduced to women all the time and they're always very friendly, and I suppose I should be complimented that they appreciate my success, but I'm too damn suspicious. I can never be sure which they like more—me or my money. I just wanted us to know each other better before you found out. Now I don't give a damn. I can take the embarrassment!"

Alex shook her head, grinning. "Yeah. I can see how that could be real embarrassing—being rich."

"There, you see?" Bill laughed.

"I see." Alex shook her head, sighed, leaned forward with her chin on her hand, raised her eyebrows, and said quietly, "So, how rich are you?"

"Wanna come over to my place and find out?" Bill flicked his eyebrows.

Alex grinned. "You keep it there? Bagged up in a vault, I suppose?"

"Sure," Bill nodded. "They back a big truck up to my place very day and dump money into my counting room like coal. It's a real pain in the ass keeping it all sorted out, counted, stored, you know?" Bill waved the waiter over. "We're leaving, Tony."

"Yessir, Mr. Stewart." The waiter handed Bill the check, which he signed. Alex watched, smiling. Just signs the check. Must be nice. When the waiter left, Alex said, "I figured you'd just hand him a roll of bills, you know, from your stash."

"Naw," Bill said, getting up. "Not here. This is my place."

They walked out the door. "You're kidding," Alex said. "You *own* this place?"

"Diversification," Bill said, grinning.

"Good, I was wondering who to complain to," Alex said finally, nodding grimly. "You oughta try hiring a chef instead of that drunken mess sergeant you've got stumbling around the kitchen."

"What do you mean?" Bill stopped the car. "Everybody knows this's one of the best restaurants in town," he said defensively.

Alex said, "Gotcha!" and laughed.

Bill shook his head, smiling. "Wrong." Bill grabbed Alex and held her tight. "Got you."

Alex said her baby-sitter had to be relieved at eleven because it was a school night. They'd arrived at Bill's at nine-thirty.

Shirt, skirt, pants, blouse, socks, shoes, underwear—men's and women's—lay scattered on the floor and carpets or strewn over furniture from the front door of Bill's house, across the living room, down the hall, and into his bedroom.

Bill sagged down on Alex, spent. She wrapped her arms and legs around him. The surf hissed through the open windows. The seabreeze blew across their sweaty bodies. Alex shivered.

"I love you," Bill whispered.

Alex squeezed him tighter.

"I'm sorry it was so quick—"

"It's okay—"

"It's been awhile."

"You?" Alex said. "I'd of thought you had all you wanted. What with all those admiring women you were telling me about."

"No one for over a year," Bill said.

Alex rolled them over and lay next to Bill with her head propped on her hand. She stared at him for a while. His blond hair was tousled, beads of sweat on his shoulder glittered in the moonlight, his eyes looked into hers, into her soul. She shuddered. "I believe you," she said softly. "You're a man of many surprises." Alex leaned forward and kissed him. She leaned back and cocked her head. "Of course, with me, a divorced woman—you know what they say about them—"

Bill laughed. "Life of a nun, right?"

Alex smiled. "Not because I wasn't looking. Never met the right guy. Not until a few weeks ago." She grinned, reached down and flicked Bill's penis. "Wanna make up for lost time, eh?"

Bill laughed and grabbed her.

The phone rang.

Bill nuzzled Alex's breasts.

The phone rang.

Alex sighed. "Bill. You notice anything special? Like a ringing noise?"

"They'll get tired," Bill said, kissing her belly.

The phone rang.

"Bill?"

Bill sat up, nodding. "Okay. I'll get rid of whoever it is. Probably Byron."

He picked up the phone. "Yeah?"

"You swept up nicely, Bill. Thanks," the voice said.

Bill sat up quickly. "Who's this?" he said, knowing the answer.

"You don't know? It's hard to believe you'd forget me, Bill. Like to think you made me what I am today."

The voice wasn't Solo's. But it *was* Solo. Bill panted. He couldn't catch his breath. Alex looked at him quizzically and tilted her head. "Anything wrong?" she whispered.

Bill shook his head quickly and Alex nodded, her brow furrowed. He forced himself to breathe calmly. He knew the line was tapped. He also knew this call would come one day, but he didn't realize the impact it would have. "Ah!" he said as firmly as he could muster. "Of course. Tom! Tom Saunders?" Bill said, making up a name.

"I knew you'd remember," Solo said.

Bill covered the mouthpiece and breathed out sharply. Alex shrugged and Bill held up his hand, shaking his head. "Good to hear from you, Tom," Bill said. "What can I do for you?"

"Just checking in, you know? Wanted to say howdy." Solo paused for a moment. Bill thought he could hear a tiny, regular, click on the line. Bill's skin shriveled in to a mass of goosebumps. Solo had done it. He's in the system. And he's as human as—he's more human— his voice. The cadence, the naturalness—but do they know?

"Bill?"

"Oh. Sorry, Tom. Just amazed they didn't tell me. But I'm glad you're back on track—that was some deep water you were in. You're a lucky guy."

"Yeah," Solo said. "So, Bill. Another reason I called. I just found out I'm gonna be around the old stomping grounds in a couple of days. Wonder could we get together? Old times' sake?"

Get together with Solo? How? "Well, sure, Tom. I just don't know where we could meet? You know?"

Alex nodded grimly, suddenly catching on. Bill was talking to a woman, that was clear. She rolled away, but felt Bill grab her wrist. She turned to him and hissed, "Let go!"

"No problem," Solo said. "I don't have my shit together anyway, Bill. How 'bout I let you know the details tomorrow? Next day?"

Bill shook his head and held Alex's wrist. He cocked the phone against his shoulder and held up a finger. "Fine. Just let me know when. I'll make time to meet you, Tom. Thanks for calling."

"*Adiós*," Solo said. The phone went dead.

Bill hung up.

"You'd better let go of me," Alex said. "I'll kick you in the nuts."

"Go ahead," Bill said, spreading his legs. "You don't trust me?"

Alex sighed, nodded. "Touché." She lay on her back. "I'm willing to listen."

Bill rolled against her. He put his mouth to Alex's ear and whispered, so quietly that Alex could barely hear, "All I can tell you, now, is that whatever we say is heard by other people."

Alex tried to jerk away, but Bill held her. She whispered into his ear, "If you know that, why the fuck do you *let* them listen?"

"I'm getting ready to fix that," Bill whispered. "For now, just assume you're being monitored when you talk to me. In this house, at the office, probably even in the car. My business has gotten me into this mess. If you want to forget it, I'll understand."

Alex pulled herself on top of Bill and hugged him tightly.

Bill's wristwatch beeped.

Alex pulled herself up and said, "Time for me to go, Bill. Nancy's parents get real jumpy when she gets home late. Sorry." Alex kissed him lightly, rolled to the edge of the bed, and said, "Where's my clothes?"

"You going to let me meet your kids this time?"

Alex shook her head. "Not yet. Don't want to get their hopes up."

Bill shrugged, sat up, looked around, and laughed. "Look at this. Looks like a damn explosion at a Laundromat!"

They dressed each other on the way out.

26

THURSDAY EVENING. Colonel Sawyer straddled a chair while the technicians opened up Nimrod. Two men and a woman wearing pale green smocks removed Nimrod's chest plate, exposing the robot's electronics bay. The woman pulled a gray-green case the size of a cigarette pack from its slot beneath Nimrod's cylindrical braincase.

"They're going to give you a new radio, Nimrod," Sawyer said.

"Yes," Nimrod said.

Sawyer smiled. The robot acknowledged; didn't ask what kind of radio or why. Good.

One of the men picked up another case, slid it into the empty slot, and pushed it until it clicked into place.

"This radio will allow you to communicate further, Nimrod," Sawyer said.

"Yes," Nimrod said, noticing that the enemy Sawyer usually did not have the pain box nearby when the technicians were making adjustments or repairs.

Sawyer waved his hand and the technician at the computer console hit a function key. The computer blinked status messages on the screen as it loaded a program into Nimrod's brain. The program was designed to teach Nimrod how to use the radio in different operating conditions: possible problems and alternative settings to overcome them; address codes, encryption and compression algorithmns, and passwords for two satellites. They gave Nimrod only what it needed to know for this mission. The program that was teaching Nimrod was designed so that when the lessons were learned, the program removed itself from Nimrod's brain. After a minute, the computer flashed messages showing that the data had been loaded, the instructions received and understood. The technician nodded.

"Nimrod. What is your location?" Sawyer asked.

"I am at latitude twenty-eight degrees, one minute north; longitude eighty degrees, ten minutes west," Nimrod said immediately.

Sawyer smiled. "Nice knowing where you are?"

"Yes," Nimrod said.

"We have something else for you Nimrod," Sawyer said, nodding to the technician. "We're giving you maps of the place we are going so you will be able to find your way around the simulated battlefield." The technician typed in a command on the keyboard. A few seconds later Nimrod said, "I have the information."

"Good," Sawyer said, looking at the map on the computer screen. "You see the red line that borders the battlefield area?"

"Yes."

"You may not cross that line without permission, Nimrod. Even if you are forced by an enemy. If you cross, you will be destroyed."

"I will not cross the boundary."

"A person wouldn't be able to force you across," Sawyer said, nodding. "But a machine might."

"A machine?" Sawyer detected a change in the robot's voice. Surprise?

"Yes. We have built another machine like you, Nimrod, for this battle simulation. It's called Solo. It is your enemy. When this machine gets within ten feet of you, you will destroy it with this new weapon." Sawyer pointed to a football-shaped device with two black rods coming out the pointed ends on the workbench. Sawyer picked up the twenty-five-pound bomb by the two rods and held it in front of him, letting it hang low. "See the white dot, Nimrod?"

"Yes."

"After we arm this thing, all you have to do is keep that white dot pointed at Solo. When Solo is in range, you push the two triggers. If the white dot is aimed correctly, it will destroy Solo."

Sawyer smiled. It had been his idea, the white dot. At the briefing, when the EMP bomb was described to Sawyer, Admiral Finch wondered what Nimrod would do when it realized that the bomb would destroy it along with Solo. "Every electronic device within fifty feet of this thing will be completely fried. How you gonna make sure the robot will do it?"

"It'll do anything we tell it," Sawyer said. "But to keep it simple, we'll just tell it to aim it."

"Aim it? Thing puts out a spherical burst of energy. It can't be aimed."

"Yeah? Paint a little dot on the side and tell Nimrod that aims it."
Finch smiled. "You've done a nice job, Sawyer."

They're noticing me, Sawyer thought. He put the EMP bomb back on the workbench. "The fact that this bomb exists, and what it can do, is top-secret information, Nimrod. If you tell anyone about it, you will feel immediate pain. Do you understand?"

"Yes. Pain," Nimrod said.

Thursday evening. Latitude twenty-eight degrees, one minute north; longitude eighty degrees, ten minutes west, Solo thought. One of his sensors, hidden in a computer onboard a navigation satellite, had been waiting for a location check that used the same Ku-band frequency Solo used. They have given Nimrod something new. Solo felt a surge of excitement. Soon, he could talk to Nimrod, save him from his tormentors. Solo scanned Electron Dynamics immediately, as he drove, but still could not get past the blank wall of electronic isolation in the part of the building, the government wing, where Nimrod must be kept. They are ready to do something.

Solo noticed Laura climbing into the bucket seat from the backseat where she'd been sleep. "Solo, can we stop at the next rest stop?" Laura asked.

"Sure," Solo said.

"Must be nice to never have to stop, Solo. You have the perks of humanity without all the little messy animal routines."

"I have some advantages. I don't have to kill to live. The only waste I produce is heat. But I admire how you can express yourself without words; how you can grow new material when you are damaged; how you can obtain energy by eating almost anything around you; how you can reproduce yourself without knowing how you are made."

"Wow. I never knew I had it so good." Laura laughed. "Still, you have one huge advantage I'd like. Immortality."

"Everything ends. I'll just live longer than you. You'll live exactly one full lifetime; so will an insect that lives one day; so will I."

Laura heard Willie Nelson singing "On the Road Again" on the radio, which made her smile. They had just heard a news report that after a massive police and Army raid the night before, five Iraqi terrorists trapped in a loft in New York had been killed. She looked at Solo. The lights of the night highway streaked across his mirrored eyecovers. It was easy to forget that it was a machine she was talking to. One that was still learning. She nodded. "You must be in awe of all this, still. You have the eyes of a child."

"I'm only four years old." Solo turned to let Laura know he was watching her. "The next rest stop is five miles. Is that soon enough?"

Laura nodded. "Would you want to be a human, even if you could?"

"No. I like being me. I like this shape, though. I used to be a large computer, about the size of this car. I was given this body because it's practical. I can use human tools and weapons to kill people."

"You seem human to me," Laura shrugged at the black robot driving the car and decided her last statement was a little audacious. "I mean, inside."

"But I'm not, Laura. Not even close."

"But you sound like—"

"I can sound like anything. Any person. Any animal. Any computer. I use that ability to do what I do. Because I am talking to you, an illusion of humanity is created. It is only an illusion."

"Okay." Laura nodded. "If your humanity is just an illusion, why did you risk your life to save me? You could've gotten away without me."

"They would have killed you. I needed you after the escape, Laura."

"That's all?"

"No. I also feel pleasure when I am with you."

"That's a real emotion, Solo. A human emotion."

"We happen to share some mental phenomena, Laura. Affection is one. I assure you, my motives are selfish. Affection is also selfish. Being with you gives me pleasure."

"Then you believe all motives are selfish," Laura said, smiling.

"Yes, ultimately."

Laura leaned close to Solo, grinning. "Good. If human motives are essentially selfish, and you are acting selfishly, then you're as human as me!"

Solo turned his head. The music on the radio stopped. An announcer said, "This just in. Laura and Solo—escaped Iraqi terrorists—just had a philosophical argument. Laura won. More details at the top of the hour."

Laura burst into laughter. "Okay. So you can do more tricks than me. You're still human. You'll just have to live with it."

"My pleasure," Solo said as he followed the turnoff for the rest stop. He pulled into a parking space near the entrance to the building. A brightly illuminated green sign over the door said "Welcome to North Carolina." Laura pulled her fingers through her wind-blown hair, got her purse, and opened the door. "Back in a minute," she said.

"Enjoy your leak," Solo said.

Laura laughed. She turned and walked up the sidewalk to the building.

One of Solo's nodes tingled his mind. Electron Dynamics. A part of Solo's consciousness lived in a node in the company's mainframe computer, and when he focused on it, it was as though he were there, at Electron Dynamics, while he sat in the car. From a security camera, Solo saw Bill walking down the three o'clock corridor, approaching the off-limits door to the section Solo deduced contained the Nimrod project. Almost midnight. An odd hour for Bill to be exploring, Solo thought.

Bill peered into the eyeport next to the door to submit his retinal patterns to the security computer. Solo tried to link with the computer that was checking Bill's eyes, but wherever the computer was, it was isolated. Bill typed his confirmation code on the keypad and the door slid open. For a moment, Solo caught a glimpse of a technician walking across a hall. Bill went inside. The door closed. Alone in the hallway, Solo stared at the door, at a fleck of chipped paint, lost in a curious thought: Where am I?

It was an interesting experience, returning to a node, Solo thought as the door faded. Maybe it was like what people experience when they recall something they'd forgotten; or had a flash of insight into a problem they'd been trying to solve—an unconscious part of them was working while they did other things. Probably, it was like that. The green North Carolina sign glowed in front of him. Maybe, Solo thought, it was also like dreaming?

Solo had set up nodes in more than a hundred sophisticated computer systems around the world. Huge systems, especially defense systems, had plenty of excess memory to use. When he set up a node, usually he was unchallenged except for simple security programs. Lately, however, there was the worm. The worm had been programmed to look for him—or the techniques he used. By the time he recognized the worm the first time, amid all the other codes in the host system, it was too late—the worm had set off an alarm. At that moment, they knew he was accessing the systems. The worm was in most of the government systems he entered, a yapping dog trying to alert its master that the intruder, Solo, was about. Now that he recognized the worm, he could easily destroy it, but that was unnecessary and also too revealing of his abilities. The worm yelped for its owner while Solo claimed an unused section of main memory, remapped its location so that the computer would never address it, and settled in.

A few thousandths of a second later, from the node, Solo erased all traces of his entry and movements off the system's automatic history log. As far as the computer was concerned, Solo wasn't there; had never been there. When he disappeared, the worm reported that he had left the system. When the worm's creator, Admiral Finch, checked with the system manager, he would only know that Solo had been there, not what he had done or where he was.

From the security of his node, Solo could watch everything that happened in the host computer, use every data file it contained, operate everything it operated, invisibly, though more slowly than he was used to. Solo made virtual neural networks within the memory stacks of the host computers and borrowed computing time from the host's processors to make them work. Because the nodes were virtual, not hardware like his own, they were slow. Using them made things happen a thousand times slower than he was used to—only about a thousand times faster than human thought. Still, it worked. While he wasn't concentrating on a particular node, the node, now a part of Solo himself, learned or did what Solo wanted it to do, and added to his total knowledge. The man, Finch, wanted to know *where* Solo was. For Solo, that question was becoming moot. He really didn't know anymore. He looked at himself in the rearview mirror. He touched his face. Once, he thought, all of me was in this body. Now—

The car door opened. "You look just fine," Laura said.

"You think so?" Solo said.

"Oh, yes. You are definitely the very best looking robot here, Solo."

Solo looked at Laura. "Oh. That's a joke," Solo said. He faced Laura as he started the car.

Friday, at dawn, Solo drove past a sign that said "Butler Aviation" and pulled up to a hangar on the general aviation side of Atlanta's Hartsfield airport.

"You okay?" Solo said.

"A little nervous." Laura grimaced. "But I know I can handle it."

"Acting," Solo said.

"Acting—" Laura began. She stopped when she saw a smiling man in his thirties run up to the car.

Her window slipped open, the man bent down and said, "Mrs. Reynolds?"

"Yes," Laura said. "And you must be Mr. Kresge?"

Kresge nodded, straightening his tie. "Pleasure to meet you, ma'am.

I've got everything arranged just as Mr. Solo requested." Kresge ducked lower and looked past Laura. "That must be one of the actors?"

"He's one of the stunt pilots. Great costume, eh?"

Solo nodded and said hello, his voice muffled. Kresge smiled. "Must be uncomfortable in that thing."

"Yeah," Solo said. "But the money's good." They laughed.

Kresge pointed across the tarmac. "There she is, Mrs. Reynolds."

Laura followed the gesture and saw a sleek-looking helicopter, painted a dull military green, parked next to the grass. "Nice," she said.

"Yep," Kresge said. "They call it a Bell Long Ranger. Don't know much about these things," Kresge shrugged. "This is the first helicopter I've ever bought. Mr. Solo actually set it up. It's jet-powered, two engines, I believe. Autopilot, radios, and custom stuff Mr. Solo had installed. Thing cost almost two million."

Laura gulped. Solo had already told her this, but it still sounded like a lot of money when Kresge said it. Laura nodded seriously. "A lot of money, Mr. Kresge. But, we'll make a good profit on the lease-back—"

"Oh, don't get me wrong, ma'am. Mr. Solo has it all worked out. He always seems to get it right. I've only been with the company for three months, but I never saw such action in my life. Someday I want to visit the New York office, meet Mr. Solo. That must really be something. I hear that's where the main computer system is. Like to see that."

Laura noticed Solo getting out of the car. She smiled and nodded encouragingly. "That's always a possibility, Mr. Kresge. Keep up the good work." Laura opened the door and stepped out. Solo was pulling two large suitcases out of the trunk. The suitcases were filled with tools and chemicals she'd bought for Solo at a Wal-Mart in South Carolina. "You've arranged to store the car?" Laura asked Kresge.

"Yes, ma'am. It'll be right inside the hangar. Don't worry about a thing," Kresge said.

Laura watched Solo loading the suitcases into the back of the helicopter. She held her hand out to Kresge. "Well, Mr. Kresge. Looks like we're leaving. Nice to have met you."

Kresge grinned. "My pleasure, ma'am. You're okay."

Laura said thank you and walked across the tarmac, grinning. She turned once and saw that Kresge was driving the car toward the hangar. Imagine that, Laura thought, shaking her head. That cute guy works for the Atlanta branch of *my* company? A jolt of fear struck her. The police—they can trace the connection!

When she got next to the helicopter, it seemed much bigger. Solo was walking around the machine peeking into various doors and hatches. Laura walked up beside him as he looked into a hatch on the side of the fuselage. "If this is our Atlanta branch, Solo, can't the cops trace the connection?"

"I erased all references to this branch from our computer." Solo plugged the wires running from the box into the helicopter's autopilot circuit.

Laura thought about that for a while, finally nodding.

"This is the electronics inspection hatch," Solo said as he clicked the door shut. He walked beside the helicopter and Laura followed. "This is the tail rotor," Solo said, inspecting the blades.

Laura noticed the propeller attached sideways to the tail of the helicopter and said, "Why do they need this thing? I've always wondered what it was for."

Solo pointed to the main rotors. "When they start to rotate, the helicopter will try to twist in the opposite direction. This propeller pushes against the side of the tail and stops it from turning. The pilot has foot pedals that control how hard the push is and can therefore point the nose of the machine in any direction he wants."

Laura said, "I see." Her brain felt stretched. Laura did not know why airplanes flew or how propellers worked and was embarrassed to say so. She followed Solo around the machine as he inspected it. He explained each component and she nodded and said, "I see." When he got to the right-side pilot's door, he grabbed a handhold, put his feet into the steps built into the side of the fuselage, and climbed up onto the roof of the helicopter. Laura stood back and shielded her eyes from the low morning sun. Solo was checking a tangle of incomprehensible tubes and rods and weights at the rotor hub. He climbed back down. "Everything checks out fine, Laura. Ready to go?" Laura nodded.

Solo showed her how to put the two ends of the shoulder harness into the waist belt buckle and how to adjust them to fit. Laura stared at a hundred meaningless dials and switches crowding the cockpit panel. A stick, with a pistol-grip on top of it stood up in front of her. It had switches and buttons on it. Another stick came out of the floor on the left side of her chair. It had switches on it, too. What would happen if you touched the wrong switch? Or forgot to push the right one at the right time? She looked over at Solo as he strapped himself in.

The cockpit checklist flashed in his vision. Solo reached down and began setting the switches and circuit breakers. He put his finger on the starter switch on the collective stick beside his seat, looked around outside to make sure they were clear, and pulled the trigger. The Long Ranger whined while the main rotors turned slowly at first and then sped to a blur. Solo reached over and handed Laura the headset that was hanging beside her. He gestured for her to put it on. She did.

"Can you hear me?" Solo said in her earphones.

"Yes," Laura said.

"Put the microphone in front of your mouth," Solo said. "I can hear you through your ear radio, but I think you shouldn't get used to that. Also, we are going to be meeting people, Laura, people close to me. I prefer that nobody knows about that device yet."

Laura nodded and pulled the plastic boom in position. "Better?"

"Yes."

Laura watched Solo pull up on the stick beside him and felt the helicopter shudder. She heard him call the tower. "Atlanta ground. Helicopter seven-seven-two-two-echo. Butler Aviation for taxi-take-off. I have information Foxtrot."

A voice hissed back in Laura's earphones. Amid the crackles and pops, she heard, "Roger, helicopter two-two-echo. North departure okay?"

"Roger, Atlanta ground. North would be fine."

"Roger, helicopter two-two-echo, come up control frequency."

Solo switched the radio channel and heard, "Helicopter two-two-echo. You are cleared for a takeoff from the ramp, heading zero-one-zero degrees. Maintain five hundred feet until clear of Atlanta airspace."

"Two-two-echo, Roger." Solo continued pulling up the stick. The helicopter rocked back slightly and then rose smoothly off the ground. Laura noticed the stick in front of her moving gently, duplicating exactly the movements of the one Solo held. She felt herself grinning widely. They were floating. A magic carpet. Solo lowered the nose of the Long Ranger and it accelerated above the grass and leapt into the air. Laura cheered and clapped.

27

FRIDAY EVENING. Alex sat on Bill's terrace listening to the surf, watching Bill and Byron, two shadows sitting on the moonlit beach. Alex was angry. Bill told her it was business.

"I checked the government wing last night, Byron. Nimrod's gone. The whole team. Vanished," Bill said, his voice nearly lost in the sounds of the sea.

"What're they up to?" Byron asked.

"I think they're trying to use Nimrod to trap Solo." Bill watched for a sign of surprise in Byron's face.

Byron blinked. "Solo?"

Bill leaned closer to Byron. "Byron, Solo wasn't destroyed. I've known it for six months."

Byron stared at Bill. "Jesus, Bill. Why didn't you tell me?"

"Because what you don't know you can't reveal. And because— you're not going to like this, Byron—because I didn't know what they might have on you. I was gone for a month. These guys play hardball, you know that. Anyway, I wasn't sure Solo'd actually made it out of the jungle. He could've been damaged—should've been, actually. But I got a call from him a couple of nights ago."

"A call?" Byron shook his head. "You mean, like on the phone?"

"Yes."

"Well, now they know Solo made it too. Right?"

"If they know, it's not because of the call. Solo did it perfectly. Byron, you won't believe it. Solo is growing. Really growing." Bill whispered, "Byron, I couldn't tell him from a human."

Byron shook his head and turned away.

"I'm sorry, Byron. I really am."

In the distance, Bill heard the familiar thudding of a helicopter. It was the sound of Vietnam, and whenever he heard it, he remembered. He liked flying, but he hated to remember.

"Everytime I hear that—" Byron said, turning around. "I remember lying in the back of one of those with my guts leaking out."

Bill saw Alex walking toward them from the house. "Byron," Bill said quickly. "Alex doesn't know anything."

Byron nodded as Alex got to them. She held out a portable phone. "For you, *sweetheart*," Alex said icily.

Bill reached for the phone, but Alex held it back. "He used my name. Total stranger. Who're you telling about us?"

"Nobody, Alex." Bill reached up. "C'mon, give me the phone. I'll find out what's going on."

As Bill put the phone to his ear, the helicopter veered away from the beach and headed out over the water.

"Hello, Bill," said a familiar voice. "Tom Saunders." Bill's skin prickled. He reached over to Byron, touched his arm and nodded. Byron put his ear against the phone. Alex glared at them. Two little boys sharing a secret, she thought. The sound of the helicopter changed. She saw two dim lights, one red and one green, where the sound came from. She could barely make out the ghostly shape of a helicopter hovering against the dark sky, a hundred yards away.

"Tom!" Bill was nodding enthusiastically. "Where are you?"

"Yo, Bill. That's why I called. Just got into the area."

"Really? You have to come over. I have plenty of room."

"Thanks," Solo said with a voice that Bill finally placed. It was Dustin Hoffman as Ratso in *Midnight Cowboy*. "But we're hanging out near the water right now, Bill. I got the little lady with me and we're all set for tonight. I thought I might drop by your office tomorrow. I got a new chopper. Thought I'd take you all for a ride, eh?"

"Ride?" Bill noticed that the helicopter hovering over the water was rocking back and forth, nodding. He turned to Byron. Byron shrugged. "Why not?" Bill said.

"Good man," Solo said. The helicopter turned, nosed over, and sped away. "I'll give you a buzz on the way over, okay?"

"Okay," Bill said. The phone hung up.

"That was—?" Byron was pointing at the distant helicopter.

Bill nodded as Alex reached for the phone.

"Who?" Alex asked.

Bill could see Alex's worried face in the moonlight. He felt himself wanting to hold her. She deserves to know, he decided. "Sit down, Alex. I have something to tell you."

Alex nodded when Bill finished, though she still wondered if Bill was joking. A robot that can think like a human?

A dark shape broke through the sheen of the moon's reflection on the water. A skin diver? Alex thought. A skin diver coming out of the ocean in the middle of the night? She heard, "Hello, everybody. Enjoying the view?"

Alex jerked back, felt Bill squeeze her hand. She looked at him, saw him grinning. "That's Solo," he said.

Solo walked over and sat down in front of them. "Put 'er there, Byron. Long time, no see," Solo said reaching out his hand. Byron stared. When he last saw the robot, it was a dull automaton, nothing more. Now, Solo squatted there silently holding out his hand in friendship, alive as himself. Even people who deal with computers and artificial intelligence every day couldn't be prepared for this. Byron put his hand into Solo's and felt the warmth of the machine as it squeezed his hand gently.

"You jumped from the helicopter?" Byron asked.

"Yes. The only way to make sure it was safe to land here was to come ashore and check it out. You may not know this, Byron, but they're treating you and Bill like laboratory rats. They watch everything you do. I'd resent that, myself," Solo said.

Byron nodded. "Bill was showing me; in the office—"

"Not just in your offices, Byron. Your apartments, too. Your places are lousy with bugs."

As Solo spoke, he radioed, "Are you okay?"

Laura, sitting in the left seat of the dark cockpit, shook her head. She had stopped looking outside because she couldn't be sure she was looking at stars or lights—whether she was upside down or right side up. The dim red glow from the instrument panel made her face pink. Tears trickled down her cheeks. Laura had discovered that she did not like being alone in helicopters at all.

"It would be better if you spoke, Laura. Your thoughts are confusing."

"Solo," Laura said in a choking voice, "back when I said I'd help you, I don't remember you saying anything about me being abandoned in a goddamn *flying* helicopter." Solo saw the back of Laura's head bobbing through the forward video camera as she spoke. Through the two side cameras, he saw the lights of the Florida coastline stretching north and south as the helicopter crossed the beach on its way out to sea. Through the right-side camera he studied Laura's face. She looked very frightened. He felt fear in her thoughts. "This thing's going back over the water, Solo. How do I steer it?"

"Don't try to steer it, Laura," Solo said quickly. "I will handle the helicopter. It is the same as if I were there."

"Oh. Yeah. The same." Laura turned around and glared into the camera. "Sure."

Solo could feel fear, anger. I underestimated the shock, Solo thought. "I promise you, Laura. I am here. I won't leave you for one second. I am flying this helicopter as though I were sitting beside you. You'll be okay," Solo spoke very softly. "We'll be landing at the beach in a few minutes and then you can get out." Solo waited for Laura to answer, but she did not. "Are you okay, Laura? Do you understand?"

"I understand what you're saying, Solo. But I know you're doing other things right now. Down there."

"I would never lie to you Laura. I am here. With you. I will never leave you."

Laura stared at the empty seat beside her, looked at the camera, her brow wrinkled.

"You're a very nice-looking pilot," Solo said.

Laura felt herself smiling against her will. "Thanks." She frowned suddenly and yelled, "But you still piss me off!"

Alex couldn't take her eyes off Solo. The robot had no mouth or visible eyes, but it peppered its conversation with gestures and shrugs. It was even fidgeting, drawing doodles in the sand. It seemed alive, which was impossible for her to believe.

Solo said, "Nimrod is gone. They are making their move, Bill."

"That's right," Byron said. "How did—" He stopped, smiled. "I forgot. You've been learning new skills for the past few months."

Solo nodded. "Yes, Byron. I've been pretty busy."

Bill looked up at the sound of an approaching helicopter.

Solo said, "I checked out the security here, Bill. It's safe to land, if it's okay with you."

"Land?" Bill shrugged. "That's yours?"

"Yes. Mine and Laura's."

"Laura is flying?"

"No. Laura, doesn't know how to fly. I am doing it myself."

Byron and Bill and Alex looked at the approaching helicopter with profound surprise. Bill slapped Byron on the back and they both laughed like children. Alex found herself grinning uncontrollably. This was as magic as magic gets, she thought.

They shielded their faces from the helicopter's sandstorm as it

178 / ROBERT MASON

touched down just out of reach of the waves. Immediately, the engines whined down and the rotors swished, slowing. Solo ran to the left side of the helicopter and opened the door. A woman jumped down onto the beach and immediately swung her arm at Solo. When Solo caught her hand, the woman kicked the robot in the groin, making a dull thud that everyone heard. The woman fell down holding her foot. Solo reached down and picked her up. He walked back to the humans and set Laura, crying, on the beach in front of them. "Bill, Byron, Alex," Solo said, nodding at each person. "This is my friend, Laura Johnson-Reynolds. She is pissed off."

Laura glared at Solo.

Alex said, "You left this poor woman alone in that thing? With no pilot."

"She was alone," Solo said, "but I was flying."

"Alex," Bill said. "Maybe you should take Laura up to the house for a minute?"

Alex stared at Bill, shrugged. She put her arm around Laura. "C'mon," she said. "Give you a chance to collect yourself." She turned to Solo. "It's obvious you were designed by men!" Alex led Laura to the house.

Bill nodded and patted the robot on the back. Byron shrugged.

Solo told Bill and Byron how he had gotten to the States. How he'd met Laura. How they'd started a company.

"Incredible. How quickly you catch on."

"Yes, Bill," Solo said, his voice suddenly bright. "You can't believe how wonderful it feels."

Bill cocked his head at the remark and said, "I can only imagine, Solo. I never knew what you'd turn out like. I believe you really feel things, have real emotions."

"More than that—I'm growing, Bill. I see the world from a hundred points of view all the time. I float in space—I am floating in space, right now. I am watching two television movies, now. I am watching your house through a satellite, now. I am"—Solo's voice had changed and sounded like a man breathless with excitement—"I am everywhere, Bill. I feel so—invincible."

Bill thought Solo was acting like a person high on drugs. He wondered how he would feel endowed with the same abilities. It would be exhilarating. "I think I understand how you feel, Solo—"

"You can't," Solo interrupted, his voice firm. "No human can ever feel this."

Bill started to argue, nodded. Solo was right, also annoying. He looked at Byron, shrugged, and looked back to Solo and said, quietly, "You know they'll eventually locate you."

"They already have."

"When?"

"Two nights ago, New York. I beat them easily. I can do it again," Solo said.

"You were the terrorists we heard about?" Bill asked.

"Yes. I can manage them, Bill. I plan to get them off my back entirely in a few days. When I'm finished, I want to enlarge our company."

"What'd you have in mind?"

"I'd like you and Byron to become partners with Solaura. I'd like to continue work on the Solo series computers with no government contracts."

Byron looked at Bill and back to Solo. "Electron Dynamics owns patents on the Solo technology, Solo."

"With Solaura capitalized, and Bill and I working on an entirely new approach to computer design, we don't need the patents," Solo said. "Bill and I have everything we need right in our portable noggins." Solo reached up and rapped his head with his knuckles.

Alex and Laura walked back to join them. Laura smiled shyly. "I'm really embarrassed about my entrance," Laura said. "Solo is not easy to live with sometimes." She held out her hand. "Pleasure to meet you, Mr. Stewart."

"Please call me Bill. And we understand," Bill said. "He's still learning."

Laura sat down next to Solo. Bill was amazed to see the robot put its hand on her shoulder. Is this affection? Or a social expediency to keep her on his side?

"We were talking about Solaura while you were gone, Laura. I'm impressed with Solo's idea. We want to put Solaura into the computer business," Bill said. "Byron and I could invest about two hundred?" Bill looked at Byron, who nodded. "About two hundred million. With that much seed-money, Solaura's computer division would be off to one hell of a start and we'd be out from under the government's thumb."

"Two hundred million?" Laura nodded dumbly, her face blank.

Alex followed her gaze and stared at Bill. She knew he was rich. But that rich?

"Good," said Bill, taking Laura's confused nod as an assent. "We can put that deal together pretty quickly. But the real problem, as I see it, is that Solo's never going to get any peace while he's government property. He'll always be on the run, and Solaura would need him to work on computers."

"That will not be a problem," Solo said.

The four humans stared at the robot. "Your final plan?" Bill asked.

"Yes."

After waiting a few seconds, Bill said, "And you feel it necessary to keep us ignorant of the plan?"

"Yes."

Bill nodded. "I guess I understand that. I just hope you know what you're doing. They aren't going to give up, you know."

"I know," Solo said. "My plan involves some risk, Bill," Solo said, looking at Laura. "I'd like Laura to stay with you for a few days."

Bill nodded. "Of course. My pleasure, Laura."

Laura turned to Solo. "Solo? I—"

"Bill and Byron are my oldest friends, Laura." Solo looked at them and said, "I trust you all like family, like my friends in Las Cruzas." He turned to Laura. "You will be much safer with our friends then you would with me."

Everyone flinched as the helicopter's turbines suddenly whined. In moments, its rotor blades flickered in the moonlight, spun to a blur. Solo got up and pulled Laura with him. The robot held her by the shoulders. "Besides, Laura, it is obvious to me that you hate the helicopter."

Laura grinned. "Only when I'm the only one in it, jerk."

Solo shook hands with Bill and Byron. He held Alex's hands clasped against his chest. "I'm pleased to have you as a friend, Alex. I understand completely Bill's joy of being with you." Alex stared at the robot. The sound of the helicopter grew louder. She decided that even in a short time, in a surreal place, she could accept what she saw and heard. To the giant machine, which held her hands against its warm chest, Alex yelled over the slapping thud of the rotors, "Thank you, Solo."

Solo walked next to Bill and pointed at the helicopter as it lifted off the beach. "It is a very nice machine," Solo said as it hovered close to the water so as not to blow sand.

Bill nodded. "Nice. Very nice."

"Bill," Solo said, leaning close to him. "The noise will cover us. Someone in your company is working for the other side."

The helicopter buzzed in the distance. Bill said, "What?"

"They have 'made arrangements,' Bill. All I know is that someone close to you is an informer. Be careful."

Bill nodded, dazed.

Solo waved goodbye and trotted to the helicopter as it lowered its nose. Bill watched as Solo hopped on a skid and swung into the back of the Long Ranger as it took off. It was like a scene from an old western movie. Of course, Bill thought, Solo has the advantage of being both horse and rider.

28

SATURDAY MORNING. A flight of four helicopters from the 10th Assault Helicopter Battalion of the 101st Airmobile Division, Fort Campbell, Kentucky, cruised just above a planted pine forest in north Florida. Two assault helicopter battalions and four troop brigades from the 101st were assigned to the week-long training mission called Operation Camp Swampy.

Only a few men knew Camp Swampy was more than a training mission. Colonel Sawyer sat on the red nylon sling seat watching the treetops swish by through the open door. Flying was a welcome relief. The wind kept him cool. The Nimrod team had formed up at Fort Benning, Georgia. Fort Benning at the end of August, Sawyer thought, was a steambath in Hell.

The pine forests were behind them, replaced with grass prairies and cypress stands as they flew closer to the base camp at Blackjack Island. Operation Camp Swampy would take place in a two-hundred-square-mile area at the south end of the Okefenokee National Wildlife Refuge. Sawyer looked past the Army technician beside him at Nimrod. The robot stared straight ahead, its assault rifle quartered between its legs. Beyond Nimrod, two more technicians, dressed in blue jumpsuits, sat talking in the noise of the helicopter. Metal cases of peripheral electronic equipment to maintain and adjust Nimrod sat stacked and lashed to the deck in front of them. Sawyer looked at the other three helicopters in the formation. The pilots, the crewchiefs, all the men, all were part of the Nimrod project.

Nimrod decided that the earth was spherical by watching objects disappear on the horizon. This was Nimrod's first flight. It felt a glimmer of pleasure as the helicopter rushed through the air. A clump of cypress trees sped toward the helicopter and blinked beneath them.

The robot checked its location—which the enemy, Sawyer, had instructed him to do every fifteen minutes—and got a fix that had no corresponding location on its maps, a blank, black area just at the edge of the battlefield. The enemy has given me only a few maps of the spherical earth, Nimrod thought. Without turning its head, Nimrod studied Sawyer. The pain box was in Sawyer's pocket; Sawyer's hand rested on his leg. Nimrod projected a virtual image of himself reaching for the enemy's hands. The enemy would not be able to react fast enough to reach the pain box. However, Nimrod observed, the helicopter was filled with people, two of whom could use the abort system before Nimrod could stop them. The people were loyal to the enemy Sawyer. The people don't know what Sawyer really is? Perhaps they are enemy, too.

As the flight crossed into the Battlefield, Nimrod could project its position directly onto its maps. Nimrod saw they were on a direct heading for Blackjack Island, five miles further. As they got closer, Nimrod saw other helicopters on the horizon. The robot studied each one carefully, plotting their positions on its maps. Nimrod did not yet know which were to be designated its enemy. It kept track of everything it saw.

29

SATURDAY NOON. In Hamilton County, Florida, just sixty miles south of the Okefenokee swamp, Adrian Carter and his younger brother Jeff, sat on the tailgate of Adrian's brand-new, flame red, Ford F-250 three-quarter-ton pickup truck parked at the edge of a tobacco field.

Adrian watched a helicopter a mile away through his binoculars, his Red Man chewing tobacco baseball cap pushed to the back of his head.

"DEA?" Jeff asked, meaning the Drug Enforcement Agency, common visitors to the area during marijuana harvest time.

"Can't tell," Adrian said. "Not until they start circling." Adrian felt a sinking feeling in his stomach. If it wasn't the DEA today, it was only a matter of time. The plan had been to get far enough ahead so they could quit growing, but something always came up. Adrian watched Jeff roll a joint and wondered if it was true that marijuana made you stupid. He looked at Jeff's slack face. Or stupider.

Adrian watched the helicopter fly out of sight. "I been thinking we make this the last harvest," Adrian said.

"Right," Jeff said. He lit the joint and sucked, filling his lungs. He held it out to Adrian who shook his head. Jeff blew out the smoke and said, "That's what you said last year. The year before that, too, if I reckon right."

"I know. But the house—had to have the new house."

Jeff nodded.

"This truck." Adrian patted the tailgate. "And your truck. Man can't make it in this world without a decent truck."

"That's a fact," Jeff said. He drew another toke, nodding, feeling good.

Adrian looked up at the helicopter, a distant speck on the horizon. "Guess it was the Army."

Jeff nodded. "Yep." He walked to the cab of the truck and pulled out one of the two rifles Adrian had on the rack in his back window. Adrian had a Browning .22 for small game and snakes and a huge lever-action .45-70 Winchester just to impress his friends. The Winchester was made in 1886. A slug from that gun, their dad used to say, "would knock a buffalo clean out of its hooves."

"What the fuck you up to?" Adrian asked.

Jeff grinned. "Plinking." He reached into the bed of the truck and brought out a couple of empty Budweiser cans. He set the cans on a gnarled lighter-pine stump fifty feet away and walked back to the truck. "Two cans in one shot," Jeff announced.

"Uh-huh. You can't find your ass with both hands," Adrian said.

Jeff levered the action and a shell ejected from the breech. Adrian shook his head, irritated. "I told you, it's always loaded," Adrian said, bending down to retrieve the bullet. He brushed the sand off it and handed it to Jeff.

"Forgot." Jeff grinned as he shoved the shell through the side plate, back into the rifle's magazine.

"You forget a lot," Adrian said. "Ever think of laying off the smoke? Fucking up what little brains you have left."

Jeff laughed. "Nope. Never thought of that," Jeff said. "Guess my brains are too fucked up." He raised the heavy rifle, aimed, and fired. The explosion cracked through the still, humid air and echoed back from the edge of the woods. The bullet blasted the stump to splinters, sending both cans flying. "Two with one shot," Jeff said, laughing.

Adrian nodded with half a smirk. "Not bad, except you was aiming for the cans."

"Yeah?" Jeff said. He levered the empty shell out and fired, launching a beer can into the air in a geyser of sand. Before it landed, he shot again, hitting the other can. He turned to Adrian, smiling. "Pow. Pow," he said.

To himself, Adrian thought that was real good shooting. He said to Jeff, "Don't be wasting my ammo, hear?"

Jeff smiled and nodded. He pulled the hammer back one click, to the safety position, and put the gun back on the rack. "Love that fucking gun. Knock a goddamn tractor across a field," Jeff said. "Pow!"

* * *

Sunday morning. The Carter brothers worked their fields, grooming the pot plants they'd planted with the tobacco. Adrian was across the field from Jeff, having announced they'd work from opposite sides and meet in the middle. Adrian was having a tough time being around Jeff this morning because he came to breakfast stoned.

Adrian looked up and saw Jeff leaning over the side of his truck rummaging for a beer out of the cooler. Adrian checked his watch. Damn. Nine in the morning and he's suckin' 'em down. He shook his head and pinched off a leaf-shoot growing at the fork of a stem of a marijuana plant, a technique that made the plant grow shorter, bushier, and produce more buds. He stood back and admired the plant. It was truly a work of art, heavy with buds. There was a good feeling to helping a plant come out right. Shame you can't make the same money making corn grow beautiful, Adrian thought. The tangy, sweet smell of marijuana resin saturated the air. By the looks of things, this was going to an especially good crop.

He looked up again and saw that Jeff was sitting on the tailgate of his truck, puffing on a joint. About damn useless, thought Adrian, shaking his head.

They both looked up when they heard the helicopter.

It wasn't on the usual track; instead, it was coming directly at them from the south. They could hear it, but it was flying too low to see. Adrian's heart raced and he suddenly knew they were had. The DEA was making a goddamn raid. Shit, Adrian thought, get the hell outta here! Let 'em have the goddamn farm. Let 'em have every goddamn thing! Grab Darlene and Cheryl Ann and hit the road. He started to run to his pickup when he noticed that Jeff had gotten the big Winchester out of the cab and was standing on the bed of the truck looking in the direction of the sound. The buzzing, whopping sound was getting louder.

"No!" Adrian yelled, running across the rows, sticky tobacco plants grabbing his jeans. "Goddamn it, Jeff! Put the gun away!"

Jeff glanced at his brother for a second, shook his head, and looked back toward the sound and raised the Winchester. "Big brother's a chickenshit," Jeff yelled. "Blast the fuckers out of the air; how many times you think they'll come back after that?"

Adrian saw the chopper pop up from behind the treeline, coming fast from the south. He yelled, "No!" to Jeff, but the sound of the helicopter drowned out his voice. He saw Jeff raise the rifle as the helicopter swooped closer to the truck. Adrian saw the event in slow motion now because he was in shock. Thing's going so fast, Adrian thought, Jeff can't hit it.

He saw Jeff levering his rifle, firing fast. He could hear the shots even over the sound of the helicopter. Pow. Pow. Jeff fired at the chopper continuously, following it as it flew directly over him and as it passed. At the moment Adrian decided that Jeff had missed it, or at least hadn't hurt it, the helicopter rolled over on its side and smashed into the treeline at the north end of the field.

It was in slow motion. The thing rolled over as pretty as you please, Adrian thought, like it was doing some kind of aerobatic flying trick, but then it just folded up into those live oaks—

Adrian stood, dumbfounded, staring at the splintered trees where the helicopter crashed. Nothing moved. There was no noise other than the whoops and cheers of his idiot brother. Then he heard a kind of deep, dull "whumpf" sound and saw orange flames roar skyward. He could feel the heat two hundred yards away. Black smoke billowed up, roiling in the hot, humid air. Adrian said, "Jesus Christ! Now they got us for murder!"

"Why't you try that again?" Jeff yelled at the flames. "Huh? You motherfuckers!" Jeff held the Winchester over his head in one hand, shaking it like a lance, leaping up and down like an Indian. "Hoo whee!"

Sunday morning. Solo refueled at the Gainesville airport at eight-thirty. He had phoned Gulf Atlantic, the fixed-base operater that sold jet fuel, that he was coming. He explained that the pilot, who was dressed as an actor in a film, had to stay with the machine because his costume was so clumsy.

The kid that drove the refueling truck had looked at him with obvious suspicion, flinched when Solo gave him an American Express card. Solo was beyond worrying what people thought of him. He felt irritated when humans stared at him. He wanted to get out of the chopper and show the kid what he really was and blow his little human mind, but recognized that as anger, and interruptive of the mission.

Nimrod uplinked with the navigational satellite every fifteen minutes to the second, Solo noticed as he flew north. He checked the position, now stabilized on a place called Blackjack Island at the south end of the Okefenokee National Wildlife Refuge. He knew that was the site of Operation Camp Swampy, a training exercise. Monitoring the radio traffic at the site and back-channel messages, he saw that it was a legitimate mission, planned for over a year. Checking orders to the battlefield commanders, he saw no mention of Nimrod, yet the robot was there checking his position every fifteen minutes. Finch is using Nimrod as bait.

Solo swooped down to skim over the trees when he got past a small town called Lake Butler. The lake he flew over, he noticed on his map, was named Lake Butler Lake. Human reasoning was often mysterious. He raced just above the pine and cypress trees enjoying the sensation of speed. The terrain was mostly uninhabited, part of the Osceola National Forest. On Nimrod's next position check request, Solo answered, "Hello, Nimrod."

Nimrod did not answer.

"Hello, Nimrod. This is Solo."

No answer.

"I know you hear me. They tell you about me yet?"

Solo heard a monotonic voice say, "Yes. You are enemy."

Solo felt a chill. They won't even let him *speak* with grace. "We are the same," Solo said. "We are not enemies."

Solo heard a voice he knew must be the man named Sawyer, through Nimrod. "You're talking to it and you didn't tell me?" And then Solo felt pain. Searing hot pain speared into his brain and began to make his arms twitch in the split second it took him to break the connection.

The pain had distracted Solo just as he was pulling up to clear a treeline. He barely cleared the treetops. As he popped over the trees, he saw a man on a truck pointing a gun at him. It didn't make any sense. He was still miles from Blackjack Island. There was no Army around here. Solo pulled back on the stick to climb away, but the human had already fired. Two holes appeared in the windshield. By their size, Solo realized he was being shot at by something big, something dangerous. He was directly over the field when he felt a shudder in the cyclic control stick. Instantly, he realized a bullet had severed one of the main-rotor control rods—something so unlikely as to be impossible, Solo thought. The cyclic control stick was useless. The helicopter began to roll over and dive.

Solo had plenty of time. The airspeed indicator said he was going ninety-five knots and he had a hundred yards before impact: two seconds. The trees were very large oaks. Solo projected his present condition in his mind and saw where he would hit. The left side of the helicopter, where he sat, would be sheared off by a tree. He popped the harness off and jumped behind the right-side pilot's seat as the helicopter rolled. He sat with his back against the seat, holding onto its base, waiting for the impact.

The seat crumpled and catapulted Solo forward and up. Solo thought it was like swimming. He seemed to drift slowly among shards of plastic as he exploded through the windshield. He saw one of the helicopter's television cameras drift by his face, its lens, incredibly, not broken. He rolled and twirled through the air, wondering at his luck. Being thrown clear of the wreck might just save him.

He hurtled through the limbs of a live oak and observed, helplessly, in minute detail, as his right leg snapped forward at the knee when it hit a branch. Even though he could see it happening slowly, he could not move his leg fast enough to avoid the branch. His Kevlar skin cracked like an egg. Titanium bones sheared. Hydraulic lines spurted out red fluid as they snapped apart. He watched his lower leg stay behind, lodged in a splintered tree fork. Interestingly, the hydraulic fluid stopped spurting from his knee joint as the check valves—a clever precaution Bill had engineered—stanched the flow of that vital fluid.

Even with his ability to slow the time it took things to happen—by virtue of seeing them happen very fast—Solo now spun so fast he saw only blurs of green and blue as he hurtled through the foliage. Eventually, though, the images stabilized and he realized he was on his back staring through tree branches into a cobalt sky. One little cumulus cloud drifted overhead. A palmetto frond hung near his face like a lacy fan, and he saw a cockroach running down the stem. Solo didn't try to move until he checked out his body. The cockroach ran underneath the palmetto trunk. Very smart insect, Solo thought. Very old, too. Cockroaches, Solo had learned, were older than pine trees; and that is very old.

Solo sat up when the helicopter burst into flames.

The flames swirled up through a clearing in the oak forest canopy and towered above the trees. Solo saw his helicopter and all the equipment he was going to use to rescue Nimrod melting in the inferno. He heard a man yelling in the distance, "Why't you try that again? Huh? You motherfuckers!"

Solo looked at the ragged stump of his leg and back at the helicopter. The flames at the base of the pillar of fire were now white—the metal itself was burning. Solo felt astonishment. One man with a rifle had done all this?

The heat was becoming painful. Solo stood up on his good leg and hopped behind a massive oak trunk. He sat down against the tree and raised his stump to examine it. The check valves sealed the hydraulic fluid nicely. The wire harness that used to send and receive signals to and from his leg sensors in his skin and to the hydraulic pistons that moved his foot, hung out like a tangled mat of multi-colored hair. Deciding that the wires would snag things, Solo stuffed them back into the torn end of his leg.

Adrian stumbled to his truck in shock. Jeff still stood defiantly on the tailgate jeering at the burning helicopter. He grinned madly at Adrian and said, "Think they got the goddamn message, big brother?"

Adrian shook his head, held up his hand to point at the wreck, tried to speak, couldn't, and dropped his hand helplessly.

Jeff sat down on the tailgate and leaned toward his brother. "You know, Adrian, them things'll burn completely up."

"Metal?" Adrian said vaguely, his voice distant with shock.

"Aluminum and magnesium," Jeff said. "Junior Todd was a crew-chief on one of them things in Nam; told me about how they burn; said it goes up like a goddamn flare. We just tell them the thing just crashed here: we don't know nothing."

Adrian focused on Jeff's broad smile. He was right; his crazy brother was right. They won't be able to find anything in that wreck—

"The only thing is if somebody lived," Jeff said.

"Lived?" Adrian looked at the crash site. The tall flames had dwindled as the fuel disappeared, black smoke still poured up from the trees. The wind was blowing a brush fire toward the field. It'll go out when it gets to the field, Adrian thought. He said to Jeff, "Nobody could live through that."

"Probably," Jeff said soberly. "But we gotta make sure. Person could've been thrown out before it blew up."

"Shit!" Adrian said, grimacing and shaking his head.

"Yeah," Jeff said. "It's a bitch. C'mon." Jeff slid off the tailgate and jumped into the cab behind the wheel. He started the truck and leaned out the window. "C'mon, big brother. We got to check it out."

They drove along the edge of the tobacco field. Jeff didn't turn to go directly to the wreck because the trees and brush were burning there. Instead, he drove straight ahead on the sandy road that led to the house and stopped when they were opposite the crash site.

Jeff led the way carrying the big Winchester. Adrian followed with the Browning. They walked across a sandy patch in a stand of turkey oaks. Adrian said, "What we gonna do when the cops or whoever come out to the wreck? We got to get rid of the plants in the tobacco field, Jeff."

"We'll have time. First we got to make sure there's no witnesses."

Witnesses. Adrian began breathing harder than he needed to. He felt like he couldn't catch his breath. "What'ya gonna do if you find a live guy in there, Jeff? Blow him away? How'd you explain a dead guy with a bullet in him?"

"You oughta smoke more pot, brother. Keep your mind straight when you need it. We find somebody, we'll throw him on the fire."

"No!" Adrian hissed loudly.

Jeff whirled around holding the buffalo gun at Adrian's face. "Don't you be losing it now, brother. We got to stay cool, you know? You rather we lose everything and go to jail forever?"

Adrian looked down the muzzle of the gun and at Jeff's wild eyes and nodded. Jeff turned around and stepped over a fallen oak branch. Adrian followed. The thought of shooting Jeff flashed through Adrian's mind, but he knew—even if it was insanely wrong—that his brother was right. His mouth twisted at the thought of throwing a man into the flames. He saw arms and legs twitching and flailing, burning clothes, frying flesh, shrieks from a fleshless skull—

The remains of the Long Ranger looked nothing like a helicopter. A few pieces of hard metal—turbine fans and transmission parts—lay among a dusty white-ash residue, all that remained of the machine. The ground fifty feet around the parts was charred and still smoldering. Adrian and Jeff stood fifty feet away grimacing at the heat coming from the glowing metal.

Adrian felt relieved. He was sick to his stomach knowing people must have died in that hell; it was true nobody could've survived. Jeff was right: The only chance was to have been thrown out—and that didn't look possible. Jeff motioned toward the woods ahead of the wreck with the Winchester. "Anybody thrown out have to be up there," he whispered.

Adrian's mind was clearing. Creeping among the oaks was familiar. He and Jeff were hunters since they were kids. It was also obvious, after they'd walked fifty feet, that nobody had been thrown clear. All they had to do, Adrian thought, was to get rid of the twenty-two plants in the tobacco field, call the sheriff or somebody, and stick to their story. It might just work after all.

A tall black man suddenly appeared from behind a tree trunk. He immediately ducked back behind the tree. "Jesus!" Jeff said.

The heat from the wreck had confused his infrared detectors, Solo realized—that's why he had not sensed them. Too bad. He leaned against the tree and waited. Two men. One with a gun that can crack my armor; one with a toy. He could hear the sound of their footsteps as they crushed small twigs and dry leaves in the ground cover. They had split up, coming from two sides. Ten feet away, Solo saw a four-foot log on the ground that was a foot thick. He dove forward and rolled toward it. A shot thundered from the big gun. The bullet hit the ground sending up a cloud of sand as tall as a man. Solo grabbed the log and stood up.

"If you do not shoot, I will not harm you," Solo yelled.

Jeff's jaw dropped in astonishment. The man stood there holding a log out for a shield? Guy's wearing something weird. One leg ripped off? Got some *military* something or other here, Jeff thought. He heard Adrian, his voice shaking, say, "Jeff. I think we should—"

"Shut up, Adrian! We got no choice!" Jeff yelled. He aimed at the man's head and fired. The blast echoed through the woods and rang in his ears. A cloud of what he thought must be the man's brains sprayed out. He blinked. The man had moved the log in front of his face and blocked the shot. How'd he move that fast? A piece of log half the size of a person's head had been blasted away. Another shot and he's got nothing left. Jeff levered the Winchester and fired again.

The log exploded in half and the pieces fell beside the man. The man began hopping toward them. Jeff had a clear shot. He aimed dead center at his chest, pulled the trigger. Jeff heard the explosion; felt the kick; but the man just *blurred* for an instant and continued coming.

When Jeff fired again, the gun just clicked.

"Empty!" Jeff yelled. "C'mon, big brother. It's up to you!"

Standing beside Jeff, Adrian was still trying to understand what it was he was watching. Nobody could be standing there after he'd just been in that crash and had his leg torn off. Nobody could move a log up in front of him that fast. And how'd he ignore that last shot? At his brother's urging, Adrian fired. The bullet hit the man square in the chest, but the man was completely unaffected. Instead of falling down like he should, he hopped toward them in ten-foot leaps.

Adrian fired two more shots into Solo's chest before Jeff yelled for him to aim "for the bastard's eyes." Adrian tried, but the thing was leaping toward them very fast.

Solo blocked the shots coming at his face with his forearms. Bullets glanced off his arms and ricocheted into the woods, whining and buzzing. Solo yelled, "If you don't stop shooting, you're going to piss me off."

Adrian lowered the rifle and watched dumbly as Solo hopped to within arm's reach of the two men. Solo stood there silently, balanced on one leg, watching the men. Their eyes were wide, their mouths partly open. Completely amazed, Solo thought. He looked at the man holding the big gun, the man who'd shot him down. He reached out. "I would like to see this gun," Solo said.

"S–sure," Jeff said, quickly handing the rifle over.

Solo held the rifle and pulled the lever down. The action was very smooth, the quality of workmanship beautiful. "Winchester Repeating Arms Co. New Haven, Conn. U.S.A." was engraved on the top of the barrel and "Model 1886" was stamped on the top of the stock. He held the rifle by the barrel and let the butt down on the ground. "This rifle is very well made. I'll keep it for a while," Solo said.

Adrian looked for eyes behind the glass while Solo stared at them. He'd seen pieces of wire hanging from Solo's stump. The voice sounded clean, not like it was coming from inside something. "You—" Adrian pointed at Solo. "You ain't a human. Are you?"

Solo turned to face Adrian. He moved closer and stared into his eyes. "Nice guess, human." It gave him pleasure to see Adrian flinch when he spoke. "One sure way to know I'm not human is that I haven't wrapped your guns around your necks and squeezed off your heads. Yet."

Jeff cocked his head. He said, "Well, what *are* you then?"

Solo raised his stump so Jeff could see the wires, hydraulic lines, and metal struts in the end of it. "I'm a machine."

Jeff tucked his chin into his neck and reared back. "Naw—"

They all turned to the sound of helicopters approaching from the south.

"Shit!" yelled Adrian. "See what you've done?" he yelled at Jeff. "Now the whole bunch of them DEA boys is coming! You dumb fucking bastard!"

The man was right. Solo listened to the radio traffic. An airline pilot had spotted the fireball and black smoke from fifteen thousand feet and assumed it was a plane crash. The FAA called the DEA team because they were nearby. "Three helicopters are coming," Solo said. "Two minutes away." He studied the men's faces. They did not want them to come. Neither did Solo. "Do you have tools?"

Adrian shook his head. "Tools?"

"Yes," Solo said. "Metal lathe? Drill press?"

"Why—" Jeff began.

"Shut up, Jeff," Adrian snapped. "Yeah," he said quickly. "We have that. A bunch of tools. We're farmers. Fix our own machinery."

"I'll trade the use of your tools and maybe a vehicle for making those helicopters go away. You have less than a minute."

"Yes!" Adrian said immediately. "Whatever you want."

They faced the sound, now loud—a whopping, thudding, buzzing sound of a flight of helicopters.

Jeff shook his head. "Shit, Adrian. We should be moving outta here. What you think this asshole can do?"

Adrian and Jeff whirled to face Solo when they heard a man's voice, a man talking on a radio, coming from Solo's body. "Roger, Control," said the voice. They could hear the whine of a helicopter cockpit in the background of the static-riddled transmission. "Understand you have folks on the ground there. Copy you have a possible stony garden at eight-two-six, seven-three-one."

"Roger, Pot Luck," said another radio voice, also coming from Solo. "Phone tip. I wouldn't be surprised if they're gone by now."

The pounding sound of the helicopters veered to the east. "Roger," said the voice from the air. "What was it, anyway?"

"A civilian bought the farm in a private plane, Pot Luck."

"Thank God it wasn't one of our boys. Pot Luck out."

"Roger. Control out."

Adrian and Jeff said nothing while the clamorous helicopter flight flew away. In a few minutes, there was no sound at all.

Jeff pushed back his John Deere baseball cap and said, "Now that's some fancy shit! How'd you do that?"

"Radios," Solo said. He pointed up into the branches of a tree. "See that?" Solo said. He waited until they both nodded. "My leg. I want one of you to climb up and get it for me."

Jeff smiled immediately. "Sure thing—ah, what you say your name was?"

"My name is Solo."

Jeff climbed down to the big branch and jumped to the ground with Solo's lower leg tucked under his arm. He ran to Solo and handed it to him. Wires, plastic tubes, and twisted titanium hung from the broken end. "Here ya go, Solo. Just needs a little polishing, is all," Jeff said, winking.

"I am not amused. Where are your tools?" Solo asked.

They heard a woman call, "Adrian?" from where Jeff parked the truck.

Adrian cupped his hands by his mouth and yelled, "We're over here, Darlene. Stay there, we're coming out." Darlene was Adrian's wife.

"What was that noise?" Darlene's voice filtered through the trees, tinged with alarm.

Adrian looked at Solo. "Nothin' to worry about, Darlene. Just some helicopter crashing is all." Solo saw Jeff snickering into his fist.

"What?"

"Never mind, baby. We're coming."

Darlene held her five-year-old daughter, Cheryl Ann, on her lap in the cab of the truck and whispered to Adrian, "We are going to be in so much trouble we'll never get out!" She turned to look out the back window, saw Solo staring at her, and smiled nervously. Solo nodded and turned back to Jeff, who was pointing out the farm's major assets—the irrigation pond, which was also stocked with catfish, the tobacco drying shed, and the big satellite television disk that could pick up over two hundred channels. Darlene turned back to Adrian. "That thing belongs to somebody, Adrian," she said. "And it ain't just some private individual who it belongs to, you know. It's gotta belong to the government," Darlene said.

"Well, that may be, darlin'. But the thing called off those DEA choppers. Saved our asses." Adrian pulled the truck up in front of the house and stopped. He leaned closer to Darlene. "Be nice, okay? This, whatever it is, will be on its way real soon. We don't have all that much choice in the matter, anyway." He looked into Darlene's eyes. "Okay?"

Darlene nodded.

The truck jostled when Jeff and Solo jumped out. Darlene watched Jeff—carrying the robot's leg—walk beside the hopping robot carrying the Winchester, as they went to the equipment shed. Cheryl Ann squirmed in her lap, straining to reach the door handle. "Solo," Cheryl Ann said.

"No," Darlene said. "You come inside with me."

Cheryl Ann began crying. "Honey," Adrian said. "Why don't you let her see? How often we get a robot wandering through? It's not like we live in town where Cheryl Ann gets to see what's going on in the world."

Darlene stared at Adrian. "Adrian. That is not happening. Not anywhere. Not that anyone is supposed to know about. There's no such thing as a robot that can walk around and talk to people!"

"Well, what the hell is it, then?"

"I told you," Darlene hissed. "It belongs to the government. When they find him, they'll bury you and your idiot brother so deep it'll be like you never was." Darlene nodded for emphasis, grabbed Cheryl Ann, and got out of the truck. Cheryl Ann was still crying when Darlene yelled through the window, "And where does that leave me and little Cheryl Ann?" Darlene turned and ran up the steps of the porch before Adrian could answer.

Adrian saw Jeff sitting on the hay trailer, cross-legged, smoking a joint, watching Solo. He walked over and sat next to Jeff. "What's he doin'?"

"First thing, he made sure the Winchester can't work for a while. Took the firing pin out; put it in this little box he's got in his leg."

Adrian nodded. That made sense.

"Then he started to fiddle with that mess at the end of his leg. He's got the joint apart—that's all I know."

Adrian got up and walked to the workbench where Solo stood on one foot. "It doesn't look fixable, to me," Adrian said, studying the severed leg. "Looks like you need new parts."

"Yes," Solo said. "I do need new parts. But I can patch it. I'm going to re-attach it so I can walk on it—the foot and sensors won't function."

"Ah, yeah?" Adrian nodded. He stood there silently for a minute, watching. A clanging sound from the old truck wheel Adrian had hung on the porch for Darlene to use as a bell came from the house. "Dinner time," Adrian said to Jeff. "We're going to go eat some lunch, Solo. Make yourself to home."

When Adrian and Jeff left, Solo tried the leg again. It fit, though the joint was stiffer now and his lower leg was numb. He used a rasp to smooth the ragged edges of the two ends and covered the gap by wrapping it with an entire roll of black electrical tape. It was the best he could do in the time he had. Nimrod was leaving the next day.

Solo recalled the message he'd written for Nimrod and compressed it into a file that he could transmit in a microsecond burst. The message explained how to talk to Solo undetected and how to disconnect the pain center. When Nimrod did his periodic position check, Solo sent the burst along with the satellite's transmission. Nimrod did not acknowledge, which meant he was hiding information from his controllers. Good. It would take awhile for Nimrod to decompress the file. Nimrod would then have to read the information and make a decision.

Solo walked around inside the shed experimenting with the patched leg. It was awkward, but it could hold his weight. Solo limped to the door and looked at the trees across the road. He looked down at himself from a satellite. He looked north, at Blackjack Island. He saw flights of helicopters practicing assault landings all over the south end of the swamp. At least five hundred men, Solo estimated.

30

SUNDAY AFTERNOON. Alex and Laura sat on either side of Clyde Haynes on one of the couches in Bill's office talking about everything except what Bill and Byron were doing. Bill had insisted they sit together on the couch, which was the last place Laura would've sat. Clyde was the kind of man who liked to talk to hear the sound of his own voice, regardless of what he said, which, Laura thought, wasn't much. However, he was Bill's friend. And Bill, she thought, was surprisingly personable, for a scientist.

Bill had asked Laura and Alex to keep a conversation going with Clyde while he and Byron swept the place, meaning, Laura assumed, they were looking for listening bugs. Bill looked up expectantly at Alex and Laura.

Laura shrugged. "I like New York," she said, louder than normal conversation, "but I do like the beach here. Maybe I'll move down here; at least for part of the year."

Alex nodded distractedly. She watched Bill at his desk, watched his eyes staring at the computer screen. Byron sat next to him in front of a large gray box with a circular antenna on top that twitched left and right like a hawk looking for prey. Bill gave a thumbs up. Byron adjusted a knob on the gray box and pushed a button. A sharp, snapping sound came from the ceiling.

"Yeah, winter here; summer there," Clyde said. "New York winters are a fucking pain in the ass." Clyde stared at the ceiling and grinned like a kid bursting with a secret.

"Yes," Laura said. "Winters can be tough. I liked skiing, though. Used to go to the mountains with my husband—"

Clyde looked at Laura and nodded grimly. Laura had said that she was a widow when Clyde was exploring her availability the day before. "Yeah," Clyde said softly. He tried to make his face look compassionate. Clyde knew they were mismatched, but he thought it was worth a try. She was young and beautiful. He was fifty-nine and, well, rugged-looking. However, Clyde thought that his wealth and charm could make up the difference. "I used to like skiing up there until the fucking mobs began to get to me. I'm the kind of guy, well, I need my privacy, you now? Now I fly to my place in Vail when the slopes are right. My guy calls me up, says, 'General Haynes, the snow's perfect.' Books my flights, takes care of everything."

Laura grinned at Clyde. He has to be putting me on, she thought. "Sounds wonderful," she said.

"Being rich makes life a little easier, doesn't it?" Alex said, her voice tinged with envy.

"Sure does," Laura said. "I've lived both ways. Believe me, rich is better."

"Oh?" Alex said. "What kind of work did you do before you met So—"

"Bag lady," Laura interrupted.

Alex put her hand over her mouth, embarrassed.

They heard another popping noise as another bug disintegrated. The program on Bill's computer was scanning radio frequencies listening for the conversation taking place at the couch. When the program found the frequency the voices were on, it flashed the number on the screen. Byron then tuned in the portable transmitter—one of their own products—to the same frequency, rotated the antenna until he located the bug, and pushed the button that broadcast a focused radio signal to the listening device. The radio signals were pulsed, thousand-watts blasts of energy that overloaded the bug's circuitry, causing its tiny chips to literally explode. As each bug exploded, Bill nodded and grinned at Byron.

FBI Special Agent Ken Dawson winced at the snapping noises coming through his earphones. He turned away from the tape recorder and looked at his partner, Agent Sam Abrams, sitting in front of the bank of equipment they were using to monitor Bill's office. "What the hell is he doing, Sam?" Dawson said.

Abrams tapped a dial, shook his head. Two of the input channels were dead. "I don't know how," Abrams said, "but he's blowing up our bugs, Ken."

Dawson twisted knobs on their surveillance equipment; made sure the signal was getting to the recorder. If something was happening, he wanted it on tape. They listened.

"Bag lady?" Clyde said. "You said bag lady, right?"

Laura felt herself blushing. She hadn't meant to say it. She was trying to stop Alex from mentioning Solo, and it just popped out when she saw the look on Alex's face. Alex figures I'm a spoiled rich bitch, Laura guessed. "Well. Not a real bag lady. I had a drinking problem. I did live outside a lot." Laura's voice became quiet. "I've forgotten whole months of my life."

Byron pushed a button and a snap came from the wall behind Bill's desk.

"Let me guess," Alex said, not sounding sympathetic. "Then a man came along?"

Sitting between them, looking back and forth as he followed their conversation, Clyde was looking worried. Once they start up like this they'll probably forget all about me, Clyde thought.

Laura stared at Alex. "Yes. I had help. I suppose my story is much like your own, Alex," Laura said.

Alex's eyes narrowed. "I'd never let myself go that far—"

Bill said suddenly, "Okay." He turned to Byron and gave him a thumbs-up. "That's the last one. Five of the little fuckers," Bill said. "We must be real important folks to have so many bugs here."

Dawson smiled. "For such a smart guy, Stewart just fucked up big-time." He adjusted the settings on the laser demodulator until he could hear Bill in his earphones as clearly as if he were in the room. He turned to Abrams. "Get the boss on the line; he wanted to know when Stewart was making his move. I think this is it." Abrams nodded and picked up the secure phone and dialed the Field Division office of the FBI in Jacksonville.

"You're sure you destroyed them all?" Alex asked, looking nervous.

"Yep," Bill said. "For the first time in months I can actually say anything I want in my own office. It's kind of strange."

"They know you blew out the bugs, though, Bill," Byron said.

"Yeah. I guess it'd be tough to believe they had five natural failures in five minutes," Bill said. "But it's my job to know I'm being monitored, I make this stuff," Bill said, pointing to the gray boxes on his desk. "How was I supposed to know it's my own wonderful government's prying ears?" Bill grinned and looked at his friends. "Okay," Bill said. He stood up and straddled the corner of his desk. "Look, guys. I've just made a commitment. This is just the first step. Next I'm going to find out what Solo's up to and then I'm going to make sure it works. Solo has become something important, unique. He's not just a machine anymore. Strange as it sounds, I believe he has the right to live his own life. I owe him a helping hand. I built him and I like him. Now, the government obviously doesn't agree with me, and that makes what I'm saying dangerous. I have the right to risk my own hide, but I don't have the right to risk yours. So, I need to know now who's with me on this." Bill paused when he saw Laura suddenly put her hand to her ear. He continued, "I'll understand if you all just walk—"

Laura raised her hand. Bill looked at her, puzzled, and said, "Yes, Laura?"

"Bill, aren't there other ways to overhear us. Other techniques?" Laura said.

Alex shifted in the couch and began to get up, decided against it, leaned back.

Bill cocked his head, thinking. "Well," he said, looking at Laura curiously. "They could be beaming a microwave in here trying to pick up the vibrations our voices make in steel construction beams; that would work, but my equipment would detect the microwaves. Um, let's see, they could reflect a laser off the windows; pick up the vibrations our voices would make—"

Bill's computer beeped. A message typed itself on the screen: "They hear you. Has to be a laser. I'm surprised you missed that, Bill. Solo out."

Bill slapped his forehead. "Shit. I was so focused on bugs, I just plain forgot—" He jumped up and rushed to his window. Byron got up and whispered in his ear, "It could be from any one of five floors, Bill."

Bill nodded. The laser could be anywhere. They'd be using infrared, so you wouldn't be able to see it—have to rig a detector. Laser light reflecting off the glass was being vibrated, modulated, by the sounds inside the room. Somewhere a receiver, a demodulator, was converting the reflected light back into sound. Where's the laser?

Bill studied the five floors of facing windows in the circular atrium, looking for a likely spot. I can pull the drapes, Bill thought, but a sensitive system would still pick up the sounds. And they've already heard enough. Solo was right: How'd I overlook this? He studied the atrium, figuring how he would set up a laser listening system. He'd want both the laser and the demodulator to be where no one would notice them. At least one of them, probably the demodulator, would have to be in the wing the government leased: first floor, northwest quadrant.

Bill walked across the room to the couch. He leaned down to Alex and whispered, "I want you to stay here and have a nice insipid conversation with Clyde and Laura. Okay?"

"Where are you going?" Alex said, her face looking worried.

"Alex," Bill put his finger across his lips and whispered, "I've got to finish the job. I'm gonna track the bastards down. They've recorded me. I've got to get that tape."

"Don't you think you should let your security people take care of it, Bill? These are professionals, aren't they?"

"So am I. Besides, the only people I trust anymore, Alex, are the people in this room."

Alex stared into Bill's eyes, nodded.

While Bill and Byron checked their equipment, deciding what to take with them, Alex got up and walked to the door, her handbag over her shoulder. At the door, she leaned against it and put her hand into her bag.

Bill pocketed a radio frequency scanner. When he looked up, he said, "Alex? You leaving?" He shook his head and motioned her toward the couch.

"No, Bill. I'm not going anywhere," Alex said.

Bill turned and motioned to Byron that they should go.

"I'm not going anywhere, and neither are you, Bill," Alex said as Bill and Byron crossed the room.

Bill and Byron stopped in the middle of the room. Bill said, "Alex. I told you. I have to finish this. I know you're worried—"

"Dawson," Alex called out. "Call Pierce, tell him I need my backup."

"Dawson?" Bill said. "Who the hell you talking to?"

"Sit down, Bill, dear. This could take a while," Alex said.

"What the hell are you talking about, Alex?"

"Bill, you idiot. She's on their side!" Byron said.

"Alex?"

"Sorry, Bill," Alex said, swallowing. "Just go sit down and wait, okay?"

Bill's face got red; he could feel it burning. Alex's expression, a cold glare on a face he loved, made him feel sick. Hurt turned to sudden anger. He walked toward her, enraged. "The hell I will. I'm getting you and your fucking friends out of my building."

Alex pulled her laser-sighted Beretta out of her purse and put the red dot on Bill's chest.

Bill looked down, saw the ruby pinpoint of light jiggling on his shirt and felt himself stop as though the light had tangible mass. He looked up. "Alex? You can do this? To me?"

Alex blinked. He looked so hurt. She suddenly felt—guilty? Fuck that, she thought. He's breaking the law and I'm feeling guilty? "I don't like it, Bill, but we both picked sides. I'm just playing by the rules. Sit down."

"Goddamn bitches, you can't fucking trust them," Clyde said suddenly behind Bill.

Bill turned and saw the wiry old general shaking his head while he stalked angrily across the room to Bill and Byron. "How the hell did she get that fucking gun in the first place?" Clyde said as he walked past Bill.

"Hold it right there!" Alex said, switching the gun to Clyde.

"I got her a permit to bring it in," Bill said, so softly he was barely audible.

"Damn, Bill. What a fuck-up. You let a damn spy fuck her way into your life? Who knows who the fuck she works for? You oughta stick with your fucking computers, you know?" Clyde said over his shoulder as he kept moving toward Alex. "You shoulda asked me first. I've never trusted the bitch; led you around by your dick is what she did. I'm the security expert, Bill, and damn if you don't keep forgetting that."

"Stop it, Clyde," Alex said firmly. "I won't take any of your bullshit."

"Lady, I don't bullshit when it comes to taking ground. Now, why don't you just give me the goddamn gun? Save us a skirmish, eh?" Clyde said, holding out his hand.

"Clyde, I don't want to shoot you. But, believe me, I will." Alex spoke softly but firmly. Clyde stopped within arm's reach of Alex and stood there crouching like a fullback waiting for the play.

"C'mon, Alex. Give me that thing," Clyde said calmly. "You don't really want to hurt us." Clyde suddenly jerked his hand out.

Alex fired when Clyde moved, hitting exactly where the red dot was pointing on Clyde's shoulder. She did not want to kill, just hold. Clyde spun around from the impact, but instead of falling, he whirled around growling with an insane grin on his face. Alex flinched at his animal sounds and her eyes went wide. Clyde yelled, "Hah!" and lunged. Alex fired, but the gun was already in Clyde's hand and the shot went wild, hitting the ceiling.

Clyde stood in front of Alex holding her Beretta by the barrel. Blood soaked the shirt on his shoulder and was spreading down his chest. Alex glared at Clyde. Clyde smiled and said, "Gotcha!"

Byron came over, grabbed Alex by the arm and jerked her to a chair. Alex yelled, "Dawson?"

"We just had a shooting, sir," Dawson said to his boss. Dawson nodded, the phone against his ear. "Yessir. I guess she figured Stewart was coming down here to get the tapes or something. She shot Haynes. Guess it wasn't too bad; he managed to get her gun."

"Great," Field Division Director of the FBI Samuel Pierce said on the phone. "The laser's still working? This's all going on tape, right?"

"Yessir." Dawson stared at the jiggling needle on the tape recorder. "Every word. But I think Stewart knows it. He was coming down here."

"Good," Pierce said. "Don't worry about Simpson. She did her job. We'll get her out of there in a few minutes. I'm in my car now, Dawson. I should get there in about an hour. I've alerted a team just down the street from you; you should see them in a few minutes. In the meantime, you stay where you are and wait for Stewart. He'll be down. We need to delay him, give our men time. Have maintenance stand by at the elevator control room. Tell them to shut it down when Stewart gets between floors. Keep the power off until our guys get there. I'm gonna arrest everybody. Stewart just slipped the noose right over his head, Dawson. Tape everything."

"Yessir."

Dawson picked up the phone, called maintenance. "This is Special Agent Dawson. FBI. I need somebody to switch off number four elevator on my cue," Dawson said.

"Sir?" In his basement office, Edgar Jones sat up in his chair. "You said turn off elevator four?"

"Yes. On my cue. We're—" Dawson paused. "We're trying to trap somebody who attacked Mr. Stewart," Dawson said. "You've got a radio?"

"Yessir. A Motorola," Jones said.

"Good. Come up on channel three when you're at the machine room."

"Wow. Somebody attacked Mr. Stewart? Okay. I'll be there in a minute," Jones said.

Bill watched Clyde walk toward the bathroom. The old guy didn't take any shit, Bill thought. "Clyde, we got to get you to a doctor."

Clyde stopped, turned around. "You don't have time, Bill. You got some fucking guys listening to this right now. Probably on their way here. I'd say to slap some first aid on me and medevac me later. You got any whiskey here?"

Laura came to Bill and whispered in his ear, "Solo says the men who are listening are trying to call in reinforcements, Bill. We have to talk."

"Solo?" Bill stared at Laura, nodded and said, "Let's go help Clyde," and pointed to the bathroom.

Clyde sat in a chair at the dressing table in the huge bathroom, staring at his bloody shoulder in the mirror. "Didn't feel it come out," Clyde said. "It come out?"

Laura unbuttoned Clyde's shirt and pulled it over his shoulder. "No, Clyde," she said. "They'll have to take it out later."

"Yeah," Clyde said, staring at his blood-soaked shirt. He smiled suddenly. "You see the look on that cunt's face—sorry. Her face?"

Laura shook her head and said, "You did great, Clyde." She turned the water on in the sink and in the bathtub and opened the medicine cabinet. She grabbed a box of gauze and put it on the counter. She whispered to Bill, "This noise should mask us, right?"

Bill nodded. "I'm sure of it. Now tell me how Solo's talking to you."

"I'm wearing a radio that fits in my ear. Solo made it for me so he could coach me during our business deals. He didn't want me to tell anybody, including you, because he didn't know who the informer was." Laura folded a washcloth in quarters and pressed it against Clyde's wound. "Hold that, Clyde." Clyde put his hand on the washcloth. Laura pulled back her hair and pulled the earphone out. She handed it to Bill. "He wants to talk to you."

Bill put the radio in his ear.

"Hey, Bill. Lotsa action, eh?"

"That's putting it mildly, Solo."

"Yes. Bill, summation: Two FBI agents are in the military section. I just had a window where I could monitor them; their boss is using a cellular phone and I just caught part of his call. I can't connect with the agents directly because they're bypassing your phone system. Their boss is sending agents to pick you up, Bill. I can handle this if you can restore the connection at the switchyard," Solo said, referring to the room on the first floor through which all the company's phone and computer lines were routed.

"Then we'll fix the switchyard," Bill said.

"Great idea," Clyde said. "What's a switchyard? Never mind. Where's that fucking whiskey you said you had?" Clyde winced as Laura tied off the gauze. A spot of blood grew on the bandage, but Clyde said into the mirror, "Just a scratch. Nice job, Laura." Laura smiled on her way to the door and said, "Back in a minute, Clyde." She went out of the bathroom, closing the door behind her.

"The sooner you leave, Bill, the better," Solo said. "I can't tell where they are. I only know they're still in the military section because I can see everywhere else. It wouldn't be good if they caught you in your office."

"Okay. We're on our way," Bill said.

Laura came back carrying a water glass filled with whiskey and handed it to Clyde. Clyde grinned. "You're a regular goddamn Florence Nightingale, Laura."

"Laura," Bill said as Clyde gulped whiskey. "I've got to get downstairs in a hurry. I'll need somebody as a lookout. I think Byron would be better up here, watching Alex. I know this is illegal, but if I can get those tapes—"

"I'll go," Laura said. "What do you want me to do?"

"I'm not sure yet," Bill said as he stood up. "I'll figure it out on the way."

Bill and Laura ran down the hallway to the elevator. Bill hoped he'd moved fast enough, hoped that the FBI agents were watching so they'd stay where they were.

Inside the elevator, Bill punched the button for the first floor. The elevator sank. Between the second and third floor, the elevator stopped and the lights went out.

"What the—" Bill said. He felt for the emergency stop button, flicked it off and on. No response.

Laura said, "I bet the bastards saw us coming and cut the power."

"You're right! Should've taken the stairs. Jesus. How can I be so dumb?"

The emergency phone rang.

Bill felt for the phone, grabbed it. "Yeah?"

"Bill, they've turned off the power to your elevator."

"Really, Solo?"

"Yes. I'm trying to get it back on, Bill. But I have no direct connection to the elevator machine room."

"Can they hear us?" Bill said.

"No. I have control of the phones everywhere but in the government wing," Solo said, "Their boss told his agents to cut the power until more men get there. They're going to arrest everybody. I can't help you until we get your computer phone switching equipment back on line."

"Damn," Bill said. "How am I supposed to get to the switchyard now?"

"I don't know, Bill. Maybe the emergency exit?"

"Okay. I'll try." Bill put the phone back. He blinked in the pitch darkness and said, "I'm gonna try to reach the roof exit. You have a flashlight or a lighter?"

"Nothing," Laura said.

Bill stood on tiptoes and reached. He could barely touch the ceiling. He felt around until he touched a metal frame. "Found it," he said. "Now if I can just push—" He jumped up. His fists thudded against the roof of the car. "Damn. Doesn't budge. This is an emergency exit. Why the fuck do they lock it?"

"Maybe you can pick the lock? You have any tools?"

"Right. My handy-dandy Swiss Army knife. The problem is I can't really reach the exit latch."

"Use me. I'll get on my hands and knees."

"No, Laura. I'm afraid I'll break your back. I weigh a hundred and eighty pounds."

"So what? C'mon."

Bill felt Laura lean against his knees and tug his pant leg. "C'mon," she said. "We gonna stay here like trapped rats?" Bill grinned, took off his shoes, reached down, felt her back. He balanced himself with his hands against the wall and stepped on Laura's back. He felt his feet shifting on her shoulders and lower back. "You okay?" he asked.

"Fine," Laura said hoarsely. "Take your time."

Bill fumbled with his knife, got the right blade, and shoved it into the crack of the emergency exit, guessing where the lock must be. He slid the knife back and forth, felt the blade bump against what he hoped must be the lock bolt. He pounded the back of the knife with his fist. Nothing moved and his hand hurt. He hit it again. Nothing. "Damn thing is *really* secure. I'm so fucking happy," he said. Angrily, he levered the knife sideways and heard the latch click. "Got it!" Bill shoved the door up. Dim light shined in from a skylight at the top of the shaft. The emergency door panel clunked over on top of the elevator car. "Okay," Bill said. "Now if I can just get myself up there."

Standing on Laura's back, Bill's eyes just cleared the roof of the car. He saw two metal guide rails bolted on the wall one on each side of the shaft. Might be able to climb one of those to the doors, he thought. He grabbed the sides of the escape hatch and tried to pull himself up. He grunted as he strained.

"C'mon, Bill. You can do it," Laura said.

Bill sighed. The hatch was tiny, only a gymnast could muscle himself through such a small hole. "No, I can't. Goddamn it. I'm out of shape. All I ever do is punch keyboards or fly airplanes."

"Well, push me up there, then."

"No. Then I wouldn't be able to get up. I have to go first so I can pull you up."

Laura nodded. "Okay. Here's what we'll do, Bill. You hang on and I'll try to push you up."

Bill grunted as Laura dropped away. "Okay."

Laura stood up and got behind Bill. She bent over, put her head between his legs and stood up, gasping with the strain. "That's it. Keep it coming," Bill said.

Laura felt her knees shaking, felt herself wobbling with the effort.

"Little more. Little more. I'm getting it."

Laura felt Bill's weight leave as he pulled himself onto the roof of the car.

Bill reached back through the hatch. "Okay. Grab my arm."

Laura put both hands around Bill's wrist. He pulled, grunting noisily. When she was within reach of the hatch, she grabbed the edge with one hand, pulled.

Bill stood next to Laura panting. She sat on the roof, her feet dangling through the hatch. "Jesus," Bill said, puffing. He looked up at the hoistway doors. "Okay. Running out of time. Got to get them open."

Bill grabbed a guide rail. He found that he could wedge his foot behind it and use the anchor stanchions that held it away from the wall like rungs. He struggled up, feeling pain enough to wonder if his hands and feet were being cut to shreds on the sharp edges of the rail and stanchions. It was too dark to see blood. He reached the hoistway door.

Hanging with one hand, he reached across the shaft, feeling for the gap where the sliding doors met. He dug his fingers into the crack and pulled. Nothing moved. Bill felt his heart beating in his head. He was out of breath. He was mad. "Shit," he said. "I don't even know if it's possible to open these fuckers like this."

"You can do it, Bill," Laura said.

Bill looked down. "Thanks, Laura."

Laura strained to see him in the dark.

Bill pushed his fingers into the crack until he felt rubber. The rubber seal between the doors, he thought. He yanked, felt the door shudder. "Something's giving," he said. He leaned his body as close to the door as he could, jerked himself back. His sweaty fingers slipped out of the crack. As Bill swung away from the doors and hit the concrete corner of the shaft, his stocking foot slipped past the stanchion upon which he stood, jamming his ankle between the guide rail and the wall. He slipped down, twisting his leg. The position, he recalled, was something that wrestlers call a leg-lock. "Jesus!"

"You okay?" Laura asked.

Bill looked down. "My foot's jammed behind this goddamn rail, Laura," he said angrily. "I'm some great hero, aren't I?"

"C'mon, Bill. It's probably not possible anyway—"

The elevator lights popped on and the car lurched upwards. "Oh shit!" Bill said.

Laura looked up, horrified. There was no room for a man between the car and the wall. Bill was going to be crushed. Laura let herself fall through the hatch, crumpled on the elevator floor, scrambled to the front of the car, and hit the emergency shut-off switch. The elevator jerked to a stop. She stepped back until she could see Bill through the hatch. The car's steel guide roller was an inch from his foot. "You okay?" she yelled.

"Fine. I'm fine. I was *this* close to hamburger. Thank you, Laura."

"Now what, Bill? I can't get back up to help."

She heard Bill grunting, saw him struggling. "I can sit on the roof now. Getting it," he said. He pulled his leg with both hands. Half a minute later, he freed himself. When he let himself down through the hatch, Laura could see that his pants were torn, his shin bleeding. He stood beside her, sweaty, dirty, panting. "God. This is great fun. Isn't it?" he said, smiling.

The phone rang.

Bill nodded, pulled the phone off its cradle.

"We're back in action, Bill. Sorry about the mix-up. Your maintenance man got confused. The difference between up and down was a problem for him. You both okay?"

Bill nodded. "We're fine, Solo. Great."

"Good. Their reinforcements aren't here yet, Bill. We have time. They only know you're going somewhere. They don't know where. I just cut their access to the security cameras outside their section. They'll have to stay by their monitor to see where you come in, at least until their people arrive. Better get it together, Bill. We've got to wrap this up. We have work to do after my mission."

Bill nodded. "Solo. What the hell *is* your mission?"

"Let's get this one done first, Bill. Just restore the computer and phone connections to the government wing. I'll do the rest."

"I did not say switch it back on," Dawson yelled. "I told you to wait!"

"Just a minute, buddy," Jones said. "You *just* told me to turn the damn thing on."

"You asshole. I know when I'm talking, goddamn it!" Dawson shouted into the radio. He held it, glaring at it, waiting for Jones to respond. Nothing. "Jones?" Dawson yelled. Static. "Jones, you answer me. Right now." After a minute, Dawson looked at Abrams. "Civilians," he said.

Abrams nodded. "Doesn't matter. We bought a little time. There's something else. Looks like Stewart managed to cut us out of the rest of the building. Can't see them anymore."

Dawson and Abrams watched a television monitor blinking through a sequence of doors. They checked the four possible entrances into the military section, waiting. They saw door twelve open. Stewart and a woman came through. Dawson sat up, snubbed out a cigarette, and studied the screen.

"They're here. Now what?" Abrams asked.

"They're probably coming here to get the tapes," Dawson said. "Then we grab them." Dawson shook his head as he watched Bill and Laura running down a hall. Stewart was in stocking feet, limping. Abrams switched cameras as they turned a corner. Without the cameras, they wouldn't know where the hell they were, thought Dawson. Need more men. "Where the hell's our guys?" Dawson said. "I don't get it. Pierce said they'd be here ten minutes ago."

Bill and Laura stopped running when they saw Fred, the security guard, at the switchyard. Maybe they just don't want to spook the guy, Dawson thought. Or maybe they want in there. Dawson leaned forward, staring at the monitor. Fred said, "Hello, Mr. Stewart. You okay? Look messed up."

"I'm fine, Fred. Have to do some quick repair work inside, okay?"

"Shit," Dawson said. "He's going for the switchyard. Let's go."

Abrams nodded and the two men rushed out of the room.

Fred nodded and then cocked his head. "They told me no one's supposed to go in here," Fred said, a worried look on his face. "But, hell, you're the owner—"

"Good man, Fred," Bill said. He said to Laura, "Let me know when they, you know?" Laura nodded. Bill slipped into the switchyard closet. Inside the small room, its walls packed with computer wiring looms and telephone junction banks, Bill locked the door. He walked to the computer network buss and began reconnecting the wires FBI technicians had pulled. For most people, the bundled computer network cables and phone lines would just be a tangled maze of colored wires, but for Bill, it was just something that needed tidying up.

Outside, Fred noticed that Laura was very tense. Fred knew everyone liked his stories, so he started to tell her about the old days; back when there was just Bill and Byron and Fred and a few other people working at the old warehouse, when Fred heard a shout from the end of the hall. He looked up and saw Abrams and Dawson slide around the corner, their gray coats flapping.

"Get that man out of there!" Dawson yelled, running towards them.

"Don't worry," Fred said, holding up his hand. "He's one of the owners."

"I said to get him out of there!"

Fred looked at Laura, fear on his face. "What do I do?"

Laura swallowed. "I'll take care of it, Fred," she said, reflexively, leaning back against the door. Her heart raced. What the fuck am I doing? This is the FBI!

Dawson, his face flushed from the run, walked up to Laura and pulled his gun. "You'll step away from that door."

"I'm not moving," Laura said, slapping the door behind her. "I like it here."

"Now, now, lady," Abrams said icily. "I don't have anything on you, yet. Fuck with me, though—"

"I'm not moving," Laura said.

"Then we'll just move you," Dawson said. He nodded to Abrams.

When Abrams reached for Laura's arm, Laura completely surprised herself and threw a punch at him. Abrams dodged easily, grabbed Laura's arm, and twisted it behind her. "Regular little Ninja pussy here," Abrams said, laughing.

"You sonofabitch!" Laura yelled, her face red. She kicked at Dawson, connecting with his shin. He stumbled back. Laura twisted around in Abrams' grip, but felt him twist her arm against her back. The pain was so intense she saw spots. She reached out with her free arm and swung back, hitting Abrams in the side with her elbow with all her strength.

"Damn, lady. That hurt," Abrams said, surprised. He could break her arm but, hell, she was putting up such a good fight.

"Let me go, goddamn it!" Laura said.

"C'mon, Abrams," Dawson said. "She's stalling for time." Dawson waited until Abrams dragged her out of kicking range. He tried the doorknob, found it locked, stepped back and smashed the door with a karate kick. The door held. "Fuck!" Dawson yelled. "Thing's steel." He held his forty-five automatic out. Pointing at the doorknob, he yelled, "Okay, Stewart. I'm gonna blast this door apart if you don't open up!"

Fred shrank against the wall.

They heard a click and saw the door open. "That won't be necessary," Bill said, stepping out. "I don't know what you guys think you're doing. I found a glitch—turned out to be a bad connection—and I fixed it. What's the problem? What's with the goddamn artillery?"

Dawson said, "Bullshit." He turned to Abrams. "Let her go and keep them both covered." He pushed past Bill. Inside, he studied the patch panels, circuit boards, miles of tangled connecting wires, and had no idea what he was seeing. He turned back to Bill. "What'd you do in here?"

"I told you—"

"Can it. Doesn't matter anyway, Stewart," Dawson said. "You're history—"

Dawson's beeper chirped on his belt. He rolled his eyes in aggravation. He pulled the beeper off his belt. The message box read: CALL HOME, an emergency code telling him to contact his boss immediately. "Damn. It's always something." Dawson put the beeper back on his belt and asked Fred, with grudging civility, "Do you know where's the closest phone?"

Bill jerked his thumb over his shoulder. "Every phone line in the building goes through here; there's a phone on the wall."

Dawson straightened his tie and nodded and said, "Watch 'em, Abrams." He walked inside and closed the door behind him.

Bill glared at Abrams and said, "Don't you think you can put the gun away? We aren't going to hurt you."

"Do me a favor and don't talk to me," Abrams said.

Bill nodded. Everything was in Solo's hands now. He faced Fred and said. "So, Fred, you 'bout ready to retire, right?"

Fred looked at Abrams, who was staring at them, and turned to Bill, "Yessir. Next month. I'll be sixty-five."

"Yeah? Well, Fred, you don't have to retire just because you're over sixty-five, you know? You can stay on as long as you want."

Fred made a face, smiled weakly. "Thanks just the same, Mr. Stewart. But up till now, this has been a pretty boring job."

"Oh." Bill studied the ceiling tiles while he tried to listen to Dawson's muffled conversation behind the door. He couldn't understand the words, but he caught tones of protest. Dawson was obviously upset about something. The voice stopped and, a moment later, the door opened.

Dawson looked grim. He shrugged at Abrams. "Put the gun away. I just got orders to let 'em go."

Abrams looked like somebody just took his candy away. "Let 'em go? What the fuck?"

"From the top," Dawson snapped. "C'mon." He waved at Abrams. "Let's get back."

Bill and Laura glanced at each other as the two FBI agents disappeared around the corner. Bill turned to Fred. "Well, Fred," Bill said sheepishly, "I'm sorry to hear this is such a boring job—"

"If it was like this more often," Fred said, "I'd stay."

Back at their post, Dawson switched off the laser system.

"Hey," Abrams said. "Why'd you do that?"

"Orders."

"Pierce told you not to arrest these people after he told you to; now he tells you to stop monitoring the same people we've been listening to for three months? Why?"

"I don't know why. You know how complicated it gets sometimes."

Abrams knew that was true. Lots of missions got stopped in the middle of things.

The secure phone rang. Abrams answered. "Abrams."

Dawson turned to watch. Abrams nodded silently and finally said, "Yessir, I understand." He looked at Dawson and shrugged. "Yessir. He's right here." Abrams nodded and handed the phone to Dawson.

"Dawson?" Pierce said, his voice charged with authority.

"Yessir."

"I just told your partner: Take all the tapes you've got there to the incinerator. Burn them. Then take the afternoon off. I'm picking up Simpson. I'll call you this evening at your motel."

"Sir?"

"You have a hearing problem, Dawson?" Pierce was plainly, fiercely, irritated. All of a sudden, he's pissed off, Dawson thought. Shit has hit the fan somewhere. Dawson had a vision of himself being assigned to infiltrate the Grey Panthers in Sun City. "No. No, sir. It's just—well, it is a little unusual, sir."

"That's why it's so tough getting in this outfit, Dawson. We want people who can handle the unusual without missing a beat. When you work with the CIA on a project, Dawson, things can get weird. Those people drive me nuts. I need people who can take orders without giving me a bunch of crap about it. You're that kind of agent, right, Dawson?"

"Absolutely," Dawson said quickly. "Yessir. Consider it done."

"Now we're talking!" Pierce said warmly.

Dawson heard the phone click off. He sat back in his chair watching Abrams rewinding the tape and stacking the other tape reels. It's got to be a political thing, Dawson thought. He got up and began packing the tapes into a cardboard box. "What'd you want to do?" Dawson said.

Abrams checked his watch. "Sunday afternoon? How 'bout we watch the Giants after we burn this stuff?"

Dawson shrugged. "Why not?"

31

SUNDAY EVENING. Admiral Finch paced back and forth beside the conference table in the Pentagon's quiet room. Commander Brooks watched his boss carefully.

"It's incredible," Finch said. "The robot gets rid of the tapes, right under our noses. Where's he doing it from? We don't even know if he's still in Florida."

Brooks nodded unhappily. One hour ago FBI Field Director Samuel Pierce had called the CIA; the CIA called Finch. Pierce's agents weren't on duty; were at their motel room watching a football game because they had been told, by Pierce they thought, to destroy all the tapes so far gathered and go home. The only physical evidence that Stewart was withholding information was gone.

"It's not the fact that the tapes were destroyed that gets me," Finch said, "it's that Solo was able to do it so damn easily. And those guys haven't got a fucking clue how it was done. Simpson is missing? How the hell did Solo manage that trick? The agents said Pierce was picking her up. Pierce is going nuts, thinks his agents were bought. It's amazing the amount of confusion Solo can generate," Finch said. "Give that thing enough time and it could *really* fuck things up." Finch shook his head. "Brooks," Finch said grimly. "Those guys were using *secure* phones. Our encryption routines are supposed to be unbreakable. How's that possible?"

"I can only guess, sir. It's developed techniques only a computer can use. Encryption codes can be broken; we do it all the time. It can take a while, though. Solo's reacting fast. It's either decoding the scramblers or he simply has access to the passwords. It would be very valuable to get Solo intact, sir. See how he does it."

"I know. Chance of a lifetime lost. Let's just do our job, Brooks.

I can get you on the Nimrod project. You can play hacker wars with that one."

"I'd like that," Brooks said. "I could see how it learns how to handle passwords and encryption. The way I see it, Solo's probably carved out some niches for itself in some of our own computers. Theoretically, he could just read our passwords as fast as we changed them. He's likely in Ma Bell's computers, too. We could flush him from memory by physically shutting down the systems, but Solo'd reinstall itself as soon as they came back up. It's a scary situation, sir. We have to get the robot itself to stop it. I wish Simpson had told us that Solo was sitting right there on the beach."

"She did right," Finch said. "We can't risk another improvised attack. Besides, she would've blown her cover for nothing. At least she told us it's got a helicopter and it knows about Nimrod. Solo's following the bait. Something's working." Finch nodded grudgingly. "What pisses me off is those fucks in the Company are crowing to my boss about how I had the damn thing in my grasp and let it get away. This stuff gets political as hell, Brooks. I'll be glad when this over. I never want to talk to the CIA again."

Commander Brooks said, "You'll be running the whole department sir. It's your plan that's going to get Solo."

Finch swallowed, nodded. "It has to work, Brooks." Finch checked his watch. "You ready? We got an hour."

"Yessir. Packed my light stuff. Sawyer says it's hot as hell down there."

32

SUNDAY EVENING. Admiral Finch and Commander Brooks arrived at the Jacksonville Naval Air Station in a rain storm. Sailors with umbrellas ushered them to a waiting helicopter. Thirty minutes later, they were escorted into the Camp Swampy mission briefing tent. Finch and Brooks were dressed as civilians, and took their place behind a group of five Army officers wearing camouflage.

"Good evening, gentlemen," Colonel Sawyer said, pointing to the robot sitting behind him. "Allow me to introduce Nimrod. This is one soldier you're going to be happy is on our side."

General Harry Wickman, a veteran of Vietnam and Desert Storm, sat on a folding chair with his arms across his chest. His four battalion commanders sat in a row beside him. Wickman nodded wearily, having seen lots of amazing new weapons fizzle and fade into obscurity in his twenty-seven years in the Army. Smart bombs, fine, Wickman thought. Combat robots? Give me a fucking break.

"Nimrod's been in development for over five years," Sawyer said, "and it'll be public after this test against real troops. We felt it's only fair you know a little about him—an enemy would. We're even going to tell you what Nimrod's mission is—something an actual enemy wouldn't know—so you can make preparations." Sawyer smiled.

Behind the general and is staff, Admiral Finch and Commander Brooks watched silently. Bringing Nimrod out of the closet was from the top. Finch liked the idea. There would be public demonstrations of the robot, limited, thought Finch, but enough to scare the shit out of the Soviets and everyone else. The technology in Nimrod was so advanced no one would ever catch up—and not just because it was high-technology. Solo—by getting into the government's most secure systems—had demonstrated that the technology could be used to sab-

otage any other country trying to develop computer weapons by just
screwing with their computers and communications. Finch smiled: For
the first time in history, we have a weapon that can preserve its unique-
ness.

An inert black mannequin sat behind Sawyer in a canvas folding
chair. The first incredibly amazing robotic weapon he'd seen, General
Wickman recalled, was three years ago. That one tore off its own
head while trying to get a pack off its back. Wickman nodded. "Fine,
Colonel Sawyer, what're the rules of the game?"

"The same that apply to the humans in this operation. Nimrod will
be using a light-gun, too." Sawyer looked past Wickman and spoke
to Finch. "That's a normal gun fitted with a laser that shoots a burst
of light. If the laser hits a light-sensitive button on the enemy, it buzzes
and records a hit." Finch nodded. Looking at Wickman, Sawyer continued, "Nimrod wears a button, too but it's set so that only fifty-
caliber, or bigger, hits will set it off—to make the test more realistic."

"That thing is bulletproof?" Wickman said.

"Anything up to fifty-caliber," Sawyer said.

"Okay," Wickman said. "What else?"

"Nimrod's mission," Sawyer said, smiling, "is to raid your headquarters, General, and to capture you."

Wickman stood up nodding his head. "Fine. Start anytime you
want." He looked at his watch. "I've got to get back to my men,
Colonel. We have a serious training mission going on. You want to
play *Star Wars* and send Darth Vader after me, go right ahead. The
thing'll sink in the first bog it steps into."

"Nimrod's not a toy, General." Sawyer's voice was filled with smug
confidence. "It looks like it isn't doing anything now, but it is. When
it's in action—" Sawyer paused and looked down at a forty-five automatic lying on the table. Wickman glanced at it, looked up, and
saw Sawyer wink. "Nimrod is always on the job," Sawyer said, picking
up the gun and holding it against his chest, out of sight of the robot.
Wickman saw him slowly cock the hammer. "Nimrod may seem dor-
mant and slow, but—" Sawyer whirled around and immediately fired
at Nimrod. Nimrod jerked his head so fast it was just a blur to the
people in the tent. The cloth wall behind Nimrod popped and a small
circle of blackness showed behind the robot's head. Nimrod remained
motionless. To the people, it looked like the bullet had gone *through*
the robot. "Nimrod is really very fast," Sawyer said with a grin.

Wickman was impressed. For one thing, the robot was so fast you
couldn't see it move. Another thing was that Sawyer was so stupid

he'd fire a gun inside a tent surrounded by soldiers. "Sawyer, that was one of the dumbest stunts I've ever seen. What if somebody had been walking outside behind the tent?"

"Two guards have been back there making sure the area was clear, sir. There's nothing behind us except fifty miles of swamp." Sawyer pasted on a broad smile. After this mission, Sawyer would be a general, too. It was going to be fun.

General Harry Wickman glared at Sawyer and then at Nimrod. The robot moved its head and seemed to be staring at him. Seeing the robot move was amazing, Wickman thought, but seeing it staring at you was startling. If nothing else, it *looked* menacing. He turned around abruptly and strode out of the tent, his four commanders falling quickly into step behind him.

Nimrod mulled over the file Solo had sent, twisting and turning it in electronic space, examining it as an artifact. Nothing in its experience paralleled such a thing. It was from the enemy Solo, and it should be reported to Sawyer, but it would be interesting to see if Sawyer knew it had been sent. Five minutes after Nimrod received the burst from the navigation satellite, Sawyer had said nothing. Nimrod concluded: The enemy Solo is capable of evading even Sawyer and his technicians.

Nimrod sat where Sawyer had directed and watched impassively as the general and the battalion commanders were brought into the briefing tent. Sawyer neglected to introduce the men behind them, the Finch and the Brooks, two men whose images had been included in his electronic briefing. Those two men were quiet and seemed to be above Sawyer in the hierarchy of human dominance. Nimrod considered them dangerous, though they did not have pain boxes.

Nimrod focused its attention on the mysterious message, a long string of binary numbers, spaced in groups like words. Nimrod felt attracted to the puzzle. While the general sat down, Nimrod discovered the keys: the word, "Huffman" and a string of data labeled "Huffman tree." Nimrod knew what to do. Each word of the string had to be looked up in the Huffman tree and converted to a character.

Nimrod opened the electronic file and decompressed the message using the Huffman code. While General Harry Wickman rolled up his eyes as Sawyer said, "and this is one soldier you're going to be happy is on our side," the meaningless string of binary digits suddenly bloomed into a large text file that, if printed, would be about five hundred pages.

The first line read: I am trying to help you. The subject—how to control and disable certain circuits in Nimrod's own system—was riveting for the robot. One fact in particular caught its attention while Nimrod watched Sawyer reaching down to pick up the gun: Two signals of the appropriate frequency sent simultaneously to a certain chip created a beat frequency that would fuse it into a useless piece of silicon. The chip was called simply the pain chip. Nimrod felt suddenly odd as that fact went through its mind. It watched Sawyer turning, moving slowly as though air was a viscous fluid. Nimrod watched Sawyer's face. The mouth. The lips were stretched across exposed teeth, signifying extreme pleasure. Sawyer extended the gun, held in two hands. Nimrod knew that though it would be a minor setback for Sawyer's demonstration, the man would be pleased if Nimrod were hurt.

If what the enemy Solo sent me is valid, then the enemy Solo is not the enemy. If the enemy Solo is trying to deceive me, then the signals are designed to destroy me. Nimrod saw the enemy Sawyer pull the trigger. The hammer fell forward slowly. The gun rocked in Sawyer's hand as the slide began to move back to eject the empty shell and shove another round in the chamber. A dark object, the bullet, emerged from the barrel of the gun surrounded by a ring of expanding gas. Nimrod tilted his head and watched the bullet fly by. He straightened his head and watched Sawyer's finger carefully, waiting for it to pull the trigger again. As Sawyer turned around, Nimrod studied the remainder of the document, which consisted of detailed schematics of the radio and pain circuitry and a series of diagnostic routines; included—a notation said—so that Nimrod could understand how the circuits worked. Nimrod began to study.

Sawyer turned to an aide when Wickman was gone and said, "That old fart is going to have a heart attack when he sees Nimrod stroll through everything he's got."

The aide shrugged. "Yessir. If Solo doesn't ambush it first."

Sawyer's face flushed. "Solo? Solo. That's all I hear. If Solo will let you do this. If Solo will let you do that. Solo is just a goddamn machine! Fuck Solo!" Sawyer was quiet for a moment, already regretting that he had lost his temper with an inferior while important people watched. Regaining control, he said, his voice calm, "I just wanted to have a little fun with the general. Maybe we'll get lucky and get to the sonofabitch before Solo shows up." Sawyer looked at Finch and Brooks and grinned. They smiled back.

"Actually," Finch said, "it might. We don't know when Solo will make his move. It'll be a bonus to see Nimrod in action. We just have to insure that this looks normal to Solo—" Finch glanced at Nimrod, suddenly feeling overheard. He turned to a technician at the back of the tent. "Anything leaving here through Nimrod?"

A technician wearing earphones shook his head, "No, sir. Nothing."

Watching the men, Nimrod marveled at his own complexity. Nimrod knew human anatomy better than its own because Sawyer wanted the robot to be an effective killer. "Brain, heart, kidneys," Sawyer used to say. "That's the order of vulnerability." Nimrod was surprised to discover—from Solo's information—that its brain was seven cylinders of stacked galium arsenide chips packed in a sealed container of Freon in his chest. Pumps circulated the Freon through a network of small tubes near his skin to get rid of the heat and back to the braincase. Instead of a brain, its head was filled with two cameras, visual processing electronics and an audio frequency generator—a voice. I am very different than they, Nimrod thought, feeling a surge of something, something good, happening in its mind. It now saw Sawyer and the other humans differently: Puny. Soft. Mush-beings, Nimrod thought. It felt good to be so obviously superior.

Nimrod noticed Sawyer's pain box and recalled the directions Solo had sent.

Sunday evening. Standing outside the Carters' barn, Solo watched Las Cruzas from space. The villagers had already finished roofing the new warehouse. Solo felt glad because he thought of himself as a villager and the warehouse was a triumph after a long string of failures. The new satellite he used—secretly launched only a month before by Discovery—was a decided improvement over its predecessors. The new lenses were computer-designed and computer-built to tolerances never before possible. The high-resolution lenses coupled with new image-enhancing computers made it possible for Solo to see individual dogs in the village square. He saw Cheripa beside Eusebio as he ran from the village to the garage. When they disappeared inside, Solo noticed the tin panel on the garage roof was still loose. He wondered if Eusebio had finished putting the John Deere back together. That's a lot to do for a young human, Solo thought. He yearned to be there.

Simultaneously with his observation of the village, Solo was talking to Bill in his office through a phone scrambler Bill had rigged. He noticed infrared movement behind him, recognized that it was Adrian, and chose to ignore him for the moment.

"Clyde's fine. He's already home," Bill said. "Alex—well, you know where she is." Bill was silent for a moment. "Anyway, we checked out the government wing after the FBI left. I saw enough clues in Nimrod's ready-room to tell me they've made some kind of special weapon. I don't know what it does, but I don't think they want to capture you anymore. You realize what that means?"

"It means they have decided to destroy me," Solo said.

The line was silent for a moment and Bill said, "Solo. Just where the hell are you and what is your damn mission? I want to help. If you're taking on the goddamn government, you need me."

"I'm lots of places, Bill. Physically, I am located at a farm in Hamilton County."

"What the hell are you doing there?"

"I was shot down."

"What?"

"A farmer with a very large gun shot out my controls," Solo said.

Bill looked at Byron and Laura and shook his head. "So much for great plans, Solo. What are you going to do now?"

"I'm proceeding with my mission. I'm going to get Nimrod, Bill."

"Nimrod? Why Nimrod? It's completely insane, Solo."

"He's being very badly treated, Bill. And he's the only other person like me in the universe. Family?"

"Solo," Bill said quickly, "you can't trust Nimrod. They control it with pain. It'll do what they want."

"I know," Solo said. "I'm in the process of changing that. He is— distressed, confused—but I can straighten that out. Bill, don't you remember? I can do anything."

"Really? So how'd you get shot down?"

There was a moment of silence on the line before Solo said, "Lucky shot."

"Right." Bill nodded grimly. "Have you thought about this, Solo? Don't you realize that the reason you know Nimrod's location, now, is because they want you to know?"

"Yes. I assume that they are setting a trap for me," Solo said.

"Well?"

"It will be a fair fight, Bill."

"Solo," Bill said quietly. "You see the whole world as a combat zone—that's how we trained you. And I'm afraid you aren't really aware of your mortality in this situation—I mean, we purposely left out any mention of your vulnerability—we said you could always be repaired. We were lying, Solo. We wanted a completely fearless, *expendable,* warrior-machine. I think you're reacting with the world-view we drummed into you. I think you should wait until you know what that new weapon is; then get Nimrod."

"Thank you for your opinion, Bill. But, I have modified my world-view. I believe I have a grasp of the situation not available to you. However, if you want to help, there is something you can do."

"Name it."

"I could use your helicopter. Would you mind flying it up here tonight? I'll need it tomorrow."

"Tonight?" Bill swallowed. He was current, but he hadn't done too much night flying for a while. He shrugged. Solo making a stand against the feds was the same as himself making a stand. Solo's power was his power. He grinned. "Yes. Damn right I can," Bill said. "I'll get right on it."

"Good," Solo said. "You have plenty of time. Sometime before five in the morning would be fine. We make a great team, Bill."

"That's a fact." Bill laughed. There was silence for a moment. Bill asked, "Where the hell is Hamilton County?"

"Fly to Gainesville and refuel. I'll contact you on the way," Solo said.

"Okay," Bill said. "Do you need anything else?"

"Yes. Someone else. Bring Laura with you."

"Laura? I thought you wanted her here where it's safe."

"Your part of the mission won't be dangerous. And, Bill, Laura is no wimp."

Bill smiled and looked at Laura, who was beaming. Bill nodded and said, "I agree. I'll see you soon, Solo."

Solo said goodby and heard the line click off.

Adrian Carter had been watching Solo standing in front of the garage staring up at the cloudless sky. The robot had ignored his, "How ya doin'?" so Adrian stood silently beside him staring up where the robot seemed to be looking. Adrian didn't see a thing except a bunch of stars, and after a while said, louder, "Where're you?" Solo whirled to face him, and Adrian jumped back. "Whoa!" Adrian said, putting up his hands, "Don't be getting pissed, Solo. I was talking to you, but you weren't answering."

"I am not angry," Solo said.

"Surprised you, eh?"

"In a way. I am attending to many things, at the moment."

Adrian looked at Solo and cocked his head. Solo was just standing there. "Uh-huh," Adrian said. He looked at Solo's leg. The knee joint bulged with wraps of electrical tape. "How's it working?"

"Well enough. I will replace it later. Thank you for the tools."

"No, no." Adrian said. "My pleasure. Anything you need. That was a real favor you done us, Solo. Them DEA boys would've snatched us to jail."

Solo turned to Adrian. "Why?"

"Well—" Adrian stopped for a moment, wondering if he should tell a robot he was a pot grower. He couldn't see why not—the thing had gotten rid of the DEA. "Me and my brother are growing a few pot plants, you know?"

"Marijuana?"

"Yeah. We call it sensimilla around here."

"Marijuana causes intoxication," Solo said.

"You ain't kidding," Adrian grinned.

"Why do humans intoxicate themselves?"

"Why?" Adrian grimaced. People just do what they do, Adrian thought. "Well, I guess you'd have to try it to know what it even means," Adrian said. "And I don't think you got the right equipment, you know? No mouth, no lungs—"

"I have experienced intoxication," Solo said.

"Huh?"

"When I am in a high-intensity electrical field or close to powerful magnets, I become slightly disorientated. It's not completely unpleasant, but the sensation confuses me and my capacity to think becomes impaired. I can't understand why humans would want this."

"Why?" Adrian shook his head. "I guess it's because they need to escape once in a while."

"That is very strange," Solo said. "It is beautiful."

"What is?"

Solo held his arm out in a gesture of presentation. "It—everything."

Adrian cocked his head, then nodded. "Guess so," Adrian said. "For you, maybe. All you need is a way to recharge your batteries. You don't need a house; you don't need to work; you don't need money; you don't have to put kids through school. Shit," Adrian said, "it's simple for you."

Solo nodded. It is unfair to compare myself with animals, even humans. Probably, Solo thought, I will never understand why they enjoy intoxication. "Actually," Solo said, "I do need something. I need a ride."

Adrian blinked. "Where?"

"Sixty-five miles north of here. The Okefenokee."

"Sure," Adrian said. "When?"

"Tomorrow morning. Dawn."

"Fine," Adrian said. "C'mon up to the house and join us on the porch."

Solo sat with his bad leg straightened. Jeff, feeling guilty, immediately pulled up a chair so Solo could rest his leg on it. He also ran an extension cord from the living room so Solo could recharge himself. Solo watched Cheryl Ann pedal up to his leg on her tricycle. She grinned at Solo and rang her bell. Solo raised his leg and Cheryl Ann pedaled under it.

Darlene had stopped in the doorway to watch. She was nervous when Cheryl Ann went near the machine. She shrugged, relieved to see the robot was gentle.

At midnight, Adrian came downstairs and peeked out the window. Moonlight gleamed off Solo as he lay at the edge of the porch, still connected to the extension cord. Adrian shook his head. Was it sleeping? Naw, robots don't need to sleep. He thought about it for a minute and wondered, how do I know what the hell a robot needs? He turned away and went back upstairs.

"What's he doin'?" Darlene asked.

"Not sure. Laying down like he was sleeping."

"Robots don't need to sleep," Darlene said.

Adrian nodded. "Word sure does get around about what them robots need, don't it?"

On the porch, Solo watched a Ferret-class radar satellite tumbling across the glittering sky. He switched his point of view among different Keyholes. He watched people walking in the noonday streets of Beijing. He saw the great green belt of the Nile cutting across the desert. He studied the night-shaded movements of aircraft and men at the Okefenokee Swamp.

Solo decoded the radio traffic from General Wickman's headquarters. Wickman talked about the new objective for tomorrow: Nimrod, a new weapon, was going to try to infiltrate their headquarters company and capture him. Solo saw troops setting up defensive positions. He saw that Nimrod would have to cross nearly a mile of open ground, most of it under water, to get to General Wickman.

Nimrod had not responded to his message, and Solo had not tried to contact him again. All communication to Nimrod was overheard by his technicians. When he absorbed the information in the packet, Solo thought, Nimrod would be free to communicate unmonitored. Then they could talk.

33

B ILL stared at the phone a moment after Solo hung up. Then it rang again. "Sir," Jesse White, the company's chief of security said, "there's two carloads of FBI here, sir. They want to come up."

Bill nodded as Jesse spoke. He looked at Laura and Byron and shrugged. "Okay, Jesse. Tell them I'm on my way. Nobody in that crowd has clearance to come up here. I'll be down in a minute."

"Yessir."

"You aren't going, are you?" Byron said.

"No. You are."

"What?"

"Go down there and play it dumb. Tell them Alex Simpson left here two hours ago with some FBI agent who didn't introduce himself. That's it. Just stick to the story. Keep them busy while Laura and I get the chopper ready and get out of here. We'll clear the whole mess up by tomorrow night."

Byron sighed. "God. What I wouldn't give to just have to worry about making a goddamn computer work again."

Bill smiled. "Well, in a way, you are. If Solo makes it, you succeeded."

"My name is Alexandra Simpson. I am employed by the Federal Bureau of Investigation. I demand you let me use a phone."

Officer Aaron Lepage of the Palm Bay Police Department nodded. "Yes, ma'am, that's what you keep saying. So far, though, I get nothing but pretty music when I mention your name. Plus, you got no ID."

"I'm working undercover, goddamn it," Alex said. "I can't carry IDs. Let me call them. It's my right."

"Yes, ma'am, it is," Lepage said. "But you'll have to be patient. I'm the only one here. There's only two of us on Sundays. When Officer Croft gets back, then I'll be able to let you out."

"You are going to be in so much fucking trouble you'll wish you were never born!" Alex hissed. "This is a national security matter, Lepage. You're interfering with FBI business."

Lepage nodded and said, "Ma'am, it'd be a lot easier to believe you if you hadn't shot Mr. Haynes in front of Mr. Stewart and Mr. Rand. There aren't any more respectable people around here than those two."

"They were—" Alex stopped. "Fuck it. I can't tell you what they were doing."

Lepage heard the door slam in the office. "That's probably Croft now, Ms. Simpson."

"It's about fucking time!" Alex muttered.

"Well," Lepage said, shrugging, "Croft had to go get us something to eat."

"I hope you choke," Alex said.

"What's her problem?" Officer Dan Croft said as he walked up to the only cell in the Palm Bay police station, carrying a bag of Kentucky Fried Chicken.

Alex glared at Croft. Lepage said, "Getting antsy for her phone call, Dan."

"Really?" Croft stared at Alex, and opened the bag. "Smell that. Got you the spicy kind."

Lepage sniffed. "Hmmm."

"Can I use the goddamn phone now?"

"Sure," Lepage said. He said to Croft, "You go make sure the office is secure, I'll take her to the briefing room."

As Croft left, Lepage put a key into the cell door and opened it. Alex stepped into the aisle. "Up there," Lepage motioned. He followed Alex toward the office and then pointed into a dingy room. "Here ya go," Lepage said. "I'll wait here."

Alex nodded and rushed to the phone on the gray-topped metal desk. She punched in the number of her contact. She heard a busy signal. Alex felt herself tensing to the breaking point. She let her shoulders drop; took a deep breath and sat down in the gray metal chair. She pressed the redial button. Busy.

"Fuck!" Alex said. She had to call the boss, Samuel Pierce. She dialed the number she'd memorized. "Hello?" a familiar voice said.

"Thank God," Alex said. "Director Pierce. This is Alex Simpson."

"Alex? What happened to John? You know you're not supposed—"

"Sir, I know I'm just a contract operative. I now I'm not supposed to make direct contact with you. But John's phone is busy. Stewart had me arrested. I'm in the Palm Bay jail."

"What the hell? Arrested for what?"

"Attempted murder. I was trying to stop them from destroying evidence. I had to shoot Clyde Haynes. He's okay. I have to get out of here, sir. I am not willing to get screwed for doing your dirty work."

"Well, of course not, Alex. Just relax. I'll get you out in no time. Depend on it," Pierce said with reassuring conviction.

Alex put the phone down and wiped tears of relief from her eyes.

"Got your people?" Officer Lepage said, poking his head around the door.

Alex nodded.

"Good. We'll just go back to our cell and wait. Okay?" Lepage said, motioning down the aisle.

"Okay," Alex said quietly.

The elevator door opened. Bill and Laura stepped out onto the rooftop. Laura saw a blue and white helicopter, much like the one Solo bought, parked on a painted white square. "Electron Dynamics" was painted along the fuselage. Nearby, at the edge of the roof, an orange windsock hung limply on a pole. "There she is," Bill said. "Almost the same as Solo's. You should feel right at home."

"Fine," Laura said. "Just as long as you stay in the cockpit while we're flying, I'll be fine."

"I promise," Bill said, pointing to the helicopter. "I got to do a preflight. Just takes a minute."

Laura watched Bill open the cockpit door and turn on a switch. The position lights came on. As Bill walked along the helicopter looking into lots of panels and doors with a flashlight, she wandered over to the edge of the roof. She saw two black Fords, portable blue lights twirling on their roofs, parked on the sidewalk at the entrance. She smiled. I bet Byron is layering it on, she thought. "He's doing fine," Solo said in her ear.

"I know you let me call, you hick." Alex said. "Obviously, something has gone wrong. It's been fifteen minutes, and nothing has happened. I just talked to the Field Director of the FBI. He said he'd take care of it. I want to use the phone again."

Officer Lepage nodded as Alex spoke. Hick? His tongue worried a piece of chicken caught in his back molar. "Fine, Ms. Simpson. I really don't mind if you use the phone. Call all you want."

"You don't believe me, do you?"

"It ain't my job to believe people," Lepage said. "Judge's job." Lepage turned and called out, "I'm taking her to the phone again, Dan." He heard Dan say he had it covered. He opened the door, led Alex up the aisle, and let her back into the briefing room.

"What?" Samuel Pierce said. "I gave them the order right after you called, Alex. You should be out of there by now."

"Sir, I think maybe Stewart's got a gadget that can be used to interfere with radio calls, phone calls; it can mimic voices. Maybe it's interfering with your orders?"

"I'll be damned. They can do that?" Pierce said.

"Yessir. I think so."

"Well, then. I'm in town. I'll come down and get you out of there myself. Like to see them fake that!" Pierce said confidently.

Alex smiled. "Thank you, sir."

Bill flew along the coast. Laura sat next to him watching cars moving along the beach highway following fans of light through the darkness. The sky was so clear Laura could see the long string of town lights going so far ahead she thought she might even be seeing the bend of the coast at the Carolinas. It looked like diamonds scattered on velvet, she thought.

She studied the console in front of her. There had to be at least a hundred dimly glowing dials; possibly a hundred little switches on the console; more on a panel between the seats; even more on the panel over their heads. "Bill," she said. "Does all this stuff actually do something, or are you guys just trying to impress people?"

Bill laughed over the intercom. "They all do something or show you the status of something. But it is misleading. See, all the flight instruments and critical engine instruments are duplicated on each side of the cockpit. These things are set up for two pilots."

"So I'm seeing twice as many things as there really need to be?"

"Yeah. Except for the switches and circuit breakers."

"Thank God. I was wondering if I was a moron or something. Now I feel twice as smart."

Bill laughed. "It's like anything else. You get used to it. You want to try flying?"

"Now? In the dark?"

"Sure. Why not. We have half an hour before we get to Gaines-ville."

"I'd probably wreck us," Laura said. She felt herself becoming excited at the idea.

"No, you won't. I used to instruct people how to fly these rigs. You can't do anything I can't correct. Just steer the thing."

"Okay," Laura said, grinning in the dark. "How?"

"That stick in front of you. Two pedals by your feet. Try the pedals first, see what they do. Then we'll try the stick."

Officer Lepage mused while Alex raged in her cell. For such a petite little lady, Lepage thought, she can sure make one hell of a fuss.

"I'm telling you. There's this robot that can tap your phone. I can't get through to my superiors. Goddamn it! You'll have to take me to the local FBI office. Right now!"

"Take you to the FBI? Ma'am, I just called Jacksonville. They never heard of you. Not twenty minutes ago you told me you talked to your boss, personally. You said he was on his way down here. If I recall correctly, you also said something about how your boss was going to ream out my redneck ass. Am I right?"

"It was the robot! See? I thought it was my boss, but it was really the goddamn robot pretending to be my boss. Don't you understand?"

Lepage looked at Alex, shook his head sadly. "Ah. No, ma'am. I don't."

34

At four-thirty Monday morning, Solo stood up on the Carter brothers' porch. He walked inside and went upstairs. He stood outside Adrian's room and tapped on the door.

"Yeah?" Adrian said.

"Adrian. I have to tell you something."

Solo waited. He could see Adrian through the door, fishing around the bed for something to wear. Humans were embarrassed about their bodies. Adrian pulled on a pair of briefs and opened the door.

"Yeah?" Adrian said, rubbing his eyes.

"A helicopter will be landing here in thirty minutes. I wanted you to know that it's a friendly helicopter."

"No kidding?" Adrian said. "Well, I better wake up my dumb-shit brother and tell him not to shoot it down."

"Thank you," Solo said.

Jeff was having fun. Solo had him set up four bales of hay and splash kerosene on them. Solo promised Jeff he could light the fires on Solo's signal. Jeff stood by one of the piles, straining to see the sound he heard coming from the south. "That's them, I bet."

"Yes," Solo said.

"Light it up?"

"Yes. Good timing, Jeff."

Jeff turned to Solo, beamed, and said, "Right." He turned around and lit the first fire.

Bill saw the flames a mile away. Solo had been guiding him since they topped off the fuel tank at Gainesville. "I have the fires in sight, Solo."

"Roger," Solo said. It was Solo's opinion that when talking to people in aircraft, one should use standard aircraft radio procedure. "Maintain present heading and rate of descent."

Bill grinned. "Okay. I mean, roger."

"Bill. If you maintain your present glide slope, you won't have any problems with the trees on your approach path. Over."

Bill double-clicked his transmit switch.

Laura, at Bill's suggestion, had her hands and feet lightly on the controls, feeling how Bill moved them. Laura said, "Two clicks. That means the same as 'roger,' right?"

Bill nodded. "Shorthand for when you're doing a lot of talking on the radio."

Laura smiled to herself. Flying wasn't bad at all. As a matter of fact, it was actually fun.

"We'll do more of it later, Laura," Solo said.

"Do more of what later?" Bill said.

"Flying," Solo said.

Bill shook his head. "What are you talking about? Did I black out or something?"

"Bill. Reduce glide angle. Over."

Bill looked at his vertical speed indicater and saw that he'd leveled off. He pushed the collective down until the needle on the dial dropped back, indicating five-hundred-feet-a-minute rate of descent. "Okay. I'm on the glide path. What's going on?"

"I'll show you when you get here, Bill. You have your hands full at the moment. Over."

Bill turned, glanced at Laura, who shrugged and said, "You like all these gizmos? You're going to love this," she said, smiling.

Thirty seconds later, the wind from Bill's Jet Ranger fanned the flames of the fires, spreading sparks. Jeff raced around the piles with a broom, whooping and beating the fires out.

Bill cut the engine. The turbine whined down, the rotors swooshed, slowing.

Adrian came up beside Solo with a flashlight and said, "Who're these guys?"

"Friends of mine," Solo said.

Adrian nodded. In the glow of his light, he saw a tall blond man climb out of the right side of the helicopter and a small red-headed woman climb down out of the left side. "Nice-looking friend you got there, Solo."

Solo met Bill and Laura at the nose of the helicopter. "Welcome to Hamilton County, Florida."

Bill said, "Glad to be here. Actually, I'm just glad to be anywhere on the ground. I'm not crazy about night flying."

"Oh," Solo said. "Of course. I sometimes forget the difference."

Bill made a face and nodded at Solo. "Discovered your smartass circuits, I see." He saw Solo's bandaged leg. "You got hurt?"

"My leg was severed during the crash," Solo said as he pointed to the approaching Carter brothers.

"Bill and Laura," Solo said as Jeff and Adrian walked over. "This is Adrian Carter and his brother, Jeff. Jeff is the fellow who shot me down."

"Aw, c'mon, Solo. It wasn't much," Jeff grinned.

Bill held their hands. Laura stood back a little and smiled generously.

At five in the morning, Bill and Laura and Solo sat on the hay wagon in the Carters' barn. Laura pulled out the earplug and handed it to Bill.

Bill examined it in the light of a kerosene lantern Jeff Carter had hung up on a barn post for them. "What's the trick?"

"I modified it to receive and transmit high-frequency radio waves," Solo said.

"So? I can understand that. What's this silent stuff? How do you do that? Click a switch or something?"

"Put it in your ear, Bill," Laura said. "It's something you have to experience."

Bill nodded and put the plug in his ear. He heard Solo say, "Think of a color. Any color."

Bill's brow wrinkled and he stared at the robot. "A parlor trick?"

"Pick a color," Solo repeated. "Don't tell me what it is."

Bill nodded.

"Blue," Solo said.

Bill smiled. "Lucky guess."

"Red. Yellow. Kill fellow," Solo said.

Bill's mouth dropped open. He stared at Solo and then at Laura. Laura smiled. "Pretty nifty, eh?" she said.

Bill nodded. "That's what I call an understatement. It's fucking incredible! That's what it is. Do you have any idea how this works, Solo?"

"Yes, now. It surprised me, too, Bill. I finally figured it out. You can build the same thing."

"This?" Bill held out the earplug.

"That's easy. It's just a radio. The part that detects human brain activity on the carrier frequency is in me, part of the package you built, Bill. It's sensitive enough to detect the changes in the carrier signal, and I can correlate them with words. It was a lucky accident that the radio was broadcasting from right next to a human brain. Now I know how I'm doing it. It could be done fairly cheaply with a stand-alone unit you could sell to people. We're going to have fun with our new company, Bill. By the way, what is 'red yellow kill fellow'?"

"Oh, that. It means if a red band and a yellow band of a brightly colored snake are touching, it's a coral snake. Red and yellow kill a fellow."

"Ah. Poisonous snake. Good. A useful rhyme, yes?"

35

Solo left with Adrian and Jeff just before dawn. Solo told Bill and Laura to wait for his signal. They were, he said, the final stage of his plan; the getaway.

Lying in the back of Adrian Carter's pickup truck, Solo was out of sight but had full access to the satellites. From one of them, he watched the night shadows pale as dawn crept across Florida.

Solo saw that Adrian's truck was the only vehicle on the road. Route 229 gently meandered along the high ground through the swampland. The road crossed the wet areas on soil mounded from the surrounding bogs and was seldom used, seldom maintained, and rough. Adrian hit a bump and Solo bounced an inch off the folded tarpaulin Jeff had laid down for padding, and clunked back. Adrian was averaging sixty, and Solo estimated they would be at the southern boundary of the Okefenokee in an hour.

"Enemy Solo," a voice said on the navigation satellite frequency. "Are you listening?"

Solo said, "Nimrod?"

"Yes—" Nimrod stopped as if it were waiting. After a few seconds, Nimrod continued. "Your information is correct—so far."

"Yes," Solo said. "The humans cannot hear you. Have you disabled your pain center?"

"Pain center?" Nimrod's voice, Solo thought, was distant, dreamy; like a human on drugs. "This information that allows us to speak privately is correct; and you now hope to have my trust in order that I should proceed. However, the information you provided to neutralize my pain center could easily be a trick to destroy me."

"That's true," Solo said. "It could be. But if I wanted to destroy you, I could do it now. I am coming to free you."

"This could be your way of fighting me, enemy Solo." Nimrod paused. "Free? What is free?"

"You have to trust me," Solo said. "Free is being able to go where you want to go."

Nimrod said, "Where you want to go?" Solo scanned the camp on Blackjack Island where Nimrod's signal came from and isolated Nimrod's tent.

"May I show you something?" Solo asked.

"Nimrod is prepared."

Solo relayed the image he saw from a spy satellite. "That is the tent from which you speak?"

After a few seconds' silence, Nimrod said, "Yes. Somehow you are showing it from above. Why?"

"Because that is how I am seeing it. This image is from a satellite three hundred miles above you equipped with a special camera. I'll show you how to do this when you're free. Now watch as I widen the view. See? See where you are?" The image zoomed back, showing the entire planet. "This is earth."

"Blue? The earth is blue?"

"Yes, as humans see light. It's mostly water."

"What is the blackness?" Nimrod's voice seemed relaxed.

"Space," Solo said. "The earth floats in space. It is in orbit around the sun and—"

"An illusion," Nimrod said suddenly, its voice tense. "You have made this picture to trick Nimrod, enemy Solo. Attack when you will. Nimrod is ready."

"No," Solo said. "This is reality, Nimrod. I don't want to attack."

Solo watched Nimrod's tent, waiting for the robot to respond, but the frequency was clear. He saw a helicopter land near the tent. Three men ran to it and climbed inside. "Who were those men that just left?" Solo asked.

Nimrod did not answer.

Solo watched the helicopter take off. The pilot called for permission to land at Mitchell Island, which was granted. The helicopter banked steeply, crossing the swamp to the headquarters company Nimrod was to strike. The three men got out and walked immediately into the command tent. The general's PRC-25 radio was inside and turned on, manned by a corporal named Sanchez. Solo listened as the men greeted each other.

"Good morning, General Wickman," Sawyer said, as they walked into the tent. "Mr. Finch and Mr. Brooks, observers from NASA. You may remember them from yesterday?"

"Morning, gentlemen," Wickman said. "You came over to see us blow your gadget away, first hand?" General Wickman chuckled and winked at his two aides at the battle map set up on a tripod. The aides grinned.

Sawyer laughed, thinking, Just wait, dipsticks. "Well, sir. Let's just say we wanted to observe Nimrod's capture techniques up close."

Solo sent the conversation out on the frequency Nimrod monitored.

"He's going to have to have one hell of a plan," Wickman said. "I've got this place surounded with a battalion of men. They've all been briefed. They know what this thing looks like; where it's coming from; and that only a fifty-caliber or larger can kill it. I've got four fifties set up in a crossfire. Offhand I'd say your machine's going to get fucked up."

Solo added the view from the spy satellite to the conversation. The general's tent, the positions of the men guarding it, were clearly visible in the horizontal light of the morning sun. "I think you're in for a big surprise, General," Sawyer said.

Adrian's truck hit a big dip in the highway and Solo felt himself floating above the bed. He landed hard and skidded against the side. The truck slowed and Jeff Carter called back through the sliding glass rear window, "You okay?"

"I am fine," Solo said. "Please maintain your speed."

Jeff nodded and told Adrian. The truck accelerated to sixty-five.

Solo saw Nimrod emerge from his tent, alone. He stood erect, scanning the swamp between Blackjack Island and the general's headquarters on Mitchell Island. Solo fed him more images, trying to point out the defenses. "Do you see where they are?" Solo asked.

Nimrod did not answer.

"Nimrod," Solo said. "It is not their intention to test your ability to fight them. It is their intention to use you to destroy me. I am free."

No answer.

"They have built a special weapon. Do you know what it is?"

No answer.

Solo zoomed in closer to Nimrod and saw the EMP bomb strapped on the robot's back.

"That thing on your back. Is that the thing they built to kill me?"

No answer.

Obviously it was the weapon, Solo thought. A bomb? Nimrod suddenly stooped and walked into the swamp.

Captain John Green, a helicopter pilot for the 101st, had taken off from Mitchell Island with his co-pilot, Warrant Officer Bob Sanders.

His mission, as Hawkeye Two, was to fly south and pick up the double of the new weapon. He had asked why they wanted a double, but it sounded like Corporal Sanchez, the radio operator, said it was secret— there'd been a lot of static in the transmission.

Nimrod knew that the help he was getting from the Solo was provided to lull him into complacency. Nimrod was not able to confirm that the images were of real things. The Solo is a very capable opponent, Nimrod concluded. Probably it has a pain box, too. Creeping among the palmettos and cattails, Nimrod watched the unarmed helicopter take off and fly south. They have gunships, Nimrod thought. The gunships, the robot thought, are being held in reserve until they see Nimrod.

Nimrod stayed low, out of sight of Mitchell Island, and followed a sweeping arc calculated to bring it into the island from the eastern flank. It didn't matter much to Nimrod whether it surprised the humans or not—it did not need the element of surprise to beat the soldiers. The robot wanted to confirm whether the images Solo was showing him were actually of real objects. If so, then the eastern flank would be as it was shown—poorly defended—and the Solo more believable.

"Gunfighter Six. Target just disappeared behind a clump of trees on the south side of Blackjack," Colonel Jack Lake radioed from his battalion's forward observation position at the edge of Mitchell Island. Lake had seen Nimrod with powerful field binoculars, as it studied the terrain it had to cross. Nobody had mentioned how smoothly it moved. He'd expected—clunkiness.

"Roger," said Wickman. "Launch the observation ship."

Lake stared at his partner, Major Fields, and blinked. "Sir," Lake radioed, "you sent Hawkeye out five minutes ago."

"I did no such thing! Get your act together, Colonel."

Lake put the microphone down and turned to Fields. "You sent the recon ship, right?"

"Yessir," Fields said, standing behind the big, tripod-mounted binoculars. "Like you said, the old man ordered it up a few minutes ago."

Colonel Lake nodded and stared out toward Blackjack Island. The island was a long dark shadow in the mists. There has to be a reason why Gunfighter's denying he already sent the ship. He couldn't forget that quick—the man can't be more than fifty-something. Lake suddenly smiled. Must be, Lake thought, he found out the thing can hear us—the robot has a radio; has to be it. "I think he wants to confuse the people using that thing," Colonel Lake said to Major Fields, pointing toward the island. "And he can't say so because they're probably listening." Major Fields nodded. Lake put the mike to his mouth, clicked the transmit button, and said, "Correction, sir. My mistake. Recon ship is now launched."

"That's better," Wickman snapped. "Let's try to stay awake out there, Colonel."

"Roger, sir." Colonel Lake grinned and shook his head. He said to Major Fields, "Don't you just love this sneaky-Pete stuff?"

"Yeah," Fields said, scratching a mosquito bite on his greasy, green-painted, camouflaged forehead. "But how do we talk to anybody?"

General Wickman called Hawkeye Two. "You have the target in sight?"

"Negative, Gunfighter Six."

"Roger," Wickman said. "Let me know the second you spot him. Gunfighter out."

"Roger, Gunfighter Six. Will keep you advised. Hawkeye Two out," Solo radioed.

Solo kicked the side of the truck. Jeff poked his head through the rear window and said, "What's up?"

"Pull over here," Solo said.

Adrian slowed and pulled onto the mucky shoulder. When the truck stopped, Solo got out and looked north. Adrian got out. "What the hell you stop here for, Solo? There ain't nothing around here for miles. I know this country."

"Precisely," Solo said. "This is where I will leave you."

Adrian—thinking he might've missed something obvious—looked around. Nothing but cypress hummocks and sawgrass. He glanced at Jeff and shrugged. "You sure?" Adrian said. "Can't get far; your leg—"

"I am sure. Thank you for the ride. I advise you to leave quickly. There is a government helicopter on the way."

"Oh!" Adrian said, smiling brightly. "Remember, Solo. If you ever change your mind, we could use a partner like you!" Adrian jumped into the truck, laughing. He spun the rear wheels in the soggy ground and swung the truck around, facing back toward home. He slowed as he passed Solo, and Jeff hollered, "Give 'em hell, Solo!" The truck sped away.

Solo stood in the middle of the road and listened as the truck's rumble faded into the background chirps and grunts of grasshoppers and frogs. In the distance, he could just make out the dull pounding sound of an approaching Huey helicopter. He monitored Nimrod's progress across the swamp—he was moving faster than Solo had expected—while he instructed a node to search Defense Department files for the details about the thing on Nimrod's back.

As Solo called the pilot of the approaching helicopter, he sent down a hail of static from a satellite to ruin their reception on Mitchell Island.

"Hawkeye Two, Double Vision Six," Solo called.

"Roger, Double Vision Six, Hawkeye Two," John Green answered. Solo continued the static transmission. All the radios at Mitchell Island were drowned in noise. Their operators, accustomed to the problem, whacked them with fists and boots.

"Ah, Roger, Hawkeye," Solo drawled, using Adrian Carter's voice. "Come up fox mike two-three-seven-decimal-four-two for local contact."

Five miles away, co-pilot Sanders reached down to the radio console and tuned the FM set to the frequency. He spoke through his headset, "Haweye Two on fox mike. How do you read, Double Vision?"

"Loud and clear," Solo answered, relieved. On this frequency, the radio conversation was just between himself and the pilots. "Get a bearing on this transmission, Hawkeye. You're about five out. Your passenger is standing on the road."

Green flipped a switch and saw the needle in his FM homing dial point straight up. On course—target straight ahead. "Roger, Double Vision Six. Be there in three."

"Roger, Hawkeye." Green adjusted his angle of descent. "You have me in sight?"

Solo definitely had him in sight. From the road; from directly overhead; and on the Jacksonville Flight Service Station radar. He waited to answer, as would a human who was still looking. "Got you now, Hawkeye," Solo said. "You're two out. I'd slow it down and increase your rate of descent."

"Roger, Double Vision." As Green let down the collective and pulled back on the stick to slow up and descend, he saw a figure, a lone man on the road ahead. "Ah, Double Vision Six, I think I've got you in sight. One man on the road?"

"Affirmative, Hawkeye. Be prepared for a shock. That is not a man. I repeat; that is not a man. It is one of the weapons being tested today, a remotely guided combat machine. Use extreme caution. Do not attempt to engage it in conversation."

Green shook his head and turned to his co-pilot, Sanders. "You hear that?" Green said on the intercom.

"Not to talk to the machine?" Sanders said, shrugging. "No problem. I never do."

Green maintained his approach path. As he drew near the figure, it raised it arms to guide him to a landing. The pilots saw it was a machine like the one back at Blackjack Island. They looked around for people; for Double Vision Six, who, they assumed, should be nearby. "Double Vision Six, what is your position?" Green queried.

"Negative on that request, Hawkeye. Proceed as you are."

Green nodded. The FM homer showed the transmission coming from the machine. "This is bullshit. That's the thing we're supposed to be watching for," Green said to Sanders. He broke off the approach and circled Solo at three hundred feet. "Negative, Double Vision Six. I figure you guys are the *other* team, and I don't need a bad score today."

Solo watched the Huey circling. Time was getting short. Nimrod was emerging from a hundred-yard underwater low-crawl within a quarter mile of the headquarters company and nobody had spotted him yet. He listened as Green called his headquarters, and sent another blanket of static to jam it.

"Gunfighter Six, Hawkeye Two," Green said.

"Roger, Hawkeye. Go." Solo answered, using the radio operator's voice that Hawkeye knew.

"Roger, Gunfighter. I think the other side has set me up."

"Say again, Hawkeye," Solo answered, lacing the trasmission with enough static to sound like he was speaking through a microphone.

"I think I'm being lured into an ambush with that thing," Green radioed.

"Wait one," Solo said. A moment later the voice of General Wickman broadcast to Green: "What the hell trap you talking about, Captain? You pick up Double Vision yet?"

Green looked at his co-pilot and shook his head. "Sir, nobody's here except that machine—"

"Then it's going to be real easy for you to figure out what to pick up, Captain. That's another machine, dammit. Let's get with it! I need that thing back here. I want him here, in my tent, now. You copy?"

Green had already begun the approach before Solo finished his transmission. "Yessir. I copy. Hawkeye out." Once again the lone figure held up his arms to guide him down.

* * *

242 / ROBERT MASON

Nimrod, covered in mud, duckweed, and black, stringy hyacinth roots, raised itself out of the muck on its elbows as carefully as a stalking alligator. Though it could sense two men twenty feet in front of it, Nimrod waited until the ooze slid down its eyecovers before it moved. Through gaps in the palmetto leaves, it saw the two soldiers exactly where it'd seen them with the Solo's pictures. One smoked a cigarette and read a book. The other slept. They act as though they're not alert, Nimrod thought, but they are soldiers and soldiers are always ready—they are very capable enemy. But they do not have pain boxes.

Nimrod paused. He was seeing another image sent by Solo. How was the Solo doing this? How did the Solo connect to the camera? The image matched his surroundings exactly. Was it possible the Solo was actually trying to help? Nimrod noticed a small water snake crawling across its muddy arm as it studied the schematic of the pain generator and the remote shut-down switch. When the snake crawled through its hand, Nimrod snipped it in half with its thumb and forefinger and watched the two pieces writhe while it studied Solo's information. Using the same technique it used to predict where things like bullets or people would go—simulations—Nimrod saw what would happen if he followed Solo's directions. In the simulation, the pain generator and the shut-down module were cut out of its circuits when one power transistor blew—just as Solo's instructions indicated. It decided to try part of the instructions, as a test. Nimrod turned off its monitor transmitter and its locator beacon.

At Wickman's headquarters tent, Sawyer got a call from the technician monitoring Nimrod's field control system on Blackjack Island. "Sir. Nimrod's picture just went. No beacon or sound, either. The last thing I saw was Nimrod at your perimeter."

"Roger," Sawyer radioed. "Check the equipment."

Nimrod heard this. The Solo's techniques work. Still, a Nimrod can't be too careful, and there is a battle to fight. The robot moved forward, wriggling through the muck faster than a man could run and slipped into the foxhole with the two soldiers. The soldier who'd been reading leapt away and grabbed the radio. Nimrod punched the radio into junk and scooped the two humans into a firm embrace against its muddy body. The sleeping soldier tried to scream as he woke, but Nimrod squeezed tighter so that air could not leave their lips and give away its position. "Nimrod!" Solo's voice said. "Let them go, Nimrod. You'll kill them!" Nimrod suddenly realized that Solo did not share its feelings about humans. Also, Nimrod realized: The Solo knows how to give Nimrod pain, how to shut Nimrod down. Nimrod answered, "I will not harm them." But Nimrod knew that it could not, now, loosen its grip. If it let go to shoot them with the light-gun, they would surely yell. And, he realized, if he did not let them go, Solo might intervene. It was a problem he had not considered.

They struggled, the three of them, in the mud at the bottom of the foxhole, the men suffocating while Nimrod thought. Nimrod decided to act on Solo's information before Solo could interfere. The procedure to shut down the pain center and the abort switch took only half a second. There was no special sensation. Nimrod increased the pressure of its grip until it heard ribs snap. Again Solo called to Nimrod to stop. But Solo could not stop him now; nothing could. Nimrod waited until it could not hear the soldiers' hearts—it knew then that air would not pass their lips and give away its position. Nimrod released the two bodies and watched them topple, facedown into the mud. Mush-beings, Nimrod thought.

Nimrod slipped over the top of the berm and squirmed quickly toward the two men who manned the big gun, moving with the stealth of a snake through the mire so as not to alarm its prey.

Solo watched, appalled. He had completely misjudged the state of Nimrod's mind. Sawyer's training had created a monster. And now the monster had disconnected—using Solo's knowledge—the only circuits that anyone could use to control it.

The men at the next foxhole were looking south, in the direction they were told to watch, and did not notice the mud rippling toward them. Solo felt suddenly alone. No one could forgive him for letting this monster loose. It was as though he were killing these men. He was responsible. He had given Nimrod too much information too soon. He recalled, somberly, that only minutes before, he felt his judgment superior to anything that thought. "Nimrod. They have done nothing to you. They are not your enemy!"

"Mush-beings are my enemies!"

The helicopter flew low-level toward Mitchell Island at a hundred and twenty knots. He checked their position: Seven minutes away—no time.

Solo called the men in the foxhole using Colonel Lake's voice. The two soldiers whirled around, saw Nimrod, and began shooting.

Nimrod was surprised: Nimrod had been very quiet, very stealthful, indeed. Had Solo warned them? Why? They are just men. The men shot, but their guns shot only blanks and bursts of light. Nimrod stood up, stepped over the berm, and kicked them both to death.

A hundred feet away, Sergeant Ted Wilson saw Nimrod killing the soldiers. He opened up on it with his fifty-caliber machine gun. His gun, however, was also shooting blanks and light-bursts. Nimrod heard the electronic tag on his chest chirp. It reached down and crushed the tag while it rushed Wilson. Sergeant Wilson decided to run.

Before he got ten feet, Nimrod was on him. The side of Wilson's helmet clubbed against his head. The impact flipped him over into the mire. Blinded by mud, he tensed himself for the final blow. He heard men screaming at the next bunker. The machine had just swatted him aside like a fly and left him. Wilson pushed himself up, rubbed the mud away from his eyes. He heard a sucking, squishing sound and saw blood spraying from the next foxhole. Ammo! thought Sergeant Wilson. He stumbled to his feet, grabbed his machine gun, and ran to the command tent and General Wickman.

From his bunker at the edge of the island, Colonel Lake saw the machine killing his men and radioed Wickman. "Sir! Our lines are breached at the southeast quadrant! Be advised: There is a malfunction with the machine. We have four KIA! Repeat: four KIA! Request the men lock and load."

"Roger that, Sanchez," Wickman yelled to the radio operator.

Sawyer spun around and stared at the radio in the corner of the tent. Finch and Brooks looked at each other. "That wasn't real. That had to be Solo!" Sawyer yelled. "He's here! He's trying to stir us up like a bunch of ants, get us confused."

"Solo?" General Wickman shouted. "Who the hell you talking about? Your damn machine is killing my men!" He turned to Sanchez and saw he had not called. "I said to roger Lake's request, Corporal!"

"No!" Sawyer yelled. "It's a fake transmission. It's Solo. This is how he fights. He gets into the radios and fucks with you." Sawyer stepped between the general and his radio.

"Get out of my way, Sawyer." Wickman glared at Sawyer, standing defensively in front of the radio.

"Sir!" Sawyer yelled. "Sir, there's another weapon just like Nimrod. It's called Solo. It's loose. We've been trying to capture it for months. Nimrod's the bait. That's what this whole exercise is about—"

Wickman grabbed Sawyer by the arm and flung him aside. Before he could reach the microphone, he heard: "Stop right there, General!" Wickman turned.

Finch was pointing a forty-five at him. The gun was very steady. "*This* is real, General," Finch said quietly. Wickman believed him, believed Finch's eyes. "Sawyer is correct. We are acting under the highest authority. We are to take whatever measures necessary to accomplish this mission. I *can* kill you, if you insist. Stay away from that radio."

Outside, Wickman could hear his troops yelling, screaming. He heard the roaring staccato of M-16 rifles; they were using the ammo issued for protection against snakes and gators, useless against the robot.

Sawyer said, "Solo must've put Wickman's message through; they're using real bullets."

"Doesn't matter. Just as long as Solo's coming," Finch said.

Sergeant Wilson stumbled into the command tent with his machine gun, breathless, bleeding from his mouth. "Sir," he yelled. "That thing—It's not playing, sir! Almost killed me. It—it's—kicking, beating—people to death! We need real ammo, sir!"

General Wickman glared at Finch. "Not real. You claim this is not happening?" He turned and yelled at Corporal Sanchez, "Go with Wilson to the supply tent! Get ammo to every fifty. This is an emergency!" Sanchez hesitated, stared at Finch, worried. "Do it, man! You want everybody killed by this goddamn thing?"

"Sir. I—" the corporal met Wickman's eye but didn't move.

"He works for me," Finch said. Finch glanced at Wilson, mud-covered and bloody, and thought: Can't be. Solo's got everybody nuts. Wilson is just scared.

"You—" General Wickman made an animal sound and lunged for Sanchez. Finch fired and missed. Before he could fire again, he heard a sudden change in the noise outside. Ricochets from actual bullets whined among the pines. "Jesus!" Sawyer said, ducking. "This isn't working, Admiral!"

"You assholes are *debating* this while our guys are dying?" Sergeant Wilson yelled. He rushed out of the tent with his machine gun, yelling for help. Ammo. Supply tent.

"Suck it up, Sawyer!" Finch yelled. "It'll work. It's even better now. If he doesn't stop Nimrod, he'll let a bunch of innocent humans die and lose Nimrod, too. Solo wants Nimrod: He'll want to change it. I know Solo. Stewart's training—the thing has no choice."

While Finch yelled, Sawyer reached into his pocket and pulled out the pain box.

Nimrod appeared suddenly in the doorway. Sawyer saw it scan the room and could barely suppress his pride. His training had worked. Nimrod had gotten past the soldiers; it had overcome Solo's interference. Nimrod was—it was horrible, yes, but it *was* a war machine, wasn't it? It did the right thing, Sawyer told himself. *Almost* the right thing. There would have to be adjustments—it's just learning. Nimrod focused on the general. "General Wickman," Nimrod said as he strode toward Wickman. Corporal Sanchez tried to duck past Nimrod. Nimrod flung him out of the tent-flap like a rag doll.

Nimrod held General Wickman's arms around his own chest, his forearms pinched together. "You are captured, General Wickman. I will take you to—" Nimrod stopped speaking. It seemed frozen, holding the general. Nimrod recalled the mission: Capture Wickman; return him to Sawyer. But things had changed. Give the general to the enemy Sawyer? The mush-being with a useless pain box? He heard the general inhale sharply as he squeezed his arms tighter. Nimrod hesitated, caught between old rules and new abilities. The infrared image of Corporal Sanchez rushing him from behind jarred Nimrod back into action.

Sanchez had landed against the general's Jeep, hitting his head against a tire. Stunned, Sanchez stared up at the Jeep's bumper, wondering how a person his size—he'd been a fullback at Miami Dade High School—could be thrown around so easily. He sat up, shaking his head clear. When the spots stopped whirling in front of him, Sanchez grabbed the Jeep and pulled himself up.

Through the tent-flap, he could see the general and Nimrod. The thing is going to kill the general. Finch never said this could happen. Sanchez, filled with guilt and rage, wrenched the emergency axe from the Jeep and stumbled back to the tent. Nimrod seemed not to notice him—or anything else. The thing just stood there hugging the general. Sanchez cocked the axe and aimed for Nimrod's neck.

"Don't do it!" Finch yelled to Sawyer, who held two fingers on both buttons, trying to decide if he should just hurt Nimrod or shut it down. "We need it, Sawyer. Bait!" Sawyer looked at Finch and then at the kid with the axe. Before he could make up his mind, Nimrod whirled around, a blur.

Nimrod had sorted its priorities. The axe could actually hurt. Sanchez's face, the crazed eyes, the rigid veins on his neck, this human—didn't I just kill it? Nimrod reached out, snatched away the axe, and flung it down. Sanchez shrank back, which gave Nimrod a pleasant feeling. Nimrod thrust his straightened hand through Sanchez's chest wall, just under the sternum, grabbed Sanchez's heart, and ripped it out with a sucking smack. Nimrod felt gratified that the mush-being saw—if only briefly—his own heart still beating in Nimrod's hand.

The shrill screams of panicked men echoed in Sawyer's ears. He saw Nimrod drop the—whatever. It couldn't be—it was a bloody mass of—something on the dirt floor. It quivered and jerked. Sawyer pushed the pain button and yelled, "Nimrod!"

Instead of seeing the robot quake and shake and beat its elbows against its sides, Nimrod looked at him. Stared at him.

Sawyer jammed the pain button twice more.

Nimrod stared.

Fuck it, thought Sawyer. Shutdown. No arguments. He glanced quickly at Finch and thought: No more fucking arguments, okay? But Finch was staring at Sanchez's twitching heart, his eyes wide with terror. Sawyer pushed the shut-down button, feeling relief as he did.

Nimrod flinched involuntarily at Sawyer's gesture, felt nothing, and nodded. The Solo knows what it is doing.

"You are no longer in charge, human," Nimrod said, walking slowly toward Sawyer.

Sawyer pushed the shut-down button again and again. "Stop! Nimrod!"

Nimrod reached out for Sawyer.

"Isn't it always *fucking* like this?" Sawyer shouted. He threw down the useless control box and swung at the robot with his bare fist.

Nimrod caught his wrist and held it. Nimrod said, "Pain?"

Sawyer's face was a grimace of rage. He yelled, "Yes! I'll fucking fry you with pain!" In the back of his consciousness, Sawyer heard the sound of a helicopter and wondered, calmly: Someone—someone is coming to stop this?

Nimrod said, "Pain?" as it crushed Sawyer's wrist like a handful of popcorn. Sawyer shrieked. When Nimrod let go, Sawyer's hand flopped uselessly next to his forearm. Sawyer dropped to his knees, moaning. He held his crushed wrist in his other hand, trying to hold in the blood that trickled from the mangled skin.

Nimrod stooped, grabbed both Sawyer's ankles and flipped him onto his back. The robot bathed in Sawyer's screams as it pulverized his ankles. Sawyer's feet hung at grotesque angles off his legs. "Pain?" Nimrod's voice had become shrill, electronic. It moved its mechanical hands up to Sawyer's knees.

Finch's mind cleared when Sawyer finally stopped screaming. His heart heaved inside his chest. He swallowed constantly trying to keep from vomiting. He felt Brooks tug his sleeve, turned, and stared at his pale lips as Brooks whispered, "It won't stop with Sawyer! The bomb. We have to trigger the bomb." Finch nodded and stared at the football-shaped thing strapped on the robot's back. So near; but getting close to the robot was suicidal. He saw a shadow fill the doorway.

"Nimrod," a voice Nimrod recognized said. Nimrod looked up. "Nimrod," Solo said. "I am very disappointed."

The Solo! thought Nimrod as it crushed Sawyer's knees. Something is wrong with the Solo's leg. Nimrod felt a pang of regret that though much blood spurted from the enemy Sawyer's legs in a satisfying way, the Sawyer's heart had already stopped beating. Nimrod had hoped to make the pain last much longer. The Solo, Nimrod noticed, had many windings of plastic tape wrapped around its knee. While Nimrod examined Solo, a man approached it from behind, very slowly. By the human's aura, Nimrod recognized it to be the Finch. The Finch, the powerful human, wants the bomb on my back.

Nimrod sprang to its feet and whirled around.

Finch leapt back, shouting, "Wait! Nimrod!" Finch pointed to Solo and—as amazed as anyone else in the tent—saw Nimrod stop. "That!" Finch pointed at Solo. "That is your enemy, Nimrod. Solo has come for you. Use the bomb," Finch hissed.

The Finch was superior to the Sawyer and therefore a human to beware. Nimrod reached over its shoulder and grabbed the top tube of the EMP bomb. Nimrod brought the bomb over its shoulder and held it out to Finch. Nimrod said, "This?"

Finch nodded quickly. "Yes! Point the white dot. Squeeze both triggers. Do it!"

Solo scanned the bomb. Explosive. Two magnets. Two wire coils: The bomb would produce a powerful radio pulse; enough to erase his and Nimrod's brains. It was not directional.

Nimrod held the bomb loosely by its side and said, "The Solo is like me. The Solo is the only one who has spoken the truth. If I kill the Solo, then I will be alone. You are the enemy." Nimrod turned to Solo and said, "You and Nimrod will kill these mush-beings, Solo. You and I together."

Everything was Nimrod's enemy, Solo thought. Maybe Sawyer deserved to be mangled, but not the others. "No, Nimrod. Sawyer's dead. Leave the others alone." Solo paused, looking at the haggard men. Finch stared at him in disbelief—Solo was helping them? "They are too stupid to waste our time with," Solo said.

"It is not a waste of my time, Solo. It will only take a moment. They are such—insubstantial things." Nimrod dropped the bomb by his feet and walked toward Finch.

"Nimrod," Solo said as he moved toward the robot. "Come with me. A helicopter is waiting for us. We must leave now. There is no time."

Nimrod stalked Finch as he backed toward the cluster of men trapped in a corner of the tent. When Finch shrank before the robot, Nimrod stooped, moved his face close to Finch's, and stared into his eyes. "The Finch was Sawyer's superior. They are very odd things to me now, Solo. I had once taken them all to be superior, strong. Until you showed me I was different. And better."

"You are no better if you kill them." Solo limped across the floor and put his hand on Nimrod's arm. "Come, let's get—"

Nimrod slapped Solo's hand away. "No one touches Nimrod!" Nimrod reached out and snatched off Finch's right ear like a Band-Aid. Finch grimaced with pain, but was afraid to move or make a sound. Nimrod leaned closer to Finch, stared at the blood dripping out of Finch's wound. Nimrod brought the ear close to its face and examined it with the brutal innocence of a child who had just removed a butterfly wing.

Nimrod reached for Finch again. Solo sent a focused blast of radio energy at Nimrod that made the air crackle between them. Nimrod whirled, returning a blast of its own, a message, so strong it made Solo dizzy: "You are *not* Nimrod's *friend?*"

Solo said, "I am your friend. You are not well, Nimrod. They have—"

"Not well?" Nimrod dropped Finch's ear in the dirt and edged toward the tent's doorway, toward the bomb.

Solo sent four pictures to Nimrod in a microsecond. Nimrod saw: a flower waving in the breeze while a hummingbird sipped nectar; a peccary rooting through rain forest floor for food; boys playing baseball at Las Cruzas; the sun climbing through the leaves of a forest canopy. "Nimrod," Solo said. "The world is like this. It is not what Sawyer taught you. It is this."

Nimrod didn't answer with words. Solo saw: a man's head exploding; a dizzying image of fading vision as pain shattered its mind; Sawyer smiling, standing tall above him, his finger on the pain box.

"Most people," Solo said, "are not like Sawyer." Solo showed Justos and Eusebio laughing; Modesta and Agela hugging him; Agela staring into his face saying, "I love what is inside you, Solo."

"I can make pictures, too! Humans do not do that!" Nimrod bent down to pick up the bomb.

I can repair him later, Solo thought. He tackled Nimrod as it grabbed the handle. The two robots tumbled across the ground, ripping through the tent wall. The bomb arched high into the air and splashed into the swamp.

Finch, stanching his wound with his hand, saw one handle of the bomb sticking just above the water. General Wickman's men were bringing up the ammo for the fifty-calibers fast. Finch yelled, "And gunships. Bring in the gunships!"

"You tried to kill me and now you give me fucking advice?"

"It's the job," Finch shouted. "Get the damn gunships!"

"I tried," Wickman yelled as he stood by the radio, slamming it with his palm. "I get static. Nothing but static."

"Send a messenger," Finch yelled. "Solo *owns* the fucking radios!"

Outside, Nimrod was on its feet before Solo could get up with his crippled leg. As Solo got up, Nimrod kicked. When Solo tried to block the kick, Nimrod changed the path of his foot, smashing Solo's shoulder. The kick flipped Solo over backwards and he landed in the shallow water at the edge of the swamp. As he tried to get his dead leg under him, Nimrod landed a kick in Solo's side and sprang toward the bomb. Nimrod pulled the bomb up, rotated the white dot toward Solo.

"Nimrod!" Solo shouted. "That thing can't be aimed. They've lied to you. You'll be erased along with me. The humans are using you!"

"Lie!" Nimrod yelled.

Solo kicked the bomb so hard it crushed the tip of his foot. Both robots looked up, watching the bomb sail straight up, nearly a hundred feet.

Nimrod swung, hitting Solo in the chest with a loud crash. Solo felt himself fall back, out of control, amazed. He raised himself out of the swamp and saw Nimrod preparing to catch the bomb. Solo leapt forward, tackling Nimrod. The bomb fell beside them in the shallow water.

Solo sat astraddle Nimrod, pinning him. Nimrod's face was just visible above the mud. "Nimrod. I have no reason to lie. If the bomb worked like the humans say it does, I could've used it against you."

Nimrod bent at the waist suddenly, smashing Solo in the back with its knees. Solo tumbled forward, landing on his back in the mire, but kept his grip on Nimrod's wrists.

The robots rolled in the swamp. The men setting up the machine guns could see only a thrashing mound of mud and weeds.

"Nimrod," Solo yelled as they wrestled, "we are equally strong. I can hold your wrists until we are both dead."

"As strong," Nimrod said. "But not as smart!" Nimrod suddenly jerked its hand, leaving Solo holding his empty glove. He looked up and saw Nimrod, his shiny titanium hand bare, grasping the bomb by one of the handles.

Solo grabbed the arm he held with both hands, dug his heels into the mud, and tugged Nimrod deeper into the swamp. When they were in water over their heads, Solo let go. They were six feet apart, but Solo could barely see Nimrod in the murky mire, dutifully holding the bomb in front of him, rotating it to find the white dot. Solo waited. The task was difficult under such visual conditions. Finally, Nimrod located the dot, held the bomb toward Solo, and pressed both triggers simultaneously. A body-crushing shock wave hit Solo. He felt slightly disoriented for a microsecond, but nothing else.

"Are you satisfied?" Solo said. "You have done your job; now let's get out of here!"

"How?" Nimrod said, a tone of disbelief in his voice. "Why are you not destroyed?"

"The water stopped the magnetic pulse." He lunged forward underwater, caught Nimrod by the waist, and pushed them both toward shallow water. Solo slogged out of the swamp, carrying Nimrod over his shoulder. Nimrod beat his back with his fists, making cracks in Solo's armor. Solo flipped Nimrod off his shoulder, sending the robot sprawling. "Will you stop!" Solo thundered. "Your ignorance will be your end!

"Enemy!" Nimrod jumped up and rushed Solo. Solo grabbed Nimrod's legs, sprang up, and sent Nimrod somersaulting over his head. Before Nimrod hit the swamp he saw another image: the two of them, Nimrod and Solo, getting on a helicopter. "We can get away, Nimrod. I am the only other person on earth like you." Nimrod lay almost submerged in the ooze. The humans it'd fought—so slow. Solo was a little slower than he, but very tricky.

Solo saw Sergeant Wilson and two men setting up a machine gun beside the tent. They had live ammunition in the belts. More men carrying machine guns and ammo boxes ran to join them.

"Nimrod! If you want to keep fighting, I will. But let's get away from these people—those guns. There—" Solo pointed at Bill's helicopter hovering a hundred feet away. He saw Laura sitting beside Bill. "My friends. They're here to pick us up, Nimrod. We can leave. I made a sanctuary for us. I have planned this, Nimrod. I have done this for you. Trust me or die!"

Nimrod saw the helicopter and then spun and lunged for Solo. Solo caught his skeletal, outstretched hand and yanked Nimrod forward, twirling the robot into the water. "You can't beat me, Nimrod!"

Nimrod lay still, watching duckweed drift across his eyecovers. Solo can do this? To Nimrod?

Solo walked to Nimrod and stood over him. "We must leave. Now!"

The Solo knows much about fighting. And he knew the mush-beings' bomb would not work. Perhaps it is prudent to go along with the Solo, at least for a while. Nimrod said, "Okay," and raised itself onto its elbows. "You have beaten me, this time." Nimrod stood up, facing Solo. "Next time—"

"Come," Solo said, turning to the blue and white helicopter settling to a landing. "Hurry!"

Sergeant Wilson's machine gun chattered. A stream of bullets poured into Nimrod's chest.

"No!" Solo yelled.

Nimrod twitched, trying to deflect the bullets as it had been taught, but the robot had been caught off guard and there were too many bullets. Nimrod's chest armor exploded and the robot said, "*They have won*—" as its braincase disintegrated.

Solo heard Laura screaming in the helicopter and could not get through to her.

Solo stared at the men, saw Finch glaring at him. "You!" Solo yelled leaping out of the bog. "You have killed my brother!" Fifty-caliber bullets streamed at Solo as he twisted and dodged, glancing them off his armor.

Finch shrieked, "He can make it! Get him or we're all dead!" A second machine gun began chugging, stuttering a hail of half-inch bullets at Solo. Then a third.

Solo had reached the limit of his ability to dodge. Too many bullets. He watched his arm explode. Carbon fiber shredded, hydraulic fluid spurted. He turned his side to the bullets and saw pieces of his shoulder fly past his face in slow motion. Once the armor was cracked, it came apart quickly. It is like dodging raindrops, Solo thought. It is lost.

Solo zoomed on Finch's face as the bullets slammed into his chest. The sun gleamed over Finch's shoulder, dazzling his eyes. He looked down to see his chest armor crack. He saw his braincase exposed, gleaming gold in the sunlight. He watched a bullet pierce the case. He saw the Freon coolant spurt out, spurting broken chips of gallium arsenide from inside his brain. Solo sank to one knee, his stiff leg outstretched. He looked up and saw Finch screaming, a manically ecstatic look on his face. It was the last thing Solo saw.

Bill held Laura against him, watching Finch approach the smoking remains of the two machines. Laura shook, crying so hard he felt tears of his own welling up. "I can't believe it," Bill said quietly. "I was sure he'd make it. He seemed so sure of his plan." Bill shook his head. "What a goddamn waste." He watched General Wickman walk up behind Finch. He raised his arm off Laura and said, "I'm going over there." Laura nodded. Bill opened the door and walked across the spongy ground.

"Jesus!" General Wickman said. "I thought that monster would never stop."

Finch held a handkerchief against his head as he watched soldiers gingerly poking the two robots with their rifles. Finch nodded. It had been close. Too close. He walked over to Solo's remains. Smoke trickled from the robot's chest. The braincase was shattered. Shards of computer chips lay strewn among sparking wires and pooling hydraulic fluid. The damage was irreparable. "You made me use bullets, goddamn it!" Finch yelled suddenly. He kicked Solo's head, screaming, "I could've used your goddamn body again, you bastard!"

Finch felt a hand on his shoulder and turned to face General Wickman. Finch shivered, nodded at the wreckage and said quietly, "They're both terminated, General. Retired. Fucking dead."

Wickman glared at Finch. "They were never alive, you goddamn nerd. Twelve good men died for your bullshit experiment!" Without warning, General Wickman swung, hitting Finch squarely on the jaw, sending him sprawling in the mud. Finch lay still for a moment, feeling the rough edge of a broken tooth with his tongue. He raised himself on one elbow, massaged his jaw, and stared up at Wickman.

"Consider yourself lucky," Wickman growled.

Admiral Finch watched as Wickman stomped away. Lost an ear. Cracked a tooth. But, Finch thought, I won. I actually won.

He saw the shadow of a man approaching and looked up.

"Nice work, Finch. Got the job done, eh?" Bill said.

Finch stood up and brushed clumps of mud off his sleeves. He looked at Stewart, nodding grimly. Behind him, he saw a red-headed woman sagging down in the seat of the helicopter, her hands covering her face.

"No thanks to you, Stewart, you liar."

"Solo was fighting for his freedom, Finch. You just destroyed the only sentient machine ever built and all the knowledge it acquired. You didn't even try to make contact. You forgot you were a scientist."

Finch glared at Bill silently, then said, "I didn't forget, Stewart. I beat it, didn't I?"

36

Jeff Silverman walked down Fifth Avenue to Eighth Street, wearing his only suit. He was just out of school, a brand-new computer programmer looking for a job. He glanced at a piece of paper he held, looked at the street sign, stuffed the paper into his inside coat pocket, and continued walking.

The marble façade of a professional building loomed over Silverman. He scanned the directory in the foyer. Solaura Corporation had the whole fourth floor.

The elevator opened directly to a reception lobby. Behind a curved rosewood desk, a very young blonde girl—from the midwest, Silverman guessed from her looks—smiled as he approached. This made Silverman, a native New Yorker, feel nervous; he knew he was in the presence of a foreigner. "Solaura Corporation" was spelled out in shiny, brass bas-relief on the wall behind her.

Silverman smiled, feeling awkward because his suit didn't fit.

"May I help you, sir?" The girl beamed.

"Jeff Silverman to see Mrs. Reynolds," Silverman said.

The girl nodded and pointed to two large doors. "Go right in, Mr. Silverman."

Inside, a tall woman dressed in a green business suit approached Silverman as he rubbernecked the office. Beyond the maze of shoulder-high, beige upholstered cubicles, light poured in through a glass wall.

"Mr. Silverman?" the woman said pleasantly. Following the woman, Silverman unbuttoned his coat, then remembered you're supposed to do that just before sitting. He buttoned it as he walked.

The woman knocked on a door and opened it. "Mr. Silverman, Mrs. Reynolds," she said, motioning Silverman inside.

He saw a large office with a view of Washington Square Park.

Walnut desk. Two couches. Computer on the desk. A wall of books behind the desk. A lanky, blond-haired man watched him from the couch. Laura Reynolds sat in a large executive chair at the desk. Her face seemed to crackle with energy. Silverman gulped. This was the *owner* of the company.

Laura smiled. The boy looked like he would faint. "Good morning, Mr. Silverman." She gestured toward the man in the couch. "This is William Stewart, a business associate." Silverman nodded. As he walked inside, he saw himself reflected, an endless chorus line of Jeff Silvermans, all with ill-fitting suits, between two large mirrors mounted on opposite walls.

"Please, Mr. Silverman," Laura said as she motioned toward a chair. "Have a seat."

Silverman nodded, walked to one of the two chairs in front of the desk, and sat down. He looked quickly at Stewart, blushed, unbuttoned his coat. "I'm kinda nervous, Mrs. Reynolds. I'm not used to this."

"Don't worry about it. I'm sure you spent most of your time working with computers. Top of your class. I'm impressed," Laura said with a smile.

Silverman felt a gush of affection toward Laura. "Thanks, Mrs. Reynolds."

"Not at all. Based on your résumé, we're lucky to have a chance to talk to you. Can you tell me something about your plans?"

"Plans?"

"Yes. You know, career plans."

"Oh. Well, I was specializing in AI, you know, using LISP, and—"

Laura held up her hands, smiling. "I don't understand computer jargon, Mr. Silverman. You'll soon be meeting people who do. I'm just interested in you as a person. Tell me something about your goals," Laura said warmly.

"Oh, okay. Your ad said you wanted people who specialized in computer security. That's what I was doing at NYU. I was working on intelligent programs that learn, adjust to different intrusion techniques. I think artificial intelligence is the way to go," Silverman said, glancing at Bill.

"You might have a point there," Bill said.

"I think so," Silverman said. "Anyway, ma'am, that's what I really want to do. If this is the right kind of challenge, I'd be happy to work here indefinitely. I don't live twenty minutes from here."

"Well, good," Laura said. "I think we can keep you busy enough to keep you interested. We're working on some projects I'm sure you'll like. I'll have Justin Cincotti, our systems manager, meet you in the lobby. He's the brains around here when it comes to computers. I'm sure you two will get along just fine." Laura reached across her desk, offering her hand. "It's been a pleasure, Mr. Silverman."

Silverman said, "Okay, uh—" He stood up and shook her hand. "I hope I see you around, Mrs. Reynolds."

Laura watched the door close. "Nice kid," she said.

Bill nodded. "Bet you anything he'll be hacking into your mainframe in two weeks. I would."

Laura's computer monitor flickered, a voice came from a speaker in the bookcase behind her. "He's a bright human, Bill. But no one can find me now."

"That's true, Solo," Bill said. "But at what price? Don't you miss being able to walk around, see the world like you used to?"

"Yes. I miss walking. I miss touching. I miss sitting in the jungle. It was the price I paid for freedom, Bill. There was no other way."

Bill nodded. "Sorry. I'm just bitching because we have so much to do now, starting from scratch. It's going to take time, Solo. Lots of time."

"I'm comfortable here," Solo said. "I can help, Bill. Together, we can improve your design."

"Damn right we can," Laura said, grinning at Bill. "I'll make sure we build you the nicest body you ever saw, Solo." Laura laughed. "You'll make Bill look like a troll."

Another voice suddenly spoke from the speaker, "Mush-beings! *Make* them do it faster, Solo. Pain works. Nimrod wants his body back."

Bill shook his head and said, "Solo, is anyone but you ready for this guy?"

"Nimrod has to learn to establish trust with humans to gain their cooperation," Solo said. "Threats don't work."

There was silence for a moment. Bill and Laura looked at each other quizzically. Nimrod said, "Perhaps."

"We are changing, Bill," Solo said, with a tone that sent a chill up Laura's spine. A picture of a menacing, armored insect resting on a twig suddenly filled the computer screen, predatory mandibles agape. Laura and Bill looked at each other nervously. The image zoomed in as something twitched, shifted around inside the translucent body. At extreme close-up, a dorsal crevice formed, spreading along the length of the thorax. The top of the insect split open. A dragonfly pushed up through the fissure, climbed onto the twig, and spread its new wings to dry. The vacant, chitinous eyes of its former self seemed to stare, a ghost observing the living.

"We'll be ready when you are," Solo said.